THE BOOK
OF GUILT

ALSO BY CATHERINE CHIDGEY

In a Fishbone Church
Golden Deeds
The Transformation
The Wish Child
The Beat of the Pendulum
Remote Sympathy
Pet
The Axeman's Carnival

FOR CHILDREN

Jiffy, Cat Detective
Jiffy's Greatest Hits

CATHERINE CHIDGEY

THE BOOK
OF GUILT

JOHN MURRAY

First published in Great Britain in 2025 by John Murray (Publishers)

1

A CIP catalogue record for this title is available from the British Library

Hardback ISBN 978-1-399-82361-6
Trade Paperback ISBN 978-1-399-82362-3
ebook ISBN 978-1-399-82363-0

Typeset in Stempel Garamond by Palimpsest Book Production Ltd,
Falkirk, Stirlingshire

Printed and bound in Great Britain by Clays Ltd, Elcograf S.p.A.

John Murray policy is to use papers that are natural, renewable and recyclable products and made from wood grown in sustainable forests. The logging and manufacturing processes are expected to conform to the environmental regulations of the country of origin.

Carmelite House
50 Victoria Embankment
London EC4Y 0DZ

www.johnmurraypress.co.uk

John Murray Press, part of Hodder & Stoughton Limited
An Hachette UK company

The authorised representative in the EEA is Hachette Ireland, 8 Castlecourt Centre, Dublin 15, D15 XTP3, Ireland (email: info@hgbi.ie)

Research for this novel was supported by Creative New Zealand.

ARTS COUNCIL OF NEW ZEALAND TOI AOTEAROA

For Bill Manhire

Contents

PART ONE

The Book of Dreams

Vincent

Before I knew what I was, I lived with my brothers in a grand old house in the heart of the New Forest. It had blue velvet curtains full of dust, and fire surrounds painted like marble to fool the eye, and a panelled Entrance Hall hung with old dark mirrors. An oak griffin perched on the newel post of the creaking staircase; we touched its satiny wings for luck whenever we passed, and whispered the motto carved on the scroll across its chest: *Verité Sans Peur*. We can't have been far from the ocean – I realise that now – but we'd never been beyond Ashbridge, never seen the water. We dreamt of it though, the three of us, conjured a gentle hushing as constant as the hushing of our own breaths, our own blood. Close, we thought, to the sound children heard before they were born, so that something in us – some old instinct – made us long for it. One day we'd go there, we said, to the place where all life began.

The house was one of the Sycamore Homes purchased in 1944, after the war, to accommodate children like us – although numbers dropped over the years. Perhaps you've heard of the Scheme . . .? But then again, perhaps not. For the most part, for decades, everyone ignored us – never gave us a second thought. And afterwards, people didn't like to talk about the Homes because they didn't like to feel guilty, which I can understand. Anyway, they're all gone now: boarded up or bulldozed, or turned into flats that bear no trace of what happened there.

Ours was for boys. It stood on the edge of the woods just across the river from Ashbridge village, and was called Captain Scott after the great doomed explorer. The outside was painted white, but here and there it had flaked away, and you could make out the rust-red brickwork showing through. The grounds were enclosed by a high flint wall with broken glass set in the top to keep us safe; we were very special, our mothers told us, and needed looking after. If we went outside early enough we could see the low sun shining through the pieces of glass, shards of amber and emerald alight in the quiet morning, and the flint opaque, like chunks of gristle in a white rind.

My brothers and I spent a lot of time in the garden, collecting horse-chestnut leaves big enough to cover our faces, cutting worms in half to find out if they would regenerate, digging for ancient coins and treasure because we'd heard of farmers unearthing fabulous hoards, and who knew what was under our feet? We trapped centipedes and kept them in matchboxes and jars, caught peacock butterflies and blew on their powdery wings that were patterned with eyes to scare away predators. We made sacrifices to the garden gods: little cairns of beetles, moss pressed into the shape of a bird, a circle of heart-shaped petals plucked from the white camellia bush, a snail rammed onto a sharp stick like the head of a traitor on a pike. In the fernery we studied ourselves in the gazing ball – a mirrored sphere that changed us into peculiar creatures and stretched the Home behind us out of all proportion. Good boys, helpful boys, we gathered peppery watercress from the nearby stream to put in our sandwiches, and mushrooms to make the stew go further, but we knew not to touch the death caps, or even the false death caps, which were also poisonous. When we were quite alone we poked at patches of long grass in the hope of flushing out adders, though we kept that to ourselves. From the ancient lemon tree we picked the knobbled lemons and took them to

Mother Afternoon, who cut them in half and juiced them by hand on the glass lemon-squeezer, pausing every few moments to scoop out pips or pulp. The discarded skins gathered at her elbow, their insides all silky and ruined, and she poured the juice into ice-cube trays and froze it.

We never dreamt of trying to escape. Those days were happy days, before I knew what I was.

Our mothers had their own quarters in the North Wing of the house, which we hardly ever saw, and each day they came to look after us in shifts. They weren't our real mothers – we understood that from the start – but they seemed to love us as their own; often they said they'd like to gobble us up. At any time we were permitted to take the albums from the shelf in the Library and look at the photos of them holding us as babies on their laps, shaking rattles at us, bathing us, testing the heat of our milk on their wrists to make sure we wouldn't burn our little mouths. It was all documented. There we were, lined up with the other Captain Scott boys in our highchairs, banging our spoons on our teddy-bear plates. We had no memory of these scenes, but our mothers told us how hungry we were, how they used to tickle our tummies and say *You'll pop! You'll explode!* In the albums, too, curls of our downy hair tied with ribbon – how white it was, how fine – and labelled *Vincent, William, Lawrence*, because otherwise you couldn't have told one curl from another. Our first teeth, also labelled, also identical. We knew how special we were when we looked at the precious little bits of us our mothers had saved. Oh yes, they loved us. If they had favourites, they never showed it.

Mother Morning's shift began at 5 a.m., when we were still sound asleep. Silently she unlocked the door in the upstairs passageway separating their wing from ours, then crept down to the Kitchen to relieve Mother Night. They had a quick chat, keeping their voices low so as not to risk waking us, Mother Night passing on to Mother Morning any information that might be useful for her to know. One of us was talking in his sleep, one of us had wet the bed again – ordinary things like that, we supposed. While we slept on, she made her way to the Laundry, where our dirty clothes waited at the bottom of the chute to be washed, and our clean clothes waited to be ironed and folded and given back to us – green shirts for Lawrence, red for William and yellow for me. We were always nicely turned out; that was important, Mother Morning said, because people judged other people on things like clothes and hair and fingernails – it was just human nature.

At half past six, tucking The Book of Dreams under her arm, a floral housecoat buttoned over her plain skirt and blouse, Mother Morning tiptoed up the stairs to our room.

Sometimes we woke before she entered, and we made ourselves lie there still as stones and think of our dreams and only our dreams. Underneath us the sheets had wrinkled and twisted, and we longed to wriggle our bodies clear of the bulky seams where the candy-striped cotton had been repaired – but if we started to move, if we so much as opened our eyes, the dreams might trickle away to nothing, and we'd have to say we were sorry but we couldn't remember. Mother Morning would speak to us in her sad voice then, as if we had hurt her, jabbed at some soft and secret part of her with the nail scissors that were not a toy. More often, she woke us, touching our shoulders and whispering our names. On those mornings we scarcely knew she was there; we were recounting our dreams to ourselves, we felt, still more asleep than awake. Lawrence slept nearest the door, so she went to him first, sitting on the edge of his bed and opening her Book, entering the date and his name, waiting for him to speak. Next she went to William, who slept by the old fireplace, and at last she came to me, over by the windows. I had to block my brothers' voices as they gave their accounts, otherwise their dreams would creep into my own, and that would really mess things up, said Mother Morning. That would seriously muddy the waters.

'Vincent,' she'd murmur when it was my turn, her pen poised, her freckled face and auburn curls beginning to take shape in the brightening room. 'Tell me everything you remember.'

6

'I'm wandering across the empty heathland and out of nowhere a pony rears up in front of me,' I'd reply, or 'I'm eating my lunch and I bite down on something hard, and it's one of my teeth come loose,' or 'I'm wrapping a present and I want to keep it for myself, but Mother Afternoon says that's as good as stealing.' My brothers and I always spoke in the present tense for our sessions with Mother Morning, pretending we were still dreaming the dreams, because that was how she preferred it. The past tense, she said, distanced us from the material; it was full of forgetting. 'I'm trying to light a fire, but the matches won't work. I'm sewing name tags into my new clothes, and every time I look the pile is bigger, and I don't know how I'll ever wear that many jumpers.'

She wrote it all down in her Book, day in, day out. All the nonsense, the garbled fragments. Sometimes, when I think of those mornings now, they smudge and flatten into one long morning, one long dream. Our sleepy voices. Our crochet blankets made by Mother Night slipping from our beds. The feather pillows that huffed out invisible dust. Mother Morning's pen scratching across the page as she noted every detail.

You probably don't remember your own ancient dreams, let alone somebody else's, so you might not believe me when I say that I remember one of Lawrence's dreams with total clarity. It's such a long time ago now – March 1979 – but I remember it because it was the first I heard of *her*.

'I'm chasing a girl through the woods,' he said, still half asleep.

'A girl?' said Mother Morning, something different in her voice. Something brittle. 'How old is this girl?'

'About my age – about thirteen. It's springtime, and I've picked a bunch of bluebells for her.'

William said, 'Lawrence has a *girlfriend*,' and I laughed even though I should have been concentrating on my own dream.

'Quiet!' hissed Mother Morning, who never spoke to us like that. 'Lawrence, go on. What does the girl look like?'

'Skinny. Bare feet. Long black hair.'

'And her clothes?'

Lawrence was silent.

'What is she wearing, Lawrence?'

A pause. The air in our bedroom taut, charged. 'Nothing,' he whispered.

I laughed again; I couldn't help myself.

'*Will* you be quiet!' said Mother Morning. 'Now, Lawrence my darling, do you catch this girl?'

'No. She keeps looking over her shoulder at me, laughing, but I can't catch her. That's the end.'

'Nothing else?' said Mother Morning. 'Are you certain?'

'That's the end,' he repeated.

After we'd made our beds and washed our faces and gone outside for Morning Exercise, William and I tried to find out more. Was she a sexy girl? Was it a sexy dream? We'd just begun to have those, the three of us, losing control of our bodies as we slept, waking to wet sheets that we bundled down the laundry chute. At first we were worried we might be sick, or even dying, but Mother Morning said it was just something we had to take in our stride, unpleasant as it might be for all concerned.

Lawrence shrugged off our questions and did the stretches we had to do at the start of Morning Exercise so we didn't injure ourselves. He grimaced when he rotated his shoulders, circled his hips, raised his bent knees to his chest; his joints had been hurting for a few weeks. She was just a girl, he said. Nothing special. Even when William and I sat on him – making sure that none of our mothers could see us – he made the sign for zipping his lips. He could be stubborn like that, especially if we ganged up on him.

We did our press-ups and star jumps, shaking off the cold of the March morning. A half-moon still hung in the sky, which always seemed wrong, no matter how many times we saw it. We squinted and tried to make out the flags our mothers had told us were flying

8

up there, the American, the German and the British, planted into the moon's dust in 1957.

Later, as we waited in the Library for Lessons, William started asking about Lawrence's dream again, but Lawrence busied himself with choosing half a dozen coloured pencils from the treacle tin and sharpening them one by one. He was blushing, though. Blushing about the girl with no clothes on.

I wandered to the back of the room and peered at the photographs that hung next to the Equipment Cupboard. For as long as I could remember, we'd lined up outside once a year so Mother Morning could take a picture of us all for Dr Roach's records. She used a big, proper camera – every Home had one – and we stood in a row by the lavender beds. I looked at the photo from three years earlier, back when we must have had forty boys left. I could see the Jones twins, the Brown quads, the Smith triplets – all gone to the Big House in Margate. John Wilson and David Collins, who had no brothers so everyone felt sorry for them but at the same time didn't want to be their friend – also gone. Paul Brown was wearing the Aran jumper Mother Night had knitted him for his birthday; he loved it so much he wore it till the waistband unravelled and the cuffs rode way up past his wrists. Richard Jones had removed his glasses but his brother hadn't; they'd always tried to differentiate themselves in little ways. Roger Smith was grinning from ear to ear because he knew what William was going to try – and there he was, my beautiful brother, at both ends of the long row of boys. First he'd stood on Mother Morning's far left, smiling for the camera, and then, as it panned across us, he'd sprinted to her far right. But who was the boy next to me? And the one next to him, for that matter? I realised I couldn't remember their names, now that they'd gone to Margate. Could barely remember them at all. And no newcomers had joined us in years – at Captain Scott, we were the last.

'Right, boys,' said Mother Morning when she arrived for Lessons, 'take out your work, please. We've a lot to get through today. How are we feeling? Bright-eyed and bushy-tailed?'

Yes, we nodded, no problems. No real problems. I felt a little flutter in my chest.

We were finishing off World War II that week, and Mother Morning took Volume 7 (SEV–ZWI) of The Book of Knowledge from the shelf and turned to the section on the Gothenburg Treaty. 'On 16 November 1943,' she read, 'Adolf Hitler was killed by a bomb concealed on the person of Major Axel von dem Bussche. Bussche was modelling the Army's new winter uniform for Hitler and carried the modified landmine in a backpack. On approaching the Führer he activated the detonator, clearing his throat to cover the sound of the hissing. As he embraced Hitler, the blast killed both men instantly.'

William hissed air through his teeth and grabbed Lawrence in a hug, then made a noise in his throat like a bomb and hurled himself to the floor, taking Lawrence with him.

'Yes, thank you, William,' said Mother Morning. 'Very realistic. Take your seats, please, boys.'

'He hurt my wrist!' said Lawrence, though he knew that complaining never got us anywhere.

'Take your seat,' said Mother Morning, twirling her finger at Lawrence's chair and reading on. 'In the wake of the assassination, the conspirators executed senior Nazi leaders and established an interim government. Two weeks later, peace talks began in Gothenburg, Sweden, with the Western Allies. The American President, Franklin D. Roosevelt, initially demanded nothing less than Germany's unconditional surrender, but after complex negotiations, Germany agreed to withdraw from France and not to resist an Allied occupation, which afforded them protection from full-scale Soviet invasion. Germany also agreed to democratic elections before the end of the year; these saw Claus von Stauffenberg take over as Prime Minister and Field Marshal Erwin Rommel as Chancellor. Following the urging of our Prime Minister, Lord Halifax, the Allies then acquiesced to Germany's retention of Sudetenland, Austria and Alsace-Lorraine. Minister of Defence

Winston Churchill regarded this compromise as a bitter pill to swallow, but Halifax declared, "The hour of urgency is upon us. Further delay will cause only further suffering: we must act to bring about peace, whatever the price."' Mother Morning's voice dropped several notes when she spoke these words, and she paused. 'In this world,' she said, 'it's not possible to have everything we want. Everything we think is right. Sometimes we have to make difficult decisions. Yes?'

We nodded, though we weren't entirely sure what she meant.

'Who won the war, then?' said William.

'Well,' said Mother Morning, 'nobody.'

'Somebody must have won,' he said.

'Nobody won and nobody lost,' said Mother Morning. 'That's what the Gothenburg signatories agreed to. And many wonderful things came of the Treaty,' she went on. 'Not only a swift end to the war, but the sharing of all sorts of important research. As we know, crucial advances in the biological sciences had already been made in the wake of World War I, when millions of soldiers and civilians were lost and terrible diseases ran rampant. Scientists had scrambled to . . .' Here she faltered. 'Scrambled to stamp out those diseases, and were beginning to achieve miracles. Things the world had never dreamt possible. Penicillin mass-produced by . . .?'

'Nineteen thirty,' we said.

'A polio vaccine by . . .?'

'Nineteen thirty-eight.'

'DNA's double helix discovered in . . .?'

'Nineteen thirty-nine.'

She beamed at us; she was always pleased when we remembered material from earlier Lessons.

'And then,' she said, 'with the collaborations made possible by the Treaty, huge progress was achieved. Our own Dr Roach made astounding progress in – in his field, with access to studies conducted in the camps before and during the war. Terrible information, some of it, but of immense scientific value. So you see, those poor people did not die in vain. They live on, in a way – we can think of it like that. We must keep in mind the greater good.'

We nodded again, and then she looked at the clock, and it was Break Time. She went to the Kitchen to cut us up our apples and cheese, tip the raisins into the little blue bowl and measure out our medicine.

William took down Volume 1 (A–BON) of The Book of Knowledge and found the entry for Adam and Eve. We'd often studied it when we were alone, mainly for the nude painting, though it was just a hazy reproduction – a black-and-white copy that dissolved into fly-dirt dots if you held it too close.

'Is this what the girl in your dream looked like?' he asked Lawrence. 'She has long dark hair. Maybe this is where you got her from.'

Lawrence sighed: we weren't going to drop the matter. He considered Eve's fleshy arms, her generous hips. 'Too lumpy,' he said. 'And I still think Adam's trying to grab her bosoms.'

We'd had this argument before. 'He's trying to stop her from taking the fruit,' I said.

'And grab her bosoms.'

William slid the Book back into its place and sat on the edge of the windowsill, picking at the glass eye of the ornamental goat we'd made on Craft Day. It stared back unblinking, strangely human. 'I think I might have dreamt of her too,' he said.

'Who, Eve?' said Lawrence.

'The skinny girl, running through the woods.'

'What?'

Other sets of brothers had shared dreams before, but not us.

'You never told Mother Morning,' I said.

'No.'

'Did you forget it?'

That happened now and again – we forgot dreams and later they returned to us, triggered by something we saw or heard, and we reported them to whichever mother was on duty so she could make a retrospective entry in the Book.

'No,' said William. 'I was . . . a bit scared of her.'

'Mother Morning?' I said. She could be strict, but was never frightening. Not really.

'The girl in the dream.' He was still picking at the goat's eye, and finally it fell from the wooden head, the wire at its root clogged with glue.

Lawrence was frowning. '*Scared* of her?' he said. Nothing scared William.

'I thought if I talked about her, I'd be . . . making her real.'

I could tell William was spooked. 'It was just a stupid dream – it doesn't mean anything,' I said. I took a tube of glue from the Equipment Cupboard and fixed the goat's eye, feeding the wire back inside its head. 'I know what we'll do. This afternoon, when we've finished lunch, I'll be you and you can be Lawrence and he can be me. Okay?'

We'd done this ever since we were little – pretended to be one another to see if anyone noticed. Sometimes they did – we'd answer to the wrong name, which is to say the right name, or we'd forget to hide a tell-tale rash or bruise – but mostly we got away with it. That's how alike we were.

I needed to use the lavatory, so I flung open the Library door and strode into the passageway, saying, 'The hour of urgency is upon us. Further delay will cause only further suffering.' As I passed Mother Afternoon's ikebana arrangement of plum branches, hydrangeas and buddleia that represented the cosmic balance between abundance and emptiness, I almost collided with Mother Morning. She raised her eyebrow at me – we dreaded the raised eyebrow – and carefully set down the tray of apple quarters, cheese, raisins and medicine before telling me that she'd heard what I'd said, and while I might think I was being funny I should show some respect for our British heroes like Prime Minister Halifax. He had made the best of a bad situation, and our country had benefited – *science* had benefited – thanks to the decisions he'd taken.

'Do I need to write you up, Vincent?' she asked.

'No, Mother Morning,' I said, and the weakness came over me. Another flutter in my chest. 'Sorry.'

'Hm. Very well. But watch yourself.'

'Yes, Mother Morning.'

We trembled at the thought of being written up – for just as our dreams were recorded, so too were our crimes. The Book of Guilt sat on the bottom shelf of the Library, next to the photograph albums, and in it our mothers wrote all our bad behaviour; things we should feel guilty for. Lying, kicking, interfering with ourselves, displaying the wrong attitude. When I think about it now, no punishments were ever meted out. Being written up was the punishment. Disappointing our mothers was the punishment.

That day, after lunch, we disappeared to our room and swapped our clothes – Lawrence took my yellow shirt, William took Lawrence's green one, and I took William's red. The dark-haired girl all but forgotten, we giggled as we looked at our changed reflections. Wicked creatures, we whispered – wicked, wicked. When Mother Afternoon came on duty at one o'clock she noticed nothing out of the ordinary, and we didn't change back into ourselves until bedtime.

Nancy

In March 1979, on Nancy's thirteenth birthday, her mother handed her a tiny parcel wrapped in pale-pink tissue paper. What could possibly be inside? Was her mother playing tricks on her, and really the parcel was empty? But when she opened it, two sparkling studs no bigger than pinheads fell into her palm. 'Are they real?' breathed Nancy, because they seemed too lovely, too precious.

'Real glass,' said her mother, 'and quite old.'

Nancy had seen ladies on television wearing earrings like these: little points of light that flashed with every movement.

'We thought they'd look nice with your special frock,' said her father, gesturing to the silvery-green dress Nancy was wearing because it was her birthday.

'But I don't have pierced ears,' she said.

'That's the other part of your present,' said her mother.

She sat Nancy down at the kitchen table and draped a tea towel over her shoulders to protect the dress, then drew a dot on each earlobe with a blue biro. 'Kenneth,' she said, 'the ice.'

Nancy's father twisted a cube from the tray in the freezer, and her mother pressed it to Nancy's left lobe.

'You don't want to numb *yourself*, Marjorie,' he said. 'You'll need the use of your fingers.'

'You're quite right,' said Nancy's mother.

She capped the top of the cube with tinfoil while Nancy's father lit a candle and held a sewing needle in the flame. Watching the little hot tongue as it flickered and bent about its sharp heart, Nancy could not tell if her ears were burning or freezing.

'What's that for?' she said, but her parents simply smiled and said it would all be worth it in the end.

Her father waved the needle through the air to cool it, and then her mother held it to her ear and said, 'Can you feel anything?'

'No,' said Nancy, though her chest felt full of tiny winged creatures trying to bash their way out: hummingbirds, honey bees, blowflies.

'Now,' said her mother, 'you must sit very still. Don't move a muscle.'

'What if I need to sneeze?'

'Do you need to sneeze?'

The creatures thrashed themselves against her ribs, scuffed her throat with the tips of their frantic wings.

'No,' she said. 'But what's the needle for?'

'It'll be over before you know it. Perfectly still now.'

And it was not pain she felt. Not pain, exactly, but a dragging sensation, a strange shifting and parting of the structures of her flesh. And then it was pain.

'Still now! Still!' said her mother, and she whisked the needle out and there was blood on her wrist, and Nancy's father handed her an earring and she pushed it through saying, 'Easy as pie!'

Her father was smiling, nodding. 'You see?' he said. 'Didn't we tell you?'

'I don't want the other one,' said Nancy.

Her parents glanced at each other. 'But goodness me, poppet!' said her mother. 'You can't go around with just the one!'

'How silly would that look?' said her father. 'All lop-sided and peculiar.'

'I don't want it!' said Nancy.

Her mother was already icing the other ear.

When it was done, her parents stood back and regarded her in a way they often did. Assessing, considering. Measuring her up somehow.

'Would you look at that, Marjorie?' said her father after a moment. 'I think you've got it just right.'

'Just right,' her mother said, and took Nancy's photograph.

Vincent

All our lives we'd wondered about the village just over the river.
From our upstairs corner bedroom we could see across the heathland and woodland and down to Ashbridge, where the clock told
four different times on its four blue faces, and the church steeple
rose above the red roofs. On rainy days the clay tiles looked shiny,
slick as wet leaves, and in winter the smoke rose from the chimneys,
the fires inside the houses keeping all the families cosy and warm
– so we imagined. As little boys, when we'd asked our mothers
why we couldn't go there, they'd told us we were delicate; our
health was delicate. If we ventured beyond our gates we might
catch something from the villagers, which could prove very
dangerous indeed. So that was the rule.

Then, in the spring of 1978, everything changed: provided we
were well, we could accompany our mothers when they needed to
visit the bank or the Post Office, or treat themselves to the new
Woman's Realm when they'd saved up enough money, or find us
some new shoes because we were growing like vines. That was the
new rule, which replaced the old rule.

We could hardly believe it. We asked Mother Morning exactly
who had decided to let us out – had she?

No no, she said; she possessed no such powers.

Dr Roach, then?

No, she said, certainly not Dr Roach. The government had decided, although she doubted they'd be the government for much longer.

So a new government could change the rules back?

Perhaps, she said.

And would a new government also start sending boys to Captain Scott again? So we wouldn't be the last ones?

She didn't know, she said. She couldn't see into the future.

At first we were nervous – we worried we'd pick something up from the villagers. But no, Mother Morning assured us: as long as we felt healthy, and maintained the right attitude, there was no danger. And how thrilling those first outings were! How strange to see the flint wall from the other side, and to leave the Home behind us as we walked with Mother Afternoon along the narrow road! We jumped when we heard a car approach, but it slowed right down to pass us, the driver peering through the window with a puzzled look on his face. Mother Afternoon told us to ignore him. We skipped along by the hedgerows, passing the sleepy-eyed cows and the skittery ponies that flicked their tails in the green air, and the crab-apple tree that was hollow at the heart but still growing, and then we crossed the stone bridge that separated us from the village. Through the high-street windows we saw whole sides of pork and whole jars of sweets, mannequins wearing real clothes and painted-on hair, tins of rice pudding arranged in precarious stacks, and, in the bakery window, a little automaton dressed in a white apron and white hat, nodding his head and tapping on the glass with a wooden spoon. But although we were locals – we'd lived in Ashbridge our whole lives, after all – the villagers never really warmed to us; they gave the briefest of nods if we said hello, and the schoolchildren in their smart uniforms nudged one another and stared wide-eyed, and the shopkeepers stonewalled most attempts at small talk. One man hurried his daughter across the street to avoid us, and when she said that we looked quite normal, he muttered, 'They're not like you and me.' Another man said to his wife, 'They'll be wanting the right to vote before too long. The right to marry. You mark my words.' And Lawrence soon learned not to try to pat people's dogs.

'Rise above, rise above,' Mother Afternoon told us. 'You're a hundred times better than they are.'

Only Mr Webb the baker was friendly, slipping an extra cream bun into the bag near closing time, asking if I had a young lady yet, because what was a handsome chap like me doing without one? Mother Morning said he was simple – a bit touched – but I thought he was kind.

Very occasionally, if our mothers were busy – and if we were feeling well – we were allowed to go to the village on errands by ourselves, though we had to promise perfect behaviour. Mother Afternoon would want a card of buttons or a bit of elastic, or she'd decide we'd earned a treacle tart or custard slice for good manners. Mother Morning would discover someone had used the last teabag, so there were no teabags for anyone else, which was a sorry state of affairs.

I remember the first time I went to the village alone: early that summer, in 1979. A new government had indeed come to power, and my brothers and I were worried that they'd say we couldn't go out any more, but the days passed and nothing changed. How lucky, we said; we didn't think we could return to the old rules. When Mother Afternoon needed some wire to support the flowers in a new ikebana arrangement, she gave me some money and told me not to dawdle. I knotted the coins inside a handkerchief, pushed them deep into a pocket so they couldn't fall out, and set off. Wild strawberries were ripening under the hedgerows, and I stopped and ate as many as I could find, careful to check for weevils. I wiped my fingers on the grass rather than on my trousers, which would have been thoughtless and made more work for Mother Afternoon when she had quite enough on her plate.

In the high street, two young mothers were pushing their babies in gleaming white prams, and they watched me as if they'd never seen me or my brothers before. When they'd passed I heard one murmur to the other: 'Pitiful creature really – he's never known love.' Her friend said, 'Of course not! They don't respond like we do!' Did they mean me? Was I the pitiful creature? I wanted to run back and tell them that even though we were orphans and sometimes felt poorly, we'd known love. We *knew* love. We had three mothers. Three! Who else could say that? But we weren't allowed to make conversation with people unconnected with our errands.

The bell above the corner-shop door jangled as I let myself in. I could smell the bacon that Mr Kendrick sliced on the big silver machine, and the cheese, and the loose biscuits in their tins on the counter. The sweets shone in their jars – rhubarb and custards, aniseed balls, humbugs, sugar mice. I lingered beside the straw-filled wicker basket where the Lucky Bags were buried, each containing an assortment of sweets and a plastic toy. I longed to plunge my hand in and feel around for the most promising bag; who knew what you might get? A tiny deck of cards, a whistle, a compass – I'd seen village children pull out such treasures. At home I kept my one and only Lucky Bag – empty now – folded away with my private things, along with the toy I'd found inside: a plastic soldier with a parachute that used to bear him safely to the ground, before it tore.

Mr Kendrick appeared from the back room, and I thought I saw something pass across his face – a flicker of uneasiness, perhaps, or even fear – but it happened so fast I couldn't catch it.

'Good afternoon,' he said. 'William, is it? How may I help?'

'I'm Vincent,' I said.

There was that look again.

'Vincent. How may I help?'

'I need some florist wire, please.' I took out my knotted handkerchief, and he eyed it as if he might catch something, though I didn't have a rash of any kind at that time – just the weakness and the occasional flutter in my chest, which nobody could see. 'It's money,' I said. 'See?'

All the same, he pushed my change across the counter rather than placing it in my waiting hand. And I said thank you and wished him a pleasant day, because I remembered my manners and I knew we must never give people reason to find fault with us.

'Aren't you an angel,' said Mother Afternoon, smiling her big warm smile when I handed her the wire. She was sitting at the Kitchen table, her crinkly dark-brown hair pulled into its usual bun. From her apron pocket she took the Spot the Ball coupon that she'd clipped from the newspaper. We weren't allowed to read the paper, which was for grown-ups, but Mother Afternoon let us help her with the contests. She spent many minutes poring over the photograph – a football game with the football removed. 'What do you think?' she said, and I sat down next to her and squinted at the picture of the men running about and leaping into the air for no apparent reason.

'Here?' I said, pointing just in front of a player's raised boot.

She shook her head. 'Look at these three. They're watching something up here.' Her pen hovered in the empty sky.

And really, the ball could have been anywhere. A smaller picture showed the result of the previous contest – nowhere near the spot Mother Afternoon had chosen.

She marked the coupon with an *X* in six different places and tucked it back into her apron pocket, where she kept all her bits and bobs. Then she gave me a kiss. She smelled like pastry.

'Why would Mr Kendrick be scared of me?' I asked.

'Scared?' she said. 'Of you?'

'I thought so.'

'Nonsense. He's a grumpy old thing, that's all. He's like that with everyone.'

'A lady said something too.'

'What lady? In the village?'

I nodded.

'What did she say?' She was studying me closely, I realised.

'She said I was a pitiful creature who's never known love.'

Mother Afternoon was silent for a second, then let out one of her loud laughs. 'Couldn't be further from the truth, could it?' She ruffled my hair. 'Could it?'

'No,' I agreed. 'Maybe she meant someone else.'

'Must have done.'

'What will you buy if you win Spot the Ball?' I said.

'A little cottage,' she said. 'A pet porcupine to keep me company.'

The answer was always a little cottage, but the animals changed each time.

'And what about us?'

'You can come and be my slaves. Cook and clean for me. Sharpen the porcupine's quills.'

One of those silly games that families play – I'm sure you have your own.

Anyway, she never won. Not that I know of.

If we were feeling poorly we had to take it easy. No Lessons, no running about the garden like mad things, and certainly no errands. We stayed in our pyjamas and dressing gowns and sat quietly in the Playroom downstairs, drowsing in front of the gas fire. Sometimes we listened to our *Peter and the Wolf* record on the radiogram, or read a volume of The Book of Knowledge that wasn't needed for Lessons that day, or did the Mona Lisa jigsaw. It was quite old, the pieces chipped and peeling, and it was missing the piece where her left eye should have been. Each time we started it we thought the eye might have turned up – but each time we got to the end and saw the hole in her face that we could not fix. We preferred the Stickle Bricks; even though we agreed we'd outgrown them, we also agreed we could still play with them when we felt poorly. We tipped them out of their shoebox and ran our fingers across the rows of bendy plastic spikes, imagining what we'd press them together to make. A castle? A cathedral? A submarine? A rocket ship? I'd once made a Stickle Brick Mother Morning, with spiky green hands and spiky red hair and one spiky raised eyebrow.

I showed it to John Wilson, who was poorly that day too, and resting on the daybed; I thought it might cheer him up, but his face turned even paler, and he said he'd have to report me because if anyone saw it they might think he'd been involved. I pulled it apart then and threw all the pieces back in the box and refused to speak to him. I think he went to Margate soon afterwards.

We didn't know the name of our sickness, and its symptoms varied from month to month and boy to boy: we just called it the Bug, as if we might catch it like the shieldbugs we caught in jars. We'd watch them crawling around in circles, looking for a way out, until one morning we'd find them on their backs, legs in the air, motionless even when we poked them with a pin. In The Book of Knowledge we read about Man's Deadliest Foe: the Microbe. *Not all germs are harmful to Man; indeed, many are his most active servants in the cultivation of crops and the destruction of putrefying matter. But others start a work of destruction as soon as they enter the human body.* If we had a sore throat, our mothers made us a hot drink with one of Mother Afternoon's frozen lemon-juice cubes. If we had a headache, they brought us cool flannels. They rubbed arnica on any bruises that appeared, and filled hot-water bottles to press to aching joints, and held bowls for us if we vomited, and let us lie down if we were feeling drowsy. And, of course, they gave us our medicine – sometimes pills on an empty stomach, or syrup with breakfast or last thing at night, or even clear solutions that dripped into our veins over several hours and came in different colours, like fruit squash. Now and then injections, the glass ampoules rattling gently in their box. This might sound strange to you, but whenever I have to get an injection these days, I almost enjoy it. I remember Mother Afternoon swabbing the crook of my arm, humming under her breath, or Mother Morning chattering away about something from The Book of Knowledge to distract me as she pushed in the needle – How the Wooden Horse Came to Troy; The Wonderland Beneath the Waves; The Daring Assassination of Adolf Hitler – and truly, I hardly feel it. How gentle they were.

Boys did die. If they failed to eat everything on their plates, or failed to do Morning Exercise to keep their bodies strong, the Bug could pick them off quick smart. It might start with a simple rash, a bit of an upset stomach, a swelling of the tongue or a fluttering in the chest, and then: lights out. We'd seen some boys lose all their hair; they looked like little old men. We had to be constantly on guard, our mothers told us. Even the wrong sort of attitude could set the Bug running rampant inside us.

If we did everything right, however, and managed to beat the Bug for good – well! Then we could go to the Big House in Margate, like all the Sycamore boys and girls before us. Nobody knew how many floors it had; we'd heard that they just kept adding more, building higher and higher as necessary. We'd personally seen dozens of Captain Scott boys improving before our very eyes, the blood returning to their cheeks and lips, their ribby chests expanding, filling with the future. And if one boy began to get better, his siblings did too because of their identical makeup – twins, triplets, quadruplets, all recovering together. We asked them: what was the secret? How could we get better too? They shrugged as they packed their toothbrushes and polished their best shoes for the journey. You just had to believe, they said. Which was very little help.

At Margate the ocean stretched away forever, and at the same time the waves rushed in and in. You could build sandcastles and collect shells – limpets and cockles and whelks just lying there for the taking – and at the souvenir shops you could buy tiny ladies made entirely of shells. You could visit the Dolphinarium, where Britt, Turk and Speedy leapt over sticks and walked on their tails. And you could descend underground to tour the Shell Grotto – a curious network of passageways decorated with ornate shell mosaics. We'd read about it in The Book of Knowledge: was it a rich man's folly? An astronomical calendar? A temple? An oracle cave? A pirate lair? Nobody could say who'd made it or why, and it might have been the Phoenicians or the Romans, and it might have been a secret society; there was simply no telling. Lawrence liked the idea of a secret society – a special club, he said, that let in only certain people. Nature-lovers. Animal-lovers. People who might seem quite ordinary up above, going about their quiet business, so you'd never guess they led a secret life underground. We'd pored over the pictures of the mosaics and traced the shapes noted in the captions: a womb, an anchor, a tree, a serpent, a setting sun, a skeleton. The journey of the soul through birth and life and death, perhaps, and on into a new life amongst the stars – that's what some people thought. I imagined the textured walls bristling, the spiralling whelks, the mussels darkly iridescent, the oyster shells slippery like the roof of my mouth. The strange Altar Chamber with its full moon, its setting sun, and the high Dome with its rings of white shells and grey shells. The opening at the top that showed a bright disc of sky.

And when you emerged from underground, you could visit Dreamland. My brothers and I talked about the amusement park so often I felt as if I'd been there already. As if I'd plummeted down the Helter Skelter, crashed about in the Dodgems, cheered on the daredevil motorcyclists who careened no-hands around the Wall of Death. I could almost remember strolling the Magic Garden at sunset, its electric snowdrops and glass oranges lit from within. And hadn't I seen the great hulk of the *Queen Mary* – a building in the shape of the ship – turning to shadow as darkness fell?

A boy knew he'd been selected for Margate when he found the brochure on his pillow – placed there by one of our mothers, we were certain, though nobody ever witnessed the delivery.

Discover the sun at Margate! the first page read. *Vast expanses of golden sand are just waiting to be played on, lazed on or dug up. It's a children's paradise, with trampolines, roundabouts, swings, rock pools, seawater swimming pools and the sunniest and driest weather anywhere in Britain. The Dolphinarium and the Shell Grotto promise cool retreats on the hottest days, while Dreamland boasts no less than 20 acres of fun. All the fairground favourites are there: the Scenic Railway rollercoaster, the River Caves, the Dodgems and the Sky Wheels. Boys and girls will love the mischievous monkeys and the bicycle-riding birds – but watch out for the dinosaurs that roam the park! After a day's enjoyment, the Big House offers first-class views of the sun setting over the bay.*

There were pictures of children eating ice creams and riding donkeys on the beach, screaming on the wooden rollercoaster, cheering Turk the dolphin as he leapt to sound a note on a horn. *Performing in natural sea water, the Dolphins jump in sheer ecstasy, play music, retrieve objects – and even talk!* On the merry-go-round at Dreamland a boy sat astride a great swan and clutched its throat, its wings spread wide, and a dozen cheerful friends ate toffee apples at the entrance to the sideshows. *Excited boys and girls queue to see Mademoiselle Yvette the Headless Lady: Alive and Human.* Pictures of the Big House showed the smart blue-and-white awnings that shaded the windows, and the panels of stained glass at the front door that shone with golden grapevines and open-mouthed fish. A girl marvelled at the high Dome in the Shell Grotto, and another stood dwarfed by the massive silhouette of the *Queen Mary*. In the Shooting Gallery a boy took aim at a mouth full of painted teeth, trying to knock them down. My favourite picture was the boy buried up to his neck in sand – *This young chap's in trouble when the tide comes in!* – and Lawrence's favourite was the boy clapping as a bright-green parakeet rode past on a tiny bicycle and studied the camera with its glossy black eye. William liked the girl holding out her candy floss to a Tyrannosaurus, its massive jaws wide open. *Come to Margate*, read the last page, *where children can have the time of their lives just being children.*

Each night I checked for a brochure on my bed; I couldn't understand why we hadn't been chosen when every other boy from Captain Scott had gone. The Jones twins, the Brown quads, the Smith triplets, and all the ones who had no brothers. 'When will it be our turn?' I asked Mother Afternoon. She was leading us through the woods on a Nature Walk, identifying butterflies: yellow brimstones,

chocolate-brown ringlets, silver-washed fritillaries. It wasn't her decision, she said over her shoulder, but she was sure we'd get to Margate
one day, and in the meanwhile she was going to enjoy our company
for as long as possible. She stopped, pointed at something poking
through the leaf litter like a bone: an antler cast from a fallow deer.
All three of us dived for it, Lawrence tripping over a root, William
trying to shove me aside, but I got there first. It was grooved with
tooth marks from mice and hares, and heavier to carry than I expected,
weak as I was. Still, I lorded it over my brothers, holding the twisted
and bony crown to my brow for as long as I could manage. I still
have it, packed away in a box. I never look at it.

In Free Time, on rainy days, we wandered through the house.
We peeked behind narrow doors to see masses of dusty pipes and
wires, the hidden guts of the place, and we examined the ancient
piece of needlework that hung in the corner of the Playroom, every
stitch dimmed to brown. It commemorated Martha Emily Phillips,
who had died in 1832, aged three, and sometimes, for a dare, we
murmured the embroidered words: *In the silent Tomb we leave
her till the Resurrection Morn, when her Saviour will receive her
and restore her lovely form.* In the Upstairs Common Room we
marvelled at the gigantic pike stuffed and mounted in a glass case,
its varnished body thick as a boy's thigh, its teeth sharp as the glass
shards on the flint wall outside. The back of the case was painted
in watery blues and greens, and reeds and rushes sprouted from
its base to suggest the faded fish was still swimming in a river. And
didn't it look like the stained-glass fish at the door to the Big
House? And mightn't that be a sign?

We explored the other boys' rooms, too – the deserted rooms.
Our voices sounded too loud in them, hollowed out somehow,
echoing off the walls and floors. Sometimes, on the bare mattresses,
we could make out the faint shape of the person who used to sleep
there. We found things left behind: a drawing of a battleship, a
desiccated beetle in a matchbox. Once, in a downstairs bedroom,
initials scratched into the skirting board: *TC, LC, PC 17.5.75.*

'Wasn't there a Tony someone a couple of years ago?' said William.

'And a Peter, I think,' said Lawrence. 'Peter Carter? Peter Connor?'

They came back to us then – tall, sandy-haired brothers who were always getting into fights. Tony put pine cones in people's beds, or frogs. Peter dumped a plate of jelly and custard on a younger boy's head because he thought the younger boy had been given too big a helping. And they'd done worse than that, much worse. Tony took an actual shit in someone's bed – we couldn't remember why, but we remembered Mother Morning devoting half a page to it in The Book of Guilt, which hurt her more than it hurt him. And Peter had pulled the chair away just as John Wilson was sitting down to lunch, and John had needed five stitches in the back of his head, which meant a rare trip to hospital. Tony and the other brother – Lionel? Yes, Lionel – had howled with laughter. 'Make sure you ask the doctor to check for a brain while he's at it,' they'd told John. Why did they get to go to Margate?

In one room, I remember, we came across an abandoned nest that a boy must have found on a Nature Walk, the three tiny blue eggs still intact. They looked perfect, and we wondered whether they might hatch if we kept them warm. They were starling's eggs, Lawrence said – he wanted to be a vet and knew these things from studying The Book of Knowledge – and starlings were clever birds: maybe we could make pets of them, train them to eat from our hands. But when I picked up one of the eggs it broke, the shell tissue-thin, and the inside was rotten through and through. I'll never forget the stench; for days I thought I could smell it on my hands.

We found clothes, too – serge trousers gone shiny at the knees, and winter vests, winter socks mended with Mother Afternoon's tiny careful stitches. Aran jumpers knitted by Mother Night, no two ever the same. If we found things we liked, and they were the right colour – green for Lawrence, red for William and yellow for

29

me – we claimed them for ourselves. It took no time at all to unpick the old names and sew our own in their place.

We must have been in Paul Brown's room one day, because I found his favourite Aran jumper – the birthday one he'd worn till the waistband unravelled and the cuffs rode way up past his wrists. There was no mistaking it: I could see his name sewn in the back of the neck.

'Why would he leave this behind?' I said, and Lawrence and William agreed that it seemed odd. But then, we said, you wouldn't want winter things in Margate, would you? You'd have no need for a heavy jumper there, where it was always sunny and you could walk around stuffing yourself with candy floss and plunge into the sea at any hour.

On those wet days the rain pelted the fernery out in the garden, bouncing the fronds this way and that, splashing on the rocks, trickling down the gazing ball. The droplets crashed onto the high flint wall, shattering into spray on the pieces of broken glass. We closed our eyes then and listened, and we might have been at the beach. How much quieter the Home was without all the other boys, we said; how rowdy they'd been. We could have had our pick of the bedrooms, upstairs or downstairs, now that so many stood empty – our mothers had told us so. Didn't we want to spread out a bit? Enjoy a bit of privacy? Especially since I wasn't sleeping well? But no. No. We chose to stay together.

When the kidney-red car glided up the driveway, the sun flashing off the snarling jaguar on the hood, I leapt from the Library window-seat.

'He's here,' I called.

'Front door!' said Mother Morning, and the three of us scurried along behind her to the Entrance Hall as she whipped off her housecoat and peered into one of the old dark mirrors, dabbing on a bit of lipstick and smoothing her auburn curls. She looked us up and down. 'Socks!' she commanded.

We pulled up our socks.

'Hair!'

We flattened our cowlicks.

'Shirts!'

We tucked in our shirt-tails.

'William, how do you have ink all over your fingers? Never mind . . . too late to worry about that. Line up, line up. Quickly now.'

We positioned ourselves at the foot of the stairs, the griffin on the newel post brushing my back with its open beak. Above us the family who had first lived in the house gazed down from their crackled portrait: a lady sat in our Playroom at a table laid for afternoon tea, her mauve silk gown adorned with rosettes and ruffles, white lace spilling from her sleeves. She held the waist of a little girl who stood unhygienically on the tablecloth; we decided she must be the Martha Emily Phillips of the faded needlework, waiting for the Resurrection Morn. To their left, if you looked closely, you could make out the grey-veined fire surround painted to look like marble; real flames blazed in the grate, because the gas was still far in the future. A little boy in a dress restrained a spaniel that was trying to sniff a plate of cake, while a second boy, also in a dress, dragged a wooden horse along on a string. A gentleman stood behind this boy, his hand resting on the child's golden head. Often we looked at that hand, its kind fingers, the way they cupped the skull. The hand of a father.

Smiling her most charming smile, Mother Morning opened the front door. 'Dr Roach,' she said, 'welcome back.'

He must have been eighty by then, but he climbed nimbly from the car, bag in hand, pushing his thick silver hair back from his forehead. As usual, he wore a three-piece suit that seemed one size too large for his small-boned frame. 'Ahh,' he said, closing his eyes and inhaling. 'So good to breathe the country air again. London is a *cesspit*, and so is Berlin.'

A fox terrier shot out after him and ran up the steps.

'Hello, Cynthia darling!' said Mother Morning. 'You're very frisky!' She bent to pat the dog even though she hated the thing because it clawed her stockings.

'Boys,' said the doctor, shaking hands with the three of us, gently in case we were feeling sore or weak. He never remembered which boy wore which colour, and he never pretended he could tell us apart. We liked him for that. 'How are we today?'

'Fine thank you,' we said, because that was polite and all he wanted for now.

'You must've shot up by a foot at least. Enormous creatures! What are they feeding you? Eh?'

Questions like this didn't require an answer.

'Please,' said Mother Morning, extending her arm to usher him into the Gun Room, where Dundee cake and fondant fancies and ginger snaps waited on a tiered stand. She always went overboard for Dr Roach.

We only ever used the Gun Room when he visited; the rest of the time it was strictly off limits, though Mother Afternoon went in there every Friday to wipe the leaves of the philodendron plant and dust the china horses. The tall, shallow cabinets that lined one wall were empty of guns now, but we could still make out the indentations of the stocks in the threadbare velvet padding, and a few pellets of lead shot rattled around the ammunition drawers. We'd found the old game book caught at the back of the bottom drawer, too. It listed everything the original family had shot: page upon page of partridges, pheasants, grouse, hares, foxes, deer. And once, I remember, Richard Jones crept in and rearranged the horse figurines into obscene positions, breaking a spindly leg off one of the foals in the process, and there was hell to pay. Mother Morning had to send the foal to London for invisible repair, but you could always tell.

Dr Roach seated himself on the good sofa – the chintz one – and accepted a slice of Dundee cake. 'Just the ticket,' he said. 'Don't stand on ceremony, chaps – help yourselves.'

As Mother Morning poured the coffee we dug into the fondant fancies, ignoring any nausea from the Bug, biting through the soft pink coating to the cubes of buttery sponge inside. Heaven.

'Cynthia, down!' said Dr Roach as the little dog tried to scrabble up onto the good sofa. '*Down.*' When she settled at his feet, he fed her a morsel of cake. 'I know I shouldn't,' he said. 'But look at that face.'

We all looked at Cynthia's face.

'Is she . . .' began Mother Morning. 'Is she . . . different?'

'I was wondering if you'd spot it,' he said.

I looked more closely – and she did seem different. Her coat smoother, her eyes brighter. Not so stocky around the middle.

'Here, girl,' said Lawrence, fluttering his fingers down by the floor, but she wouldn't go to him for back-scratches and paw-shakes the way she usually did.

'She'd reached her teens, and everything was starting to fail,' said Dr Roach, the faintest quiver in his voice. 'I had to make a very difficult decision.'

He cleared his throat, straightened his waistcoat. A look passed between him and Mother Morning, and I knew they wanted to protect us from the truth, and the truth was death.

'But here she is,' said Mother Morning. 'Bright-eyed, bushy-tailed.'

'Here she is,' said Dr Roach. 'Almost one year old.'

A different dog, then. A new Cynthia.

'What?' said Lawrence.

William and I rolled our eyes at each other. 'She just looks the same,' I said.

'What?' Lawrence repeated, but we knew the truth was dawning.

'It was the kindest thing,' Mother Morning said to Dr Roach. 'You were looking after her in the best possible way.'

'Yes, the kindest thing,' he said. 'And it really is as if I have her still.'

The little dog leapt onto his lap, and he fondled her gingery ears.

'I do hope I'll be around long enough to look after her,' he said. 'Was I selfish to get her, at my age? Before I'd even lost the other one? Was I cruel?'

'Not at all,' said Mother Morning.

Dr Roach had been coming to Captain Scott once every two months for all our lives. He was in quite a few of our baby pictures, listening to our hearts or peering into our mouths or taking our blood, beaming in the background like a grandfather while we tried to grab Cynthia's tail. He'd sit us on his lap and say, 'Shall I have a look at you, my little rabbits?' and we'd feel his hand cool at the back of our necks. When we were a bit older he'd let us tap his knees with the reflex hammer, holding dead still, then shooting a foot straight out to make us laugh. We knew he travelled around the country, visiting the other Sycamore Homes, but we didn't like to think of sharing him with other children. As far as we were concerned, he was ours.

'Can we take Cynthia out to the garden?' asked Lawrence.

'Be my guest,' said Dr Roach. He needed a bit of time to chat to Mother Morning about our symptoms, our medicine, and to go over the notes from the last two months.

'Cynthia! Cynthia!' called Lawrence, fluttering his fingers again, but she didn't seem to know her name, so he picked her up and carried her outside.

As we left the room, Mother Morning opened The Book of Dreams and Dr Roach took out his notebook and pen.

'Let's see what you've been getting up to in your sleep, eh?' he called over his shoulder. He was always very interested in that; he'd told us once that he had a whole department of people studying our dreams, and then Mother Morning had said we shouldn't let that piece of knowledge go to our heads.

The garden was alive with bees looping through the buddleia and the lavender, crawling in and out of the foxgloves. The mossy panes of the old glasshouse – dangerous and out of bounds – glowed bright green, lit from within. Lengths of wisteria drifted on the vines like feather boas, and clusters of saw-toothed pinks released the scent of cloves. In the vegetable patch the cabbages grew fat under the insect-proof mesh; without it, caterpillars would bore through their hearts, and wouldn't that be a dreadful waste? Wouldn't that make you weep? Birds landed on the broken glass at the top of the flint wall, perching there on the sharp bright edges and looking this way and that, too light to hurt themselves. Then they flew to the oaks and horse chestnuts and pecked at the seed balls we'd hung from the branches. We'd made them one Craft Day with Mother Afternoon, when she was teaching us the importance of being kind to wildlife – we'd grated suet and added it to poppyseeds and linseeds, oats and millet and maize, then squashed and pressed the mixture until the warmth of our hands made it stick together. And the birds really did love it, and they didn't starve in the snow, and we knew that we were kind.

Lawrence found a stick and threw it for Cynthia, and soon she got the idea. He couldn't throw it very far, but she bounded away across the grass, faster than we'd ever seen her, and returned moments later to drop the stick at Lawrence's feet and stare at him until he threw it again.

'Can I have a go?' said William, and of course Lawrence handed him the stick straight away because that's just how he was.

William drew back his arm and said, 'Are you ready, girl? Are you ready?' and Cynthia's whole body tightened with anticipation, and then he flung his arm forwards and off she shot – except he hadn't thrown it. He laughed his head off, and then he did the trick again. And again.

'Come on, William, let her have it,' I said.

'Okay, okay. It was just a joke.' He hurled the stick with all his might, and it disappeared into the fernery.

Cynthia raced after it, plunging into the lush fronds; we saw them shaking as she searched back and forth, back and forth.

'Where is it, eh girl?' said William, jogging over. Lawrence and

35

I followed more slowly; he'd been sore in his joints, and I was still feeling some weakness, experiencing a few flutters in my heart. Sometimes the Bug affected us more than our brother. I did my best not to dwell on the flutters; our real parents had both died from heart attacks at a young age, and I knew from The Book of Knowledge that *any extra strain, especially when emphasised by ill health or disease, may prove too much.*

'You're really a bit thick, aren't you?' William was saying as we came up behind him. We could see that Cynthia had shaken loose one of our sacrifices to the garden gods – a tiny bird's skull threaded onto a length of long grass and hung inside the green core of a fern. 'It's right here, idiot.' William picked up the stick and waved it at her – and then he stamped on her hind paw. The noise she made sounded almost human.

'What the hell are you doing?' said Lawrence.

'She hurt herself,' said William. He crouched down and patted her, soothed her, and she buried her snout in the crease of his hip.

'She didn't hurt herself.' Lawrence pushed past me to get to Cynthia, but William picked her up and said, 'You're all right, girl. No harm done.'

'Vincent, you saw that, didn't you?' said Lawrence.

They were both looking at me, waiting for me to reply.

'I . . . I'm not sure,' I said. 'I think she must have hurt herself.'

'Why do you always take his side!' said Lawrence.

'There are no sides,' said William. He held Cynthia up to the gazing ball, and she growled at her warped reflection, then wriggled free and ran off.

'I'll tell Mother Morning,' said Lawrence.

'I'll say it was you.'

'Vincent will back me up.'

'Stop it, both of you!' I said. 'Cynthia seems fine. Let's leave it at that.'

We came back inside through the Laundry so we could clean the soles of our shoes rather than dirtying the whole place. At our feet, crawling up through the drain in the floor, was a cockroach. I didn't say anything, but Cynthia began to sniff at it, and then William noticed. He nudged it with the tip of his shoe.

'You know what I think?' he said. 'I think if I told Vincent to eat that, he would.'

'Don't be horrible,' said Lawrence.

'You would, though, wouldn't you, Vincent?'

'No!'

'We should get back,' said Lawrence. 'They'll be ready for us.' He always tried to keep to the rules; he felt safer that way.

'Sure. As soon as Vincent finishes his elevenses.' William picked up the cockroach and held it out to me. Its slick thorax glinted, and it moved its hair-thin feelers, trying to get its bearings.

And I took the thing from my brother.

And even as Lawrence grabbed my arm and said *Don't, don't,* I closed my eyes, put it in my mouth and swallowed.

After that, we went upstairs to our room and undressed to our underpants so Dr Roach could examine us. He had the softest hands – small and pink, cool but never cold.

'Let's have a look at my last little Captain Scott rabbits, then,' he said.

Lawrence's face fell.

'What's the matter, old chap?' said Dr Roach.

I knew what was coming because Lawrence had voiced it many times over the years.

'That we're the last,' he said. 'What happens to all the other orphans at risk of the Bug? Do they just die?'

'Of course not,' said Dr Roach. 'I'm as disappointed as you are that we can't bring more children to the Homes, but the previous government withdrew funding, and the new lot won't reinstate it.'

Lawrence gave a half-smile, and I knew he was still worrying – he always had the softest heart. William and I teased him for it in private. I'm ashamed of that now.

As usual, Dr Roach chatted away while he worked: his grand-daughter, who was our age, wanted to be a doctor, and he was trying to dissuade her because there were too many in the family already, and she needed to understand that once you were a doctor, you were a doctor for life – no escape. She simply wasn't cut out for it, he said. Didn't have the right character. He wasn't in the business of crushing dreams, but better to find out earlier rather than later, didn't we think? Before one took the wrong path?

These questions didn't require answers either. While Mother Morning watched from the doorway, he moved his stethoscope over our bare chests and backs, looked in our ears and our eyes, and then we lay down and he pressed on our stomachs, felt all around our necks, took our blood. He always took Lawrence's first, to get it over with; Lawrence hated needles. On the ceiling, I noticed, a water stain had spread. It looked like the outline of some unknown country. Every time it rained it spread a little more, but there was no money to fix the roof.

Dr Roach asked us if the dizziness and nausea had resolved, even though he had already chatted to Mother Morning about our symptoms, we knew.

Almost, we said, pleased with ourselves; we hated having to disappoint him with our poor health.

Any headaches, fever, breathing problems?

No, we said, even more pleased with ourselves.

What about fearfulness? What about nightmares?

We shook our heads.

'And still some joint pain for you, Vincent?' he said.

'Joint pain for Lawrence,' Mother Morning reminded him. 'Weakness and occasional insomnia for Vincent, along with a flut-tery heart, and a bit of bruising for William.'

'That's right,' he said. 'Let's see this bruising.'

William lifted his arm to show Dr Roach the black blotches underneath.

'Any pain?'

'No.'

'Excellent, excellent,' he said, and turned to my bed. 'Vincent, what about this weakness still hanging about? That's no good, old chap, is it? All right, I want you to push as hard as you can against my hand. Resist me. Resist. Hmm. Now the other way.'

'Cynthia hurt her hind paw,' said Lawrence.

'What?' Dr Roach dropped his hand, and I was pushing so hard I lurched to the side. 'Why didn't you say? Cynthia! Cynthia!' The little dog appeared from under Lawrence's bed, and the doctor fell to his knees and checked her paws. 'Which one was it? Which *one?*'

We realised he was asking us, not Cynthia.

'Back right,' said Lawrence.

Gently Dr Roach lifted the paw, felt it all over, checked for blood. Moved it backwards and forwards. Then he came and sat on my bed and called her to him, and she ran across the room without limping. 'How do you mean, she hurt it?' he said.

'Oh,' said Lawrence, and I caught his eye, gave the tiniest shake of my head. 'I'm not sure. We just heard her yelp.'

'But you knew which paw she'd hurt.'

'Oh,' said Lawrence again, then faltered.

'She was licking that one,' I said. 'There must have been a sharp stone. Maybe some thorns.'

Something quivered inside me. Moved its hair-thin feelers.

Dr Roach stared into Cynthia's eyes as if expecting her to speak – but Cynthia wasn't telling. He sighed. Opening his bag, he handed a box of glass ampoules to Mother Morning. Injections this month, then. 'One each morning,' he said, 'in the gluteal muscle.'

Lawrence's face fell once more.

'Don't you want to feel better, old chap?' said Dr Roach. 'I really think this will help. We must keep trying.' He had to leave us then, he said, as he was flying to Dresden for an important conference – often he travelled abroad, sharing his work with other doctors in the hope of curing the Bug.

The following day, after we'd told her our dreams, Mother Morning took three ampoules from the box and snapped their glass necks. She drew the medicine into the syringes while we lay on our sides and pulled down the waistbands of our pyjama bottoms, baring our hips for her. Right before she pushed in the needle she said, 'Just a little sting coming now,' so the pain would not take us by surprise. Then she went to the Kitchen and made our breakfast, and we went to do Morning Exercise, and when we came inside to the Refectory we found mugs of cocoa waiting for us on the long pine table where we always sat, and William poured loads of sugar into his, and Lawrence none at all. They both drank theirs scalding hot while I waited for the skin to form on mine. Because we weren't the same. We weren't.

Nancy

The girl whose name was Nancy tried not to squint. Tried not to move.

'Where's that gorgeous smile?' said her father.

Her arm ached from holding the elephant-shaped watering can above the bed of cornflowers, but she looked up at the camera and did her best.

'Good,' called her mother. 'Tilt your head a little to the left. A little more. Perfect.'

The glare from the glass conservatory hurt her eyes. The garden was too hot, the sun too bright, and she'd emptied so much water on the cornflowers that they were drowning, the dark earth hollowing out around their roots. But the sooner her father got the pictures, the sooner she could go back inside the cool house and take off the gingham pedal-pushers and white blouse that she wasn't allowed to get dirty, and have a glass of fizzy drink garnished with mint to make it seem grown-up.

'Now you're laughing,' called her mother. 'Daddy has made a joke, a very funny joke, and you're splitting your sides.'

Nancy didn't know any jokes that funny, but she held one hand to her chest as if she couldn't breathe for laughter.

'Yes!' called her mother. 'Kenneth, look! Are you getting it? Exactly right, poppet.' She came over and straightened the satin bow in Nancy's hair and asked her to sit on the grass, legs crossed, leaning her chin on her left fist. But careful not to wriggle about! She didn't want to dirty the pedal-pushers!

Then the roll of film was finished and Nancy's father was helping her to her feet and her mother was taking the elephant-shaped watering can and returning it to its special hook in the potting shed.

'Did you get some good ones?' Nancy asked. 'Do you think?'

'They'll be the business, all right,' said her father, and he tucked her hair behind her ear.

She hoped the pictures would turn out well. Her parents would scrutinise them when they came back from the chemist, noting the way she held her mouth when she smiled, the way she crinkled her nose when she laughed. Whether her dimple was showing itself or not. Whether her long black hair was falling over the correct shoulder.

'Turn your studs, poppet,' her mother reminded her.

Months had passed since Nancy's birthday, but the earrings still hurt. She turned them every few days so the holes wouldn't close over.

'What would you like for your tea?' asked her mother as they retreated into the house, where net curtains softened the light from every window, blurred the view to the outside.

And Nancy said, 'Beans on toast,' even though she didn't much care for them.

Vincent

That June, three months after Lawrence's first dream of the girl in the woods, I began dreaming of her too. She was running through the trees in a long wispy dress, tangled hair flying out behind her, the ends of it brushing my outstretched fingers. Moonlight filtered through the leaves, and night birds called to me in human voices.

'What are they saying?' asked Mother Morning.

'I . . . I can't remember,' I said. 'I keep telling the girl to slow down – warning her that she'll have an accident. It starts as a game, but then it's not.'

'Why is it not a game?'

'We shouldn't be out so late at night. Nobody knows where we are.'

'Does she have a name?'

'No. No name. And then she trips and hurts herself. I'm trying to help her, and she won't stop crying. That's the end.'

Mother Morning wrote it all down.

My brothers and I had no idea who the girl was; we supposed we'd just invented her – bits and pieces of the village girls, and Eve in The Book of Knowledge, and the girls in the *Woman's Realm* knitting patterns that we'd sneaked a look at once or twice, even though the magazines, like the newspaper, were for grown-ups only. That was how it worked, wasn't it? A bit from here and a bit from there? So Dr Roach had told us, and he should know, with his whole department of people. Lawrence's dreams of the girl were more pleasant than mine – they were running through the woods in springtime, and the sun shone down on her naked skin, and she was pale as toothpaste, and bumblebees drifted amongst the blackthorn blossoms.

Only William was scared of the girl, scared of his dreams of her. Only William never reported them. I tried my best to cheer him up, reminding him she wasn't real; I hated seeing him so affected. I would have done anything to help him.

My heart was still fluttering at that time, and I'd begun feeling weaker than ever; some mornings I could scarcely push back the covers and get out of bed. I'd have liked to stay there all day, drowsing under my crochet blanket, finding my way back into my dreams so I could catch the girl when she fell – that part always made me uneasy – but I forced myself to get up. You couldn't let yourself become a lazybones, because that was just the kind of attitude that would see the Bug win, and if that happened then quite frankly you deserved it. First thing every day, no matter the weather, I put on my shorts and vest and headed out to the garden for Morning Exercise with my brothers. After our warm-up stretches we touched our toes, did our press-ups and star jumps, taking turns to count them off in sets of ten, and then we ran round and round the inside of the flint wall till we couldn't breathe. If Lawrence could keep going despite his sore joints, then I could keep going too.

In Lessons that week we were doing our world maps, which Mother Morning had traced for us on baking paper from the fold-out one in The Book of Knowledge. We spread them on the big splintery table we used each Craft Day, but the baking paper kept rolling back up, so we had to hold it flat with our left hands and colour in the landmasses with our right – except William got it wrong and started colouring in the oceans. Well, he said, how could you tell the water from the land when it was all just outlines?

And this was very true; he had a particular way of looking at the world, my brother. Mother Morning said she couldn't give him a fresh map because she didn't have any spares, they didn't grow on trees, and William – smiling his beautiful smile – said weren't they made of paper? And Mother Morning said she could see where he was going and she had no time for it.

She wrote *ANTARCTICA* on the blackboard and underlined it twice, then took Volume 6 (ORG–SER) of The Book of Knowledge from the shelf and turned to The Immortal Story of Captain Scott – one of our favourites, since we were Captain Scott boys. As we filled in the sliver of Antarctica at the bottom of our maps with our white and grey and pale-blue pencils, she read to us: 'On 29 March, 1912, three men lay dying in a little tent far away in the frozen Antarctic continent – three heroic men who had reached the South Pole.' We loved picturing the little tent, and we loved the part about Scott's last letter – 'his imperishable farewell to England, in which he said, "I do not regret this journey, which has shown that Englishmen can endure hardships, help one another, and meet death with as great fortitude as ever in the past. We have been willing to give our lives for this enterprise, which is for the honour of our country." But let us not forget his comrade Captain Oates,' Mother Morning went on: struck down with frostbite in his feet and hands, he sacrificed himself to save the rest of his party. He knew he was slowing them down, so he folded away his reindeer-skin sleeping bag and calmly and politely said *I am just going outside and may be some time*, and then he stepped from the tent and into the blizzard to face certain death. A true Briton, beamed Mother Morning; an example to the rest of us. No fuss. No fanfare.

I kept going over the same patches with my pencils, layering grey on blue on white on grey to suggest endless snow, endless ice, till the paper gleamed like the skin of an apple. My hand felt tired when I'd finished.

Then I saw it.

'Mother Morning?' I said, raising my good hand.

She paused in her reading of Scott's final instructions to his wife regarding their son – *you must guard him from indolence. Make him a strenuous man.* 'Yes, Vincent?'

'There are two New Zealands.'

'I beg your pardon?'

I showed her my map, pointing to the New Zealand on the right-hand edge and the New Zealand on the left-hand edge. 'And look, two Russian peninsulas.'

She seemed flustered. 'Well, that can't be right.'

'Is it from when they signed the Gothenburg Treaty?' said William. 'After they blew Hitler to bits, and some countries got more land and some got less?'

She began to flick through Volume 8 (FACT INDEX) of The Book of Knowledge as if she might find an answer.

And why hadn't we noticed it before? Two New Zealands, and two Russian peninsulas jutting out into two Bering Seas. Was it true? Could there be places in the world exactly the same as other places? All the mountains and roads and rivers identical, all the shops and houses, all the people?

'Ah,' said Mother Morning, finding the original map in the FACT INDEX and folding it open, tapping the page. 'Here's the reason – of course. The map is just showing us that those two edges meet up. You have to imagine it as a globe.'

'Like the gazing ball in the fernery,' said Lawrence.

'Exactly right! Excellent!' she said.

'Or the group photo,' I said. 'With William in it twice.'

We turned to look at the photograph that hung next to the Equipment Cupboard.

We were silent for a few seconds.

'I don't think that's quite the same thing as the maps,' said Mother Morning.

'It was funny, though,' I said. I nudged William. 'Wasn't it?'

William was frowning at his map and didn't reply. Something was wrong with the world.

'What's that meant to be?' I asked him at Break Time. His Antarctica was mostly scribbles, with one tiny figure sprawled on the ice, gnawing at a bone.

'A sledge-dog eating one of the ponies,' he said.

'I wouldn't let Mother Morning see.'

'It's historically accurate.'

Laying my head down on my arms, I didn't reply. I was so tired all of a sudden, so weak.

'Are you all right?' asked Lawrence. He stroked my hair with a kind hand.

'He's not a baby, stupid!' said William, so I sat up and tried to make a joke of it.

'I am just going outside,' I said, 'and may be some time.'

Mother Morning came back with our elevenses and medicine right at that moment – and of course she heard me, because she heard everything. I was expecting a telling-off, the raised eyebrow, but she said, 'You've been struggling lately, Vincent.'

I nodded.

She excused me from Lessons and told me to go and rest on the daybed in the Playroom – except that didn't help, and nor did the soups and broths Mother Afternoon prepared for me over the following days, the crustless toast cut into soldiers. I wouldn't touch the treacle tart that Mr Webb the baker sent home with her for me, even though I agreed it was a very nice gesture. On Chicken Day, which was my favourite day of the month, I couldn't even bite the meat from the bone; Mother Afternoon had to cut it into little pieces and feed me.

'Goodness gracious,' she said, 'when I win Spot the Ball, and buy my little cottage, you won't be any use to me, will you? I need strapping young slaves who can lift my pet alligator into the bath. Brush his teeth twice a day.' She always pretended she'd need our help, but in truth she was stronger than any of us, with sturdy legs and broad hands. She never got sick.

My brothers were struggling with the Bug more than usual too.

William had come out in hives all over his chest and was scratching himself till he bled; Mother Afternoon scrubbed at the spots on his vests, soaking them overnight in cold water to get out the marks. Lawrence said his throat felt pinchy and tight, so she made him a hot drink with one of her frozen lemon-juice cubes, but the next day he said he thought his throat might close over, and then his tongue started itching and his lips swelled up. As soon as that happened Mother Morning gave him an injection – not our medicine but something else – and summoned Dr Roach, even though he'd visited only the week before. He came early now and then, if we were really suffering with the Bug – if we were in grave danger because we had failed to eat our vegetables and do our Morning Exercise and maintain the right attitude. This time he arrived in a matter of hours, the tyres of the kidney-red Jaguar flinging gravel off the driveway as he zoomed up to the house, the new Cynthia catapulting herself from the passenger door as if she sensed an emergency. Lawrence was fine again by that stage, but quick smart Dr Roach decided that clearly our injections weren't working, and all three of us needed different medicine, better medicine, in order to keep on top of things. He gave us some canary-yellow pills to start the next day, and said Mother Morning had been right to call him. Then he whistled to Cynthia, who leapt back into the Jaguar with him, and we waved them off from the front steps.

'Vincent, do you feel well enough to join us for Lessons?' asked Mother Morning, and I said I'd give it a try, because it was Thursday, which meant we had Ethical Hour. 'Good boy,' she said. 'Back to the Library, then.'

'Mother Morning,' said Lawrence, still finishing off a few raisins from Break Time as we took our seats, 'wasn't there a boy who died when his throat felt tight and his tongue started itching? A couple of years ago maybe?'

'I don't think so,' said Mother Morning.

'But I remember his lips swelled so he could hardly speak,' said Lawrence, 'and other boys said he looked like a goldfish, and then he died. Joseph someone, Jason someone . . . his name began with J, definitely.'

'I really don't recall,' said Mother Morning.

Then she wrote that week's question for Ethical Hour on the blackboard: *A building is on fire. You can rescue a trapped child, or you can rescue a valuable painting and sell it in order to raise enough money to save twenty children from starvation. What should you do and why?*

We'd discussed such questions before: was it ever right to kill, for instance? To sacrifice one for the sake of many? We never could settle on the right answer – which was itself the right answer.

I couldn't sleep. I threw off a blanket and punched my pillow into shape, tried emptying my mind of all thoughts. I pulled the blanket over me again, lay on my side, lay on my back. Nothing worked. Lawrence and William were breathing in time, dead to the world as usual, and I hated them for it. We'd been on the new medicine for almost a week by then, and while my fluttery heart had settled and the weakness had improved a little, the Bug was still making me wakeful.

I sighed, climbed out of bed. Under my feet I felt the rag rug Mother Afternoon had knotted from her sewing scraps – little bits of cloth left over when she made us our trousers and shirts and pyjamas. The knot from Philip Cole's blue striped shirt pressed into my sole; it sat a little higher than the others, and normally I tried to avoid that spot. He'd worn the shirt the day he left for Margate, so excited that he pushed the buttons into the wrong buttonholes. Mother Morning had fixed it for him – we couldn't be sending our boys out into the world looking like street urchins! What would people think?

'Don't worry, it'll be your turn soon,' Philip had called to me as he climbed into the Van.

William said something in his sleep – impossible to make out – and Lawrence laughed, then both fell silent once more. I pushed aside the curtains. In the garden the gazing ball gleamed like a fallen moon, and all the greenery was black: black ferns, black flowers, black willow trailing like black whispers. Somewhere in amongst it, our little sacrifices to the garden gods, the holes we'd dug looking for treasure. I couldn't say why, but in my mind I heard the noise Cynthia made when William stamped on her paw – not an accident, I knew. I knew. He'd done the same to me before, bringing his boot down on my bare foot, and I'd let out similar yelps. I hadn't told anyone about that either; for whatever reason, I realised I needed to keep William's cruelties to myself.

'I don't understand why you protect him,' Lawrence had said once. He was rubbing my hair with a towel after William had held my face under the bath tap.

'Because he's my brother,' I'd said.

'So am I.'

'He does stupid things sometimes. Acts without thinking. That's all.'

Lawrence didn't answer. He just kept rubbing my hair dry, gentle as ever, then hung up the towel in its proper place.

Lawrence never spat in my sandwiches the way William did; he never hid worms in my slippers, or wrung my wrists till the skin stung, or kicked the back of my knee to make my leg collapse. It was William who'd torn the parachute on the plastic soldier from my one and only Lucky Bag so that now he plummeted to the ground. And yet, I loved William better. I still can't explain that, but perhaps you can understand – perhaps you have loved in that way too.

Out there beyond the flint wall, further than I could see in the dark, the ponies moved across the heathland. Sometimes, in the daylight, we watched them from our bedroom window nuzzling their foals, grazing amongst the patches of bracken and gorse. We'd seen them in the village, too, walking down the high street, bunting the hanging baskets of petunias and nasturtiums, blocking the way on the stone bridge. The villagers just ignored them the way they ignored us – but at night we knew the ponies were there; we could hear them nickering, sense their muscular bulk. On our Nature Walks, Mother Afternoon told us they were not wild in the true sense of the word but were owned by local people who let them roam where they liked – they seemed wild to us, though, and that is how we thought of them. Once, as we lay in our beds and waited for sleep to come, William said, 'Do you reckon we could catch them? Jump on their backs and ride away?' But the ponies were not to be touched; they could bite children, kick them, trample them.

Lawrence and William breathed on and on, their eyelids quivering. I closed the curtains and stole into the passageway.

Two rooms along, in the Upstairs Common Room that we rarely used now, Mother Night sat knitting. Her needles clicked out the rhythm of every stitch, and at her elbow the radio played something soft and classical, all blurry violins. The stuffed pike glared down from amongst its reeds and rushes.

'I can't sleep again,' I said, and she looked up, nodded to the armchair opposite her.

'Are you warm enough? Shall I turn up the gas?'

'No,' I said.

'No you're not warm enough, or no I shouldn't turn up the gas?'

'I'm warm enough,' I said.

'And?'

'And thank you.'

'That's better.'

We hadn't really known Mother Night as little children. Her shift started at 9 p.m. and finished at 5 a.m., and she kept to her quarters the rest of the time, or went into the village, so for many years she was a shadowy figure to us – someone who materialised to check our temperatures if we were feverish or change our sheets if we wet the bed. As we grew older, though, if we woke in the night from a dream, we learned to call for her – not with our voices, which would have woken everyone else, but by reaching for the buttons next to our beds. We had one each: a little black disc that said *Press*, like a doorbell, and it would sound in the Upstairs Common Room, lighting up the correct boy's name on a console, and then she would come. She would sit on the edge of the bed and open The Book of Dreams, her torch flaring on the page like a tiny sun as she recorded everything we told her: floating through the River Caves at Dreamland and turning to ice in the Ice Cave; a life-size lady made of shells, her sharp skirts scraping the ground as she walked; birds circling a faceless girl, trying to land on her head.

'What are you knitting?' I said now.

'An Aran jumper.' She held up the few rows of red stitches: only a waistband so far, and the stumps of cables that would twist up the body.

'For William?'

'He's outgrown his old one.'

'So have Lawrence and I.'

'You'll be next.'

She didn't need to look at her knitting as she worked; her hands knew the patterns. How lovely she was: brown eyes pale as acorns, long elegant limbs, wavy black hair secured with tortoiseshell combs. I could picture her balancing a cigarette holder between her tapered fingers, laughing on a yacht with other fabulous persons. While Mother Morning wore housecoats to protect her clothes from chalk dust, and Mother Afternoon had her aprons to catch the spatters of soup and stew and the smears of furniture polish, Mother Night was different. She dressed in houndstooth skirts and silky blouses, patent-leather shoes with heels that made her taller than she really was. A tiny gold watch glimmered on her wrist.

'Why don't you wear a nightdress?' I asked, drawing my legs up underneath me. The gas breathed its warm breath at us, and in the dim light the painted fire surround could have been real marble.

'Because your night is my day, of course,' she replied. 'I need to convince my body to stay awake. I need to trick it.'

I watched her looping the wool around her fingers, pushing the needles in and out. *Click-click-click, click-click-click.* 'Don't you ever feel sleepy?'

'Not if I get enough sleep during the day. No boys running about the place, yelling and screaming like mad things.'

We were supposed to keep quiet between 5 a.m. and 1 p.m. so we didn't wake Mother Night: that was the rule. No shouting *You're It!* in the garden, no racing one another down the stairs. If we forgot about the rule and began to yell and scream like mad things – if something in us took over and we simply couldn't help it – then Mother Morning would appear, jabbing a finger in the direction of the North Wing and reminding us to rein ourselves in. 'Don't make me write this up,' she'd warn.

Mother Night finished a row of stitches and swapped the needles over. 'There's a story,' she said, lowering her voice, 'about these jumpers. Do you know it?'

'I don't think so.'

'They were worn by fishermen originally,' she went on. 'Knitted by wives, sweethearts. Mothers. Each family had their own pattern, so that if a man was lost at sea and then washed up some time later, they could identify his body.'

'Couldn't they just look at his face?'

She shook her head. 'Not if he'd been in the water for weeks. Beaten against rocks. Nibbled on. Bloated with brine.'

'*Nibbled* on?' I said.

'Fish,' she said, glancing at the sharp-toothed pike. 'Crustaceans.'

I shivered.

'It's probably just a story,' she said.

'The nibbling?'

'Oh no, that's true. The nibbling happens. Outright biting, I expect. No, the part about the different patterns to identify the loved ones.'

Mother Night was full of information about the world; I used to wonder if she read The Book of Knowledge while we all slept.

I had begun to long for the insomnia just so I could sit up late with her when everyone else was sleeping, though I knew not to mention our chats to anyone; she'd been very clear about that.

I worried at a loose thread on my pyjamas and imagined a waterlogged body. Sand in the mouth, seaweed choking the throat. Tiny creatures underneath the clothes, all pincers and teeth.

'You'll make a hole,' she said.

The radio at her elbow burbled softly about Schubert, who had left his eighth symphony unfinished, and then the music crept through the speaker, the opening notes dark and low.

Her hands worked the wool and the needles, *click-click-click*, regular as a machine. 'You're like the little baker in Mr Webb's window,' I said. 'The automaton in his white hat, tapping his spoon.'

'I find it soothing,' she said.

'Mother Morning called Mr Webb simple. A bit touched.'

'To his *face*?'

'No, just to us.'

'He's a kind man,' she said.

'Yes,' I said. 'A kind man.'

A sad and pretty tune began to float over Schubert's restless strings – an oboe, I thought, or maybe a clarinet. I knew a little about such instruments from The Book of Knowledge.

'Why don't the villagers like us?' I said. 'Apart from Mr Webb?'

Mother Night paused in her knitting. 'They're just different,' she said.

'How?'

'They think you don't deserve basic human rights.'

'But what have we done?'

'Nothing. Nothing.'

'I thought we might be able to make some new friends,' I said. 'Boys our age.'

'You know you can't chat to anyone unconnected with your errands.'

'But *why*?'

'It's not safe. You know that.'

'The Bug,' I said, and she nodded. 'I just thought . . .' I sighed. 'Tell me about when you were growing up, then.'

'I had a very ordinary childhood,' she said. 'Nothing memorable.'

'I'd still like to know.' We had a deep curiosity about ordinary people – children with ordinary parents who hadn't died young from heart attacks. That's understandable, don't you think? Even though we weren't allowed to talk to them?

She gazed at me and gave a smile, a sad little smile. 'Well,' she said, resuming her knitting, *click-click-click*, 'maybe if you ask me a specific question, I might remember some details.' She pulled on the thread of wool, letting out another length, and the ball spun and tumbled on the parquet floor.

'Okay . . . what games did you play?'

'Ah, games,' she said, settling further back into her chair. 'I loved croquet. I was a croquet champion. We had a huge lawn at the back of our house, and my sister and I would push in the wire hoops and clear away anything that could send the balls off course. We were scrupulous in our preparations, so there could be no arguments about twigs or pebbles getting in the way. Mostly I won, but now and then I threw the game because Emma got so upset. I'd whack the ball in completely the wrong direction, and she'd say *Frances, you silly, the hoop is here, look.* I'd say *They're hard to see, though. Remember Mr Hill?* And we'd recall the awful day that Mr Hill had visited, and had hooked his toes through a croquet hoop and fallen flat on his face. *The blood! His glasses, smashed to bits!* So it seemed quite reasonable that I might fumble my shot once in a while. Oh, and skittles – we played skittles too. Our father painted the pins to look like our family, so we had the four grandparent skittles, and then the two parents, and then Frances and Emma and our baby brother Reggie. We hated hitting him, but we lobbed the ball at each other no holds barred. You know how siblings are. Sometimes they let you win, and sometimes they knock you clean over.'

On she talked – about the gloves she and Emma had knitted on toothpicks for their dolls, and Honey the cat, who scooped gold-fish from the pond, which was terrible but also just the way of things – and then the unfinished symphony finished and I could barely keep my eyes open.

'Come along,' said Mother Night, leading me back to my room. 'And we'll keep our night-time chats to ourselves,' she reminded me in a whisper. Yes, I nodded, my head a boulder. Then she tucked me into bed and kissed my forehead, and I caught the scent of her face cream – clean and cool, a little waxy. Then I fell fast asleep.

The Minister of Loneliness

The Minister scrutinised her reflection. 'Can you make me look a bit . . .' she said, gesturing at her face. 'You know, a bit . . .'

'Younger?' said the makeup girl.

'Kinder,' said the Minister at the same time. A tissue was working its way loose from her collar, and she pushed it in again to keep herself clean, then sat back in the chair and tried not to frown at her dark circles, her wilting jowls. Frowning would only make things worse.

The makeup girl fluttered her fingers over the trays of pancake foundation, the blushers, the shadows, the shimmers. The little discs she used most were worn down in the centres, like chalky cakes of paint in a paintbox. The Minister remembered one she'd owned as a child: a long flat tin with a picture of circus animals on the lid and, inside, a blunt brush too stiff to paint anything good. Anything lifelike. Her mother scolding her: *You've mixed the colours together, Sylvia. You should have rinsed the brush each time. Now they all look like mud.*

'We'll brighten you up,' the makeup girl was saying. 'Something peachy for the cheeks, and a soft pink lip. Nothing garish. Nothing harsh.'

'Do you have a family?' the Minister asked as the girl dabbed and blended. 'Children, I mean.'

'No, but I have a fiancé,' she said. The tiniest diamond, hardly visible from some angles, glittered on her ring finger. 'Close your eyes, please.'

While the girl worked her magic, the Minister ran through the things she needed to say in the interview. Hard decisions had to be made. The Homes had run their course – reached their natural end point, if you like. They were a relic of an earlier era – an earlier administration – and the current government could no longer justify the considerable taxpayer expense, et cetera. Then she'd smile and say that something good could come out of the Scheme finally winding down, and this was where she, the Minister, had a role to play. The residents of the Homes – the children, the *children* – could be rehomed to approved families or individuals, and could provide that thing so vital to human wellbeing: companionship. There was a range of skin colours and temperaments for applicants to choose from, she'd say, and a range of ages: eight to thirteen. And there was absolutely no danger to the public. It was win-win.

In the studio the Minister took her place as the interviewer scanned his notes. He was wearing makeup too – up close he looked terracotta, but you never noticed that when you watched him on television. The lights glared into the Minister's face and somewhere beyond them the cameramen crept about like great black insects. It was a pre-record, she told herself – not live. She sucked in her stomach, angled her body. After her first TV appearance, her mother had rung to ask if she'd gained a great deal of weight.

'No,' she'd said.

'Really?' said her mother. 'Really and truly? My goodness, you looked enormous. I said to your father, isn't she the image of Aunt Audrey? She was dead at forty-three from the weight.'

'Welcome back,' said the interviewer. 'Tonight, with special permission from Downing Street, we cover a topic normally kept out of the headlines: the Sycamore Scheme. I'm joined by Sylvia Dalton, Minister of Loneliness, who today confirmed rumours that she plans to disestablish Britain's Sycamore Homes. Minister, over the years there have been skirmishes *within* the Homes, but since the regulations were relaxed last year, residents allowed out on errands have been causing concern in villages across the country. Now you'll be releasing them into the community on a permanent basis. What do you say to those viewers, those ordinary people, who are terrified at the implications of all this?'

'Good evening, Brian,' said the Minister. 'If I can just put you right, the disestablishment is the Prime Minister's initiative, but of course I'm delighted to implement it for her.'

'So you're only following orders, is what you're telling me?'

The Minister forced herself to smile. 'The thing is, the Homes are the relic of an earlier era and have run their course – reached their natural end point, if you like. They were a coalition initiative, established in the years following the war, and we simply inherited them. And for a while, they worked – let's not forget the good they achieved under the periods of our governance. But the previous administration had already started winding down the Scheme eight years ago – only a few residents now remain in each Home – and, looking at the cost-benefit analysis, it's clear we can no longer justify the taxpayer expense.'

'So the decision is purely fiscal.'

'Not at all, but at a time when hard choices have to be made about programmes that place a burden on the taxpayer, the Sycamore Homes cannot escape scrutiny. And the fact remains that the buildings – in many cases historic – and the large areas of land attached to them could be put to better use.'

The interviewer fixed her with that look he had. 'Three dead in Flamborough,' he said. 'Three families, devastated.'

'Flamborough was an unfortunate anomaly, and of course we extend our heartfelt—'

'An *anomaly*? What about Lavenham? What about Ambleside, and the other incidents since the regulations were changed? Not as catastrophic, perhaps, but still troubling.'

'The previous government – a shambolic minority government – were the ones who changed the regulations,' said the Minister. 'It is now up to us to put things right. These incidents that you mention, Brian, arose because a vigilante member of the public spoke out of turn. Everybody knows the illegality of fraternising with the Sycamore residents beyond brief transactional exchanges. Certainly, everybody knows the illegality of sharing sensitive information with them, and the harsh penalties for flouting this law.'

'But that's just my point, Minister. Over the past year we've seen the consequences of the residents having contact with ordinary people – and now you're asking us to welcome them into our homes?'

'It's true that some individual residents have reacted undesirably when provoked by one of these ordinary people – people choosing to sensationalise certain details about the Scheme, or acting out of a sense of misplaced compassion. We regret this – of course we regret this. Anyone with a beating heart couldn't fail to be moved by such incidents. But they were *isolated* incidents, and the residents concerned were taken care of appropriately, and all remaining residents will be very carefully vetted before release.'

'You admit they're potentially dangerous, then. Are we not, in fact, taking a risk in even covering the story?'

'Not at all. The residents – the children – have no access to television. On special occasions—'

'Children?' said the interviewer. 'Come now, Minister – you can't be asking us to think of them as we think of our sons and daughters.'

The Minister surprised herself then. 'Perhaps that's just the shift in mindset we need,' she said.

The interviewer laughed. 'And where would that end? Legal citizenship? Intermarriage?' He shook his head.

'Regarding television coverage of the story,' the Minister said, 'on special occasions the children are permitted to view certain items – the Queen's Christmas message, for instance – but nothing beyond that. The same is true for radio and newspapers. And as you yourself said, the topic is normally kept out of the headlines.'

'But what happens when they're living in the community and discover the truth?'

'Most likely they never will. The same laws around non-disclosure of information will apply. The same deterrents. Up until last year, ordinary people knew the rules and just got on with things, never giving the Scheme a second thought.'

'Until they came face to face with the residents and had to give it a great deal of thought,' said the interviewer. 'Until Flamborough happened.'

'As I said, Flamborough was an isolated incident, and the resident involved has been taken care of. Besides, the residents, the children, will be placed in loving homes, which our research suggests will make all the difference. And if they do discover anything, the families will frame the narrative in terms of heroism – each and every child having done their bit.'

'Like the carriers of genetic diseases who, post-Gothenburg, have opted for voluntary sterilisation?'

'A bit like that, yes.'

'But what these *isolated incidents* demonstrate, Minister, is that the Sycamore residents are unpredictable creatures. One has to wonder whether Alastair Roach really knew what he was doing back when he let the genie out of the bottle.'

She was starting to feel very hot under the lights. Sticky between her fingers, her face turning to wax. 'As you know, Brian, the Homes have not been part of my brief until now, so you'd really need to ask the Prime Minister about the historical side of things, or indeed Dr Roach – but I can assure you, and assure the public, that the residents pose absolutely no danger. Some of them already *are* in the community, after all. Cleaning our streets. Scrubbing our lavatories. Nannying, even – looking after people's *babies*.'

'Taking jobs away from British citizens who are crying out for work, in other words.'

'Well, I wouldn't—'

'Besides, they're the older generations. The ones you plan to release are different. You really can't compare the two populations.'

'As I said, they'll be very carefully vetted, and we're planning Socialisation Days between the different Homes so the children can practise real-life scenarios together. And what an opportunity—'

'And is it the case that hospitals will pick up where the Homes leave off?'

'I understand a clinical model has been in development for some time, yes, but again, that's a question for the Prime Minister and Dr Roach – I can't speak for them. What we should be focusing on, what we should be *celebrating*, is the opportunity this represents for people in desperate need of companionship. Childless couples, or those with an only child longing for a sibling. The elderly, the bereaved. It's win-win.'

'You're saying that these . . . these individuals will suddenly understand kindness?'

It had sounded that way. 'Yes,' said the Minister, aware she was promising something she almost definitely couldn't deliver. 'That's exactly what I'm saying.'

At home, her husband was watching the darts with the sound down. A man in a gold shirt took aim, his hand graceful as a white bird. He hit the treble 20 once, twice, three times, the darts so close to one another that surely they'd landed in the same hole.

'Well, I'm glad that's over,' she said.

'What's over?'

'My interview.'

'Was that today?'

She couldn't blame him; she'd been downplaying the whole thing.

'How was it?'

'A bit tough. A few traps.'

'You always know what to say, though. How to weasel your way out.'

'Do I?'

'Oh yes. You're a crafty one. When does it air?'

'Tomorrow night – I'll be back from Captain Scott to see it. Why are you watching the darts?'

'It reminds me of my dad.'

On the television a man with luxuriant sideburns made little practice jabs in the air, then let the darts fly. The treble 20 again, one two three.

'Why don't they aim for the bullseye?'

He shrugged. 'Something to do with the scoring – they have to get to zero exactly.'

'How is zero a score?'

'I don't know. Mum would never let me play. You're going to learn the bassoon and make something of yourself, she said.'

Sylvia went upstairs to the powder-blue bathroom and ran the hot water till it stung, then rubbed away the makeup. It smeared across the flannel like mud. She was fast asleep before her husband came to bed.

The next day she dressed in her navy suit and cream suede heels. Perhaps a risk – they marked so easily – but she was only going to Hampshire. It wasn't the jungle; it wasn't a coal mine. It wasn't Flamborough, for that matter. Quite safe, she reminded herself. Quite, quite safe. All the same, that morning she'd told her husband she loved him and slipped a vegetable knife into her handbag.

'Could I have a little air please, Evans?' she asked her driver when they reached the outskirts of London. The day was hot, her suit far too heavy.

'Of course, madam. Anything I can do, just sing out.'

Can you take me somewhere else? she wanted to ask him. Can you not leave me there?

But in no time at all they were approaching the high flint wall, and a pretty young auburn-haired woman in an unremarkable grey dress was opening the gates.

Vincent

We knew something was up because all three of our mothers were sitting at our table in the Refectory. We almost never saw them together.

'What's happened?' I said. 'Is it Dr Roach?'

He was old and getting older; he told us so just about every time he visited. He couldn't kick a ball around the garden any more; he couldn't bowl us his leg breaks while we waited at the end of our makeshift cricket pitch, bat poised, trying to guess his strategy. When we tugged on his sleeve to draw him outside, he protested that his knees and hips were gone and his back was going. Bit by bit he was leaving us. We dreaded the day when we lost him altogether.

'Dr Roach is fine,' said Mother Morning, who appeared to have powdered her face; her freckles looked fainter. 'In fact, he'll be here in a little while.'

No reason for him to visit us again so soon. Our symptoms had settled, hadn't they? A bit of insomnia, some lingering bruising and weakness. Occasional nausea. Nothing worrisome.

'We've some exciting news to share, boys,' said Mother Afternoon. 'We're expecting a very important guest after lunch. A Cabinet Minister, no less.'

She didn't look excited. Nor did Mother Night, who stared at the toast cooling in the rack.

'The new government wants to make some changes to the Sycamore Homes,' said Mother Morning. 'We should feel honoured that the Minister has chosen to visit ours to see how they work.'

'What sort of changes?' I said.

'Oh, this and that,' said Mother Morning, bending to rub at a scuff mark on the green linoleum. 'I imagine she'll give us more details when she's here.'

'Is the Minister a female?' said William.

'And why wouldn't she be?' said Mother Morning. 'Remember Joan of Arc.'

She'd read to us about her from The Book of Knowledge, her face alight as she recounted how Joan, *the girl heroine clothed in armour, with the golden-lilied banner of France waving above her head, led an enthusiastic army to the relief of the walled city of Orléans.*

'And our new Prime Minister is a woman too,' she went on. 'A woman, and the daughter of an ordinary teacher. What a magnificent example.'

'Perhaps they'll burn her at the stake,' murmured Mother Night.

Mother Morning shot her a look. 'She is going to make sweeping reforms,' she said. 'I for one am full of hope. *Full* of hope.'

Mother Afternoon said, 'I don't think the likes of us . . .' and then trailed off.

Mother Night straightened a piece of toast that sat crooked in the rack.

'Do we bow?' said Lawrence.

'What?' said Mother Morning.

'Do we bow to the Minister?'

'Goodness me, she's not the Queen!' said Mother Afternoon, who adored the royal family and cut pictures of them from the *Woman's Realm*. Her eyes went all dreamy then, and I expected she was imagining the Queen coming to visit, or poor sad Princess Margaret, who was Mother Afternoon's favourite because she hid her sadness almost completely but you could just tell. She sighed.

'I should finish my ikebana,' she said, and she went out to the garden to clip some lengths of willow for her arrangement that would express the tension between extravagance and simplicity with the clever use of negative space.

'Well now, eat up,' said Mother Morning.

The toast was stone cold and so were the scrambled eggs, but we weren't to waste a scrap and we weren't to complain. Some children had nothing to eat at all. Some children had never seen a scrambled egg in their lives. We were to count ourselves lucky.

'If they have nothing to eat at all,' said William, 'how are they even alive?'

'They're not,' said Mother Morning. 'They've starved to death.'

'I feel sick,' said Lawrence.

'No you don't,' she told him. Now and then the Bug made him vomit, but we knew from her tone that there was to be no vomiting today.

At two o'clock, we were sent upstairs to change into our best shirts – green for Lawrence, red for William and yellow for me. We tamed our cowlicks with water and cut our fingernails down to the quick with the nail scissors that were not a toy. Then we came downstairs, touching the wings of the griffin on the newel post for luck, and went and waited in the Gun Room. Mother Afternoon was arranging the tassels on the cushions and giving the china horses an extra dust even though they didn't need it. One side of the philodendron plant was bushier than the other – the side that got the most light, because that was how photosynthesis worked – so after she'd wiped each leaf she turned this better side towards the chintz sofa where the Minister would sit. A diamante hairclip sparkled in her hair.

We started when we heard a car crunching up the freshly raked gravel driveway, but of course it wasn't the Minister, because how would she have got through the gates?

Mother Afternoon, who had run to the window, said, 'False alarm – just Dr Roach,' and that made sense because he had his own key. 'Settle down now,' she told us, her big round face flushed, her eyes slipping to the window every few seconds.

'Good afternoon,' said Dr Roach, his gold cufflinks flashing. He stifled a yawn. He was just back from meeting his fellow physicians in Potsdam, he said – a late flight the previous night – so we'd have to excuse him. Certainly, he seemed more subdued than usual.

'Did you find a cure?' said Lawrence. 'In Potsdam?'

'We're working on it,' said Dr Roach. He took a seat on a damask armchair, Cynthia at his feet. Normally he sat on the chintz sofa, but someone must have told him it was reserved for the Minister, or he must have realised this himself. He took a bag of sweets from his pocket – milk teeth, our favourites, because they looked like real teeth and gums – and set them down on the mantelpiece next to a china mare. 'For later,' he said. 'If you're good little rabbits.'

We protested when Mother Afternoon whisked them away, but she pointed out that the Minister wouldn't want to see a bag of teeth, and we agreed that this was probably the case.

At ten minutes to three, Mother Morning made her way down to the gates. We could see her in the distance, patting at her hair, smoothing her best dress, checking her watch. At five minutes to three she pressed her face to the wrought iron and peered down the road. Three o'clock came and went, and then ten past, and then quarter past, and perhaps the Minister wasn't coming after all; perhaps at the last minute she had chosen a different Home with better children. Finally, at half past three, the black car appeared, and Mother Morning was unlocking the gates and sweeping her arm to indicate the way to the house, though that was quite obvious. She locked the gates again and hurried along behind the car in shoes we hadn't seen before, the high heels slipping on the gravel.

The Minister was smaller than we'd expected; we towered over her, and I thought I saw her flinch when she shook my brothers and me by the hand. She had short, no-nonsense brown hair and pale-blue eyes that seemed to see everything, and she wore a brooch pinned to her lapel: a filmy-gowned angel hovering in the air, two sleeping babies in her arms.

'Do sit down,' said Mother Morning in a voice not quite her own. She gestured to the chintz sofa next to the three of us, but the Minister mustn't have understood that this was where she was supposed to sit, because she settled herself into the other damask armchair, where she couldn't even see the philodendron plant.

Mother Morning wavered, as if she might invite the Minister to sit on the chintz sofa after all. Then she composed herself and said, 'Would you care for some refreshments?'

She poured the Minister a cup of tea, adding the milk last. 'Some people think it proper to start with the milk,' she said. 'But this is a misconception. Back in the eighteenth century, the potter Josiah Spode – born a pauper – began manufacturing his fine bone china. It really is made of bone, by the way, from cattle and other herbivorous animals raised for their flesh. All meat scraps are removed and sold as pet food, and the bone thoroughly cleaned, then heated to over one thousand degrees to sterilise it, burning off any residual matter in the process. After that it's ground into bone ash. At any rate, Spode's china proved strong enough to withstand boiling water, so the wealthy, who could afford it, poured their tea in first, while those less fortunate, with inferior clay cups that would crack from the heat, had to pour their milk in first.'

There was a brief silence.

'How interesting,' said the Minister.

'And in fact,' Mother Morning went on, flipping over a saucer to show the manufacturer's mark, 'I am *holding* Spode bone china.'

'My word yes,' said the Minister.

'Sugar?'

'Please.'

Mother Morning plucked up a sugar cube with silver tongs shaped like bird claws and dropped it into the tea, which splashed out onto the saucer. 'Oh dear,' she said.

'No matter, no matter,' said the Minister as Mother Morning blushed right through her face powder to the roots of her hair.

'How was your journey down?' asked Mother Afternoon.

'Really rather pleasant, once we left the A4,' said the Minister.

'Ah, the A4,' said Mother Afternoon, as if she travelled it regularly and knew its shortcomings.

'Dreadful congestion around Chiswick,' said Dr Roach. 'You should ask the Prime Minister to do something about it.'

I thought he was joking, but his face was stony.

The Minister said, 'Roading is on her radar, certainly. I'm so sorry I was late.'

'Quite all right,' said Mother Morning, waving an airy hand.

'You could have driven down together,' said William. 'That would have saved time.'

'Mm,' said the Minister.

Mother Afternoon nodded towards the dainty sandwiches on the tiered cake stand and said, 'They picked the watercress themselves, our boys.'

'They're most resourceful,' added Mother Morning, handing a side plate to the Minister. 'Fondant fancy?'

Only Mother Night was silent. I kept glancing at her, and I couldn't shake the thought that she wanted to burst into tears – but perhaps that was just because I wasn't used to seeing her in the daytime and understanding the way her face moved and changed in natural light.

The Minister ate one fondant fancy and half a sandwich. Mother Afternoon tried to persuade her to try the Dundee cake – she'd made special patterns with the almonds on top, and I knew she was disappointed to see it untouched – but the Minister insisted she couldn't manage another bite, delicious as it looked. Being in the public eye, she said, she had to watch her figure. She held her hand over her side plate as if to deflect anyone attempting to slip her a piece of Dundee cake.

'She's in the *newspaper*,' Mother Morning told Mother Afternoon.

'She's on *television*. But you look lovely, Minister, of course,' she added. 'Very trim.'

'Have you ever met Princess Margaret?' asked Mother Afternoon. She felt for her diamante hairclip, checking it was still in place.

Mother Morning glared at her.

'Just the once, at a garden party,' said the Minister.

'What did she say?'

'She said she thought it might rain, which would be a pity.'

Mother Afternoon said, 'She's used to perfect weather, of course, on the tropical isle of Mustique, where she goes to escape her sadness.'

Mother Morning closed her eyes for a moment.

Dr Roach polished off three slices of Dundee cake, which was good of him, though he still seemed out of sorts.

'Well,' said the Minister at last, 'I expect you're all wondering why I'm here.' Then she turned to me and my brothers and gave a tight little smile. 'You boys will have heard, from your . . . your mothers that our Prime Minister wants to make some changes to the Homes, yes?'

Yes, we nodded, our mouths still full, our fingers sticky though we knew not to lick them.

'Here it comes,' said Dr Roach.

The Minister's hand strayed to the brooch on her lapel, and she fiddled with the fine little chain that hung from it. 'Since the Prime Minister took office in May,' she said, 'she has been committed to improving the lot of our citizens. She recognises that many Britons feel helpless – they believe that our once great nation has somehow fallen behind, and it's too late to turn things around. But this is untrue. We are rich in natural resources – coal, oil, fertile farmlands, gas. And we are rich, too, in human resources.' She stopped. Perhaps she could tell that we weren't following. 'We as a Party support family life,' she said, 'and we know that many are struggling to raise the deposit for a mortgage. Our tax cuts will help thousands of families into their first homes, but also – since it costs much more to subsidise a new council house than to give tax relief to a home buyer – we expect a significant saving to the British taxpayer.'

She stopped, fiddled with the brooch again. 'Places like the Sycamore Homes, though,' she said, '*cost* the British taxpayer a lot of money. They are expensive to run, and the land and buildings they occupy are very valuable, and when only a handful of residents remain in each . . . well, you see what I mean.'

'Yes,' we murmured, though we had no idea.

'Crystal clear,' said Dr Roach.

'Who is he, though?' said Lawrence, who hadn't vomited so far. 'The British taxpayer. Maybe if the Prime Minister talked to him . . .'

'Oh,' said the Minister. 'Oh, no – the taxpayer isn't just one person.'

'We've studied taxation,' said Mother Morning. 'Haven't we, Lawrence. Import duties, salt tax, window tax, the Corn Laws, death duties – the whole lot. I do apologise, Minister. Please go on.'

'Well, what the Prime Minister proposes,' she said, 'is that the Homes themselves – the buildings and grounds – are put to better use, and that the residents' – she smiled at the three of us – 'are rehomed in the community.'

Dr Roach pursed his lips.

'I beg your pardon?' said Mother Morning.

'Rehomed?' I said.

'Quite so,' said the Minister, beaming now. 'Rehomed.'

'So we won't live here any more?'

'We'll find good homes for you all,' said the Minister, as if she were talking about unwanted dogs. 'Wouldn't you like to have real parents – form a real family? Haven't you dreamt of that?'

'What about Margate?' said William.

'They're already part of a family,' said Dr Roach. 'They already have a home.'

'Nevertheless,' said the Minister, her voice bright, 'this is what the Prime Minister proposes. And it won't happen immediately, of course – you'll have many weeks to adjust to the idea. We'll use that time to organise Socialisation Days with one of the girls' Homes.'

Dr Roach snorted.

'What's a Socialisation Day?' said Lawrence.

'A chance for you boys to mingle with other young people – with young *ladies*,' she said. 'So you can practise your conversation skills and nice manners and so on. Now,' she continued, before anyone could comment, 'we'll need to produce a catalogue of the available children for the parents to consult, and after that I expect there'll be home visits to ensure a good match.'

'But they are my life's work,' said the doctor. 'I've made that very clear to the Prime Minister this past week.' A strand of silver hair fell across his forehead, and he shoved it away. 'I have donated millions over the decades, not just to your administration, and this is how I'm repaid. It was bad enough when the last lot stopped any more children coming to the Homes. Now you want to shut me down entirely! And exclude me from any new scheme!'

'Nevertheless,' repeated the Minister.

'And their medication? They can't just stop taking it! Who will oversee that?'

'It won't be an issue,' said the Minister.

'What if we pass on the Bug?' I asked. 'Or succumb to it?'

No one replied. Mother Afternoon was holding her hand to her chest, and Mother Morning looked rather less full of hope.

'Don't you know how valuable these boys are?' the doctor demanded. Then he glanced at us and shut his mouth. He'd been going to say something else, but he shut his mouth.

'Yes,' said the Minister, 'I know how valuable they are.'

For a moment no one spoke. Cynthia twitched and growled in her sleep, chasing something, hunting something.

'And what of us?' asked Mother Morning, staring at her lap.

'We'll endeavour to find suitable positions for all carers.'

'All *mothers*.'

'All mothers, yes.'

A fly landed on a fondant fancy. Nobody shooed it away.

'But . . . they'll be coming with us,' I said.

The Minister shook her head. 'Each approved family will already have a mother, a real mother. Trust me, this is best for everyone. You'll never look back.'

'Do they live in Margate, the families?' said William.

'What do you mean?' said the Minister.

Then Mother Night spoke. 'I think it's a good idea,' she said. 'A new start for them. A new chance.'

'There you are, you see?' said the Minister.

'This makes no sense,' said Dr Roach, and I too was puzzled. Mother Night loved us. She *loved* us.

Mother Afternoon wrung her hands. 'I think once the boys and I have shown you around the Home, you'll see just how efficiently we run the place. How frugally.'

'You really think a vegetable patch and some crafts are going to make a difference?' said Dr Roach. 'They've already made their minds up. It's signed and sealed.'

'All the same,' said Mother Afternoon.

In the Kitchen we showed the Minister the drawer where we kept the smoothed-out tinfoil, washed and ready to use again, and we opened the freezer and pointed to the lemon-juice cubes for when we had sore throats, and the scraps of carrots and celery that we'd boil up with bones to make stock. Mother Afternoon had forgotten she'd shoved the bag of milk teeth into the pantry, but she explained that Dr Roach had purchased them for us as a rare treat, and everyone needed a treat now and then in order to feel they mattered – but it wasn't all bags of sweets, by any means. It wasn't all fondant fancies and Spode china. See the plain Digestives? The chipped but serviceable dinner plates? The mushrooms picked in the woods? The watercress, which the Minister had already enjoyed in her

sandwich? And look, there on the cooker, the jar of beef dripping
– delicious spread on toast, and it turned the roast potatoes extra
crisp. The Playroom next, with the Mona Lisa jigsaw and the Stickle
Bricks – we didn't need more toys and games than those, we were
quite content with those – and the daybed with the blanket
crocheted by Mother Night for when we were feeling poorly, and
the candy-striped sheet repaired by Mother Afternoon because
there was still plenty of wear in it, and the radiogram so we could
listen to *Peter and the Wolf*. In the Refectory, the pots of jam
Mother Afternoon made from the plum and apricot trees, and the
chafing dishes that we no longer used to keep the food hot, because
there were only three of us now and that would be a waste of fuel.
In the Entrance Hall, the ikebana arrangement made from bits and
pieces found in the garden.

'How lovely,' said the Minister, trailing a finger over a length of
willow.

'It's ikebana,' I said. 'It's Japanese.'

'I see.'

'It expresses the tension between extravagance and simplicity
with the clever use of negative space,' said Lawrence.

'Does it.'

'There was an article in the *Woman's Realm*,' said Mother
Afternoon. 'I'm not Japanese.'

'No.'

'And along here is the Library, where the boys have their
Lessons,' she said, showing the Minister down the passageway.

I said, 'The love of the beautiful in Nature and Art seemingly
inborn in the Japanese people is in puzzling contrast to the ruth-
lessness with which they wage war and the cruelties they can
perpetrate in cold blood.' I was only quoting The Book of
Knowledge – the section on The Artistic Genius of a Strange People
– but Mother Afternoon glared at me, and I knew I'd said something wrong.

We'd hardly set foot in the Library before Lawrence vomited

straight into the treacle tin of coloured pencils. William laughed. The Minister turned pale.

'Oh my God,' said Mother Afternoon, grabbing Lawrence by the elbow and bustling him away. 'William,' she called, 'clean that up, would you?'

He scowled and went to fetch a cloth.

Then it was just the two of us.

'The library, is it?' said the Minister, looking around with her pale-blue eyes that seemed to see everything. She moved to the opposite wall, pretending to be interested in the blackboard, but somehow I felt she was uneasy.

'Yes, the Library.' I pointed to the ornamental goat on the windowsill. 'We made that on Craft Day. It's an ornamental goat.'

'But where are all the books?'

'Right here,' I said, crossing the room to show her The Book of Knowledge on the shelf just beside her. 'We have the full set. Everything in the world is in it. You see – it starts with *A1* and ends with *Zwingli*. Everything. And if it's not in here, it's not important.'

'Yes, I see,' she said, watching me. She drew a little closer and rested her palm on the spine of GERM–LOCK as if calming a small animal.

'BOO–CRO is missing page 504, though, which is a real shame,' I said.

'A real shame,' she agreed.

I found the spot for her. Some other boy must have torn it out, I explained – some angry boy who wasn't displaying the right attitude. Our mothers had fixed things as best they could, though, blacking out the corresponding entry in the Index so as not to cause confusion.

'Yes, I see,' she said again. 'And those?' She pointed to the lower shelves.

'Those are our dreams, and those are our crimes.'

'Ah yes, I have heard . . . may I?'

Already she was opening The Book of Guilt and reading the terrible things we'd done. Lawrence had spat out his mashed parsnips when Mother Morning had taken the time to prepare a healthy meal for us. I'd shoved William when he wouldn't let me past on the stairs, and he could have fallen and broken his neck though he didn't. William had punched Lawrence when we were playing Charles I and William was Charles I and Lawrence was the masked executioner. William had defaced the portrait of the family who'd first lived in the house, sticking a toilet-paper moustache to the lady in the mauve silk gown. And then the Minister was flicking back through the Book, back in time to when other boys had lived here. Mark Brown had yanked the bathmat out from under David Collins, and David Collins had cut his head open on the tiles. Graham Young had left the shed skin of an adder in his brother's wellington boot. Michael Lewis had trapped a woodlark and snipped off its feet. Colin Wright had forced the finger of another child into the beak of the griffin on the newel post, causing injury to the finger (newel post undamaged). Terrible things, wicked things, all written up so nobody would forget them. I blushed, even for the crimes that weren't my own. They looked worse written down, as if they weren't really in the past but kept on happening over and over.

'And this?' said the Minister. She picked up a photograph album – the one from 1972, when we were six. 'Is that you?'

'No,' I said, 'that's Lawrence. He'd just learned to ride our bicycle.' I was leaning in to her and I could hear her breaths, quick and shallow.

'And who's this?'

I looked at the picture of the grinning boy holding a cricket bat and pointing to a large round blotch on his knee. 'I can't remember his name,' I said, 'but I think Dr Roach has just bowled him out LBW. That means Leg Before Wicket.'

'So it does,' she said.

I was close enough to make out all the detail on her brooch –

the angel in the filmy gown holding the sleeping babies. I could see the sash carved at the angel's waist, the tendrils of hair drifting behind her, the toenails on her bare feet, the shape of her body beneath her gown.

'She's very beautiful, isn't she,' said the Minister in a quiet voice.

'Very beautiful,' I said.

'She was carved from a shell. Look how the artist used the dark upper layer for her hair, and then carved deeper to the white layer for the rest of her.'

'Yes,' I said. I'd never seen a brooch like it. 'Who is she?'

'Nyx, the Greek goddess of Night.'

We'd never learned about her; I didn't know her. 'And the babies?' I said.

'Her children, Hypnos and Thanatos.'

I studied the tiny chain that hung from one edge, a tiny pin fixing it to the lapel. 'What's that for?'

'In case the main pin fails – so I don't lose the brooch.'

'Has it ever failed?'

'Well, no.'

I moved closer still. 'Made from a shell?'

'A real shell. It's called a cameo.'

I took down Volume 8 (FACT INDEX) of The Book of Knowledge and looked for the word – *Camellia, Camelopard, Camelot, Camembert, Cameo* – and then I turned to the entry in BOO–CRO. 'An engraved gem or seashell bearing a design cut in relief,' I read aloud. 'The art was at its height in the 1st century AD . . . The industry degenerated with the end of the Roman Empire, and there was no real revival until the Renaissance . . . But after the end of the 18th century few further cameos were made, as forgery was easy, and the art fell into disrepute. It is little practised today.'

'Oh,' said the Minister. 'I don't think mine's a forgery.'

'I'm sure it's not,' I said – but how could you tell? 'Is it from Margate?' I asked.

'Margate?'

'Where we go when we get better.'

She was looking blank.

'Where the Big House is. With the stained-glass windows of grapevines? And fish with their mouths open?'

'Fish,' she said.

'They have all sorts of things made from shells there.'

'Oh. I don't know,' she said with a fleeting frown. 'It belonged to my grandmother – my mother never liked it, so she gave it to me. She is not a kind woman, my mother. I don't think she ever wanted children – well, I know she didn't, because she's told me so many times. No, not kind. But sometimes we love those who are not kind to us.'

I reached out a finger and touched the cool, polished surface of the brooch. The folds of the gown. The ridges of the feathers. Faintly, ever so faintly, I felt her trembling.

Nancy

The girl, Nancy, held up her arms. 'Skin a bunny,' said her mother as she pulled off Nancy's nightie in one go and tucked it under her pillow. The silvery-green dress hung on the bedroom door in its special bag that protected it from moths and sunlight and dust and sticky fingers. Nancy could see the shape of it through the cotton, the stiff skirts pushing against the inside of the bag. It wanted out. It wanted to be worn. But she hadn't tried it on in months, not since her thirteenth birthday, and perhaps she had grown too big.

Her mother lifted the dress free and examined it, pressing the silk flowers on the bodice back into shape, smoothing out the tulle where it had snagged on itself. It was a Sunday-best dress, a dream of a dress, with ruched organza sleeves and silver embroidery that trailed daisies from the waist down to the scalloped hem.

'Arms up again,' said her mother, and she lowered the dress over Nancy's head, and Nancy smelled its musty smell – a little like old books, a little like soured milk. She pushed her hair to one side so it wouldn't catch in the zip. As long as she hadn't grown too big.

'Breathe in,' said her mother. 'Hold it . . . hold it . . .' Her hands fussed at Nancy's back, easing the zip up tooth by tooth. 'And there we are – it still fits. Didn't I say so?' She fastened the tiny hook at the top, plucked at the sleeves to make them sit right.

'No wiggle room, though.'

Her mother fluffed the skirts. 'You don't need wiggle room.'

'I can't really move.'

'Nonsense.'

Nancy peered down. In some lights the dress looked white, but if you looked closely you could see the tinge of silvery-green – seafoam, her mother called it. Was that a tiny patch of rust forming around a daisy? The metallic thread starting to corrode, to eat into the tulle? She looked away again. Best not to mention it.

'Oh,' said her mother now, stepping back and clasping her hands together. 'Oh, let me look at you.'

Nancy stood very still and tried not to let her fingers rest on the fabric. She knew she mustn't get it dirty or damage it in any way.

'Don't you feel special?' her mother asked.

'Very special,' said Nancy.

'Kenneth! You can come in now!'

Her father must have been waiting at the bedroom door because it opened straight away. 'Well, there she is, large as life,' he said.

'Not too large, though,' said her mother. 'It still fits her.'

'Oh goodness me yes,' said her father. 'It's perfect. You're off to the ball, I expect! Off to a fancy party!'

He didn't mean it, of course. In all her thirteen years, Nancy had never left their bungalow in Belgrave Close. She could play in the high-hedged garden, as long as she kept nice and quiet, and she could sit in the conservatory, which had a glass roof and glass walls that her mother kept so clean you could imagine they were nothing but air. But she couldn't go beyond the gate and out into the dangerous world.

'What's so dangerous about it?' she asked her parents from time to time. 'Why can't I go to school, like ordinary people? Why can't I have *friends*?' Her voice would rise, and her cheeks would flush, and her mother and father would tell her to calm down, to control herself. 'You're terrible people!' she'd shouted at them one day. 'I hate you!' She'd flung a glass to the kitchen floor, but it hadn't broken, only bounced its way across the linoleum to nudge at her mother's slipper.

'You don't hate us,' her mother said. 'We'll pretend we never heard that.'

'Heard what?' said her father, giving Nancy a wink.

Nancy refused to speak to them for the rest of the day. In the evening, her father came to her bedroom and sat on the edge of her bed.

'We're doing our best, love,' he said. 'You'll understand when you're older.'

'Will I be allowed out when I'm older?' she asked.

'Just be patient.' He stroked her hair. 'Your mother's very upset, you know.'

This was how it always went – Nancy became angry because she wasn't allowed out, and shouted awful things at her parents, which made her mother cry, which made Nancy repent and behave. One day, she told herself, she'd see the world – but for now she could watch it on television.

Her favourite programme was *Jim'll Fix It*, where real children wrote to Jim, telling him their wildest dreams, and then he chose the best ones and made them come true. A boy sank under the water in a Royal Naval submarine; a girl saw how dolls are made; two boys rode the Queen's drum horses; a girl flew through the air; a girl lay on a bed of nails; a girl hid in a postbox and grabbed people when they posted their letters. The children all took home big silver badges that said *Jim Fixed It For Me*, so they could wear them whenever they liked and everyone would know how lucky they were. Nancy's second favourite programme was *Mork & Mindy*, with Mork the alien who travelled to Earth in a giant egg and said shazbot in place of swear words, and she also started saying shazbot, because it felt a bit disobedient, a bit thrilling, but even though it had no meaning her parents told her they didn't like it and it wasn't a nice word for a young lady to say. There was *Rainbow*, with Geoffrey the presenter, who was a person, and

Bungle the bear and George the hippopotamus, who were animals, and Zippy, who was neither. He had a zip across his mouth, and when he talked too much one of the others would yank it shut and Zippy would make desperate muffled noises that you couldn't decipher – Nancy didn't much like that part.

She didn't much like *Give Us a Clue*, either, where the contestants had to act out book and film titles without speaking, and sometimes their fellow contestants guessed straight away and sometimes they had no idea despite all the comical gestures of the person who could not speak. She loved *The Generation Game*, where families competed to win all sorts of fabulous prizes that trundled by on a conveyor belt, as long as they could remember what the prizes were. And she never missed *Antiques Roadshow*, where people brought in their old and occasionally mysterious things, and the experts would turn them over and open them up and inspect them through tiny spyglasses and say, 'Do you have any idea what this is worth? Are you sitting down?' Those were the best episodes, when the people would look like they were going to faint because their murky old painting of a bull would bring in five thousand pounds at auction and possibly much more when restored; their big ugly vase that had always just sat in the passageway holding the wet umbrellas had belonged to a Chinese emperor. Sparkly earrings turned out to be diamonds, not glass. Old books turned out to be first editions with priceless notes from the author tucked inside. And even though Nancy would never admit it, she also loved the episodes when an expert had to tell someone their item was a fake and not worth ten pounds, though perhaps of course it had great sentimental value. Usually the person pretended it didn't matter, and insisted that the thing would always be precious to them because of the family connections, but Nancy could see the disappointment slumping their chest and dulling their eyes. How foolish they had been. And now everyone knew.

Her parents watched the news each night to keep up to date with how the government was ruining the country. They sat on the plastic-covered sofa, blowing on their tea, the replica Tiffany lamp casting its soft light on the occasional table while Nancy drew pictures with her Spirograph set: complex circling designs that spread across the paper like flowers, like fireworks, like strange deep-sea creatures nobody had names for. She'd pin one of the transparent rings to the page, then place a smaller wheel inside, interlocking the teeth of both, and then, pushing a coloured pen through one of the tiny holes, careful not to slip and wreck everything, she'd move the wheel around the ring and draw loop after loop until she was back where she started.

If certain stories came on the news – certain sad stories – her mother would leap from the sofa to snatch at the TV. She turned the volume right down and stood in front of Nancy, and she and Nancy's father watched the soundless images and shook their heads and said, 'There's no need for that. Or that. Goodness me, they have no shame.' Nancy could tell the stories were sad stories, but still her parents watched them; they couldn't help themselves. If she peered around her mother she might glimpse a lonely place – a moor, a clearing in the woods – and once she saw a photo of a little boy in a school uniform, and once a burnt-out car, its boot propped open like a black mouth. That had made her feel strange, like she couldn't get enough breath. Afterwards, her mother had sat down next to her and put her arm around her shoulders and sobbed. 'Now then, now then,' her father had said, opening a box of Cadbury Milk Tray and offering it to them, not even taking the orange crème for himself.

Nancy knew that it wasn't just the news stories that upset her mother; she knew she herself was somehow to blame. 'Why do I make you sad?' she asked her once. And her mother, eyes glistening, squeezed her tight and said, 'Oh, poppet. You make me happy. *Happy.*'

She was studying Nancy in the seafoam dress now. 'You'll break hundreds of hearts,' she said. 'Don't you think, Kenneth?'

'Hundreds of the things,' said her father.

Vincent

The week before the young ladies came for our first Socialisation Day, my brothers and I lay awake talking about what they might be like. Would they be triplets too? Would we be able to tell them apart? We hoped they'd be pretty, of course, with delicate little ears and graceful necks, slender wrists we could encircle with a thumb and forefinger. There'd be ribbons of some kind, we supposed, and perhaps floaty scarves. Hairclips in the shape of fruit, like the ones the girls in the village wore. Soft musical voices. And breasts? said William. Probably, yes, there would be breasts – six of them, all told. Bare arms, and maybe bare legs, or legs sheathed in gauzy stockings that stopped somewhere above the hemline. The scent of flowers rubbed on pulse points, and tiny beaded purses holding nothing more than a handkerchief and a palm-sized mirror. Thin-strapped sandals that buckled at the ankle, and a beauty spot on the cheek or temple, and maybe a few freckles. Definitely no pimples. No bad breath or wonky teeth.

But how would they look at us? The way the Ashbridge girls looked at us? Sidelong, from a distance? Whispering amongst themselves as they hurried past? No, we decided: the young ladies would be happy to give us the time of day, because they were Sycamore girls just as we were Sycamore boys. They would not back away if we dared to smile at them. They would let us take their hands and lead them around the Playroom in a waltz or a foxtrot like ordinary people.

Maybe, said Lawrence, they were lying awake in their own room, talking about us. We felt a churning deep in our stomachs then, a kind of hunger.

I closed my eyes and could sense my brothers near me in the almost-dark, conjuring the young ladies from the shadows in the blue velvet curtains, the water stain on the ceiling.

'What should we talk to them about?' I asked after a while.

William didn't answer, and Lawrence said only, 'Mmm,' before he dropped off to sleep too. I lay there for a while longer and tried not to move, willed myself to think of nothing, but the insomnia held me in its fist.

Pushing open the curtains so I could see a little better, I reached under my bed for the cake of soap and the paring knife I'd hidden there. I was quite pleased with my work so far – the way a figure was starting to emerge from the piney, pale-green block. I balanced it on the windowsill, next to the antler I'd found, and cut away a sliver here, a sliver there. In the moonlight my hand looked strange, non-human – grown, perhaps, from the antler's bony palms. The blade of the knife seemed to move of its own accord. I carved as much of the body and hair as I could, but the face was too risky – and I still wasn't tired.

The rich, bright notes of a trumpet trickled from the Upstairs Common Room when I opened the door. Mother Night sat in her usual armchair, tapping her foot in time to the quiet radio. She was crocheting a new blanket, though we hadn't needed any more blankets in years; dozens of them occupied the wardrobes and drawers in the unused bedrooms, tucked away with sachets of lavender to repel the moths and also the silverfish which in fact are insects. Next to the radio stood the old console that lit up when we pressed the buttons next to our beds. I ran a finger over all the names, the rows and rows of names. A few of them, belonging to boys who'd left for Margate very early on, had been covered over with waterproof tape the colour of skin so new names could be written on top. One night, I remembered, William and I had slipped into the room of a departed boy and pressed the button, then dashed off, trying to smother our laughter. Lawrence had stayed in bed – he wasn't going to break the rules, he told us, so we called him a spoilsport and walloped him with our pillows before stealing away. Afterwards, when we heard Mother Night walk along the passageway and enter the deserted room, we peeked from our own doorway, shoving one another with our elbows, giggling till we cried. Then William beckoned to me, whispering that I should follow him for a closer look – and there was Mother Night kneeling on the floor and weeping in silence, her cheek pressed to the departed boy's pillow, the tortoiseshell combs working their way free of her hair. Her breath snatched at her throat when she noticed us, and she just stared for a second, and then she spoke. Had our mothers not done their best to teach us compassion? Did we think such actions were compassionate? No, Mother Night, I said, hanging my head to show that I knew I should be sorry for what I'd done. William, though – William was still giggling. He couldn't stop. As she steered us back to bed, she said she feared for us, which we later agreed was a strange thing to say and not especially compassionate. We felt certain she'd write the incident up in The Book of Guilt, but nothing appeared, though we checked every day for a week. Later, when William wanted to try the trick again, I said no to him for once in my life. Lawrence also refused. William sulked about the place for ages.

'Who's the blanket for?' I asked now.

'It keeps my hands busy,' said Mother Night.

Soft and lacy, it was, and the palest shade of lemon – the kind of blanket you'd make for a baby before it was born, when you didn't know what it would turn out to be.

I picked at a loose thread on my pyjamas, and Mother Night

told me it was a very bad habit, and I'd unravel the whole seam, but I kept picking at it anyway.

'Why did you say to the Minister that rehoming us is a good idea?' I asked.

'Because it is a good idea. You can live in the real world.'

'But you can't come with us.'

'No, I can't come with you.' Her face expressionless, her eyes fixed on her crochet.

'And we don't get to go to Margate.'

'A family is even better than Margate. Trust me.'

I scowled.

'*Trust* me.'

'What will they be like, the families?'

'Ordinary people, I imagine. Compassionate people.'

'Like the family in the picture above the staircase?' The mother letting the little girl stand on the afternoon-tea table. The father resting his hand on the head of the boy in the dress.

'Not as wealthy, perhaps.'

'How will we know what to say to them?'

'That's what the Socialisation Days are for. So you can practise.'

'But we'll just be practising with other Sycamore children.'

'Mm.'

The radio murmured that it was time for some Chopin, and a piece of piano music started.

'When the young ladies come,' I said, 'do we shake their hands?'

'I think that would be polite,' said Mother Night.

'And what happens then?'

'Well, you invite them to sit down. Enquire about their journey, perhaps. Tell them your name.'

'But how do we dance with them if we're sitting?'

'I don't imagine the dancing will start as soon as they walk in the door. You'll chat a bit first.'

'I see,' I said. I felt I should be writing this down. 'And do we tell them they look nice?'

'Yes.'

'Even if they don't?'

'Yes.'

'But that's lying.'

'Sometimes we lie to be kind.'

I nodded; we'd covered that in Ethical Hour. 'And how will I know which is my one?'

'My goodness,' said Mother Night, her crochet hook catching at the lemon wool, 'we haven't *assigned* them to you, like . . . like portions of chicken on Chicken Day. It should just happen naturally. You'll chat a bit, and then Mother Afternoon will put on some music, and you'll ask one of them, "Would you care to dance?" and she'll say, "Delighted," and off you'll go. Then later you'll ask a different one to dance, and so on.'

'If they're triplets, how will we tell them apart?'

'By their clothes, I expect. But I don't think they're triplets.'

'What if William hogs the pretty one?'

'There'll be no hogging.'

'I bet he will, though.'

'I'm sure they're all equally nice. In their own special ways.'

First thing in the morning, I thought, I'd go down to the Library and look up *Conversation* so I'd know how to talk to the young ladies, since Mother Night wasn't much help in that regard. I hoped it wasn't the page that was missing from BOO–CRO; that would be terribly bad luck.

She shifted in her chair, and I noticed it then: the corner of something poking out from under her hip. Something hidden in a hurry. 'What's that?' I said.

'Sorry?'

'That thing you're sitting on.'

'Just a book. Nothing. Nothing.'

'Why are you sitting on a book?'

Gentle as rain, the piano music pattered around us. Mother Night frowned at her crochet, undid her last stitch.

I'd seen books before, of course – Mr Kendrick sold them in the corner shop, his graceless displays featuring paperbacks about doctors and nurses, or tight-trousered men flanked by powerful dogs. 'What are they?' I'd asked Mother Morning on our first visit to the village, and she'd said they were rubbish and nothing I needed to concern myself with. And another day, when she and Lawrence and I were crossing the street, a schoolboy had passed us, and a book fell from his unbuckled satchel. Without thinking I picked it up. It was small and light and rather scuffed – not looked after the way we looked after The Book of Knowledge – and the cover said *The Horse and His Boy*.

'Hey!' yelled the schoolboy. 'That's mine!'

'I wasn't *stealing* it,' I began, but he snatched it from me and kicked my shin.

'Didn't even hurt,' I said, so he punched me in the stomach.

I gritted my teeth, refusing to react.

'You really feel no pain,' he said.

I shrugged.

His face had turned hard then. 'Freak,' he hissed, and ran off.

'I wasn't stealing it,' I told Mother Morning, and she said she was quite aware of that, but I shouldn't have touched it all the same, and anyway, there was nothing in it – nothing in any of the books we might see in the village – that we couldn't learn from The Book of Knowledge. How lucky we were, I'd thought, to have those eight volumes at our disposal; we didn't need to consult any others. In a way I felt sorry for people who had to buy a book here and a book there, piecing together their understanding of the world in dribs and drabs.

'Why are you sitting on a book?' I asked Mother Night again. She sighed. 'I'm reading it. I read at night when you're all asleep.'

'What do you want to know?'

'Know?'

'Well, why are you reading it? What are you trying to find out?'

'How it ends, of course. What happens.'

'Something beginning with Z, I expect. Those things always come at the end.'

Mother Night put down her crochet hook and peered at me. 'I don't know whether to laugh or cry,' she said at last. She pulled the book out from under her and held it on her lap, resting it on the unfinished baby's blanket that was still too small for an actual baby but just the right size for the book. *Ulysses* was its name.

'Just between us, yes?' she said, and I nodded. Then, turning to page one, she began to read aloud.

I'd never heard anything like it. The words were all jumbled and strange, like words in a dream. They twined in and out of the soft pulse of the piano, now rising, now falling, a curious night-time music. Sometimes, as I listened, I had the impression Mother Night was singing to me. There was a man with a mirror and a razor who blessed the mountains, and a man who may have killed his mother because he would not pray for her on her deathbed. I think they lived in a tower, these men, and the sea was a great sweet mother, and from the tower they watched the white breast of the dim sea. I had no idea what it meant.

'Was it on sale?' I said. 'Marked down? I'm sorry, Mother Night, but I don't think it's any use at all.'

'Just listen,' she said. 'Just let it wash over you.'

And as she read, I felt myself loosen inside my skin, and my worries about the young ladies drifted away, and slowly, slowly, the insomnia slackened its fist.

'We needn't tell anyone,' Mother Night reminded me as she ushered me back down the passageway.

I felt my way to my bed, letting the knot in the rag rug from Philip Cole's scraps press into my sole.

Maybe you have bad dreams from time to time, or maybe you have them most nights; maybe you're predisposed to them for reasons you don't care to examine. As we grew, they began to plague William, and I remember exactly when he had his first real nightmare: it was the night before the young ladies came. In the small hours I woke to him shouting in his sleep: *Stop it! Stop it!* Lawrence woke too and said, 'Tell him to shut up,' and then, grumbling, climbed from his bed and headed for the lavatory while I headed for William. I found my brother flailing his fists in the gloom, trying to hit something that wasn't there. The sheet was wound tight around his body.

'William,' I whispered, touching his shoulder. 'William, it's all right. Wake up.'

Absolutely against the rules – to wake another boy from a dream.

He flinched, stared as if he didn't recognise me.

'You had a nightmare,' I said. 'It's not real.'

The whites of his eyes glimmered: pale pieces of moon, pale sails on black seas.

'I could see a knife,' he mumbled. 'Someone running through the trees. That skinny girl. I slipped in the blood . . .' He gazed at his hands, turning them this way and that in front of his face.

'Just a bad dream,' I said, but he sounded so terrified that I hardly believed my quavering voice; it had only just broken, and sometimes it changed back to the voice of a little child who doesn't know a thing. Clearing my throat, I unwound the sheet, climbed into his bed and wrapped my arms around him. 'It wasn't real,' I said, my forehead pressed to the nape of his neck. I could smell the pale-green soap we used, and the soft warm scent of his pyjamas.

The door opened, and light spilled in from the passageway. 'William?' said Mother Night, and then she was standing beside the bed, pulling her pearl-buttoned cardigan around her. 'And Lawrence?' She placed a hand on my shoulder. 'Where's Vincent? And what are you doing in here? You know the rules.'

And I could have put her right – spoken my own name, taken the blame for waking William. Instead, making sure my voice held, I said, 'Vincent went to the lavatory, and William had a bad dream – he was scared.'

'What sort of bad dream?' said Mother Night. 'Scared of what?'

'There was a knife, and someone running, and a . . . a girl, and he slipped in the blood.'

She froze, then bent over the bed and stroked William's hair, kissed his forehead. 'You forget about that,' she said. 'Both of you. All right?'

Still she did not recognise me, and I curled in closer to William and felt my breathing match itself to his.

'Don't you need to write down my dream?' murmured William.

Dr Roach and his department were especially interested in the bad ones; we knew that for a fact.

'No,' she said. 'We need to forget it. Promise me.'

'All right,' said William, practically asleep.

'All right,' I said.

'You can't stay here, Lawrence,' she reminded me. 'Disturbing each other's dreams. I'd have to write it up.'

So I climbed into Lawrence's bed, wished her good night, let her kiss my forehead. Then, when she'd disappeared, I crept back to my own bed, which had turned cold in my absence.

The next thing I knew, Mother Morning was waking us. I heard her saying Lawrence's name, asking what he'd dreamt, and he told her he was scratching the back of a dog's neck and combing his fingers through its rough coat, and then somehow he *was* a dog, wolfing down piles of meat, burying bones.

'And you, William?' she said, coming to sit on his bed.

I opened my eyes just a crack, even though we weren't supposed to: that was how dreams vanished.

William rolled over, rubbed his eyes, and his face crumpled as he remembered his bad dream. He let out a quiet whimper. 'I can see—'

'I don't think he dreamt anything,' I said. 'Did you, William.'

'Sh!' said Mother Morning. 'What's got into you? He must tell me himself.'

He let out another whimper.

'Are you a dog too?' said Lawrence.

'Shhh!' said Mother Morning.

'I've forgotten it,' said William.

Mother Morning's hand dropped to the page. 'Forgotten?'

'Mmm.'

'But you were about to tell me something.'

'No,' said William.

'I think you were.'

He sighed. 'Just a stupid nightmare. Mother Night said I should forget it.'

'Did she?' said Mother Morning smoothly.

'Yes.'

'And have you?'

'Yes.'

She sat there for a moment longer, then came to my bed. 'Can you remember William's nightmare, Vincent?'

I pulled Mother Night's crochet blanket up over my shoulder. 'How could I remember what someone else dreamt?'

'If he told you, of course.'

'He didn't tell me.'

'Lawrence?'

'I was using the lavatory.'

Her weight pulled the covers tight across my chest; I couldn't move. 'And your own dreams, Vincent?'

'Gone. Sorry.' Which was true.

'I see. Well, that's a shame. You'll have to let me know if they come back to you over the course of the day. Both of you.'

'Yes, Mother Morning.'

'Yes, Mother Morning.'

She gave us our medicine then, dropping the canary-yellow pills into our palms and handing us our glasses of water. Watching us swallow.

Down in the Library, I couldn't find anything about conversation.

Convection, Convent, Convention, Converter, Convex mirror.
Useless.

'Just in here,' said Mother Afternoon, smiling her big warm smile
as she showed the young ladies into the Playroom. We'd pushed
the daybed into the corner and tidied away the Mona Lisa jigsaw
and the Stickle Bricks. A jug of orange squash sat sweating on the
refreshments table, along with a plate of butterfly cakes and some
sausage rolls. For the mantelpiece Mother Afternoon had done a
special ikebana arrangement: spikes of triumphantly upright
delphiniums interspersed with dahlias and full-blown roses to
symbolise the transitory nature of existence.

'Now then,' she said, 'this is Vincent, Lawrence and William.'
She gestured to each of us in turn, glancing at our clothes to tell
us apart – Lawrence in his checked green shirt that looked a bit
like a cowboy's, William in his belted red waistcoat, me in my
yellow poloneck that used to be Graham Young's before he went
to Margate. 'And we have Diane, Jane and Karen, yes?'

The young ladies, who lived at Edith Saunders Home for Girls
and weren't triplets, nodded. 'How do you do?' they said, which
everyone knew was never a question. We all shook hands.

What curious creatures they were – nothing like the girls in the
village with their supple tresses and their bright complexions, their
lacy white socks, their halter necks and berets. Diane wore spectacles that made her eyes too big, like you couldn't get away from
her, and she kept scratching at patches of rash on her hands and
face. Her cardigan fastened with bear-shaped buttons. Jane's pinafore flattened her chest, and her hair hung in one long dun plait.
Her skin looked wax-white, even her lips all but colourless, and
she kept twitching them across her sharp little teeth. Karen was
fat. Unfortunately, she too wore a yellow poloneck.

'You all look nice,' I said. 'Do sit down.' I directed them to the
stacking chairs we'd brought from the Refectory. 'How was your
journey?'

'I'm very well thank you,' blurted Diane.

'We came on the motorcoach,' said Jane. 'Have you ever been on a motorcoach?'

We shook our heads.

'You're up so high, you can see the whole road ahead of you. But you get thrown about a bit. You have to hold on when you go round corners.'

'There are windows in the roof,' said Karen. 'They pop them open for fresh air. You can't open the windows by the seats, in case you stick your head out and get decapitated, so they have the ones in the roof.'

'And stretchy white covers on the tops of the seats,' said Jane, 'to protect them from people's muck and grime. They must take them off and wash them, I suppose. I'm not sure how often though.'

'If you got decapitated,' said Diane, 'you could get a job at Dreamland, like Mademoiselle Yvette the Headless Lady: Alive and human.'

We discussed where we'd go first at the amusement park: Karen said the River Caves, because you got three for the price of one: the Ice Cave, the Venetian Cave and the Smugglers' Cave. Jane said that was a stupid reason, because you didn't have to pay at Dreamland anyway. She'd head straight for the Sky Wheels, and she wouldn't even hold on. Diane said the Magic Garden with all the twinkling flowers and butterflies, and the peacock made of light, and the glass oranges that glowed on the trees – as long as we were allowed out after dark. We checked with Mother Afternoon, who nodded and said she imagined we would be; she was practically certain. She busied herself with the sheer cloth that kept the flies off the refreshments table, adjusting it so it didn't smear the cream on the butterfly cakes.

'I have a question,' said William. He leaned over and plucked at the wrist of Karen's yellow poloneck. 'Are you wearing boys' clothes, or is Vincent wearing girls' clothes?'

Diane giggled.

'I borrowed it from Mother Morning,' said Karen.

'What?' said William and Lawrence.

I was puzzled too. Why was Mother Morning lending her clothes to a stranger? And anyway, she never wore polonecks. She wore plain cotton blouses, and her floral housecoats over the top.

'Mother *Morning*,' said Karen, like we were deranged. 'Our *mother*.'

'But she's our mother,' said Lawrence.

The young ladies exchanged glances.

'Every Home has a Mother Morning, stupid,' said Jane.

'Oh,' we said.

'And a Mother Afternoon and a Mother Night.'

And of course we knew this was true, but somehow it felt strange to hear it.

'They're quite right – I'm nothing special,' murmured Mother Afternoon, her broad hands tucking a strand of crinkly hair back into her bun.

'Mother Morning said you might like to know the origins of the name of our Home,' said Karen. 'By way of conversation.' She waited.

'Now you ask her what they are,' said Diane.

'What are they?' said Lawrence.

Karen said, 'British scientist Edith Rebecca Saunders co-discovered genetic linkage in the early twentieth century, and our own Dr Roach drew on her findings in his ground-breaking work in the 1920s to '30s.' She nudged Diane.

'What are the origins of the name of your Home?' asked Diane.

'You know – Captain Scott,' I said. 'The Immortal Story of?'

The young ladies shook their heads.

'He was trying to reach the South Pole,' said William. 'Everyone died. The sledge-dogs ate the ponies.'

'Now then,' said Mother Afternoon.

Lawrence said, 'No story in the history of exploration has so stirred the hearts of all who have heard it as that of Captain Scott's tragic expedition to the South Pole.'

'Idiot,' said William.

'You must be peckish after your trip,' said Mother Afternoon. 'Please do dig in.'

'Mother Morning packed us some sandwiches for the motor-coach,' said Karen. 'Normally we have fish paste, but today she made us cheese and tomato for obvious reasons.'

'I'd like a sausage roll, please,' said Jane.

'Of course, dear,' said Mother Afternoon, whisking away the fly cover so we could help ourselves.

'What are the obvious reasons?' said William, peeling the crimped paper case from a butterfly cake and biting off both wings at once.

'Well,' said Karen. 'Well, she didn't say.'

'How about you, dear?' said Mother Afternoon. 'Can I tempt you?'

'I'm watching my waistline,' said Karen.

William smirked. 'Clearly you're not. Clearly you haven't watched it for quite some time.'

Mother Afternoon marched over and grabbed his elbow. '*What* has got into you?' she whispered. 'Apologise at once!'

'Sorry,' he said, still with a smirk on his face.

Karen's chin was trembling.

'I think you look very pretty,' said Lawrence. 'All of you.'

I stared at the leg of Karen's Refectory chair: a smear of egg from a distant breakfast had congealed on the chrome. Something felt ruined.

'Who's Martha Emily Phillips?' said Jane, peering at the ancient needlework hanging in the corner. 'In the silent tomb we leave her,' she read. 'Creepy.'

'We think she's the little girl in the painting in the Entrance Hall,' said Lawrence.

'We don't *know* that,' said Mother Afternoon.

'But we're pretty sure.'

'Maybe she died in *this very room*,' said William.

'Let's have a cheerful time,' said Mother Afternoon. She put a record on the radiogram – not *Peter and the Wolf*, which wouldn't have been suitable, but one of her own LPs that she kept in her quarters in the North Wing and played for us on Music Appreciation Day. We weren't allowed to touch those records; she slid them from their sleeves herself, only ever holding them by their edges, and she kept them free of dust with a red velvet cleaning pad that had a little stylus brush hidden in its handle. We weren't allowed to touch that either. Today she'd chosen her Richard Clayderman LP for us to dance to – piano music that wasn't too fast and wasn't too slow. It was called *Rêveries*, which was French, because Richard Clayderman was French even though his name didn't sound it. He was actually born Philippe Pagès, Mother Afternoon had told us one Music Appreciation Day, but he'd changed his name for his international audience, who wouldn't be able to pronounce French despite the advances achieved since the signing of the Gothenburg Treaty. Mother Afternoon knew all about Richard Clayderman. He gazed from the record cover, golden hair swept back from intense blue eyes, his lips slightly parted in a sultry fashion. A candelabra blazed beside him.

The music started, and Mother Afternoon caught my eye and nodded. I put aside my sausage roll, removed a crumb of pastry from my poloneck, panicked as I looked from one young lady to the next, then went over to Jane.

'Would you care to dance?' I said, my voice going high on the last word, like the voice of a little boy.

'What?' she said, her mouth stuffed with butterfly cake.

I was holding my hand out to her, and she scowled as if I'd offered her a sneezed-in handkerchief. 'Would you care to dance?'

She rolled her eyes and pointed to her mouth and kept chewing for a few seconds. I wondered if I should sit down again. Then she shrugged and took my hand.

'Lawrence, William,' said Mother Afternoon, cocking her head at Diane and Karen.

We began to move around the Playroom, the six of us, more or less in time to Richard Clayderman. Pearl earrings were screwed to Jane's downy lobes, I noticed, and a matching strand shimmered at her throat, white on white.

'You're more graceful than your brothers,' she said.

'I make mistakes,' I replied, aware of the warmth of her shoulder blade through her pinafore.

'Who taught you to dance?'

'My mother.' We both glanced over at Mother Afternoon, who was fluttering her hand back and forth to the music.

'Natural pearls are very rare,' I said, nodding at Jane's necklace. 'Pearls that form without any human intervention. Thousands of opened oysters are discarded with never a find – that's why they're so expensive.'

'I see,' said Jane, and her eyes drifted to the refreshments table.

'Monks in China,' I said, 'inserted minute figures of Buddha into oysters' shells. Then, when the deposit of pearl had covered them, they were sold as natural curiosities.'

'Were they,' she said.

'Yes! And they weren't natural at all!'

'They were, though. In a way.'

'Yours must be cultured pearls,' I said, ploughing on. 'Made with the help of Man. They're much more common, and therefore much cheaper. Or much cheaper, and therefore much more common.'

Jane laughed for the first time, throaty and sly, and I liked her better then. 'Actually,' she said, lowering her voice, 'it's even worse than that. They're faux.'

'Faux?'

'Not real, stupid. It's French.'

'Oh.' Richard Clayderman would have known what faux meant. I peered at the pearls as they caught the light. 'I'd never have spotted it. People are so clever, aren't they?'

Lawrence and Karen passed us. She was saying something about the cool of the evenings, how summer seemed already on the turn, and he was smiling at her as if he'd never heard anything so interesting.

'Higher please, William,' called Mother Afternoon, and William raised his hand from the small of Diane's back – virtually her bottom – to just above her waist.

'Do you like to read?' I said.

'As long as someone dies,' said Jane.

I wasn't sure that was something a young lady should admit to, but I said, 'Which volume's your favourite?'

'BOO–CRO. It has the story of the *Bounty*, with the sailors turning mutinous and starting their own colony on the remote island of Pitcairn, *and* it has the coffin of the Egyptian priestess Ta-Ahti, *and* it has Caesar giving up against his assassins when he sees his friend is one of them, *and* it has Careers at a Glance. I want to be a Record-keeper, which requires a willingness to care for pieces of paper, parchment or cardboard as precious things, and Diane wants to be a Mannequin, displaying fine clothes to men and women who are expert and critical buyers. Have you done Your Personality Profile to find out what you should be?'

'No,' I said, which was a lie; I'd done it several times. *Sense of duty (very conscientious? does not care?). Memory (learns easily? usually forgets?). Strange places (desires, enjoys? fears, avoids?). Hope (optimistic? pessimistic?).* I'd never liked the outcome.

'Well, you should have a look. BOO–CRO.'

I was about to say that I wasn't so fond of BOO–CRO because of the torn-out page, but I stopped myself; I felt embarrassed about our damaged volume.

'A–BON is very interesting too,' I said. 'It has Thieves of the Bird World, Jeremy Bentham's mummified head kept under a glass bell, and the Bayeux Tapestry with all the corpses.'

'Mm. They're just embroidery, though.'

'But the battle did happen. They really did die.'

We fell silent for a few moments, and I listened to the soft thudding of our feet. I wondered if I should mention the strange book Mother Night was reading about the men who lived in the tower, and the white breast of the dim sea, because someone died in that: the man's mother died when he would not pray for her on her deathbed, and now he dreamt of her ashy-wet breath. But no – keep it between us, Mother Night had said.

Jane closed her eyes. 'A tiny pearl Buddha made by an oyster,' she said. 'Imagine that.' And then, before I could answer, a whisper: 'Sometimes I think about running away.'

My stomach lurched; I almost tripped on the edge of the rug. I wasn't sure I'd heard her correctly. When we were well past Mother Afternoon again I said, 'What do you mean?'

She moved closer to me, her breath sweet and milky from the butterfly cake. 'After dark I'd pack my things in a pillowcase and steal the grocery money they keep in the biscuit tin. Then I'd climb out the Laundry window and over the wall and disappear.'

I remembered the time William asked if we thought we could catch the wild ponies. Jump on their backs and ride away.

Jane was watching me, waiting for me to reply.

I imagined galloping across the heathland, letting the pony take me somewhere I'd never been, where the people might treat me like an ordinary person – like one of them.

'But then you'd never get to go to Margate,' I said. 'Or to a family. Whichever comes first.'

'I'd find my own way to Margate. I'd copy the map of England from The Book of Knowledge.'

'It's wrong to steal money,' I said. 'Haven't you talked about that in Ethical Hour?' Mother Morning writing on the blackboard: *What should you do if you find a purse in the street? What do most people do? What would you do?*

'It's not always wrong,' said Jane. 'If it's to save someone's life, for instance.'

William and Diane had stopped dancing while Diane scratched the rash on her wrist. Tiny dots of blood appeared.

'I had that rash once,' I said to Jane. 'All over my chest and back. Dr Roach prescribed me some cream, but it didn't really help, so Mother Morning gave me the fork from a pair of salad servers to scratch the places I couldn't reach.'

'What did you use for salad, then?' said Jane.

'Our hands.'

'What?'

'A pair of tongs.'

'Oh.'

'We're not animals.'

'No.'

'I only had it for a few months, though,' I said. 'Now I get insomnia and a bit of weakness. What do you get?'

'At the moment, bleeding noses.'

'We've never had those.'

'You might still.'

'Yes. You never know what the Bug's going to do.'

She looked at me sidelong, a strange expression on her face like I'd said something astonishing. 'Haven't you figured it out yet?' she whispered.

'Figured what out?'

But the music stopped then, and Mother Afternoon announced that we should swap partners. Jane went to William and Diane to Lawrence and Karen came to me, and soon Richard Clayderman had started up again and Karen was talking about the cool of the evenings, how summer seemed already on the turn. I nodded my head as she chattered away, but I wasn't really paying attention. William had a bit of blood on his sleeve from Diane's wrist. On the mantelpiece the full-blown roses were showing their spidery stamens. Figured *what* out?

When the record finished William asked if we could take the young ladies out to the garden.

'I suppose that would be all right,' said Mother Afternoon. 'It's a lovely day.'

'A little cooler in the evenings now, though,' said Karen.

'So it is, dear. Well, off you go. And remember your manners, boys.'

She followed us along the passageway but turned into the Library where she took The Book of Guilt from the shelf, and I knew she would be writing up William for his comment about Karen not watching her waistline.

We filed through the Kitchen, and Lawrence held the back door open for the young ladies, bowing to them as they passed.

'Idiot,' said William.

We led them through the fruit trees to the vegetable patch with the insect-proof mesh, and then to the lavender beds, which were past their best but still smelled nice if you dragged the flowerheads through your fist. In the oaks and horse chestnuts our seed balls had been all but pecked away; the string hung slack, knotted around the branches like string around a finger to remember something. The bare spots on the lawn marked our cricket pitch, we explained, though we didn't have enough boys left for proper teams, and Dr Roach insisted he was too old to bowl to us these days.

'I expect he'll die soon,' said Jane. 'That's what old people do.'

We didn't want to think about that, except now she'd said it we couldn't stop the thought. Who would find a cure for the Bug? And who would look after Cynthia? She would be devastated; her little heart would break from loneliness. We all agreed that Cynthia deserved an owner who wouldn't die, and perhaps the Minister could arrange something, since she was the Minister of Loneliness, after all, and she must know how rehoming worked because she was rehoming each of us. Really, said Jane, it had been irresponsible of Dr Roach to take on the new Cynthia; he hadn't thought about her needs but only his own, and that wasn't love.

'Perhaps she can come with us,' said Lawrence. 'When we go to our family.' He'd have given anything for a pet of his own.

'Have they found you a place already?' said Karen.

'Are you going together?' said Diane.

'Calm down, calm down,' said William. 'They haven't even done the catalogue yet, have they.'

Jane said, 'I asked if I could go with Diane, because we're best friends, but Mother Morning told me that was unlikely, and most families would only want one.'

'And then,' added Diane, 'even if they've picked out a particular boy or girl from the catalogue, they might still change their minds during the home visit. So you just never know.'

'You never know,' echoed Karen.

'But there could be families who have no children,' I said. 'They might want to order three at once.'

'They're not families, though,' said Jane.

We considered this.

'What about Mother Afternoon's little cottage?' said Lawrence. 'Maybe we'll go there, to be her slaves, and crack walnuts for her pet macaw. Scratch her pet rattlesnake behind the ears.'

'That's only if she wins Spot the Ball,' said William. 'It's all just pretend.'

'I think my family will have an indoor swimming pool,' said Diane. 'And probably a butler.'

'Can you swim?' I asked.

'No, but the butler will teach me. And a colour television! They'll have one of those, maybe even two.'

'Mine will have a dog,' said Karen. 'Probably a St Bernard. They're very loyal and can save you from avalanches.' She and Diane were beaming, breathless.

'Wait, you *want* to leave?' said Lawrence.

'Don't you?' said Karen.

'Why would we want to live with strangers?'

'They won't be strangers,' said Diane. 'They'll be your family.'

'No. Our family is dead. Our proper family.'

'Car accident?' said Jane. 'Shipwreck? House fire? Train derailment?'

'Heart attacks,' I said. 'Our mother first and our father a week later.'

'That's very unlucky,' said Jane. 'Mine were mountain-climbing and fell into a crevasse.'

'Mine crashed their car,' said Diane. 'Killed instantly.'

'House fire for mine,' said Karen. 'They threw me out from the second storey where they were trapped by the inferno, and a neighbour caught me.'

When we reached the fernery Lawrence pointed out the gazing ball, and the way the ground seemed to career up its sides when you peered into its mirrored surface, and thank goodness it was just an illusion. A song thrush landed on it and looked at us, tilting its head this way and that as if trying to decide what kind of creatures we were, before fluttering up into the plum tree where one of the seed balls had hung. It pecked at the bare string.

'We should put some more food out for them,' I said. 'That would be kind, wouldn't it?' Again my voice went high, like a child's.

Yes, agreed the young ladies, that would be kind, especially with the blackbirds and robins still nesting.

Jane picked up a fallen dahlia and slipped it into the pocket of her pinafore, which wasn't the best idea because it would only shrivel up and turn brown, but it would have been bad manners to say so.

'I know what,' said William. 'We'll play Sardines. Vincent, you're the first sardine, because you smell.'

'You're a bit of an arsehole, aren't you?' said Jane. Karen and Diane gasped, but William just laughed it off. Nothing ever seemed to get to him. I suppose I wanted to be like that.

I ran away to find a place to hide while everyone else closed their eyes and promised on pain of death not to peek. As they started to count I dashed through the fruit trees, past the vegetable patch and the old glasshouse, its cracked panes filmy with moss. We weren't allowed in there, because the whole thing could come crashing down around our ears, so on I ran. Over by the flint wall I squeezed behind a fuchsia bush and listened to the others calling my name as they spread out to look for me.

'Here, fishy fishy,' called William. 'Where are you, little fishy? I'm coming to get you.'

But it was Jane who found me first. She pushed the branches aside and poked me with her toes like something dead. Then she crawled in beside me.

The flint chilled our backs, and we held our hands over our mouths, pushing our laughter back down inside, trying not to give ourselves away. Up ahead, the house rose above the garden, and I thought I glimpsed movement in the window I knew was Mother Night's. Jane tapped at the fuchsias one by one, setting them dancing in their frilly ballerina skirts. In between us, at the base of the bush, a flower was staked to the ground with a stick, the sharp end thrust right through its fleshy pink body.

'What's that?' she whispered.

'Just a game we play sometimes,' I whispered back. 'A sacrifice to the garden gods.'

'And what do they give you in return?'

I'd never thought about that. 'Lots of cabbages?'

'That doesn't sound very fair.'

'I suppose not.' I pulled out the stick and threw it away. 'We're a bit old for that game now.'

'Fishy fishy fish,' called William, a little closer.

'Why do you think the people out there dislike us?' whispered Jane.

I'd been wondering the same thing myself. Was it really just the Bug?

'I don't know,' I whispered back. 'You seem very nice to me.'

She ran a finger along a row of fuchsia berries: tiny black globes that formed as the flowers started to fall away. Twisting one free from its stem and holding it out to me on her pale palm, she said, 'Dare you.'

'Is it poisonous?' I whispered.

'Of course not.'

I put it in my mouth and chewed. Lemony, peppery. Not unpleasant.

'At least, I don't think so.'

For a split second my jaw seized – and then I spat the berry into the undergrowth and scrabbled at my tongue as Jane rocked back and forth in silent glee.

'Let me breathe, let me breathe,' she gasped, even though I wasn't stopping her. 'Your face! Oh my God!'

'Just tell me if I'm going to die.'

'You're going to die,' she said. 'Eventually.'

I could have strangled her.

Then I remembered.

'What did you mean when we were dancing?' I said. 'Haven't I figured *what* out?'

'Here, fishy fishy,' called William, drawing ever closer.

Jane held a finger to her lips and squeezed in further behind the bush, pushing right up against me now, all but in my lap. Again I thought I glimpsed movement in Mother Night's window, a figure looking down at our hiding place. Then William was shoving back the branches and sliding in next to us. 'Don't mind me,' he said, coiling his arm around Jane's shoulder.

She pressed her mouth to my ear and whispered so softly that only I could hear. 'The medicine, stupid. It doesn't make us better. It makes us sick.'

The Minister of Loneliness

She cast her eye over the house – it must have been lovely once. Now there were slates missing from the roof and the skin of white paint was peeling off the bricks.

'The boys have a slightly odd manner,' she said to the photographer, 'but they're not dangerous. We have no concerns of that nature whatsoever.'

He snorted. 'I bet that's what they told those poor sods in Flamborough.'

'Flamborough was an anomaly.'

'If you say so.'

She didn't care for his tone, but they'd been hard pressed to find anyone to do the job.

'The most important thing is to make them look friendly,' she said. 'Healthy and friendly.'

'And are they?'

She thought of the identical triplets: their light-green eyes, their thick blond hair, their full, curling mouths. How tall they were for their age, how they loomed over her as well as over their mothers – but she had to stop calling the women that. Three full-time workers, funded by the State, to look after three boys who could surely scrub a lavatory themselves! A criminal waste of resources.

'Oh indeed,' she said. 'Very much so.'

The bleak playroom, the few toys all scuffed and grubby like rejects from a charity shop in the wrong part of town. The vomit in the tin of coloured pencils. The library with no books, just a set of children's encyclopaedias decades out of date. And dear God, the used tinfoil, washed and smoothed and saved. No wonder the one in the library dreamt of the seaside. She remembered how he'd asked about her cameo, reached out and touched it while she stood there scarcely daring to breathe, waiting for something dreadful to happen, the vegetable knife tucked in her handbag. But he'd had such a kind manner – and hadn't she told him about her mother? She rarely talked in that way – frank, unguarded. It had felt like a dream, that strange moment, and she'd thought about him often since then – his soft fingers wondering at the carving on the brooch, his gentle voice. When she'd tried to tell her husband about him, she'd got it all wrong. Made the boy sound peculiar, even threatening, but in fact she'd wanted to stay there with him, with Vincent, leafing through the photograph albums like some long-lost aunt. 'Good grief, you'll be putting your hand up for one of the creatures,' her husband had said. 'Buying him a train set and taking him roller skating. You mustn't lose sight of what they are, my love.'

The photographer had the boys sit on the chintz sofa one by one – the room had a nice diffuse light, he said; see how it softened their faces? They posed awkwardly in front of the camera even though he kept telling them to relax, just be themselves. Their afternoon carer bustled about, fluffing the pot plant next to the sofa, mouthing at them to pull up their socks, straighten their ties. At first the Minister wasn't sure which boy was hers – well, which boy was Vincent, the one from the library – until he came and stood next to her and said, 'You're not wearing your cameo brooch today.'

'Oh,' she said. 'No, I don't wear it all the time.'

'How about a big smile?' the photographer was saying. 'Nah, that's not a real smile! I can tell, mate – I'm a trained professional.'

'We met the young ladies at the weekend,' said Vincent.

'Very good,' said the Minister. 'The Socialisation Days will make the transition easier for all of you.'

'We danced to Richard Clayderman, and then we played Sardines.'

'How nice. That sounds like excellent practice.'

'Do a lot of people play Sardines?'

'I believe so.'

'Do you?'

She couldn't help laughing. 'Not for years.' She had a sudden recollection of squeezing herself into her friend Beatrice's potting shed with half a dozen of Beatrice's cousins on a drizzly day. The smell of dirt, wet wool, secateurs rubbed with linseed oil. The roll of scratchy jute twine. The slug pellets they were not under any circumstances to touch. An ancient rusty scythe.

Vincent twisted his mouth; he seemed to be considering his next words. 'One of the young ladies said something,' he whispered. 'Jane. She said the medicine doesn't make us better, it makes us sick.'

The Minister trained her eyes on the photographer, kept her expression neutral. 'What a strange remark,' she said.

'But what did she mean?'

'I'm sure I don't know.'

'Okay, show me your silliest face,' said the photographer. 'That'll make you laugh. Your silliest. Okay, here's mine.' He stuck out his tongue and wrinkled his nose.

The boy on the sofa just stared at him.

'Don't you want to look your best for the catalogue, Lawrence?' said the carer.

'I'm William,' said the boy.

'Why are you wearing Lawrence's shirt . . .? But in any case, our visitor's quite right – the families will be wanting pleasant children. Happy children.'

The boy shrugged.

'Time to bring out the big guns, then,' said the photographer. 'Knock knock.'

Silence.

'I said, knock knock.'

The Minister cleared her throat. 'Who's there?'

'Luke.'

Again, silence.

'Now you say, Luke who?' said the photographer.

After a moment, the Minister said, 'Luke who?'

'Luke through the keyhole and find out!'

Nobody laughed.

'What's he *talking* about?' said Lawrence.

'Right, let's get a group shot on the stairs, yeah?'

They all filed down the passageway with its worn parquet, here and there a piece missing, and the photographer arranged the boys on the creaking staircase. The maroon runner felt flat, threadbare under the Minister's feet, and huge old mirrors hung from the panelled walls and glinted like eels. Vincent touched the wings of a carved creature perched on the newel post – a dragon, was it? The Minister squinted to make out the motto that curled across its breast.

'If I can get you on the bottom stair, just in front of the boys,' the photographer said to her. 'Great. And everybody smiling . . . one two three . . . smiling, yeah? And looking natural. Maybe one of you could rest a hand on the Minister's shoulder. Are we okay with that, Minister? Yeah? Looking natural, smiling smiling . . . hmm. Okay, let's try something. Everybody say silk five times.'

'Silk, silk, silk, silk, silk,' said the boys while the Minister stood there wishing she had a decent prop to hold – a pair of gloves, an umbrella. She could see herself in one of the murky mirrors: her short brown hair sat flat to her head, and her handbag drooped from its strap, a deflated and useless thing. The Prime Minister always looked so glossy, with her smart white cuffs and her slippery scarves, her sleek chestnut French twist. Maybe the Minister should grow out her hair.

111

'Now tell me what a cow drinks,' said the photographer.

'Water,' said the Minister.

He glared at her. 'Right,' he said, 'it's a brain teaser, though, yeah? Most people say milk, because they've just said silk over and over. And then I tell them cows drink water, and everyone has a laugh and I get some good shots.'

'Calves drink milk,' said Vincent. 'They're baby cows.'

'Cheers, mate,' said the photographer. 'Okay, I think we'll go out to the garden for a few more headshots. Get some fresh air into you, yeah? Rosy cheeks and all that.'

'I was wondering,' said the carer. 'Do you think I could get a photo with the boys? Since we'll be going our separate ways soon?'

'Sure, why not. If you stand . . .'

But she was already placing herself between Vincent and Lawrence, her arms around their waists, their arms across her back, and all of them were beaming.

As the others headed outside, Vincent lingered at the foot of the stairs.

'I made you something,' he whispered, catching at the Minister's sleeve.

'Oh?' she said.

He bent and pretended to tie his shoe, waiting until the rest of the group had gone. Then he produced a tiny parcel wrapped in brown paper and slipped it into her hand.

'Shall I open it now?' she said.

He glanced through the door. 'If you like.'

She slid the smooth little thing from the paper, cupping it in her palm: a piece of pale-green soap, maybe two inches long. It was carved with the figure of a girl standing on tiptoe and blowing a dandelion clock, her long dress and long hair swirling around her. 'You made this?' said the Minister.

'Yes. It's a cameo.'

'I can see that. You're very clever.'

'I didn't tell anyone because it was a waste of soap. I had to cut away so much. We're not supposed to waste anything.'

'It's not a waste. It's beautiful.'

He ducked his head, blushing. 'And I couldn't do a darker colour for her hair because the soap is green all the way through, but I made quite deep cuts along the strands, so the shadows make it look dark.'

'So they do – what a good idea. Who is she?'

'I don't know. Nobody.'

'Well, she's the nicest present I've had in a long while. Thank you.'

He gave a quick smile.

'What does the motto say?' she asked, peering at the newel post on the staircase.

'*Verité Sans Peur*,' he said.

'*Verité Sans Peur*,' she echoed, following the words along the carved scroll. 'Truth Without Fear.'

'Oh,' said Vincent. 'We never knew.'

'Is it a dragon?'

'A griffin – a mythical creature, half eagle, half lion, supposed to guard hidden treasure. We touch its wings for luck.'

'And does that work?'

'I'm not sure,' he said. 'How would we know?'

She was about to head for the garden when he caught at her sleeve again.

'Why would Jane say that? About the medicine making us sick?'

She tucked the soap cameo into her squashy handbag and could feel his eyes on her. 'People come out with all kinds of things,' she said. 'I'm sure it's nothing to worry about. Sounds like a bad joke.'

'It wasn't very funny.'

'Bad jokes never are. My mother often says things she finds hilarious, but nobody laughs.' *I take it we haven't seen a salad in a while, Sylvia.*

'Like the jokes the photographer told?'

113

'Exactly! Yes, exactly like those.'
'They weren't funny either.'
'There you are then, you see?'
'Yes, I see.'

On the way back to London she wondered what she might have told him instead – what other answer she might possibly have given – but nothing came to her. She took out his present and studied it in the silvery overcast light that filtered through the car window. How finely he had picked out every detail, right down to the girl's eyelashes on her closed eyes, the arch of her bare feet. She looked like some kind of forest sprite with her wild hair and her pale-green skin, the dandelion clock breaking apart at the touch of her breath. The Minister noticed Evans watching her in the rear-view mirror then, and she slipped the soap back into her bag. She could still smell its piney scent, though, and dark trees gathered around her, their fuzzy branches rich with resin. Things rustled in the under-growth, unseen things, but they meant her no harm, and she could lie down on the soft fragrant needles and dream her dreams, and nobody would find her.

Vincent

When William started screaming I flicked on my bedside lamp and pushed back the covers to go to him, but Mother Night was already bursting into our room.

'Be quiet, be quiet!' she whispered, shaking him awake, and he opened his eyes and stared at her, terror-stricken, still half inside his nightmare. His breaths came quick and staggering. She picked up his pillow from the floor; for one unreal moment I thought she was going to smother him with it. Then she sat on the edge of the bed.

'What was it about?' she asked. The Book of Dreams nowhere in sight. One grim nod when William said it was the girl and the knife and the blood again.

Lawrence was sitting up now. 'The skinny girl with the long black hair?' he said. 'Running through the trees?'

'Yes.' William looked like he was going to be sick.

'There's no blood when I dream about her, and no knife,' Lawrence said to Mother Night. 'She keeps laughing over her shoulder at me, and I've picked her a bunch of bluebells.'

'Shut up,' I said, and Lawrence looked hurt. I hadn't wanted to be mean, but I could see the state of William.

Mother Night stroked his hair. 'It's all right,' she said. 'It wasn't real. You're here with us.'

He gave a nod, his face pale.

'And Vincent keeps calling to her to slow down, but she won't,' said Lawrence. 'It's a game.'

William groaned.

'Thank you, Lawrence – let's stop talking about her,' said Mother Night.

'Why are we dreaming about the same girl?' he said.

'Let's just lie down again,' said Mother Night.

'But why are we all dreaming about her?' he persisted.

'Girls are girls,' she said. 'Each much the same as the next. And sometimes identical siblings can have similar dreams – you know that.' She went and stood at the window, her back to us, her shoulders shaking. Had we done something wrong? We looked at one another. On the ceiling the water stain had grown, a shadow-bird covering us with its damp wings. When she turned back, we could tell she'd been crying.

'Promise me you'll keep this to yourselves,' she said. 'It's just a silly dream, of course – just a trick the brain plays – but you must promise.'

We'd never seen her so distraught.

And so, even though we knew that Dr Roach and his department of dream people needed the full record, we promised.

She kissed each of us on our foreheads and told us to go back to sleep. All the same, after she'd left the room William begged me not to switch off the lamp, not yet.

'It was just a silly dream,' I said.

'Nightmare,' said William.

'Okay, just a silly nightmare.'

'It seemed so real.'

'But it wasn't.'

'Why can't we mention it, then?' said Lawrence. 'If it was just a silly dream or nightmare or whatever, and not even real.'

None of us knew.

'And why do they write them all down every single day, and why is Dr Roach so interested, if they're just tricks the brain plays?'

None of us knew that either.

'I suppose it's because we're special,' said William.

'But *why* are we special?' said Lawrence.

'Because we're triplets?'

'Plenty of those around.'

'Not any more.'

When I closed my eyes, I could still make out the light from the lamp, like sunlight shining through closed lids on a drowsy day in the garden. She came to me then, the girl, but not as a dream – as a memory. I had called her up, this mysterious creature, carved her from the pale-green soap. Her bare feet, her skinny arms. A dress swirling around her, whirling in the wind, but the lines of her body visible underneath. The furrows cut deep into the strands of her hair to make it look dark.

I was wide awake now.

I reached over and softly switched off the lamp, and neither of my brothers stirred.

Mother Night was knitting something tiny, with fine ivory wool and the thinnest needles I'd ever seen.

'What's that going to be?' I said.

'A baby's bonnet.'

'We don't have any babies.'

'It's good to be prepared.'

The book called *Ulysses* lay open on her lap. She made no attempt to hide it this time.

'Why do you write down all our dreams?'

'Because you're special.'

'Why are we special?'

'Well, my goodness, you're going to be in a book! A full-colour catalogue!'

'But before that.'

She smiled, and didn't answer for a moment. Then she said, 'You were such a lovely newborn. I'd just started here when you arrived, and I was very nervous and *very* young – only sixteen. I thought I might break you. But you used to look at me with those big, big eyes, and you had a way of holding my finger . . . not so much holding it as feeling it, figuring out what it was for. You tried to suckle from it once or twice. Funny thing. That won't work, little bean, little bug, I told you – you'll starve.'

'How do you know that was me? Maybe you're remembering Lawrence or William.'

'No, we were careful – from day one we dressed you in your colours: green for Lawrence, red for William and yellow for you. And at bath time we tied coloured string to your wrists so we could tell you apart. We did that until you knew who you were and could say your own names.'

'String?' I said. 'Like parcels?'

'I suppose so. It sounds strange now that I say it, but it seemed the only way. Do you know, Mother Afternoon thought she might have mixed you up one bath time. Lawrence was already in the tub, and she was about to tie the string on you and William when Lawrence banged his head. He started screaming, so she turned her back on the two of you for just a second, and when she looked back you'd squirmed all over the place like grubs.'

'So I might not be me?'

'Oh, no, my love!' she said, seeing my face. 'Of course you're you. And I myself don't believe she lost track of you. She double-checked with me when my shift started, and I'm sure we got it right.' She was casting off stitches, smoothing out the finished piece of bonnet against the open book on her lap. It seemed the wrong shape for a baby's head: long and straight, with a slight bulge at one side, like the heel of a sock. I knew it would look different when she'd sewn up the seams to make a soft dome, though – like the flattened world on the fold-out map, with the two New Zealands and the two Russian peninsulas to show where the edges should meet.

The radio said, 'The prince, who had commissioned the work,

later remarked in a letter, "Beethoven's mass is unbearably ridiculous and detestable, and I am not convinced that it can ever be performed properly. I am angry and mortified." Despite this, the Mass endures as an example of Beethoven's ground-breaking departure from tradition.' A deep male voice sang the first notes, and then a gentle choir began to fill the room.

'But how did you *know* that I was myself and William was himself?' I asked.

Mother Night tilted her head to one side. 'A bruise, I think it was,' she said. 'The tiniest mark from a needle – but let's talk about something else. Shall I read you a little more?'

'All right.'

'Let me see . . . some of it's not entirely suitable . . . well, here we are.'

And she began to read me the dream-like story again, and although I didn't fully understand, I just let it wash over me as she'd suggested the previous time. *The grainy sand had gone from under his feet. His boots trod again a damp crackling mast, razorshells, squeaking pebbles, that on the unnumbered pebbles beats, wood sieved by the shipworm, lost Armada. Unwholesome sandflats waited to suck his treading soles, breathing upward sewage breath, a pocket of seaweed smouldered in seafire under a midden of man's ashes.*

Through half-closed eyes I watched Mother Morning sit on the edge of William's bed and smile her lovely sad smile. She said, 'I think someone is keeping things from me.'

'No,' said William, poking his fingers through the holes of his crochet blanket.

'You haven't had any more nightmares, then?'

'No.'

'Only I could have sworn I heard one of you screaming last night, all the way from my room.'

William shook his head, kept weaving his fingers through the blanket. He'd stretch the gaps in the crochet too far if he wasn't careful; he'd snap something.

I lay still, waiting for my turn, pretending I was asleep.

'Perhaps it was you then, Lawrence.' The beautiful sad smile directed at him now. The eyebrow raised.

'I already told you my dream,' he said from his bed. 'I'm building a sandcastle in Margate, and each time I fetch water to hold it together, the sea has crept closer. Which is quite convenient.'

'Not frightening at all,' she agreed. 'The boy I heard sounded terrified, whoever he was.'

'I didn't hear anything,' said William.

'You must have been dead to the world,' said Mother Morning. 'I know what a nightmare sounds like. I've heard hundreds over the years. The funny thing is, there's no record of it.' She checked the current page in The Book of Dreams once more, as if she might have missed it. 'Not a word,' she said. 'Well, I'll ask Mother Night. I expect she'll tell me. I expect she's just forgotten to write it in the Book. Don't you think?'

'Maybe it was a pony you heard,' said Lawrence. 'They make noises at night sometimes.'

Mother Morning ignored him. 'William, look at me,' she said. 'Stop fiddling with the blanket and *look* at me.' She grabbed his wrist. 'It's my job to write down everything you dream. It's your job to tell me.'

'There was no nightmare,' he said.

Mother Morning sighed and came over to my bed. 'And what did you dream, Vincent?'

'I'm in the garden,' I said, eyes closed. 'I'm digging for treasure behind the glasshouse, and I can hear the ocean, or maybe it's the wind in the trees. Someone is looking for me, a young lady is looking for me. I can see her in the gazing ball, which is huge, as huge as the moon, and she is picking her way along the top of the flint wall, tiptoeing over the broken glass, and whenever she takes a step closer to me, I take a step further away.'

'Who is the young lady?'

I hesitated. 'The one who visited here,' I said as quietly as I could. 'Jane.'

Lawrence and William could hardly contain themselves. They'd been teasing me about her all week, asking if I'd had any *special* dreams about her. I'd tried to tell them what she'd said about the medicine, but every time I mentioned her name they began to snigger. 'You should have seen the two of them in the fuchsias,' William had crowed to Lawrence one night when we were getting into our pyjamas. 'Her hand was in his pocket and his was up her dress.'

'It was not!' I said.

'I know what I saw. You were both having a good old rummage.'

'Ohhhh, Vincent,' said Lawrence, wrapping his arms around himself and making kissing noises, thrilled to be ganging up against me with William for once. 'I want to marry you, Vincent.'

'And she was loving it, the dirty little thing,' William went on. 'Rubbing up against him like nobody's business.'

'You're such a liar,' I said. But the more I protested, the more they teased. In the end I just shut up.

'Shh, the pair of you!' Mother Morning told them now. 'What does she look like, Vincent?'

'A long mousy plait. Pale skin – very pale, like the gazing ball. She's wearing a pinafore that's too small for her.'

'And you're sure she's the young lady who visited? She couldn't be anyone else?'

'I'm sure.'

'Very well,' said Mother Morning, slipping her pen into the pocket of her housecoat. Then she gave us our pills.

All my life I had taken the medicine. I had swallowed down the tablets and the syrup, sometimes in the morning on an empty stomach, sometimes later with a meal, now and then just before bed. I had offered up my skin to thousands of injections, and I had even sat for hours at a time while pints of fluid dripped into my veins, the needle taped to the crook of my elbow or the back of my hand, hurting if I moved. And no, I had not died – but I had not beaten the Bug, either. Would it matter so much if I skipped a day? Missed just one tiny pill? I rolled it to the side of my mouth, took the glass of water from Mother Morning. Watched Lawrence and William swallow theirs. Then I pushed the pill under my tongue where it sat like a lost tooth as I gulped my own glass of water.

'Time to rise and shine,' said Mother Morning. 'We have to finish How the World Gets its Rubber today.'

When she and my brothers had gone downstairs, I spat the pill into my palm and slipped into the bedroom next door, which had been empty for many months. I opened the chest of drawers and moved aside the socks and vests that used to belong to another boy, and right at the back I found my private things – a slingshot made from a forked hazel twig and a bit of left-over elastic from Mother Afternoon's sewing basket; a picture of a lady in her under-wear that I'd cut from a *Woman's Realm* left lying around by accident; my empty Lucky Bag; my plastic soldier with the para-chute, now torn; a drawing of the Dolphinarium at Margate done for me by Frank Harris, one of the departed boys who had been my friend. I took out the Strepsils tin where I kept all the best feathers and stones I'd collected for our sacrifices to the garden gods, dropped the pill inside, then buried the tin at the back of the drawer again where nobody would find it.

That day, all day, I monitored myself for signs of the Bug begin-ning to take hold. Was I feeling weaker? Was I hot to the touch? Were bruises forming anywhere? What about a rash? Did my joints feel sore? Was my heart beginning to race, my head to pound? Did I want to faint or vomit? Could I breathe? There were so many ways the Bug could overwhelm a boy – and yet, I felt no different. No evidence of illness, but also no improvement. Probably the Minister was right: Jane was just joking about the medicine making us sick. The Minister understood people and what made them say the things they said; you didn't get to be Minister of Loneliness, responsible for the country's wellbeing, unless you understood people. Still, I skipped the pill the next day and the next, hiding the evidence in the Strepsils tin, and then, because the Bug was keeping its distance, I went on skipping the pills. And after a week there was no denying it: I felt better. Not just improved but *recovered*. Each night I drifted off to sleep without even trying, without even thinking about it, and I didn't wake until I felt Mother Morning touch me on the shoulder and say, 'Vincent. Vincent. Tell me what you dreamt.' No more insomnia. No more weakness. I could have uprooted a tree, lifted a horse over my head. How could that be?

I found myself thinking more and more about Mother Night's book, and how different it was from The Book of Knowledge. How nice it might be to read something new.

One day, in Free Time, I crept to the Upstairs Common Room, shut the door and searched for *Ulysses*. It wasn't behind the cushion in Mother Night's chair, nor underneath the sofa or the rug, nor between the radio and the wall. The stuffed pike watched me from its case, the dried reeds and rushes disintegrating around it. My gaze fell on the console next to the radio. Wasn't the glass top with all its old names a little crooked on the base? I grasped it at either end, and the whole thing lifted away to reveal a circulatory system of wires and tiny dead bulbs – and Mother Night's book. I opened it and began to read, and its strange dreamy lines wove themselves around me. *Does he ever think of the hole waiting for himself? They say you do when you shiver in the sun. Someone walking over it. Callboy's warning. Near you. Mine over there towards Finglas, the plot I bought. Mamma, poor mamma, and little Rudy.* I knew it was telling me a story in a way The Book of Knowledge never could: there were the things that happened, as far as I could follow them, but drifting about these – like thistledown, airborne and almost transparent; like a shimmer of dust glimpsed in a certain light – were all the private thoughts too. All the secrets only ever spoken inside a person's head. Line upon line of them, printed as truth. *I was happier then. Or was that I? Or am I now I?*

Twentyeight I was. She twentythree. When we left Lombard street west something changed. Could never like it again after Rudy. Can't bring back time. Like holding water in your hand. I read until Mother Afternoon called us for tea. It was Corned Beef Day, and I was starving.

My brothers refused to believe me when I confessed to them about the medicine – when I told them what Jane had whispered in my ear.

'He's lost his mind,' said William. 'All the blood's rushed to his knob and his brain's shrivelled up.'

Lawrence started his *Ohhhh, Vincent* routine with the kissing noises and the arms, but I cut him off.

'Wait here,' I said, fetching the Strepsils tin from the empty room next door and showing them the unswallowed canary-yellow pills. 'And I feel fine. Explain that.'

'Coincidence,' said William.

'You can't just stop!' said Lawrence.

'Wrestle me. Two against one.'

They looked at each other, then launched themselves across the room. Usually William could take me down without breaking a sweat; he'd grab my head and twist it like a stuck lid on a jar, or kick my legs out from under me without warning. Lawrence, too, could bear-hug me to the ground and then sit on me, yelling that he claimed the Island of Vincent for the Queen. Today, though, they could barely get a grip on me, even working as a team. When William leapt on my back while Lawrence went for my wrists, I shrugged them both off in seconds; when they charged at me side on, shoulders braced to pin me to the wall, I pushed them aside like empty clothes hanging in a wardrobe. They sank onto Lawrence's bed, panting, eyeing me.

'Still think it's a coincidence?' I said.

'Why would they want us to feel sick?' said William. And then, in a small voice, 'They love us.'

'You tore my pyjamas,' said Lawrence, fingering a buttonhole ripped right open.

'Just try stopping the medicine for a few days,' I said. 'See what happens.'

'But that's against the rules,' said Lawrence. 'And so dangerous – you're leaving yourself completely unprotected. Aren't you scared?' His voice started to wobble, and tears formed in his eyes.

'Not any more. You've no idea what it's like to feel . . . ordinary.'

'Well, you might feel fine at the moment, but I bet you anything the Bug's biding its time, getting ready to come back stronger than ever.'

'Maybe,' I said, 'but I can fight it off now.'

'You'll be going to Margate without us,' said William. 'You won't even need to be adopted. They'll just send you there.'

I hadn't dared think about it, but I suspected he was right. Soon enough our mothers would notice that I had recovered, and Dr Roach would nod his special nod when he came to examine us and take our blood, and then one night, possibly even the very next night, I would find the Margate brochure on my bed. When I got to the seaside, when I climbed from the Van, my bag packed with only the essentials, what would I do first? Head to Dreamland and ride the Sky Wheels and the Dodgems? Or stuff myself silly with candy floss – perhaps offering it to a Tyrannosaurus, perhaps not – while I watched the no-hands motorcyclists brave the Wall of Death? Maybe the Dolphinarium, to see Britt, Turk and Speedy do their tricks? Or perhaps I would go underground first, exploring the strange passageways of the Shell Grotto, making my way to the domed centre with its opening at the very top like a memory of sky. I wouldn't need to be in the catalogue the Minister was making for the families; I'd move straight to the Big House in Margate, where they had shelves of books, probably. And they'd put me on a floor so high I could see the ocean from every window, and hear it at night, lulling me to sleep, along with all the boys and girls who had gone before me.

'What if Mother Morning finds your tin?' said Lawrence. 'Or Mother Afternoon, for that matter.'

'Yeah, you should get rid of the evidence,' said William.

'They never go into those rooms,' I said.

'Maybe he knows he still needs them, for when the Bug comes back,' said Lawrence, his face crumpling. 'We can't lose you to it, we *can't*.'

'I don't need them,' I said, sitting down next to him and putting my arm around his shivering shoulders. 'Trust me. And if you both stop taking them too, we can all go straight to Margate.'

The next day, when Mother Morning handed us our medicine and our water, Lawrence fixed me with a stare and gave a small but firm nod: *swallow it*. Again I hid the pill under my tongue and waited until Mother Morning had left our room, then spat it into my hand.

And William did the same.

Nancy

Clippings of black hair sprinkled the kitchen floor, and Nancy could feel her mother holding each length taut as the scissors inched their way across her back. Quietly she moved her fingers along the edge of the table, imagining a black piano she'd seen on *Jim'll Fix It*, imagining the tune a little girl had played while a man sat with his arm around her.

'What are you doing?' said her mother.

Nancy had thought she couldn't see her. She returned her hands to her lap. 'Nothing,' she said.

'Such a fidgeter. Anyway,' said her mother, making one final snip, 'all done. Good girl.' She poured Nancy a glass of squash, ran a hand through her own short grey hair. 'Mine used to be as long and dark as yours, if you can believe it.'

'And I *had* hair,' said her father, sweeping up the clippings.

Nancy knew her parents were a lot older than most – a lot older than the parents on television. 'I like your hair, Mum,' she said.

Her mother kissed her cheek. 'Off you go and help your father. I need to do my catalogues.'

The Fletchers' house was filled with things Nancy's mother had ordered through the post: the replica Tiffany lamp that sat on the occasional table, the *Swan Lake* coasters they placed under every glass and cup, the Black Forest cuckoo clock (Certificate of

Authenticity included) that hung on the sitting-room wall, the draught excluder shaped like a giant caterpillar. Over the years she had bought cut-glass sherry decanters, ornamental birdcages, wide-angle binoculars and zoom binoculars, dressing-table sets in presentation boxes, water-resistant digital watches, simulated leather jewel cases with automatic lift-up trays, twenty-six-piece punch sets, spaghetti jars. In the catalogues she circled the things she wanted and posted off the forms, and when her purchases arrived she unwrapped them and studied them and decided where they would go. Some items she displayed on the credenza in the sitting room – the porcelain figurines of the Shoemaker, the Blacksmith and the Tramp on Bench (Exclusive Limited Numbered Editions); the pair of pewter tankards hand-worked by craftsmen in Sheffield; the silver-plated miniature cannon and gun carriage for After Eight mints – but often, when an order arrived, she decided it didn't look as nice as the picture and was cheap and nasty and belonged at the back of a drawer with all the other disappointments.

In the sitting room, Nancy slipped a *Swan Lake* coaster under her glass of squash and inspected the train station with her father. It was part of the model village that he'd built by hand, and it needed a bit of maintenance: the roof tiles had faded, and six were coming loose. With tweezers he prised them free, applied some glue and nudged them back into place while Nancy mixed up the grey paint. They tested it on a piece of paper, her father adding a dash more black, a dash more white, until he decided it looked right. When the glue was dry enough, he let Nancy brush on the paint, and after a second coat he said that nobody, not a living soul, would be able to tell that the station roof wasn't real slate.

He reached between the curtains tacked around the edges of the trestle tables and flicked a hidden switch, and all the lights in the village came on. Then he set the passenger train going, and he and Nancy watched it looping around the pretty half-timbered houses, the school, the church, the dense forest of trees, their trunks and branches shaped on a skeleton of wire. He was most proud of the stream, which he'd built up with layers of glue that dried clear; the gushing water looked so real, it was as if time had stopped. He'd made the goods displayed in the shop windows, too: shoes and books and sweets, even little individual apples and bananas and pears. Nancy's mother had sewn the dresses for the dress-shop window, and the washing that hung on the washing lines, and also the mailbags that went on the freight train. They held real letters that Nancy and her father had written on tiny pieces of paper, looking through a magnifying glass so they could see the words. *I can't wait for my holiday abroad. Rex is such a naughty dog – last week he stole a string of sausages! Will you come and visit soon? I love you. I miss you.* Nancy's father used the magnifying glass to paint the different outfits and hair colours on the plastic people, too, some of them sitting, some standing, some riding bicycles. He had the steadiest of hands – during the week he worked at an engraver's, cutting names and dates into trophies and plaques and wedding rings. Before he left for work each morning, he moved the plastic people around the village so that no day ever looked the same. One of the children reminded Nancy of a girl from her favourite episode of *Jim'll Fix It* – the girl who had flown through the air. Sometimes Nancy imagined her climbing onto her shoulder and beginning to speak, whispering secrets into her ear, the kinds of secrets friends tell each other.

Nancy's mother came into the sitting room then and took some envelopes from the bottom drawer of the credenza. She must have made her choices from her latest catalogues.

'What's for tea?' said Nancy.

'Beans on toast.'

'Shazbot.'

'I beg your pardon?'

'Nothing.'

'You love beans on toast.'

'I don't, actually.'

'Nonsense. You've never said so before. Turn your studs, poppet.'

'I'm telling you now, I don't like beans on toast.'

'Well, if you're peckish before tea . . .' said her father, offering Nancy the bowl of fruit that stood on the credenza. A family joke: the fruit was wax – although the pear did have a bite mark in it. Evidence of tiny teeth that had dug into the flesh. Nancy's parents said she'd done it when she was a toddler, clambering up on a chair and helping herself, but Nancy had no memory of this. Oh, you were just a little thing, they said. We came into the room and caught you in the act, but how could we be angry with you? When Nancy's mother dusted the fruit, she always turned the bite mark to the inside so visitors wouldn't see it – they never had proper visitors, though, just men who came to fix things that her father couldn't. He'd crawl out from under the bathroom vanity or close the fuse box and say, 'It's beyond me,' in a hopeless sort of voice, as if something important had slipped from his grasp and drifted away. Then the plumber or electrician would have to come, and Nancy would have to wait in her wardrobe to be on the safe side. Usually it wasn't for very long, and her mother would make her a jam sandwich if she promised not to smear it on any of the clothes – the gingham pedal-pushers, the polka-dot skirt, the puff-sleeve dress, the angora cardigan with the glass buttons – but especially the cotton bag that covered the silvery-green dress. The long wall of the wardrobe backed onto the sitting room and the short wall backed onto the passageway, so depending on where the problem was, Nancy could sometimes hear the men talking. *It's a warning sign*, they'd say, and *Best to be cautious – tomorrow might have been too late*, and *I'll know more when I open her up.*

She wondered about these men. What they looked like, where they lived, whether they had families of their own. One day, when the kitchen sink was blocked and her father couldn't for the life of him fix it, she decided not to stay hidden in the wardrobe. Listening at her bedroom door, she heard the front door open, and a man – the plumber – said *Barry Sedgwick*, and her mother said

Thank goodness you're here, Mr Sedgwick, and he said *Got yourself in a spot of bother, have you, sweetheart?*

Nancy crept along the passageway towards the kitchen, and soon she could see the back of the plumber – a broad man in dark-blue overalls – but neither he nor her mother could see her.

'You just show me what's wrong,' he was saying, 'and I'll have it fixed in a jiffy.'

How kind he sounded. He bent to put down a box of tools, and Nancy saw his face. He had brown sideburns that extended halfway down his cheeks, and plump ears, much larger and pinker than her father's, and fleshy furrows across his forehead too. He hadn't noticed her, and maybe he never would, and maybe she could stand there staring at him for as long as she liked, outside of time, somehow, like the dried-glue stream in the model village, and when he left she could leave with him. Go to the shops. Go to the cinema, or even school. Then he looked up.

'Hello, princess,' he said.

'Hello,' said Nancy.

'What are you doing?' said her mother, bursting into the passageway.

'I was thirsty,' said Nancy. 'I wanted some squash.'

'Well, you can see Mr Sedgwick is here. It's not convenient.'

But the plumber smiled and waved Nancy into the kitchen. 'You don't look like trouble,' he said. 'Help yourself, sweetheart.'

'Thank you,' said Nancy, brushing past her mother, stepping over Barry Sedgwick's toolbox and opening the fridge.

'Off school today, are we?' he said.

'A bit of a sore throat,' said Nancy. 'Nothing serious.'

'We're just playing it safe,' said her mother. 'Go and lie down, poppet.'

'Do you have children, Mr Sedgwick?' said Nancy.

'Four girls,' he said. 'For my sins.'

'Are they at school?'

'All but the youngest.'

'And they go every day? But not on the weekends?'

He looked up at her, amused. 'That's right.'

'Lucky them.'

'Off you run now,' said her mother. 'We can't keep bothering Mr Sedgwick.'

'You've a good girl there, Mrs Fletcher,' he said.

'Have they ever been to the cinema?' Nancy said. 'Your girls?'

Before he could reply, her mother took her arm and led her back into the passageway, saying, 'Come along. You need your rest.'

'Get well soon,' Barry Sedgwick called after her.

Nancy stayed in her bedroom until he'd gone. *Give me a ring if you need me again, sweetheart*, she heard him saying, *and I'll come and sort it out – but remember, these problems are easy to avoid if you do the right thing in the first place.* Her blood fizzed. The world must be full of people like Barry Sedgwick, kind people who thought she didn't look like trouble. People with daughters who attended school and went to the cinema.

Nancy expected her mother to be angry, but when she came to her room she was crying. 'Never do that again,' she said through her sobs. 'You have no idea of the danger.'

'What danger?' said Nancy. 'He was nice! And he thought I should be at school. Why can't I go to school?'

Again her mother said, 'You have no idea.'

And when her father came home and learned what Nancy had done, he turned pale and shook his head and said they had to be careful, very careful, because often people were not what they said they were. Not what they seemed to be.

And that was that.

Vincent

William was right: I shouldn't have kept the pills – but I wasn't quite brave enough to get rid of them entirely. What if the Bug came back? What if I needed them in a hurry? In reality, though, I was feeling so much better, so much stronger, that in unguarded moments I thought nothing could touch me. As often as possible, in Free Time, I slipped away to the Upstairs Common Room to read passages from *Ulysses*. *He is a mule, a dead gasteropod, without vim or stamina, not worth a cracked kreutzer. Copulation without population! No, say I! Herod's slaughter of the innocents were the truer name. Vegetables, forsooth, and sterile cohabitation! Give her beefsteaks, red, raw, bleeding!* I still didn't understand it, but that only made me want to read more. To devour every page. In the Library I looked up the name of the man on the cover: James Joyce. *Irish author; remarkable for psychological analysis of character, realistic handling of themes, and a style verging sometimes on incoherence.*

William was feeling better now too; he'd started discarding his own pills in the lavatory each morning, and in a matter of days he was charging down to breakfast, no sign of the Bug in him at all. Only Lawrence still felt poorly, with headaches that smashed at the back of his eyes and made him see things that weren't there: flashing lights, zigzag lines. He rested in the Playroom for hours

133

at a time, but even the Mona Lisa jigsaw was too much for him; he just pushed the worn pieces around the floor, a bit of forehead here, a bit of chin there. He could not put her together.

We were finishing the washing up after breakfast when we heard a crash above us and a shriek from Mother Morning. Usually nothing rattled her, so we knew something must be wrong – and then, as we made our way to the staircase and touched the griffin's wings for luck, another shriek sounded. We found her in the room next to ours, sitting on a bare bed, holding the empty Strepsils tin. On the floor, the upturned sock and vest drawer. Its contents everywhere.

'I thought I might do a spot of tidying up,' she said. 'I opened the top drawer, and at the back I found all sorts of things tucked away. Hidden. I pulled it right out to see, and that's when it dropped to the floor. And that's when the tin flew open.' She was looking at me now with her lovely sad eyes, and she was saying my name, Vincent, Vincent, and I stood there staring at all my private things laid bare: my slingshot, my best feathers and stones, the picture of the lady in her underwear, the plastic soldier with his torn parachute, the drawing of the Dolphinarium from the departed boy who had been my friend. *To Vincent, I'll save you some fish, from Frank.* Mine, clearly mine. Worst of all, though, the canary-yellow pills, scattered to every corner of the room.

'This is the work of a very wicked creature,' said Mother Morning, bending to pick one up. 'You do understand that, don't you?'

'Yes, Mother Morning,' I said, and I felt my wickedness shiver inside me as I spoke, scuttle along the pit of my stomach. I sat down on the bare bed opposite her. At my foot, the *Woman's Realm* lady, all creased from many handlings. She stood with her arms raised above her head, eyes half-closed, stretching as if she'd just woken up. The flesh-coloured fabric encased her, seams dividing up her body like the cuts of meat drawn on animal carcasses in Mother Afternoon's cookery books. *A revolutionary combination of girdle and panty,* the words below her said. *Power-control panels to discipline problem areas. Nylon tricot gusset. Discreet convenience opening.* I could make that out if I squinted – two snap fasteners between her legs that would pop apart easily as anything when the need arose.

'Wicked,' said Mother Morning, rolling the pill around the shallow dish of her palm, 'and dangerous. Do you know how vulnerable you are without your medicine? And coupled with the kind of attitude you've displayed in the process . . . the Bug could swoop in and take you just like that.'

'I feel better,' I said in a low voice. I couldn't meet her eye.

'Sorry, Vincent?'

'I feel better,' I repeated.

My brothers were standing in the doorway, unsure if they should come into the room. William started to edge away, but Mother Morning raised her freckled hand and beckoned, and the two of them slunk in and sat next to me. The mattress smelled stale, unaired. On the windowsill, dead moths.

'You're mistaken,' she said.

'No,' I said. 'I feel better. I *am* better.'

'That is entirely coincidental.'

'We told him it was,' said William.

'Ah,' she said, turning her attention to them, eyebrow raised, 'so you both knew what he was up to?'

Lawrence looked like he was going to cry. 'Will you finish your tidying up?' he asked in a desperate voice.

'This isn't about tidying up, Lawrence,' she said.

'No,' he said.

Mother Morning inhaled, stared at the ceiling. 'It's the deviousness that upsets me most, I think. Pretending to swallow them down each morning. Hiding them away in an old abandoned room where you thought nobody would ever look. That took some planning.'

Little chips to the paint behind her, just above the mattress line.

135

Little dents. Our room sat on the other side of the wall, and I remembered him then: a boy who kept having nightmares in that bed, violent nightmares. He'd thrash about, kicking in his sleep, until one of the other boys in his room rang the bell for Mother Night to come. It carried on for a week or two, I think, and then he went to Margate. Though my brothers and I had been envious, we were also glad to see the back of him so we could get a good night's sleep.

'It was that crazy girl from Edith Saunders,' blurted William. 'She told him the medicine makes us sick.'

'That's not true,' I said.

He was only trying to protect me, but I wished he hadn't dragged Jane into it; I didn't want her to get into trouble too. I'd been wondering when I might see her again, hoping we might have another chance to talk – just about the medicine, I told myself. Nothing more.

'Which girl?' said Mother Morning.

'The pale one with the long mousy plait,' said William. 'Jane.'

'Jane,' she repeated, 'Jane,' and we knew she was tucking the name away somewhere safe and would not forget it.

'Yes, it's all her fault,' said William. 'She egged him on.'

And, looking at him, I began to suspect he was protecting not only me but himself too.

'I see,' said Mother Morning. 'And you wanted to please her, this Jane, did you? You like her, Vincent – is that it?'

No sniggering from my brothers. No *Ohhhh, Vincent* and pretending to kiss someone who wasn't real, a girl made of air. Lawrence was holding his fingers to his temples, trying to stave off another terrible headache.

'I . . . I do like her,' I said.

'Well,' said Mother Morning, following my gaze to the creased magazine page while I wondered if I could cover it with my foot, hide the sleepy-eyed lady and her convenience opening, 'such feelings do begin to occur at your age, and unfortunately there's nothing we can do about it. But we must take steps to ensure we are not jeopardising our health, yes?'

Yes, the three of us nodded, yes.

'That's settled then,' she said, and we weren't sure what we had agreed to. 'Pick them up, Vincent. Every single one.' She held out her hand, and I deposited the pills in her palm as I collected them from the floor, crawling under the beds to retrieve the last few, wiping the dust and cobwebs from them. 'Lawrence,' she said, 'be a darling and fetch Mother Afternoon and Mother Night.'

'It's too early,' he said, looking alarmed. 'We're not allowed to disturb Mother Night – that's one of the rules.'

'Well, I am overriding the rule, so be a darling and fetch them both for me, would you? We'll meet in the Upstairs Common Room.'

Off he went.

She slipped the pills into the pocket of her housecoat and picked up the rest of the things herself, quite calm as she moved about the room and tidied the socks and vests away into the drawer, the stones and feathers into the Strepsils tin. 'You could have used these on Craft Day,' she said, a mournful note in her voice as she shut the coppery breast feather of a kingfisher in the lid, breaking its slender spine. She barely glanced at the *Woman's Realm* lady, screwing her into a ball and making no comment, but she scrutinised the slingshot, testing the strength of the hazel twig, the reach of the elastic. 'A weapon, Vincent?' she said in her sad voice, tucking it into her other pocket and shaking her head.

'It's just a toy,' said William. 'Just for birds and things.'

But Mother Morning said, 'A thing like that can do real damage,' and he knew better than to argue.

Only the drawing of the Dolphinarium she returned to me.

Mother Night was already waiting for us in the Upstairs Common Room, and it was strange to see her there in the daytime, wearing her satin dressing gown and pink velvet slippers. Her hair hung loose, no tortoiseshell combs, and her mouth was bare of lipstick, and I thought she looked younger. She sat in her usual chair; I wondered if she might produce the *Ulysses* book and begin reading to me – but of course, she'd never do that with everyone right there listening.

I took a seat on the floor with my brothers, next to the console. I could feel the weight of the book hidden away inside it, behind all the old names. *Copulation without population! No, say I! Herod's slaughter of the innocents were the truer name.*

'Can we get started?' said Mother Afternoon. 'I need to nip to the village to post my Spot the Ball.'

Mother Morning cleared her throat and said something had come to her attention, something shocking and hurtful. 'It appears,' she announced, 'that Vincent has not been taking his medicine. Day after day he's been standing in front of me bold as brass and only pretending to swallow his pill. I found them all in one of the unused rooms, deliberately concealed.'

I thought Mother Afternoon and Mother Night would gasp, tell me I was putting myself in great danger and did I not realise I could die without the medicine? Was I not afraid?

But Mother Night said nothing, and as I watched her I thought I could make out the trace of a smile on her bare lips, like the smile that took shape on the Mona Lisa jigsaw puzzle when we put all the pieces together. Mother Afternoon simply waved a hand and said, 'What does it matter?'

'What does it *matter*?' said Mother Morning. 'Dr Roach has supplied us with a very specific protocol that needs to be followed to the letter. Those pills are life-saving!'

Mother Afternoon waved her hand again. 'They'll all be lining up,' she said. 'All the families.'

'No takers yet, as far as I know,' said Mother Morning. 'Not a single nibble.'

'They probably won't even consult us,' said Mother Afternoon, staring at the floor. She had not been her usual cheery self since we'd had our pictures taken for the catalogue.

'But we could have months left,' said Mother Morning. 'As much as a year, perhaps. Or maybe there won't be any takers at all.'

Mother Afternoon let out a sob, and Mother Night said that wasn't helpful, and we must embrace what was coming, we must welcome it, even if Dr Roach wanted to continue with his protocol and keep playing God right up until the last minute, and it must be nice to have friends in high places, friends happy to accept whopping donations. Mother Morning said it was clear that Dr Roach no longer had friends in high places, because those friends were leaving him out in the cold, weren't they, and it was also clear that Mother Night had jumped ship some time ago, and did Captain Scott mean nothing to her? All the years they'd devoted to it, not to mention to us? 'You've no business,' she said, jabbing her finger at Mother Night. 'I know exactly what's been going on – don't think I'm unaware.'

'I have no idea what you mean,' said Mother Night.

'Now then, ladies,' began Mother Afternoon, but Mother Morning cut across her.

'Not recording dreams,' she said. 'Nightmares. You can't change the rules to suit yourself, you know. That's not your decision to make.'

'We've no proof there were nightmares,' said Mother Afternoon.

'It's happened more than once,' said Mother Morning. 'Terrible nightmares. I'm sure of it.'

My brothers and I shifted uneasily; we sensed we shouldn't be there, hearing what we were hearing.

And our mothers must have realised that too, because Mother Afternoon said, 'Now's not the time,' and all three of them looked at us and said no more.

I couldn't concentrate on Lessons that day, even though we were doing How Rome Won and Lost the World. At Break Time I ate only a bite of apple and a single cube of cheese, then pushed the little blue bowl of raisins towards my brothers. I kept hearing Mother

Afternoon: *What does it matter?* And Mother Night, my own Mother Night, urging us to embrace what was coming when what was coming would separate us all. We must welcome it, she'd said. I'd never have admitted this out loud for fear of causing hurt, but she was my favourite mother – and now here she was, quite happy to leave the Home and send us off to strangers. Were we really only a job to her?

That night, after Lights Out, Lawrence said, 'How much longer, do you think?'

None of us knew.

'What if no one wants us? Not a single nibble, Mother Morning said.'

I remembered the conversation I'd had with Mother Night about the drowned fishermen, their bodies nibbled on by sea creatures. Up to the surface they bobbed in the dark, their home-knitted jumpers holding together their picked ribs, remembering their names for those back on land.

Before I knew it Mother Morning was touching me on the shoulder and asking me what I'd dreamt. My mind was blank.

'Nothing today for Vincent, then,' she said, marking a dash beside my name in The Book of Dreams. Normally she would have questioned me for longer, tried to draw back up anything that might have slipped beneath the surface, but today she seemed restless to move on. She opened the blue velvet curtains with a gentle hand – they were starting to rot in places – and passed us our glasses of water and our medicine, Lawrence first and then William, as usual, and then me. 'I wish it were otherwise, truly I do, my darling,' she said, shaking a pill from the bottle, 'but we have some catching up to do, don't we?' She pushed the pill between my sleepy lips. 'This is for the slingshot,' she said, waiting while I swallowed, then checking my mouth. 'This is for the frequently handled vulgar picture.' A second pill. 'This is for thinking you know better.' Three. 'This is for the big lie itself.' Four. 'And this . . .' She deliberated, holding the fifth pill just in front of me like one of Cynthia's dog treats. 'This is for luck.'

The Book of Dreams

I started feeling strange halfway through breakfast. My scrambled eggs seemed to quiver on the plate, reforming themselves into a pile of canary-yellow pills that kept slipping from my fork. I drank glass after glass of water until a tide swelled inside me, rising past my breastbone, and the long pine table turned to sawdust under my grasping hands. *The sea they think they hear*, I said. *Singing. A roar. The blood it is.* And then the Refectory began to curve and distort like the things seen at the edges of the gazing ball, and I slid from my chair and onto the cold linoleum.

I remembered little of the next few days – little that made sense. I came to in the Playroom once, and the walls and the windows and even the daybed were made of Stickle Bricks; I could feel the bright plastic spikes beneath me, digging into my back. Up above, drifting across the spiky ceiling, the Mona Lisa smiled her private smile, and the sky shone through the hole where her eye was missing. Then she turned into the water stain on our bedroom ceiling. Then she turned into nothing. The gas must have been turned up high, because I was boiling, but when I forced myself to focus on the fireplace – which I knew was not marble, only painted like marble to fool the eye – I saw it was quite dead. The family from the portrait above the staircase came and went, the mauve-silk lady rustling at the foot of the bed and reaching for the hand of her daughter Martha Emily, who had faded to the brown of the needlework in the corner. When I tried to sit up, the gentleman – the father – laid his hand gently on my head and said *Verité Sans Peur*. Mother Morning appeared every so often to feed me my pills, three at a time, six at a time, I could not tell, I just swallowed when she told me to swallow and tried to display the right attitude. Mother Night visited me once too, in broad daylight, and she leaned across the daybed – which was no longer made of Stickle Bricks – and whispered *I can't stay, I don't have much time, I should have told you earlier but I was scared and for that I'll never forgive myself, and you must do everything in your power to get a family to take you, and you must be on your best behaviour, you can't put a foot wrong, and Margate isn't Margate, you must never go to Margate, do you understand me, say you understand me.* She kissed my forehead, and I smelled her face cream that was clean and cool and waxy, and then I felt her reach under the covers and press something into my hand, something made of paper, a letter or perhaps money, I didn't know what.

Other times I found myself in a bedroom, one of the deserted downstairs bedrooms where I could see the old initials of the Carter boys or the Connor boys scratched in the skirting board: *TC, LC, PC 17.5.75.* I tried to get up, but I was tucked in tight under the candy-striped sheets, weaker than a newborn, my head full of feathers, full of stones. I could hear Dr Roach somewhere nearby, talking to Mother Morning, telling her it was *highly irregular, not to mention risky,* and she was saying *Edith Saunders took risks. All of your scientists took risks. Goodness me, Josef Mengele took risks! And look at the miracles you've achieved.* Little paws pattering across my chest, a little tongue licking my earlobe. *Don't get any grand notions,* said Dr Roach. *Remember what you are.* And I wasn't sure if he meant me or Mother Morning or Cynthia or someone else entirely, and I heard his car creeping past the window, and I saw the silver hood ornament rear up, the silver jaguar, life-size and ready to pounce. My brothers came and went and told me things about Rome's Period of Decadence – how the women wore silk from China and diamonds, pearls and rubies from India, how peaches and apricots came to their tables at immense expense, how the national character began to decay – and for the first time in my life I could not tell William and Lawrence apart. One of them poked at me with the antler I'd found on the Nature Walk. *He can't feel a thing,* he said. *I am just going outside,* said the other, *and may be some time.* Then the blizzard took him.

Gradually the world returned to me, and I to the world. When I was well enough to stand, Mother Morning led me to the Bathroom and ran me a lovely warm bath. How many days since I had washed, properly washed? I remembered my mothers folding back the covers and unbuttoning my pyjamas, sponging me all over with a damp flannel, but now I craved the water, silky and deep.

'Hold on to me,' said Mother Morning as I put one foot in the bath. 'You're still very weak. That's it. Now the other. And down we go.'

My legs looked pale and spindly under the water, my feet bonier than usual. I sat very still for a few seconds, until I was sure I had my balance. 'Mother Night told me you might have mixed us up once,' I said. 'When we were babies, before we knew our names. You'd lined us up for a bath, but Lawrence hit his head, and William and I were squirming about, and we might have swapped places.'

'Mother Night has had some very strange ideas lately,' she said, rubbing the pale-green soap across the flannel and washing my back. 'Anyway, it's a good thing you're all better, because the Minister wants to send a television crew to film you soon.'

'Television?' I said. 'To film us?'

'Yes, to find families for you.' She rinsed the soap off my back. 'Oh, you used to love your baths when you were little boys. You laughed and splashed, and I'd end up soaked from head to toe, but I didn't mind.' She lifted my arm to wash it, and it felt dull and heavy, not quite part of me. 'Rub-a-dub-dub,' she said. 'It's like I have my baby back again.'

'I remember that,' I said. 'That rhyme you used to say to us.'

'Do you?' she said. 'What a clever boy – you were only toddlers at the time. How did it go?'

'Rub-a-dub-dub, three men in a tub, and who do you think they be? The butcher, the baker, the candlestick maker, and all of them out to sea.'

She laughed and said yes, yes, that was it exactly.

Funny the things that return to us.

Lawrence said I was better because all the pills had knocked the Bug on the head, and William – who could no longer get away with flushing his each morning – said I was better because I'd been cut back to one per day. I didn't know what to believe. I wanted to talk to Mother Night, to ask her about the pills, and the paper she'd pressed into my hand when I was sick – the paper I could not find – and what she'd meant by *Margate isn't Margate*. But I hadn't seen her since I'd recovered; her shift started at 9 p.m., which was Lights Out, and although the insomnia was returning, I didn't dare creep to the Upstairs Common Room to sit with her while she read to me from *Ulysses*. I didn't even dare go there in Free Time to read the book myself, no matter how I longed to. *You can't put a foot wrong*, she'd said, and I'd heard something desperate in her voice.

William and Lawrence laughed at me when I told them about her strange visit.

'Your brain made it up, that's all,' said Lawrence.

'Vincent's gone crazy!' said William, leaping around, contorting himself. 'He's bonkers! He's mental!'

'No I'm not,' I tried to say, but he leered in close at me so his face went out of focus. 'Bonkers! Mental!' he yelled.

'You thought the Playroom was made of Stickle Bricks,' Lawrence reminded me.

On this my brothers agreed: the more peculiar memories from my convalescence must be dreams. And life did seem to be returning to normal. We'd heard nothing from the Minister of Loneliness about the rehoming, so we began to believe it would never happen. My dreams were ordinary dreams again too: climbing the staircase to go to bed, only it was ten times bigger than in real life and the griffin had vanished. Riding the Sky Wheels that kept going up and up until I was in the stars above Dreamland and I could still see everyone far below but they didn't realise I'd gone. Sometimes Jane appeared. Sometimes the girl running through the moonlit woods.

One day, as I was about to drop my dirty clothes down the laundry chute, I heard Mother Morning and Mother Afternoon, their voices filtering up the narrow shaft.

'He's a very lucky boy,' Mother Morning was saying.

'Is he?' said Mother Afternoon. 'Is he really?'

'Of course. When you consider the alternative.'

The next day, Mother Morning told me she thought I was strong enough to go with her to the village. 'I need to be back well before Dr Roach arrives,' she said, 'and I could do with an extra pair of hands.'

We walked along the road by the hedgerows, swinging our string bags. The crab-apple tree shone with pale-yellow fruit, unaffected by its hollow heart, and up ahead of us three bay ponies grazed, one of them suckling her foal. I picked ripe blackberries from the brambles and ate them, and Mother Morning didn't mind, and didn't tell me to be careful not to scratch myself or stain my shirt. As we crossed the stone bridge I could see trout drifting in and out of the waterweed that swayed like green hair in the river. It was good to be out in the late summer, and I felt the things I'd dreamt when I was sick dissolving into the fresh bright air.

'I'll pick up the groceries, and you get the bread,' said Mother Morning, handing me some coins. 'That should be the right amount. I'll meet you outside.'

I paused at the bakery window to watch the little automaton baker that stood amidst the cakes. He tapped his spoon on the glass and nodded his head: *yes, yes, come and buy.* Inside, the smell of yeast and sugar curled its way around me, and my mouth watered at the sight of the fruit pies and jam tarts, all the coiled Chelsea buns.

'Well, look who it is,' said Mr Webb. 'I'd like to shake you by the hand, young man.'

'What have I done?' I said.

'What's he done, he wants to know! You've only saved my grandson's life.'

I had no idea what he meant. 'I think you must be mistaking me for someone else,' I said.

'No mistake. You're a hero, that's what you are. You and your brothers.' He came out from behind the counter and grabbed my hand, shaking it so hard I felt my whole body jolt. 'They'd given him a few months at best, poor wee mite. The size of a golf ball, it was, and spread to his spine. They couldn't operate. But then they tried a new drug in his chemotherapy, and it worked. Dreadful side-effects – he felt sick as a dog, and some days he couldn't stand up for the dizziness – but it worked. And that's thanks to you.'

'I'm sorry,' I said, 'but I really don't know what you're talking about.'

'Well,' he said, frowning, 'the drug trials. You *must* know. You and your brothers – and all the ones like you. It's you that deserve the knighthoods, never mind Alastair Roach.'

'Drug trials?' I said. The air in the bakery pressed in on me like raw dough, clammy and thick.

'Oh dear,' he said. 'I've got carried away. I've spoken out of turn. They think you'll go on a rampage with a knife if you find out – how mad is that! But you really had no inkling?'

And I knew something was wrong, very wrong indeed.

I forced myself to smile. 'I'm glad your grandson's better,' I said. 'Please may I have a farmhouse loaf and a wholemeal cob?'

'Anything you like, on the house!' He whistled as he shook open a paper bag. 'And how about something for the way home? An Eccles cake? An apple turnover?'

'No thank you,' I said.

'Go on. Please. It'd make me happy.'

I needed to get out of there. I pointed to a tray of apple turnovers and said, 'One of those then, thanks.'

'Coming right up. It's a crying shame they're shutting you down, you know. Criminal, that's what it is.'

I could see Mother Morning waiting for me outside the door. I shoved the money she'd given me back into my pocket and rushed to her.

'Right, let's get going,' she said. 'We'll have to hurry. Can you manage?'

146

'I'm fine,' I said.

'You look pale.'

'I'm fine.'

'What's in there?' she asked, pointing to the extra bag.

'He gave me an apple turnover on the house.'

'What a nice man. If a bit touched.'

'Yes,' I said. 'Yes, well, he was in a good mood today because his little grandson's better.'

'Is he,' said Mother Morning, turning her head to look in the window of the dress shop.

'Yes. Completely better.'

'What wonderful news.'

'Yes.' Our reflections glided across the mannequins, the expressionless women with their painted-on hair and their stiff limbs. I pushed the apple turnover up out of the bag and took a bite. It tasted like dust, and I could barely swallow, but I kept on eating until it was finished.

I went through the motions with Dr Roach: yes, I was feeling back to normal; no, I had no more troubling symptoms; yes, I was doing my Morning Exercise and maintaining a healthy attitude. Cynthia came racing into the Gun Room and pressed against my leg when I was fiddling with a coconut macaroon I didn't want, looking up at me with hungry eyes, so I fed her a bit of it and Dr Roach said, 'Oh, you're shameless! Yes you are!'

I waited until well after Lights Out, when the house had fallen quiet, to tell my brothers about Mr Webb. His words sounded strange as I spoke them in the dark, and when I'd finished I wondered if William and Lawrence had fallen asleep, because neither of them spoke.

'So what does that mean?' William said at last.

'I'm not sure,' I said. 'What do you think it means?'

They didn't know.

Over the next two days we discussed it whenever we could,

speaking in low voices during Morning Exercise, whispering to one another as we ate.

'What are you up to, eh?' Mother Afternoon asked with a smile. 'What are you planning?'

We smiled back, but we were figuring things out. In The Book of Knowledge, under The Science and Art of Healing, I found a brief reference to drug trials: *Working together with their Gothenburg Treaty partners, Britain's scientists are at the cutting edge of modern medical research. New drugs are tested first* in vitro *(in the laboratory) and then* in vivo *(on living organisms) before being deemed safe for human use.*

And finally I understood that nothing was wrong with us, that nothing had ever been wrong with us. Jane was right: the medicine didn't make us better, it made us sick. There was no Bug. We were laboratory animals. We were sacrifices.

'They've been lying to us all these years?' William said as we lay in our beds. 'Our mothers? Dr Roach?'

'Everyone,' I said.

'Maybe our mothers don't know,' said Lawrence.

'Everyone knows,' I said.

'But what about the Bug?'

'There is no Bug.'

They digested that.

'All those boys who died . . .' said William.

'The medicine,' I said.

'Not the Bug?'

'There is no Bug.'

'So . . . so we're heroes?'

'That's what Mr Webb thinks.'

'Then why does everyone in the village look at us like we're freaks?'

'Guilty consciences,' said William.

We jumped when our door opened. 'Time to settle down now, boys,' said Mother Night. 'No more chatting.'

She came and straightened Lawrence's blankets, ran a hand over William's cheek. We could see her tortoiseshell combs shining in the light from the passageway, and her little white teeth glinted as she leaned over each of us in turn and reminded us that we needed our sleep. But what was it that we noticed? What was wrong? She looked like Mother Night, and she sounded like Mother Night. The same smile in her voice; the same quality of deep water, dark feathers. She wore one of Mother Night's silky blouses, and she even smelled of Mother Night's face cream – clean and cool, a little waxy.

Kiss.

Kiss.

Kiss.

In her patent-leather shoes she crept from the room, her familiar shape lingering in the passageway before she shut the door.

I can't remember who spoke first. Perhaps William said it, or perhaps I did.

'That's not Mother Night.'

A whisper, small as a dream, in the quiet room. We were all thinking it. We blinked in the dark, which was so thick it made no difference if we kept our eyes open or shut.

'Who is it, then?'

'I don't know.'

'I don't know either.'

'It's not her.'

'No.'

'No.'

When Mother Morning woke us, we had nearly forgotten about the mistake the previous night, the strange switch. As we rubbed at our eyes, though, and stretched our bodies underneath our blankets, we began to remember, and we realised that we'd dreamt troubled dreams: mothers in masks; kisses on our foreheads that filled us with shadows; a voice saying *no more chatting, no more chatting* as a hand clamped our mouths shut; patent-leather shoes that walked of their own accord and left behind footprints of ash. But instead of these dreams my brothers reported quite ordinary ones, ones they'd dreamt before.

'Now, Vincent,' said Mother Morning, settling herself on the edge of my bed and opening the Book, 'what about you?'

She was looking down at me, holding her pen above the page. I glanced over to William, who shook his head almost imperceptibly.

'Whenever you're ready,' she said, smiling at me.

The dream of the shoes was in my mouth, but somehow I knew I shouldn't say it. I swallowed.

'I'm passing underneath the *Queen Mary* building at Dreamland,' I said, 'and it turns into a real ship and floats away. I'm waving to everyone watching from the shore, until smoke from the funnels covers them up.'

And Mother Morning wrote *I'm passing underneath the* Queen Mary *building at Dreamland* . . .

Then we took our pills and felt nothing like heroes, and when we climbed out of bed the cool air crept underneath our pyjamas, and Mother Morning drew back the curtains, and the light caught in her auburn hair. We saw the pale sky, the hazy garden, the gazing ball shimmering in the ferns like a great eye, the same as any other day. But we knew everything had changed.

We spoke in whispers as we dressed, though Mother Morning had already gone downstairs and couldn't have overheard us. What on earth was happening? First Mr Webb's slip-up, and now the business with Mother Night. Had she really been replaced, or had we simply dreamt her up, this new mother who looked almost exactly like the old one? And if she was real, where had they found her? We tried to pinpoint what had unsettled us about her. Was it something in the way she spoke? Something about her clothing? Was she taller than she should be? Under my bare foot I felt the knot made from Philip Cole's blue-striped scraps.

'It was when she leaned over me,' said Lawrence. 'Her face. She looked older.'

Yes, we agreed, that was it. Only by a few years, perhaps, but she looked older. She *was* older.

'Mother Not,' I said.

'Mother Not,' echoed my brothers.

Perhaps, we said, we should just bite the bullet and ask Mother Morning and Mother Afternoon about all this – Mr Webb, Mother Night.

But our mothers were the ones who gave us our medicine.

And our mothers had been lying to us all this time.

So perhaps we'd be better off if the Minister rehomed us. And perhaps we shouldn't ask our mothers a thing. Perhaps we shouldn't breathe a word.

PART TWO

The Book of Knowledge

The Minister of Loneliness

'What do you think our children would have been like?' she asked her husband. They were eating their supper – a very nice fish pie that he'd made at the start of the month and frozen into individual portions.

'Our *children*?' he said, as if he'd never given the matter a moment's thought, as if children, their children, were a ludicrous notion. Back when the two of them were first married, they had chosen to focus on her career – and look how that was paying off.

'Yes, our children,' she said, spearing a bit of anchovy – his secret ingredient to give the dish some heft.

They were all but past that point now, of course; a family was really no longer a possibility, and she'd never felt it as a loss. She remembered her terror a year earlier, when certain symptoms had presented themselves out of the blue: a skipped period, tender breasts, nausea, weight gain. She'd sat motionless at her desk one morning while her telephone rang unanswered and her secretary brought papers for her to read and sign, just if she could see her way clear, just if it wasn't too much trouble. The Minister – who wasn't a Minister then, only a shadow Minister – told herself she couldn't possibly be a mother. How could she be a mother? She'd make a terrible mess of things. The child would sense it was an accident and run completely off the rails; it would torture neighbourhood pets, shoplift cigarette lighters and methylated spirits and carry a flick knife concealed on its person, and from there it was just a hop, skip and a jump to heroin addiction.

Her doctor had put her right when she'd finally made an appointment – he'd told her it was the very start of the change of life. The symptoms were easy to mistake for pregnancy, funnily enough, and her body was just playing tricks on itself. 'A shadow pregnancy, if you like,' he'd said.

She'd laughed, because he'd meant her to laugh – but for months afterwards, every time the symptoms flared, she'd imagined the shadow child inside her, its inky limbs taking shape, its tiny fingers unfurling.

'Thank God for that!' her husband had said when she'd told him they weren't about to become parents in their forties.

'Yes,' she'd agreed. 'Thank God for that.'

Now he forked up another dollop of fish pie and put his head on one side as he chewed, considering her question. 'Well,' he said, 'I suppose they'd be short, thanks to you, and ginger-haired, thanks to me. Poor little buggers.'

'And tone deaf, thanks to you, and night owls, thanks to me,' she said.

'And mean-spirited, thanks to your mother, and good at darts, thanks to my father.'

'They'd have your funny thumbs.'

'And your bad eyes.'

'Your inability to whistle.'

'And your fear of voles.'

'Horrid little claws,' she said.

'The children?'

'The voles. And long wormy tails.'

'I thought we weren't allowed to talk about voles.'

'We're not.'

'But here you are, chatting away about them.'

'You brought them up.'

He laughed. 'They'd always want the last word,' he said, winding a strand of melted cheese around his fork. 'The children. Not the voles.'

'Watch yourself,' she said.

On they went, fleshing out these phantom children until they seemed to populate the dining room, jostling for a place at the table. She passed him the last of her fish pie to finish – she was ready to burst – but when he tried to take a bite, she grabbed his wrist to stop him.

'Make up your mind,' he said.

'I saw a bone,' she said – and there it was, a sharp white needle lodged in a chunk of salmon. She plucked it out, held up the thing he could have choked on. Felt a certain pressure in her own throat.

'Nobody wants them, you know,' she said. 'The Sycamore boys and girls. We've hundreds of catalogues piled up, ready to send out to interested parties, but they're just gathering dust.'

'Can you really blame people?' he said. 'After what happened in—'

'Please don't say Flamborough.'

'—in Flamborough.'

She sighed. 'All the more reason to move the remaining older children to proper homes, homes in the community, and to start the drug trials from scratch with the very young ones in a clinical setting. That boy would never have reacted the way he did if he'd known what he was from the beginning.'

'A lack of knowledge is the reason they turn violent?' he said. 'Not their genetic inheritance?'

'In many cases, yes,' she said. 'As well as their inhumane treatment.'

'Mm,' said her husband, 'maybe. But what does that actually mean? A clinical setting.'

'Well, a clinic,' she said. 'A new medical team with new ideas – fresh blood.'

'Roach won't take kindly to that.'

'I think the PM's keen to shake things up in light of what's happened. Move it all out of the public eye. And the participants will be housed in state-of-the-art facilities, apparently, quite separate from the community. With appropriate security.'

'A prison, then.'

'A clinic, with security. And from an early age they'll be made fully aware of their role. No pussy-footing around what they really are.'

'And that's a better solution than the Homes, you think?'

'The PM is confident, yes.'

'What do you think, though?'

'It's not my area.' But she had seen the drawings of the new facilities: the high windows, the glass reinforced with wire mesh. The airless dormitories with their sheets pulled drum-tight.

'Have the rest of them been told what they are?'

'Not at this stage. The public have been very good at keeping a lid on it, by and large. The press, too.'

'Well, everyone knows the penalties. They're afraid.'

'That's part of it, yes – but until last year, most people never gave the Scheme a second thought. We knew the basic set-up, but we put it out of our minds, the same way we ignore the origins of our pork sausages. The Scheme's been winding down for nearly a decade, after all – and it's only since the children have been let out for errands that a few people have felt moved by a misplaced sense of compassion or justice or goodness knows what.'

'So potentially,' he said, 'when the children do find out, you could have another Flamborough on your hands.'

'Doubtful,' she said. '*If* they find out – and many may never – they'll be ensconced in a loving home, no longer part of the trials. Assimilation is the aim. Perhaps they'll look back on their time in the Homes as heroic – as doing their bit. That's how we'll be advising the families to frame it, in the event it does come to light.'

'They're not normal children, though,' he said.

'The remaining ones are fine. Docile. It looks good for us to be showing compassion towards them.'

He brushed the back of her hand. 'I worry about you visiting these places. The Homes. The prisons. Why couldn't she have given you one of the safe portfolios – Energy, or Transport, or even Gothenburg? That'd be a good one. We could flit off to Berlin or Rome every other week.'

'She wanted a woman for Loneliness,' said the Minister. 'She was very clear on that.'

'But men for everything else,' said her husband.

'It's an honour. An *honour*.' Her skirt felt too tight. 'I think,' she said, and smoothed the tablecloth, 'I think a couple of the children might have an inkling.'

'How do you mean?'

'Vincent,' she said. 'The boy who asked about my cameo brooch.' She didn't say *The boy who carved me a cameo from soap*. She hadn't shown that to her husband; it was still in her handbag, releasing its piney scent when she felt about for her lipstick or coin purse. 'He said he'd heard that the drugs make you sick, not better.'

'Heard it from where?'

'One of the Sycamore girls, at a Socialisation Day.'

'And you're only mentioning this now? You're lucky he didn't grab the brooch and stab you with it!'

'He's a very gentle soul.'

'A soul?' said her husband. 'A soul?'

'I told him the girl was probably just joking, and he seemed to accept that.'

'I don't like it,' he said, shaking his head. 'Unpredictable creatures. I don't like it at all.'

'The end is in sight. Once they're rehomed, I won't be involved any more.'

'Except nobody wants them.'

'We're broadening the campaign. Trying television.'

'How will that help? They're *violent*, Sylvia. Better to keep them confined to the Homes.'

'The problematic ones have already been taken care of,' she said.

'And the Homes are a relic of an earlier era. A less humane, less socially aware era. It's time we relegated them to history.'

'You sound exactly like her, you know.'

She blushed.

'And the residents – they won't put up any resistance?'

'The *children*,' she said.

'You've changed your tune.'

'If you just met them—'

'Steady on.'

'To be honest, I don't think they want to leave, no. And nor do the carers.'

'Well, you wouldn't, would you? A plum job in a country estate, all meals covered, a clothing allowance and an entertainment allowance . . .'

'The allowances were scrapped years ago.'

'But still, they've had it pretty good.'

'Perhaps. At any rate, they're not part of my brief – not part of the rehoming programme. Just the children.'

The Minister unbuttoned the waistband of her skirt. That felt better.

Vincent

Mother Afternoon had planned a picnic for our next Socialisation Day. Many people enjoyed picnics in small mixed groups of males and females, she said, and it would give us a chance to practise chatting to the young ladies again, this time outside the Home. She'd make a batch of her Scotch eggs for the occasion. Didn't that sound like fun? She bustled about, retrieving the picnic basket from a musty cupboard, cleaning off the cobwebs and airing tartan travel rugs for us to sit on. As if everything were perfectly normal. As if she hadn't been lying to us our whole lives.

'We can tell the young ladies about Mr Webb if we get a chance,' I whispered to my brothers over breakfast. 'See if they know anything about the drug trials.'

The day of the picnic was clear but unseasonably chilly, and we were glad of our new Aran jumpers. We spread out the tartan rugs next to the stream, not far from the road that led to the village. The young ladies wore puffy jackets that did nothing for them, we agreed; they looked like eiderdowns with arms, and the swishing set our teeth on edge. We tried to listen instead to the soft ocean sounds of the alder trees.

I asked how the motorcoach was, because I knew from the last time that the young ladies had enjoyed their trip, and it was polite and normal to ask about a person's interests.

161

'A man was sick into a briefcase,' said Jane.

'Was he,' I said.

'His own briefcase, or someone else's?' asked William.

'His own,' said Diane. 'He had no way of cleaning it, so he just snapped it shut and held it level on his lap till we reached Ashbridge.'

Mother Afternoon set out the food and the plastic plates, smiling away; she'd even brought the salt and pepper cellars that had S and P punched in holes on the lids so you didn't get it wrong, and paper napkins that she folded into water lilies so they looked elegant. She poured us cups of cocoa from a red thermos, but the cups had no handles and we kept burning our fingers – apart from William, who got the proper cup that screwed on top of the thermos, which wasn't fair. My brothers and I sat cross-legged, but the young ladies seemed not to know how to sit, what to do with their bodies. They fidgeted and wriggled, and the puffy jackets swished. 'You can just pop your legs out to the side, like so,' Mother Afternoon told them, leaning on her left hip and bending her sturdy legs to the right, keeping her ankles together. 'I imagine this is how Princess Margaret would arrange herself at a picnic on the tropical isle of Mustique.'

We filled our plates and began to eat; we were hungry because we'd skipped lunch to leave room for the picnic, and it was nearly two o'clock. Mother Afternoon had brought far too much food, as if other children, forgotten children, might materialise from the woods.

Karen inspected her plateful and said, 'I'm not sure this is entirely hygienic.' She took a small, tentative bite of coleslaw.

'Isn't this nice,' said Mother Afternoon. 'Aren't we having a lovely time.'

And perhaps it was because we were away from Captain Scott, away from our other mothers, or perhaps it was just the late-summer day that made us think of things changing and growing older, but we brought up the matter of Mother Night.

William mentioned it first: 'We thought we noticed something strange,' he said.

'Oh?' said Mother Afternoon. She looked around, as if she might see this strange thing.

'It was two nights ago,' he said. 'When Mother Night came into our room.'

Lawrence and I nodded, because Mother Afternoon did not look worried or angry at this topic of conversation, and really, why hadn't we raised it before now? And, for that matter, why hadn't we raised the issue of Mr Webb and the drug trials? Perhaps our mothers hadn't known about them after all; perhaps they hadn't been lying to us. We wanted to believe that. I'm sure you can think of things you want to believe too.

'What was strange about Mother Night coming into your room?' she said, untroubled.

'She looked different,' said William.

'Different?' A small shift in tone now; an edge so slight that an outsider wouldn't have noticed. I started to feel scared, though, and so did Lawrence. We tried to change the subject – the crispness of the air; how much warmer it must be at Princess Margaret's home on the tropical isle of Mustique – but Mother Afternoon was peering at William, and we knew she wouldn't let it go.

'What do you mean, different?' she said. A wariness in her voice. A warning.

And William looked Mother Afternoon right in the eye and said, 'She's older.'

Mother Afternoon paused for a split second, then laughed, waved a hand. 'My goodness,' she said. 'Looking after you three's enough to give anyone a few grey hairs. I feel about ninety years old myself.' She laughed again. 'But you really mustn't dwell on this. Commenting on a woman's age is a sign of what?'

'Poor breeding,' we said.

'*Very* poor,' she said.

So that solved that, then: Mother Night was still Mother Night, and we were mistaken. Weren't we?

I wondered if, with the young ladies there, we should take the opportunity to ask about the drug trials – but despite Mother Afternoon's breezy manner, the wariness and the warning lingered about her somehow. Lawrence and I exchanged glances and returned to our food. We'd wait to get the young ladies alone, and then we'd tell them what Mr Webb had said.

Diane had been saving her Scotch egg till last, but when she bit into it there was no egg inside, only sausage meat all the way through.

'Oh, yes,' said Mother Afternoon, 'I had some left over and didn't want to waste it.'

Diane said it shouldn't have been in with the Scotch eggs, because it was just a rissole, and it was wrong to mislead people, she knew that from Ethical Hour, and now all the genuine Scotch eggs were gone because everyone else had polished them off. Mother Afternoon said there was an important lesson here for all of us but didn't elaborate. Lawrence offered Diane his cheese and onion sandwich, but she said that was hardly the same, and anyway, she'd already eaten two cheese and onion sandwiches because she wanted to get them out of the way before enjoying her Scotch egg.

Karen saw the ponies first, picking their way across the leaf litter to come right up behind us. She let out a little scream. How quietly they had approached.

'Shh,' said Mother Afternoon, placing a hand on Karen's arm. 'You'll scare them.'

'*I'll* scare *them*?' said Karen.

'What do they want?' whispered Diane, shrinking away from the edge of the rug.

'They're just saying hello,' said Mother Afternoon. 'Checking up on us.'

'Are they dangerous?' said Karen as a pony sniffed at the container of coleslaw, its soft muzzle inches from her leg.

'They're wild animals,' said William.

'They're not wild,' said Mother Afternoon. 'Not in the true sense of the word. But you mustn't touch or feed them, or get between a mother and her foal.'

'So they *are* dangerous,' said Karen.

'They can bite,' said William. 'That one could rip your arm off. Trample you to death.' He pointed to a pony with a white blaze that was nibbling on the lush undergrowth, a piece of bracken snagged in its mane. It blinked its burnt-toffee eyes at us.

'He's being silly,' said Mother Afternoon. 'But all the same, don't touch them.'

They moved around us, nine or ten of them, the light catching in their bay and chestnut coats. We felt their heavy tread, the thud of it pulsing up through the ground. Their powerful breaths, their wild blood. The mineral smell of the roughed-up earth. Around their hooves the leaf litter skittered like moths, and we stayed very still and quiet so as not to cause alarm. After a time they made their way to the edge of the stream and drank. They seemed scarcely to touch the water, just brushing the surface with their lips. Then they crossed to the other side and vanished into the woods.

'The foals will be taken from the mothers soon,' said Lawrence.

Nobody replied.

Jane twirled an alder leaf in her fingers.

'Heart-shaped,' I said, 'but the wrong way round. The point is at the stalk.'

'I've read A–BON too,' she said. 'Being durable under water, alder wood is used for the foundations of piers and bridges.'

'And the soles of clogs,' I said.

'Obviously,' she said.

'Shall we go on a Nature Walk?' said William, and Mother Afternoon said she supposed that would be all right but we mustn't go too far. She would stay behind to look after our things, because there were some crooked types about who needed no encouragement.

'Like robbers?' said Diane. 'Or gypsies?'

'Pirates!' said Karen.

Jane scoffed. 'Are we at sea? Have we just swabbed the deck and trimmed the sails?'

We picked our way across the stream, balancing on a rotten log that felt spongy underfoot, its roots splayed like antlers.

Karen grabbed William's wrist and pointed to a moss-covered boundary stone. 'Is that a gravestone?'

'It's a boundary stone,' he said.

'What's a boundary stone?'

'It marks a boundary.'

'You're very brainy. You know everything.'

He shrugged.

In front of us the woods rose up green and black, and we felt the drop in temperature as we moved into the shade of the trees. The young ladies zipped their puffy jackets up to their necks. Tiny mushrooms the colour of bone glimmered around the roots of beeches and oaks, and they might have been death caps and they might have been false death caps, but either way we weren't to touch them.

'Watch out for adders,' said Lawrence, and Karen shrieked.

'He just said to watch out for them,' said William. 'He didn't say there *are* adders.'

'But there might be?' said Jane.

'You never know.'

'Sorry,' said Lawrence. 'I didn't mean to scare anyone. Sorry.'

'Adders are the most dangerous of all poisonous snakes,' I said. 'Most bring forth their young alive, and this has led to the tale that they swallow their young when danger threatens.'

'Idiot,' said William.

On we walked through the cool of the woods, skirting the patches of holly and brambles. We knew we needed to tell the young ladies about Mr Webb, and to see if they'd heard anything similar, but none of us wanted to be the one to raise it. To let them know what they really were.

Karen stayed close to William and kept asking him questions.

'Do you like corned beef with mustard?' she said.

'It's all right,' he said.

'I love it. I could eat it every day, but we only have Corned Beef Day once a month. How often do you have Corned Beef Day?'

'Once a month.'

'Have you ever seen a baby hedgehog?'

'No.'

'I'm going to have my own dog one day. I want a St Bernard because they're the most loyal breed of dog in the world. Do you want a St Bernard?'

'I don't know. No.'

She picked up a twig with a few leaves attached to it. 'Identify this,' she said, waving it in front of his face, tickling his chin.

'It's a twig,' he said.

She laughed, too loudly. 'This is a Nature Walk, silly! We're supposed to identify things. Wait, hear that?'

We listened – a bird sounded in the canopy above us. *Key-key-key-key-key!*

Jane and I peered up into the branches, but we couldn't see anything.

Key-key-key! it called again.

We turned in circles, squinting at tree after tree. It was like trying to find the right place on Mother Afternoon's Spot the Ball coupons. Marking an *X* here, an *X* there, hoping luck might be on your side.

Key-key-key-key-key! Key-key-key-key-key!

Louder now. More urgent.

'What *is* that?' Karen asked William.

'It's a bird,' he said.

Karen laughed again. Bouncing on her toes, she tagged William's shoulder and yelled, 'You're It!' then dashed away.

He stared after her, contemplating something. Then he took chase. 'Thank goodness for that,' said Jane. 'She's so annoying today.'

'And I'm pretty sure she ate the last Scotch egg,' said Diane.

We scuffed through the leaf litter, and nobody could think of any conversation. *Key-key-key!* called the bird, high-pitched and frantic. *Key-key-key-key-key!*

'The lesser spotted woodpecker, I believe,' said Lawrence. 'Quite rare. Though they do not sing, they have distinctive and sometimes musical calls.'

'Real birds never sound like the one on *Peter and the Wolf*,' I said.

'That's a flute,' said Lawrence. 'Not a bird at all.'

'Hmm.'

'What did William mean about Mother Night?' said Diane.

'We thought she was different,' I said, my voice slipping into its child's register. 'Someone else.'

'How is that even possible?'

'I don't know. We must've been mistaken.'

'You're used to seeing her in the shadows,' said Jane. 'People can look different then, depending on how dark it is.'

Which was true.

She reached into the pocket of her brown corduroys and took out a small orange packet: chewing gum. We'd spotted it before, at Mr Kendrick's corner shop, and in the mouths of the village girls, but we'd never tried it; our mothers said it was common. 'Care for a piece?' she said, so I held out my hand, and she squeezed a glossy white pellet into my palm. It looked like a large pill.

Lawrence took one as well. 'Now what?' he said.

'Now you chew it, stupid.'

The hard sugar coating crunched between my teeth like glass. 'Where did you get it?'

'The corner shop in our village.'

'Are you allowed it?'

'No.'

'It's not very filling,' said Lawrence.

Jane rolled her eyes. 'You swallowed it, didn't you.'

'Why wouldn't I swallow it?'

'It's *chewing* gum, stupid. How will you ever survive when they let us out?'

'Maybe we'll be stuck at the Homes forever,' I said. 'They've not had a single nibble.'

'But what about the families?' said Diane, who looked like she might cry. 'The catalogues?'

'Ugh, don't get her started,' said Jane. 'Anyway, I thought you wanted to stay.'

'We've changed our minds in light of recent information,' I said.

'They'll still close us down,' said Lawrence. 'The British taxpayer demands it. That's why they're coming to film us.'

'*Film* you?' said Jane.

'For television,' I said. 'To attract families.'

'They're not filming us,' said Diane. 'You'll get all the families, and we'll get none. That's not fair.'

Jane pushed the packet of gum back into her pocket and did a handstand up against a tree. Diane was wandering ahead, sniffling, and Lawrence hurried after her, saying he was sure lots of families had seen her in the catalogue, and very soon she'd hear something, and probably she'd be able to take her pick.

In the distance I could make out Karen's grating laugh.

I sat down next to Jane, who was still upside down, the tip of her braid brushing the leaf litter. 'I tried stopping my medicine,' I said. 'After what you told me last time. William did too.'

'How can you stop it?' she said. 'Nobody can.'

'I pretended to swallow the pills, but really I kept them under my tongue.'

'Oh, pills,' she said. 'I suppose it would work with pills.' Her face was turning red as all the blood rushed towards the ground. She looked different somehow: unlike herself.

'I felt . . . incredible.'

'Told you so.' She shifted the angle of her hands a little. Her fingernails dug into the dirt.

'You're pretty strong.'

'Sometimes,' she said. 'Depends on the medicine.'

'I thought that any day they'd notice I was better and put me on the Van to Margate.' The hazy words of Mother Night returned to me: *Margate isn't Margate, you must never go to Margate* – but then William's words returned to me too: *Vincent's gone crazy! He's bonkers! He's mental!* I shook my head, blinked them all away. 'I couldn't believe how strong I felt,' I went on. 'Is that how it is for everyone else? I mean, for ordinary people?'

'Maybe.'

'You should probably come down now. Your face is turning weird.'

'I'm keeping the blood in. The medicine gives me bleeding noses.'

'But you can't go about upside down all the time.'

I think she rolled her eyes; it was a bit hard to tell. '*Obviously,*' she said. 'But if I do it enough, I can train the blood to stay inside me.'

'Oh. Okay.' It sounded logical – back then, it sounded logical. You need to realise how little we understood.

'If you're so strong, why don't you pick that up?' She pointed with her chin to a gigantic fallen branch.

'It didn't last,' I said. 'Mother Morning found my pills.'

'Well, that was stupid of you.'

'Yes.'

'No Margate.'

'No.' *Margate isn't Margate.*

'A big fat black mark in The Book of Guilt.'

'Yes.' I cringed to think of the entry, Mother Morning's neat hand detailing my worst crime ever. 'She makes us show her inside our mouths each time now.'

'So that's that,' said Jane. 'You've ruined everything.'

'I expect so.'

'Why don't you want to stay at the Home any more?'

I shuffled closer. 'That's what I've been meaning to tell you,' I said. 'Mr Webb's grandson recovered.'

'What?' she said. 'Who?'

'Mr Webb the baker.'

'What's he got to do with it?'

I knew I was making little sense, but I suppose I thought the fact of the boy's recovery might soften the blow for Jane. 'I was in the bakery in the village the other day,' I went on, 'and Mr Webb said his grandson was better even though the cancer was right through him and they couldn't operate, and I had saved his life.'

'He sounds like a nutter.'

'No – no, listen. He said we're heroes, all the Sycamore children, because of the drug trials. They tried a new drug on his grandson, and it had dreadful side-effects and made him sick as a dog, but it worked. We deserve knighthoods, he said. And he must have seen the look on my face, because then he said he shouldn't have mentioned anything. And then he gave me an apple turnover on the house.'

In silence Jane lowered one leg and then the other. Brushed the dirt from her hands. Sat down next to me. I could hear her breaths: shaky and too fast, as if she'd been running. 'Drug trials,' she said.

'Yes,' I said.

'What does that mean, exactly?'

But I knew she'd worked it out, just as I had. She was looking at me, wanting me to tell her that I'd made it up, that I was teasing.

'I'm sorry,' I said.

She picked at the dirt under her nails. 'The people out there . . . why would they do that to us?'

'To look after their children.'

'So our mothers have been lying all this time. Dr Roach has been lying.'

'It seems that way, yes.'

'Maybe they don't know about the trials. That's possible, isn't it?'

'I doubt it.'

'And the Minister?'

'When I told her what you said – that the medicine made us sick, not better – she said you must have been making a bad joke.'

171

'So maybe she doesn't know.'

'Or maybe she does.'

'We should just ask them,' said Jane. 'Just come right out with it.'

'No,' I said, remembering the change in Mother Afternoon when William had asked about Mother Night. The fear that had crept up the back of my throat. 'No, I really don't think we should.'

Jane looked at me for a few seconds, then nodded. Gradually the colour drained from her face. We sat there listening to the sounds of the woods – the whirr of birds' wings, the rustle of water – and she reached over and put her hand in mine, and I kissed her on the lips as lightly as the ponies drinking from the stream.

Then we heard another sound in the distance – a girl shouting, 'No! Stop it!' A cry, a scream.

'That's Karen,' said Jane, and we scrambled to our feet.

Through the woods we ran, calling for her, searching for any sign of her, but she had fallen silent, and we couldn't tell where she was. In a small clearing we met up with Lawrence and Diane, who'd heard her too, and we turned and turned, peering into the trees, peering up into the branches, even, as if Karen might have shinnied up a trunk to get away.

'Maybe a horse attacked her,' said Diane. 'I didn't like the way they sniffed at us.'

'She probably just tripped on a tree root and twisted her ankle,' said Lawrence, but he sounded unsure of himself, and none of us really believed him.

'What about the robbers and gypsies?' said Diane.

Maybe something like that, we agreed, because hadn't Mother Afternoon said there were crooked types about? But then we hadn't seen anybody lurking, had we? So maybe that was a lie too.

'And she's with William,' said Jane. 'He'll look after her.'

'Yes,' I said, glancing over at Lawrence. 'She's with William.'

'Oh, perfect.' Jane was holding her hands to her face: her nose had started to bleed. 'Can you get my hanky? Front pocket.'

I slipped my hand into her soft corduroys and dug below the

packet of chewing gum for the handkerchief. It had been ironed into a neat rectangle, so I shook it open for her while she sat down and pinched her nose to stop the bleeding. Then I headed back into the trees by myself.

The woods seemed darker now, and quieter, and I was moving further from home with every step. In the distance a bird was hiccupping.

No, not a bird.

I found her at the foot of a great beech tree, sprawled across its mossy roots. Eyes closed, she was whimpering to herself, quietly, rhythmically, the way a baby does when it's exhausted from crying but its body can't quite stop. Her jacket lay nearby, turned inside out, the pale lining scuffed and dirty. Dirt on her cheek, too, and a criss-cross pattern where the side of her face had been pressed into the ground. Her blouse was torn at the hem, her jumper rucked up and her trousers pushed down around her hips, which glimmered white in the gloom, as white as death caps.

'Karen?' I said, and she flinched when she saw me and tried to back away.

'No,' she said, and at first I thought she wanted to convince me she was someone else, someone other than Karen, which made no sense. 'No no no!' she repeated as I came closer, and I realised she was terrified of me. Of someone who looked like me. She scrabbled at her trousers, trying to pull them up, all thumbs.

'It's Vincent,' I said. 'Vincent.' I retrieved her jacket for her, and she snatched it from me and spread it across her middle while she put herself to rights. I looked away.

'Where is he?' she said.

'I don't know.'

Gingerly she got to her feet.

'Are you hurt?' I said.

'Don't touch me.'

'Was it the robbers? The gypsies?'

'What?'

173

'A pony, then?'

She made a sound that was neither laugh nor sob but something in between. 'You know who it was,' she said. Her hands shook so much she could hardly tuck in her torn blouse. 'You *know*,' she said again.

And I did.

And I remembered what Mother Night had told me when I was delirious: *you must be on your best behaviour, you can't put a foot wrong*. How desperate she had sounded.

The trees were closing in, and I was plunging through the River Caves at Dreamland, the water taking me wherever it wanted: the Smugglers' Cave, the Venetian Cave, the Ice Cave, the sea.

'Please can you not tell anyone?' I said. 'I'm sure he didn't mean to hurt you. He plays a bit rough sometimes. It was just a mistake.'

'It didn't seem like a mistake.'

You can't put a foot wrong. 'Please, Karen,' I said. 'I . . . I think something bad will happen if anyone finds out.'

'What do you mean, something bad?'

'I don't know exactly. But something very bad for William.' I licked my lips – then I said it. 'And very bad for you.'

'Me?'

'Of course. You went walking with him alone. You were teasing him. *Annoying* him. We all saw it.'

She blushed right down her neck. 'I thought he liked me,' she muttered.

'Oh, he did. He does.' A lie. 'He talked about you a lot after the first Socialisation Day.' Another lie. 'Like I said, he just plays rough sometimes.'

She frowned. Zipped up her jacket. Followed me back to the clearing.

William was waiting for us there, leaning against a tree, his hands in his pockets.

'Are you okay?' Jane and Diane said, rushing to Karen, touching her arm, her hair.

'I'm all right,' she said.

'She just went a bit off course,' I said.

'Yes,' she said.

Around the edges of Jane's nostrils, dried blood.

'You'd better tell her about Mr Webb,' said William. 'Then we'll all know.'

'I told Diane,' Jane said to me.

'But I don't believe it,' said Diane.

'Who's Mr Webb?' said Karen.

So I repeated the story – my visit to the bakery, his grandson's recovery. What he'd let slip about the drug trials. The apple turnover on the house.

Karen didn't believe it either. 'We asked our mothers why the medicine made us feel worse sometimes,' she said. 'They told us the Bug was fighting it off and our bodies were fighting back.'

'Do you think that's true?' said William.

Karen shrugged. She wouldn't look at him.

'I don't,' said Jane. 'But we're usually on syrup or injections or drips. You can't hide those under your tongue, so how can we put it to the test?'

'Let's go and ask Mr Webb,' said William. 'The village isn't far. He'll give us *all* apple turnovers.'

'Is that a Nature Walk, though?' said Lawrence. 'We're supposed to be on a Nature Walk.'

'Apples are fruit,' said William.

'Mother Afternoon will worry if we're gone too long,' I said.

'It's not far,' said William.

So off we went, stopping to pick up a black acorn and an interesting leaf that was half green and half yellow, half alive and half dead, because we'd need something to show for our Nature Walk.

'Perhaps we'll find some sundews,' said William.

'Some what?' said Diane.

'Sundews. Carnivorous plants. Mind your fingers and toes!'

'You're making it up,' said Diane.

'Gobble gobble,' said William.

'We do have sundews,' said Lawrence, 'but not in the woods. We'd have to look on the heathland, where it's boggy.'

'No thank you,' said Diane.

'Are you an insect?' said William.

'I beg your pardon? Of course not.'

'Are you sure?'

'I'm a human female.'

'Then you're safe. They don't eat those.'

Now and then I glanced over at Karen, but she seemed fine. Fine.

And William was right – soon we emerged from the woods, and there was the stone bridge across the river, and the church with its steeple that rose above the red-roofed houses, and there was the blue-faced clock that told four different times. There was the high street: the chip shop with its delicious oily smells, and the corner shop where the Lucky Bags waited buried in straw for all the lucky children. There was the telephone box painted bright red, and inside it the instructions for emergency calls, and the phone that reeked of sweat and smoke. I'd picked it up and held it to my ear once. Pretended to talk to someone.

Two girls came out of the chip shop, newspaper-wrapped parcels hugged to their chests, and almost collided with us. We knew these girls – well, we knew them by sight, though we'd never been this close to them. They shrieked and nudged each other, trying to step around us, and one of them whispered something in the other's ear.

'Go on!' said the first girl when her friend shook her head.

'You do it!' said the second.

'I dared you, though!'

So the second girl glanced around to see if anybody was watching, then grabbed the side of my wrist and pinched hard. I was so surprised I didn't even react, didn't say a word, and the first girl looked at her friend and said, 'See? Told you so.'

They giggled as they raced away, lacy white socks pulled up to their knees, glossy hair bouncing.

I remembered the boy who had dropped his book – the boy who had kicked my shin and punched me in the stomach, marvelling that I seemed to feel no pain. And part of me did wonder what on earth the village children saw in us to make them treat us this way – yes, part of me did want to know what we were. But that day I also felt different: that day we had young ladies in our company. Weren't we just like any group of boys and girls? Weren't we just like ordinary people?

A woman walking a red setter stepped aside to let us pass, peering at the young ladies as if trying to place them – but of course they'd never been to Ashbridge before. Diane reached out a hand to pat the dog, but just as Lawrence told her it wasn't a good idea the woman yanked on the leash and said, 'She doesn't like strangers.' On we went, and I said, 'Sometimes the ponies wander along here. I've seen them strolling down the street as if they're doing their shopping.' And Diane said that didn't sound right, I must be making it up just as I'd made up the story about Mr Webb, but Lawrence and William said no, it was true, the ponies often came into the village and everyone knew to be wary of them.

And there at the end of the street was the bakery, its window filled with lemon drizzle cakes and Swiss rolls, Victoria sponges and finger buns, and standing amidst the trays of treats the automaton baker in his white hat and apron, tapping his spoon on the glass.

Inside, a ruddy-faced man I didn't recognise stood behind the counter. His eyes flicked from William to Lawrence to me and back to William, and he wore the slightly perplexed, slightly uncomfortable look the villagers often wore. 'Yes?' he said.

'We're here to see Mr Webb, please,' I said, making sure to remember my manners.

'No one here by that name any more,' he said.

'But he's the baker,' I said. 'This is his bakery.'

The man shook his head.

'Told you he made it up,' muttered Diane.

I could hear the little baker in the window, tapping away. 'I think you're new here,' I tried again. 'Maybe you haven't met him properly yet. He has wavy white hair, and he's tall and broad. Huge hands, for kneading the bread.'

'We have a machine for that,' said the ruddy-faced man.

'He told me we're heroes,' I went on, speaking too loudly and too fast now, I knew. 'He wanted to shake me by the hand. Because of the drug trials – his little grandson.'

'I think your brother's not quite right in the head,' the man said to William. 'Better take him home, there's a good lad. Before there's any trouble.'

A young woman came through from the kitchen and slid open the cabinet under the counter. She wore a hairnet and smock, and she began tidying away the empty trays; the bakery would be closing soon.

'Miss?' I said. 'Excuse me, miss? You've served me before. You know me. I need to see Mr Webb, please.'

She glanced at me, then continued with her work. 'Sorry,' she said. 'There's no Mr Webb now. He retired.'

'But he told Vincent about the drug trials just the other day,' said Lawrence. 'We're from Captain Scott, you see. We're the . . . the participants.'

'He gave me an apple turnover on the house,' I added in desperation. 'To thank me.'

Through the door to the kitchen I could make out a vast steel bowl with a mechanical arm inside.

'We don't give things away,' said the man.

All the while the little baker was tapping on the glass, regular as a pulse.

'I was just starting to wonder where you'd got to,' said Mother Afternoon, smiling her big warm smile as if she was someone we could trust. 'Did you have a lovely time? What did you learn about nature?'

So we showed her the black acorn and recited the things she'd taught us – that it was botanically a nut, that it stood in a cup of consolidated bracts. We told her about the bird we'd heard in the woods, and Diane mimicked its call: *key-key-key!* We'd looked and looked for it, we said, because it sounded very close, but we hadn't been able to see it – even so, Lawrence had identified it as a rare lesser spotted woodpecker just from the sound. And here was an interesting leaf, which was half yellow and half green – not quite dead and not quite alive. Around the roots of the beeches and oaks, we said, we'd seen little white mushrooms, and they might have been death caps and they might have been false death caps, we weren't sure, but both were poisonous anyway, so we hadn't touched them, hadn't gone anywhere near them.

Karen said nothing.

In the morning, when I opened the door to the laundry chute, I heard Mother Afternoon and Mother Morning again. I leaned in, submerging my body in the close, dark space that smelled of plaster, damp socks, bleach.

'What sort of complaint?' Mother Afternoon was saying.

'From Edith Saunders,' said Mother Morning. 'They're convinced something happened to one of the girls.'

'Nonsense. I was there the whole time.'

'They said you let them go on a Nature Walk by themselves.'

A pause. 'Well, yes, an educational ramble in the woods. Nothing wrong with that.'

'It was educational all right. William attacked one of them.'

'Attacked?'

'That's what Edith Saunders claim.'

'I can't believe it of him.'

'Can't you? Really and truly?'

Another pause. 'What exactly do they mean, attacked?'

'They're saying . . .' Mother Morning lowered her voice, and I leaned further into the chute, as far as I could without falling. 'They're saying copulation was involved.'

I'd heard that word before – I'd *read* it before, in the book called *Ulysses*, the book I could no longer find, no matter how I searched. *Copulation without population! No, say I!* I hadn't understood it then, but there were lots of words I hadn't understood in the story; I'd just let it wash over me, as Mother Night had advised.

'*Copulation?*' said Mother Afternoon.

'Copulation.'

The more they spoke the word the less sense it made, and at the same time I knew it must be very important.

'Ridiculous. How would he even know what to do?'

'The body knows.'

'Where's the proof?'

'Torn clothes. Dirt on her jacket and face. A fearfulness. And—'

Mother Afternoon huffed. 'There could be any explanation for that.'

'And Dr Roach examined her.'

The sound of water running. A brush scrubbing at a stain.

'She told them Vincent knew about it and advised her to keep quiet,' Mother Morning said – and I froze, my breaths impossibly loud now, and surely I would topple forwards, drop down the chute like a bundle of dirty sheets and give myself away. I felt our world curling up at the edges like something reflected in the gazing ball: the same but not the same. Beginning to stretch out of shape. 'I must say, I've a mind to have a word with Dr Roach about the girls,' she went on. 'The mousy one in particular. All the trouble started with her.'

I remembered the day Mother Morning had found my unswallowed pills – the day William had blurted about Jane. *She told him the medicine makes us sick.* Mother Morning repeating her name, *Jane, Jane,* tucking it away for future use.

'And the Ministry's insisting on another Socialisation Day,' she said. 'How they think that mixing with other Sycamore children is preparing them for the outside world, I don't know.'

The water ran, and the brush scrubbed and scrubbed.

'If he did attack her,' said Mother Afternoon, 'what will he do – what will *any* of them do – when they're released?'

'Exactly,' said Mother Morning. 'Another Flamborough in the making. Can you imagine how that will reflect on the Scheme? On us?'

'Yes, I can,' said Mother Afternoon.

'Dr Roach says we should continue as normal – go ahead with the next Socialisation Day, as well as the television clip – but then he'll look after everything.'

'Look after it?'

'Yes, he'll look after all of it. No need for the Ministry to know about the attack.'

'And us?'

'He'll look after us too.'

They fell silent, and I edged myself out of the chute. Slowly, slowly closed the door. Took my dirty clothes back to the bedroom.

Later that day, when Mother Afternoon had disappeared to the village again and my brothers and I were supposed to be sorting through the fridge, removing all the things that had gone bad, I crept to the Library and slid Volume 2 of The Book of Knowledge from the shelf: BOO–CRO. I flicked past *Bulgaria* and *Butterflies*, past *Camouflage* and *Celluloid* and *Centrifugal Force*, *Chronometer* and *Chrysanthemum*, *Clouds* and *Colours* and *Co-operative Societies*, until I reached the place where page 504 should have been. The entries jumped from *Copper* to *Coral*, and under my breath I spelled out C-O-P-U-L-A . . . And yes, *Copulation* was the thing missing, the thing torn out. The thing William had done to Karen.

The following day Mother Morning organised a Grounds Beautification Project because the television crew was coming at the weekend and the garden was out of control and beyond a joke; all summer it had grown unchecked, spreading its riotous tendrils, bursting from its beds, the green panes collapsing into the glasshouse and smashing to pieces. Once, years earlier, we'd had a gardener who'd trimmed things and trained things, keeping the lawns low-clipped and felty and the roses pruned back to their knuckles, but we'd had to let him go owing to cost-cutting measures. 'What else will they take away from us?' Mother Morning had said in a rare outburst. We hadn't answered; we hadn't known what to say. We'd thought she must love the gardener, because once, from the upstairs windows, we'd seen him offer her a camellia bloom, and then when she came inside she'd closed her eyes and breathed in its scent with a dreamy look on her face even though the camellia, we knew, smelled of nothing. 'Will you get married?' we'd asked her. 'Will you leave us then? How many children will you have?' And she'd dropped the camellia on the Kitchen table as if it didn't matter at all, and said, 'I can't have children. You are my children.' But that was a long time ago.

You might think a Grounds Beautification Project sounds quite grand and complicated, but really it was just me and my brothers assigned to different sections of the garden. Lawrence had to mulch around the fruit trees, taking care not to smother the trunks, since that could lead to rot. William had to clear the vegetable beds, the tomatoes blighted and black and the marrows turned powdery with mildew. I worked on the fernery, loosening the soil with the hand fork and pulling out the weeds, throwing them into a shaggy heap. Privately I wondered why we were even bothering – the place was about to close, after all, and the television people could just film around the messy bits, surely. But when Mother Morning came by to check on me, she seemed to have read my thoughts, because she said she was pleased we were making in-roads, and we wouldn't want anyone calling us lazy, would we? Because that would reflect very badly on the Homes, very badly on our Mothers. No, I agreed, we wouldn't want that.

'Good boy,' she said, and tousled my hair.

I kept my face neutral, normal, but I felt the fear creeping up the back of my throat again. In the two days since William had asked about Mother Night, our mothers had been kinder to us than ever, letting us have two each of the milk-teeth sweets from Dr Roach and bringing us cubes of frozen lemon juice to suck like ice lollies. I did not know what to make of it – what to make of any of the odd things that were happening at that time – but I didn't dare ask any more questions; I was too scared. You must know that.

After Mother Morning had gone, I realised I'd cut the head off a beetle, and I waited to see if both pieces might reattach – but they just lay there motionless. I resumed my digging with the hand fork, wondering if I might yet uncover something valuable; I kept watching for a flash of gold in the dank earth. Nothing. When I'd finished that job, I took a bucket and cloth and washed the gazing ball, which had gathered a layer of dust and grime. I rubbed at my bulbous reflection, moving my head so my face kept changing – my cheek swollen, my chin stretched wide. Then I saw it: a flash of brilliant blue wing feathers. A jay had alighted on the high flint wall, perching on a shard of amber glass that shone like the panels of grapevines and the open-mouthed fish at the door to the Big House. It held something in its beak – a piece of dirty paper, which it shook back and forth, then put down and began to peck at. When a breeze blew the paper to the ground, the bird fluttered after it and pinned it with a claw, and I saw what it was trying to dislodge: a chunk of fish stuck to a scrap of newspaper. We almost never set eyes on newspapers. Some lucky person must have enjoyed a meal of fish and chips, and maybe it was even one of the village girls we'd seen, with her lacy knee-high socks and her bouncy hair, and maybe she was so used to having such a meal that she didn't even feel the need to finish it. The jay pulled away the last flake of white flesh and only then seemed to notice me. It cocked its head. *Harsh harsh harsh*, it called. When I rose to my feet, it flew off.

Oil had soaked through the piece of newspaper, turning it translucent in parts. I picked it up by its torn edges and smoothed it out on my palm. *A £2000 loan for only £10.37 per week*, it read. *FREE LIFE COVER. 10 YEARS TO PAY. FAMILY PROTECTION PLAN.* Down the bottom, a dotted line enclosed a space for someone to write their name and address. *Yes, I'm interested in learning more about CreditPlan secured loans.* A pair of scissors pretended to cut around the dotted line, but they were just a drawing.

Then I turned it over.

And I saw a photograph of a little boy.

And even though he was upside down, and the bottom half of the photograph was missing, I thought I recognised him.

A serious, full-lipped creature, with curly blond hair and light eyes.

With the tip of my finger I nudged him, turned him, until he was the right way up.

Myself, aged around four, looking back at me from the palm of my hand.

Nancy

Her mother was making a cake – a rich, heavy cake like she made at Christmas time, though it was only the beginning of August. For weeks she'd been soaking the fruit, removing the bowl each morning from its cool dark spot in the kitchen cupboard and stirring the raisins, sultanas, currants, cherries and bright bits of peel through the brandy. 'Why are we starting so early this year?' Nancy had asked more than once, but her mother had just smiled and stirred and replaced the bowl in the cupboard. Now, at last, it was baking day.

'But why *are* we starting so early?' said Nancy, taking a pencil and tracing the shape of the tin onto a sheet of baking paper – tins, in fact, for this cake was to have three tiers.

'Well,' said her mother, 'it's not a Christmas cake.'

'What's it for then? Is someone getting married?'

'Like who?'

'I don't know.' Nancy began to cut around her pencilled line, keeping the scissors just inside it so the circle of paper would fit in the base of the tin. She'd already done the walls, which were much trickier; she liked to get the difficult jobs out of the way first.

'No one's getting married,' said her mother, weighing the butter on the kitchen scales, then chopping it into cubes and leaving it to soften on the sunny windowsill. 'No, we're having a party.'

'A party!' said Nancy. They'd never had a party before, though she'd longed for one. 'Can I wear the seafoam dress?'

'Of course. We know it still fits you.'

'It was quite tight.'

'It's meant to sit close to the body.'

'When's it happening? Is it soon?'

'At the end of August.'

'That's weeks away!'

'Worth waiting for, though.'

'The dress might be too small by then.'

'You won't grow much in a month. And maybe I can let out the seams.' She weighed the dark-brown muscovado sugar, adding a sprinkle more, removing a few grains, until the needle showed the exact amount.

'What about the cake? Will it still be all right?'

'Fruit cake keeps forever,' said her mother. 'Remember *Antiques Roadshow*?'

Nancy did remember. Someone had brought along a piece of Queen Victoria's wedding cake – a tiny square, no bigger than a fingertip, packed in a silver box with a glass lid like Snow White's coffin. The cake would still be edible, the expert had said, though of course it was far too valuable to eat. Oh, of course, of *course*, said the owner, and the onlookers nodded their agreement, craning their necks to see, wishing they too owned a piece of unspoilable cake. 'How much was it worth again?' said Nancy.

'A hundred pounds at auction. More on the open market.'

'And you couldn't ever eat it.'

'Never.'

'Not even if you were starving to death.'

Her mother put her head on one side. 'That's an interesting question,' she said.

Nancy lowered the paper circle into the tin: a perfect fit. 'What's the party for? Who's coming?' Every party needed guests; Nancy knew that from television. Finally, *finally*, she'd be able to meet some other people – maybe even make some friends. And those friends would invite her to their houses, and she'd say thank you, yes, I am available then.

'We're marking a very special day,' said her mother. 'At eight o'clock that morning, we'll be free.'

'Free?' said Nancy. 'Free?'

But her mother was folding a strip of thick brown paper in half and tying it around the outside of the tin to stop the edges from cooking too quickly. 'Give me your finger,' she said, so Nancy held down the string while her mother knotted it tight.

Then it was time to cream the butter and sugar until the mixture turned pale and fluffy but only just, and to beat in the eggs one by one, careful not to overbeat, and although Nancy wanted to know more about the party, and the guests, her mother had to concentrate and couldn't talk. Nancy assembled the spices – cinnamon and nutmeg, cloves and ginger and mace – and the set of metal measuring spoons that hung on a ring like keys. They went all the way down to one-eighth of a teaspoon, and even if you used only one of them you still had to wash the whole thing. Nancy recalled the little handwritten card tucked in with Queen Victoria's wedding cake: it had love hearts inked at each corner and read *To dream upon*, because if you slept with wedding cake under your pillow, the *Antiques Roadshow* expert said, you'd dream of the person you'd marry.

'What do you think would happen,' said Nancy, 'if I put a piece of our cake under my pillow?'

'It's not a wedding cake, remember, poppet,' said her mother, shaking the flour through the sieve. She'd done it twice already, and now it fell fine as dust into the china mixing bowl. 'And I think you'd probably just make a mess.'

'Probably,' said Nancy. 'But what's the party *for*? And who's coming?'

'Turn your earrings, poppet,' said her mother.

'They hurt.'

'All the same.'

Nancy knew her mother would offer up no more information about the party. Perhaps it was supposed to be a surprise; perhaps guests would fill the house – Barry Sedgwick the plumber, and all kinds of other people Nancy could only imagine. She twisted the little glass studs to stop the holes from closing over.

Her father was busying himself with party preparations too. He'd begun making tiny decorations for the model village: Chinese lanterns with orange cellophane inside to set them aglow, paper chains that he glued link by link with tweezers under his magnifying glass, streamers of crinkly crepe paper. Garlands of gauze flowers for the trains, and Union Jack bunting for the shops and houses. He hummed as he worked. Nancy had never seen him so happy.

She dreamt of the model village sometimes. She could walk around inside it, so either it had grown to the size of a proper village or she had shrunk to the size of a doll. The houses had real glass in the windows, and when she opened the doors she found real people inside, real people eating their dinners and brushing their teeth and watching television and rocking babies. 'Hello there, Nancy,' they said to her as she strolled through their rooms. 'Will you stay for a bit?' And the girl who looked like the *Jim'll Fix It* guest who had flown through the air – she was there too, whispering in Nancy's ear: 'Stay. Don't go outside. Stay. *Stay.*' But Nancy never could; a cuckoo clock just like the one in her house would strike, which meant she had to leave, only when she opened her mouth to thank the people for their kindness, no words ever came out. On she walked until she came to the shops, where there were racks of brand-new dresses and red leather shoes, jars of sweets and straps of liquorice, colouring-in books with pictures of ice creams and aeroplanes and seahorses, all different types of toothpaste and shampoo. 'Can we help you, Nancy?' the salespersons said. 'How may we help you?' Again Nancy could not speak, so she just shook her head: no, they couldn't help her. After that she followed the train tracks for a bit, waving to the passengers when they passed, watching the steam as it stretched itself into certain shapes, certain words that Nancy could not decipher. She reached the stream, and it shone with water, not dried glue; it changed shape every second, and if she picked her way down the mossy bank she could dip in her cupped hands and drink and drink. But she never went near the forest.

For a little while after she woke from these dreams she could not shake the feeling that she really had been to the village. That she knew it. Wasn't home just around the corner? If she left the stream behind, if she stopped trying to drink it dry – so cool, so silky in her throat – wouldn't she find her parents?

'Is the village real?' Nancy asked her father one day as she painted some of the Union Jack bunting for the party.

'What do you mean?' he said. 'Of course it's real, love. It's right in front of you.'

'But is it a real place? Life-size, out there somewhere?' She gestured at the sitting-room window.

'We don't need to worry about out there,' he said. 'We have everything we need in here.'

The Minister of Loneliness

'After just a few months in office,' said the Prime Minister, 'the new Conservative government is already implementing the changes our country so desperately needs. We have pinpointed areas of inefficiency and overspending, setting in motion the sale of council houses and flats, and the closure of the Sycamore Homes. We are making savings in the areas of education and science, and also on our transport, trade and arts programmes.'

The Minister of Loneliness sat at the front of the auditorium with the rest of the Cabinet and applauded. How magnificent the Prime Minister was in her gold-buttoned blazer and pearls. Her voice low and deliberate. Hair in the sleek French twist that no breeze ever seemed to muss.

'The British people crave strong leadership,' she said. 'They want someone at the helm who is willing and able to make difficult decisions. To lead them out of our country's recent period of disastrous decline. To empower them to increase productivity so that they bring home more in their pay packets. To ensure they feel safe in the streets. They have been let down so many times; we Conservatives must restore the morale smothered by the socialist years. And this is why we have begun to rebuild our Territorial Army and other reserve forces. This is why we are collaborating with our Gothenburg Treaty partners to promote free trade with those co-signatories. They'll be eating our black pudding in Munich and our Blue Stilton in Milan!'

More applause. She waited for it to die down.

'Finally,' she said, 'this is why we have voted with our consciences to restore capital punishment – and why those few vicious criminals sentenced just before its suspension will now pay in full for their actions.'

Vigorous applause. Shouts of *Hear, hear!*

'We want all our citizens, even children, to understand the difference between right and wrong. To recognise that certain evil acts must be outlawed by decent society. I personally have always voted in favour of the most punitive measures. When a man commits a dreadful act, a barbaric act, he forfeits his right to life. There are several such offenders, already sentenced to death, who have been burdening our overstretched prisons for years. We shall not allow this to continue.'

Wild applause. Cheering. The entire auditorium on its feet.

Prisoner welfare formed part of the Minister's portfolio, and she prided herself on the fact that she had visited several of the country's facilities – open prisons, where the men were not locked up and were able to undertake gainful employment during the day, such as making windows or packing plumbing parts.

'So you fill the boxes with all the pipes and . . . and flanges and so on, do you?' she'd said to one group of inmates.

'Yeah,' they'd said.

Some worked on farms, and she visited these too, viewing a range of livestock as well as crops.

'Tomatoes?' she'd said to a prisoner as she toured an enormous glasshouse bristling with vines.

'Yeah,' he'd said.

'And what do we have here?' she'd asked another man holding a piglet.

'It's a piglet,' he'd said.

The animal had lain so quietly in his arms.

Strangeways, however . . . Strangeways was another type of prison altogether. The men there spent their days untangling endless lengths of Post Office string if they were lucky, and, if they weren't, sitting locked in their cells for all but their exercise hour. Yes, Strangeways was different – and Arthur Powell was different too. Since the late 1940s he'd tortured and killed at least eleven West Midlands girls, some as young as ten years old, but he'd evaded arrest until 1964. Terrible timing: although he was sentenced to death, capital punishment was abolished shortly afterwards, and he'd languished in a cell ever since. Until now.

'How will you vote?' her husband asked her when the PM announced a conscience vote on the reintroduction of the death penalty.

'I'm in favour, of course,' she said.

'You'll be sending men to the gallows.'

'Not just me.'

And certainly, with crime on the rise, the carrying out of Powell's death sentence fifteen years after the judge had imposed it would be a triumph for the new government: he would be the first man hanged after the reinstatement of capital punishment. It was a win for justice, the Prime Minister had announced, but more importantly it was a win for the victims' families.

The Minister had seen a faded picture of him on the news after the announcement: a tall, rather handsome man with a thick beard, plentiful blond hair and large pale eyes which seemed to stare directly into the camera. Something about him made the Minister catch her breath. And now he had requested a visit from her, hinting that he'd reveal the whereabouts of the one victim who had never been found – but only if the Minister agreed to sit down with him and listen to his concerns.

'No,' said her husband as they folded back the bedspread and climbed into bed. 'Absolutely not.'

'The PM is in favour,' said the Minister. 'Imagine if we could bring home that poor lost girl.'

'Well, you could bring home what's left of her.'

'Don't be like that.'

'It's true, though. And you might not find her at all. You'd have got the parents' hopes up for nothing.'

The Minister opened her Jeffrey Archer and tried to read a few pages, but she was almost halfway through and Kane still hadn't even met Abel – to be honest, she didn't understand what all the fuss was about. 'He'll be guarded the whole time, and on the other side of the glass,' she said. 'They'll be taking no risks.'

'Why has he asked for *you*, though?' said her husband.

That she did not know.

She could smell the nearby brewery as she stepped from the car, the air yeasty and bitter. The wind whipped scraps of rubbish into the gutters, and a stocky man passed by walking a stocky pitbull. There under the low sky stood Strangeways: a castle, a fortress, its red bricks dark with drizzle while a tide of grime spoiled the white accents. In a niche above the gigantic arched doors, the Queen's golden lion and silver unicorn reared up on their hind legs, their sides gaunt with the strain. The Minister smoothed her hair, took a deep breath, then passed through the turreted gatehouse and into the star-shaped compound where the ventilation tower rose like some terrible chimney.

Arthur Powell wore the usual blue-and-white striped shirt with denim trousers and jacket. He sat very straight and still in his chair, nodding at the Minister through the glass as she took a seat opposite him. The room smelled of damp overcoats, cheap soap, fatty meat. Despite the partition, Powell seemed very close. Couldn't he simply smash his way through before the guard had time to react? Couldn't he grab a jagged shard of glass and slit her throat?

Stop it, she told herself. She positioned her solid new handbag on her lap.

'Good morning, Mr Powell,' she said, smiling. 'I understand you wanted to see me.'

She was relaxed, she was calm, this was all part of the job – but then Powell looked her right in the face with those light-green eyes, that full mouth, and she realised in a flash who he was. A breathy noise escaped her lips. Keep smiling. Keep smiling.

'I heard I might have some children out there,' he said. And of course: if you took away the beard and all the grey in his hair, he couldn't be anyone else.

'Oh?' she said, trying to make her voice expressionless.

'At one of the Sycamore Homes. Three identical boys. That's what I heard.'

'I imagine one hears all sorts of things in here.' Relaxed. Calm. Part of the job.

He smirked. From the way he was watching her, she knew she'd given herself away. 'You can't take your eyes off me,' he said.

Immediately she glanced to the guard at his back, the clock counting out its black minutes on the wall.

'You can see them in me, can't you?'

'I wouldn't say that . . .' But yes, yes, they were right there in his face, in his long spatulate fingers, in his hair that was greying now but still thick, plentiful: the boys, the triplets, and he was their future.

'Well, Mr Powell,' she said, her hand moving to her cameo brooch of its own accord, checking the safety chain. 'Well, I don't know that we can call them your children . . .'

'So they *are* real,' he said.

She opened her handbag and pretended to search inside it for something – an answer, perhaps, some way of denying what he already knew. The soap cameo, smooth and cool, brushed against her fingers. The pale-green girl who smelled like the forest.

'I want to meet them.'

'Mr Powell,' she began in her most reasonable voice, 'when you were convicted, you lost certain rights, and we—'

'I *want* to *meet* them,' he repeated. 'It's only fair, wouldn't you say?'

The Minister sighed. 'The thing is, we are currently engaged in trying to rehome the boys, and any interference with that process —'

'They're my flesh and blood,' he said. 'The continuation of my line.'

The Minister really didn't want to think of Vincent and his brothers in those terms. Yes, everyone knew the typically sordid origins of the Sycamore children, but no one ever acknowledged them; the matter was simply one of those unpleasantnesses it was better not to dwell on, like the fire-bombing of Hamburg, or force-fed veal. She shifted in her seat. Repositioned her handbag on her lap. His flesh and blood, she thought. His flesh and blood. The facts of his crimes came to her unbidden, crowding in behind her eyes. Dark-haired girls plucked from the street on their way to school, then driven to lonely woods and violated. Pieces of them cut away. Sometimes fingers or toes, sometimes worse. Always their tongues, so they couldn't talk. When he'd finished with them, he slit their throats and watched them gasp and bleed to death. Then he buried them.

'And why should we grant you this request?' said the Minister. She drew herself up in her seat, straightened her spine. She was made of iron. Iron.

'Nancy Liddell,' he said, and she could hardly bear the luxurious movement of his lips around the name.

He'd never admitted to Nancy's murder, and he'd never let slip anything that might link him to her, but it was clear he was responsible: she'd disappeared on her way to school in 1951 and her torn uniform had been recovered in the woods, dropped a short distance from a freshly dug hole. In the pocket, dreadful things: a severed tongue, a finger, an earlobe, all confirmed as Nancy's by genetic testing. The gossiping public seized upon them: imagine the parents viewing the small remains! The earlobe with a cheap earring still attached, perhaps; the finger with a mole or a scar in a particular spot, or maybe a certain shade of nail polish the girl had been wearing at the time of the unspeakable event, because she liked to doll herself up, no use pretending she didn't, and that had probably contributed. Unspeakable and dreadful, and oh, the poor mother and father who had no other kiddies and now not so much as a body to bury, just those small unnamed pieces of their daughter stuffed like dirty hankies into her own pocket, and wouldn't that send you over the edge? How would you ever go about the basic business of living after something so terrible? Police believed the culprit had shifted the body in his car because he'd heard someone approaching, which meant it could be anywhere, anywhere at all. The Minister remembered all the girls going missing when she was a girl herself, her mother showing her their pictures in the newspaper as some sort of warning.

'See, Sylvia,' she'd said when Nancy disappeared, jabbing at the front page.

Sylvia had pored over Nancy's broad, even smile and the satin bow she wore in her hair. The gingham pedal-pushers. She'd run a wistful finger over the newsprint as if she might pick up some of Nancy's glorious sheen, but her mother had scoffed and said, 'Look where all the primping and preening got her.' Better to be plain. Safer to be modest.

'Nice pedal-pushers, though, don't you think?' Sylvia was hoping for a pair for her sixteenth birthday.

'On her, I suppose,' said her mother. 'But a cropped trouser does the bulky girl no favours, Sylvia. Remember that.'

And the Minister had.

'What about Nancy Liddell?' she said now. Behind Powell the guard was staring straight ahead, but she could tell he was taking in every word. The air felt tight, alive, like the air right before an electrical storm. She hardly dared move in case she set something off.

'I know where she is,' said Powell. 'I can tell you exactly where to look.'

'Let me make sure I understand,' said the Minister. 'You're offering her remains as – what? A bribe?'

'A fair exchange. You bring me the boys, then I tell you where she is. Take it or leave it.'

In the months following Nancy's disappearance, the Liddells had begged for exactly this information. They accepted their daughter was gone, they said, but they just wanted to be able to bury her, and if the person responsible had a shred of decency left in him . . . Every few years the newspapers printed the same photograph of Nancy cross-legged in her white blouse and gingham pedal-pushers, though the family had long since fallen silent – moved to a new town, the papers said, to make a fresh start. Nobody could find them by the time Powell was arrested; they'd disappeared too. Well, you would, wouldn't you.

The Minister leaned back in her seat as she considered Powell's proposal. Did she even have the authority? And how would the boys react to the news? Might they themselves turn violent? Flamborough, after all . . . But then, if handled properly, this could be a real coup for her – a chance to make her mark. A chance to do some good, she told herself.

'I'll bring you the boys,' she said, 'after you divulge the whereabouts of the remains and they are successfully recovered.'

Would she be able to announce it herself? The police would handle that, she supposed, but she'd certainly figure prominently, favourably, in the story.

He shook his head, holding her gaze all the while. 'That won't do,' he said. 'I don't trust you.'

'Mr Powell,' the Minister began, then stopped. He was to be executed at the end of the month, and after that she would never recover Nancy.

'Very well,' she found herself saying, and as she shifted she caught sight of her reflection in the glass, superimposed over the figure of Powell. Not plain but authoritative. Not bulky but powerful.

'One more thing,' he said, and now he looked not at the Minister but at the scratched wooden ledge where his hands rested. 'The boys . . . have you found homes for them? Decent homes?'

'Applications remain open,' said the Minister.

'So you're making your way through them and choosing the very best families?'

'As I said, applications remain open.' She paused. 'We need to allow people plenty of time to decide, given what they are.'

'And if nobody ever wants them?' His voice was barely audible through the glass.

'We have the matter in hand,' said the Minister.

Powell had a point, though: what if nobody ever wanted the Sycamore children? The catalogues were nicely produced, but they weren't doing much good piled up in her secretary's office.

She'd have to hope the television clip would change all that. For a moment she wondered if anyone would recognise Powell in the boys . . . but none of the indistinct pictures in the papers or on television showed him anywhere near their age, and he had a beard in all the adult shots. Unless you saw him in person, and knew the boys, you'd never guess the relationship.

The afternoon carer came to the gates in a peculiar get-up – a lilac twinset teamed with a long black satin skirt such as the Minister wore to formal functions when dancing was required. In her hair she had pinned a bit of dried something or other that might once have been carnation and fern, and she wore rust-red lipstick that wobbled at one corner.

The day had turned cool during the drive down from London, so while the television crew set up in the garden the Minister waited in the library with the boys. She blinked to clear her head of Powell – his hands, his eyes. Yes, the boys resembled him, but that didn't mean they would become him. Did it?

They seemed more subdued today – anxious, even. 'Are you a bit scared?' she asked.

'Scared of what?' said Vincent, his eyes huge.

'Of being on television,' said the Minister. 'Really, there's nothing to be nervous about. I've done it hundreds of times.'

He nodded. 'We're not scared of that,' he said.

She asked what they'd been studying recently, so they showed her posters they'd made on British Industry: coloured-pencil drawings of aluminium smelters and coal mines, and something that might have been a bed factory.

'That one's mine,' said Vincent, standing at her side in his yellow shirt, close enough for her to smell the sandy, woody scent of his hair. 'See, the chimney sucks in the cumulus clouds, and they travel down through these pipes and into the mattress casings, which are a bit like sausage casings only they're not made of guts. Then when they're crammed full of clouds they're stitched closed, and then they're tested to make sure they're soft enough.' He pointed to a stack of mattresses piled up at the end of a conveyor belt; a stick-figure boy was jumping on them. In a vast adjoining room dozens of boys lay sleeping on the puffy new mattresses.

'What a marvellous job to have,' said the Minister. 'I think I'd enjoy that.'

'He got a D,' said the boy in the red shirt – William; William was red.

'That's not how mattresses are made,' said the boy in the green shirt, who must be Lawrence.

'Have you ever been to a mattress factory, though?' demanded Vincent.

'No,' said Lawrence.

'So how do you know?'

'I got a B,' said William, 'but *Lawrence* got an A minus even though he spelled aluminium wrong.' His voice a sneer.

'I fixed it, though,' said Lawrence. 'I drew a picture of a dead cowboy over the top.'

'That was a good idea,' said the Minister.

William snorted. 'An A minus! What do cowboys have to do with aluminium?'

'Belt buckles?' said Lawrence.

'Too soft, idiot! They'd fold in half like milk-bottle tops! Don't you know anything?'

'Well, Mother Morning thought my poster was the best, so there.'

The anxiety she thought she'd noticed vanished as they bickered. Really, they were just like ordinary siblings – ordinary young boys. She hoped the cameras would capture that.

The day had turned even cooler by the time the television crew was ready, and the Minister wanted nothing more than to run herself a deep bath in her powder-blue bathroom. She'd sink into the water until it reached her neck, breathe in the rising steam. Soon she'd hear her husband padding up the stairs with her cup of milky tea which he'd place by the hot tap along with a couple of custard creams. She didn't deserve him, she'd say, and he'd agree.

The interviewer was a young woman the Minister hadn't encountered before – someone new and hungry, no doubt, since all the old guard had declined the job. Taking her position beside a pretty patch of ferns, she kept tucking her long brown hair back behind her ears, then raking it forwards again. 'Chop shops stock chops,' she said, stretching her mouth around each word. 'A pessimistic pest exists amidst us.' She bared her teeth at the sound recordist, and said, 'Any lipstick? Any food?' The Minister suspected they were sleeping together.

No difficult questions this time; no traps. Instructions had been issued from on high. The Minister smoothed the collar of her navy-blue blazer and told herself to relax, to smile as she gave her answers. She was doing noble work, work that would make a real difference, leave a real *legacy*. She was magnanimous and kind. She possessed *vision*.

'And what motivates you to want to help the remaining Sycamore children?' the interviewer asked.

'I believe every British child deserves an equal chance,' said the Minister. 'It's my dream to see them assimilated into the community – into real homes. Let them lead normal, productive lives. They of all people deserve that.'

She could see the boys standing to the side of the camera, trans-fixed, scarcely noticing the afternoon carer fussing at their collars and hair. They were so beautiful: green-eyed and golden-skinned and fine-featured, though every so often she could make out the powerful men they would become, their adult silhouette – the silhouette of Powell – pulsing just beyond the edges of their adolescent bodies. Strange to be talking about them in their presence, when all earlier discussions had happened at several removes, in meeting rooms and television studios and the House of Commons, where the children had existed only in theory.

'And what advice might you have for anyone considering opening their home to one of these children in need?'

A breeze passed through the ferns, ruffled the chiffon bow at the neck of the Minister's blouse. 'I would say that you'll never regret a good deed,' she replied, smoothing the fabric back into place. 'You have the opportunity to change a child's life – but also the opportunity to change your own. So, if you've any questions, do get in touch with the Ministry – we are ready and waiting to allay all worries – and as I said, we can post the catalogue to you that same day.'

'Let's invite our special guests on now,' said the interviewer, and just as they'd rehearsed, the boys joined the Minister in front of the camera. Somehow she found herself opening her arms to them the way a mother might, the way she'd seen the Prime Minister open her arms to the cameras, and although she glimpsed a flicker of confusion pass across the faces of Lawrence (green shirt) and William (red shirt), Vincent led the way and his brothers followed. She reached out and squeezed Vincent's hand as if she'd known him all his life, and the three of them took their places around her while she smiled and smiled. How comfortable she was with them, how very much at her ease. How perfectly safe.

'Would you like to say hello to Britain, boys?' said the interviewer.

'It's just through there,' said the Minister in a stage whisper, pointing to the lens of the camera.

'Hello, Britain,' said the boys.

'Now let me see, I think you're Lawrence, you're Vincent, and you must be William,' said the interviewer, and they shook their heads but did not speak.

The Minister laughed a glittery laugh.

'Vincent, William, Lawrence?'

They shook their heads again.

'Well, my goodness, you're so handsome I don't think anyone would mind which one of you they got!'

The Minister could feel William's swift, disdainful exhalation, the stream of his breath on the back of her neck.

'And I understand you have quite the encyclopaedic knowledge,' the interviewer went on.

'We're doing the Evolution of Furniture at the moment,' said Lawrence. 'By the time of the Great Exhibition of 1851, there had arisen a newly rich class which sought every kind of decoration. The pieces of furniture that answered these demands are the most vulgar in the whole history of the subject.'

'Very intelligent boys,' said the Minister. 'Very gifted.'

'It certainly seems that way,' said the interviewer. 'And just think – perhaps your families are watching tonight and deciding right now that they want to offer you a home. So can I ask you to tell me – to tell *them* – what it would mean to you to be part of a real family?'

'The world,' said Vincent.

'Yes, the world,' said Lawrence.

William curled his lip. 'They're just saying what they're supposed to.'

'Oh!' said the interviewer.

'William!' said the carer.

'We can cut that bit,' said the cameraman.

'Maybe some activities!' said the Minister. 'Some non-speaking activities.'

So the crew shot some footage of them playing leapfrog and cricket, racing about and shouting *You're It!*

'Don't tire yourselves, boys,' called the carer.

They picked apples, and the interviewer suggested the Minister accept one from William and bite into it for the camera. It would make her seem human, she said. To begin with William tried throwing the apple to her, but she simply couldn't catch it; she kept lunging at it, tripping over her own feet.

'Maybe he can just pass it to you,' said the cameraman.

William held the apple back up to the branch and pretended to pick it again, then handed it to the Minister with an exaggerated bow. Well, it would probably look fine on camera – a bit light-hearted, a bit of fun – but the Minister could sense the loathing in him as he pressed the apple hard into her palm. And when she took a bite, the flesh tasted sour, and it was all she could do to chew and swallow.

Inside, the crew filmed the boys making beds and doing the washing up and dusting the carved griffin at the foot of the staircase, its motto curling around its strange body: *Verité Sans Peur*. When they'd finished, the Minister told the carer she'd like a word with her and the boys, so the carer led the way to the room with all the china horses, her long satin skirt swirling around her ankles.

'I'll put the kettle on,' she said.

'Please don't go to any trouble,' said the Minister.

'It won't take a minute. Boys, behave yourselves.'

As soon as she'd gone, William nudged at a china horse, shifting it towards the edge of the mantelpiece. It was cast in a grazing pose, head down, and he nudged it further and further until its muzzle met with nothing but air. He leapt into his seat when he heard the carer swishing back through the door.

'Now then,' said the Minister, 'I have a bit of news.'

The carer poured her a cup of tea and offered her a bought biscuit – the spread far less lavish than on her first visit, she noticed. Not a fondant fancy in sight.

'Is it good news or bad news?' said the carer.

'Well,' said the Minister, eyeing the precarious china horse, 'it's interesting news. Someone wants to see the boys.'

'A family?' said William.

'No – no, I'm sorry, I shouldn't have given that impression. Although he's family in a sense. In that you *are* related.'

They were looking very puzzled. She was making a terrible job of things.

'Your father,' she began again. 'Your natural father, if you like. He has requested you visit him.'

'We have a father?' said Lawrence.

'Everyone has a father, idiot,' said William.

'But he died. He had a heart attack.'

'Yes, a heart attack,' said the carer, nodding her head in an exaggerated fashion. 'A week after their mother.'

'It seems the attack was not fatal,' said the Minister.

The boys were all staring at her.

'Perhaps this is something we can—' began the carer, but the Minister pressed on.

'You'd already been brought here and settled in, and he had such a long and precarious recuperation that the authorities decided – and he agreed – it was better for you to stay here. The records aren't entirely clear from back then, but it seems that is what happened.' This was the story she'd been advised to tell, and it had seemed plausible to her. Plausible enough. She'd be *protecting* the boys, protecting those around them. Now, though, the words felt like dead leaves in her mouth.

'Where is he?' said Vincent. 'Will we go to live with him?'

'Goodness me, no,' said the Minister. 'No no – he's not well enough for that. He just wants to meet you. He's in Manchester.'

'Manchester,' said the carer.

'Yes, Manchester. The boys will travel there by coach on Thursday. It's all arranged.' The back entrance to the prison. The guard in ordinary clothes. 'His health is still very delicate, so you'll be separated by a pane of glass. We don't want to pass on anything nasty.'

When she stood to leave, she shifted the china horse back into place. She could still taste the apple, still feel it hard and sour in her stomach.

Vincent

It was quite clear: the boy whose picture I'd found in the garden must have been our father when he was little, which meant our father must be famous, since only famous people had their pictures in the newspaper. Perhaps he was an inventor, we thought, or an explorer – *I am just going outside and may be some time* – or perhaps he was very, very wealthy, because money made people famous even if they weren't at all interesting. He could be a member of Parliament, tending to the country's wellbeing, like the Minister of Loneliness. Maybe he'd saved a child's life – snatched a girl from a burning building or pulled a boy from the sea with no thought for his own safety. Maybe he was a painter of mountains and farm animals and thatched cottages and so on, or a renowned musician like Richard Clayderman. We studied the boy on the tiny scrap of paper, his forehead translucent where the oil had soaked through, as if we might be able to see right inside him to his secret thoughts.

On the coach we felt ravenous. At ten o'clock we ate our pieces of apple and cubes of cheese, then tipped the raisins carefully into our palms – how strange, we said, that they were wrapped in waxed paper and not nestled in the usual little blue bowl. When we'd finished, we wanted to tear into the sandwiches Mother Morning had packed for us, and we had to stop ourselves. Something about the trip had made us hungry – the early start, the giddy sense that we were setting off alone, quite alone, and not just on an errand to the village but to a big city hundreds of miles away. We'd looked up Manchester in The Book of Knowledge, of course. It was known the world over for its textiles, and in Africa and Australia people referred to their bed linens as Manchester, which seemed very odd, and had nobody thought to put them right? The Rolls-Royce was born there, we read – though now it was made in Crewe. That was disappointing. The choir stalls and screens in the cathedral were an example of medieval woodcarving matchless throughout Europe – but most of it was shattered in the Christmas air raid of 1940. Also disappointing. Still, said The Book of Knowledge, repairs were undertaken by the most skilled craftsmen in the north of England.

'That means they made copies,' said William. 'Hardly any of it would be the real thing any more.'

'So good that you couldn't tell, though,' I said.

'Maybe he was one of the skilled craftsmen,' said Lawrence. 'After the war, maybe he helped put it all back how it was.'

We considered this: our father in the shattered cathedral, the light pouring in through holes in the roof as he picked his way around the broken carvings. He'd examine the fragments to identify the shapes they made. Start afresh with a new piece of wood, finding the angels and roses and strange part-bird beasts inside it. When he stopped for his midday meal, we imagined, he'd have gone to Garden Square in the centre of the city – the great empty space at its heart – and he'd have unwrapped his sandwiches, which he had not eaten early because he understood the value of self-control, and he'd have sat there with all the other workers, enjoying the sunshine and the flower beds and probably answering lots of questions about his important and highly skilled work. Maybe that was how he'd become famous – for remaking something precious that everybody had thought lost.

And weren't we quite good at woodwork? Hadn't Mother Afternoon always praised the bits and pieces we turned out on

Craft Day? The recipe-book stand, the mug tree, the ornamental goat?

'Maybe she never meant it,' said Lawrence. 'She might have been lying, the way she lied about the drug trials.'

'I bet she was,' said William.

'So maybe we're not good at much at all,' said Lawrence.

But I thought of the cameo I'd carved from soap: how easily my knife had conjured the lines of the girl. Perhaps I had inherited that from my father. Anything was possible.

We sped along at treetop height in the coach, every second moving further away from our mothers and their stories, their lies. We looked down on the cars and felt like giants, and we leaned back and looked up at the sky slipping past like a length of blue ribbon, because there were indeed windows in the roof, just as the young ladies had said. Yes, anything was possible. Soon, I imagined, I'd be able to tell Jane about our trip – about the coach, but also about our father, who was not only alive but famous. After break-fast that day, Mother Morning had laid out ties for us to wear. Would it matter, we said to one another now, tugging the knots at our necks, if we took them off for the duration of the trip? Who would ever know? But we kept them on all the same. Tried not to crease our shirts. Checked and rechecked our nails, which we'd trimmed with the nail scissors that were not a toy.

The Minister and her driver met us at the terminus. 'Quickly now, boys,' she said. 'You're quite late, and we don't have much time.'

We hadn't realised we'd lost time on the journey, and we apol-ogised, even though it wasn't our fault, because that was polite and proper. In the back of the car we straightened each other's ties, making sure we looked presentable. The Minister took a little mirror from her handbag and checked her face, ran her fingers through her fine brown hair. I remembered what she'd said when I'd told her Jane's comment about the medicine making us sick: it was just a joke, a bad joke.

We drove through the city, crossing two rivers – or perhaps we crossed the same river twice – and then we came to a castle. That was the word we used, all three of us at the same time: a castle. The driver gave a snort, and the Minister said, 'That will do, Evans.'

Inside, a tall, broad man with wavy white hair and a neat white moustache greeted us. For one uneasy moment I thought he was Mr Webb, the baker; he could have been his twin – he even had Mr Webb's huge hands – but when I looked again I saw I was mistaken. We followed him along a corridor lined with closed doors, and he told us we had half an hour, no more, and we weren't to take any photographs.

'Famous people don't like that,' whispered Lawrence.

Though two men stood behind the pane of glass in the small white room, we knew our father at once. How like us he was; how like him we were. He had our light-green eyes and our high cheekbones, our fine nostrils and full mouth and long fingers. Under his beard we could see the shape of our jaw, and his hair curled just as ours curled, with the same cowlick, though his was mostly grey. We felt we were looking into some strange mirror that showed the future. He did not speak at first, but simply looked at us, shaking his head.

'Here they are, Mr Powell,' said the Minister. 'Just as you requested.'

He sat down then, and so did we, but the man behind him remained standing. A butler, by the looks; certainly some kind of servant. 'Thirty minutes,' he said.

'Good afternoon,' we said to our father, who nodded.

'Have you had a pleasant day?' I enquired.

He opened his mouth, closed it again. Studied each of us in turn. 'All this time,' he said at last. 'All these years, you were out there.'

His voice our own voice reaching us from a distance – through water, perhaps, or down the dark drop of the laundry chute.

'Are you good lads?' he asked.

Yes, we said; our mothers had taught us nice manners, how to be kind. We told him about the seed balls we'd made to feed the birds in winter so they wouldn't starve in the snow, and we explained Ethical Hour, when every Thursday we discussed quite tricky questions to find out what was right and what was wrong. We did the washing up after each meal, we said, and made our beds with proper hospital corners, and complimented Mother Afternoon on her ikebana arrangements that suggested the impermanence of all things and the relationship between heaven, Man and earth, even though we couldn't quite see it ourselves.

'Icky-what?' he said.

'Ikebana,' I said. 'It's the Japanese way of doing flowers.'

'Is she a Jap?'

'She learned it from the *Woman's Realm*,' I said.

We didn't mention the medicine our mothers had fed us all our lives, the things they hadn't told us. The fear we felt when we lay in our beds in the great dark house.

'We've been meeting young ladies on our Socialisation Days and asking about their interests,' said Lawrence. 'I offered Diane my cheese and onion sandwich when she discovered her Scotch egg was just a rissole.'

'You must always treat young ladies well,' said our father. 'Promise me that.'

Yes, we nodded; yes, we promised.

Young ladies were flighty creatures, he went on, who didn't know their own minds. That could land them in risky situations that they couldn't foresee. It was up to us to look after them.

Next to us the Minister was pursing her lips.

'I would have offered Diane my Scotch egg,' William said, 'only I'd already eaten it.'

'The kind thought was there,' said our father. 'Good lad.'

William beamed at him.

As he talked on about how we should handle young ladies, I remembered what I'd seen in the woods that day – Karen whimpering at the foot of the beech tree, its mossy roots bulging like green serpents, her clothing all awry and her hands shaking. No sign of William, yet at the same time every sign of him. *They're saying copulation was involved.*

'We dream about a young lady,' said Lawrence. 'She's skinny and pale with long black hair, and she's running through the trees.'

Something sparked in our father's eyes as he turned his gaze on Lawrence. 'All three of you dream about her?' he said.

'Yes!' said Lawrence. 'The same girl, only in my dream it's a lovely spring day, and in Vincent's it's night-time and she falls over, and in William's there's a knife and a whole lot of blood.'

William shot him a look, and the Minister seemed uncomfortable too – but I knew that Lawrence only wanted our father to like him. 'They study our dreams,' Lawrence went on. 'Dr Roach and his department. Especially the bad ones.'

'Do they indeed?' said our father. 'Well, what a thing. All three of you dreaming about her.'

'Twenty minutes,' said the butler, and our father flinched. He turned and said, 'That was never ten minutes just now,' but the butler pointed to the clock on the wall. When our father turned back to us, his eyes were dark with something like anger.

'What are you?' I asked.

'Beg your pardon?' he said.

'What are you?' I repeated. 'An inventor? A musician? A skilled craftsman? An explorer?'

'I'm not anything.'

'But what do you do?'

'Well,' he said. 'Well, for a long time I did nothing, but these days I untangle string.'

We looked at one another. How was that a job? How would that have got his picture in the newspaper? Was he so rich he didn't need to work at all?

'It's for the *Post* Office,' he said, as if that explained everything. When we didn't respond, he said, 'I unpick the knots and snarls until the string's as smooth as hair. Then people can use it for their parcels. To wrap up the presents they send to their loved ones. Chocolates and books and talcum powder and things.'

We were all silent for a moment.

'How is your heart?' asked Lawrence.

Confusion crossed his face. 'It's fine,' he said. 'Until tomorrow morning, I suppose.'

'What's tomorrow morning?' I asked.

He gave a short, contorted laugh. 'The knot I can't untangle.'

'Let's talk about something else,' said the Minister, but she couldn't seem to think of anything.

We sat there listening to the clock tick through the partition, every second tapping on the glass.

'Ten minutes,' said the butler.

'You've fiddled it!' said our father. 'You've shifted the hands! Lads, did you see him shifting the hands?'

He seemed to want us to say yes, we'd seen the butler reach up and change the clock. And was it possible? Had we seen him and simply not paid any attention? Even the Minister checked her wristwatch – but no. No.

My brothers and I shook our heads.

Our father sighed, examined his nails. They were longer on his right hand – for loosening the knots, I supposed. I thought of the crackled portrait that hung above our staircase – the father resting his hand on the head of his son.

He asked us what we were good at, what we might want to be when we grew up. William said he was good at cricket, so maybe he could play for England one day. Our father said maybe, maybe, and he'd been good at cricket once too, and that must be where William got it from. There was a time, in fact, he said, when he'd thought he might be able to do something with his cricket, but life or fate or his own bad luck, whatever we wanted to call it, had other ideas. The two of them chatted about wrist spin and finger spin while the clock ticked on.

'And what about you two?' he said, shifting his attention to Lawrence and me.

'I want to be a vet,' said Lawrence. 'I love animals.'

'You'll have to kill as many as you save,' said our father.

'What?' said Lawrence. 'Why would I kill them?'

'To put them out of their misery. It's the kindest thing.'

'I won't be doing any killing,' said Lawrence.

'Is that so?' said our father. 'Well, wait and see.'

'Five minutes,' said the butler.

Our father didn't even turn to him this time – he simply flicked his fingers in the man's direction as if shooing away a blowfly. 'And you?' he asked me.

'I don't really know,' I said.

'You're already thirteen years old!' he said. 'You should have some idea of what you want to be. Or do you think you have forever?'

I shook my head, and again I recalled the girl I'd carved from the soap. 'I'm good with my hands, I suppose.'

My brothers agreed; I could build the most complicated things from the Stickle Bricks, they said, and whenever we did woodwork on Craft Day I seemed to know just how to wield the tools so our projects turned out well; the recipe-book stand and the mug tree were proof of that, not to mention the ornamental goat. They described my papier-mâché model of Dr Roach's Jaguar, and the slingshot I'd made from the hazel twig even though it wasn't allowed. Our father nodded his approval, but somehow I felt ashamed. If I didn't know what I wanted to be, did that mean I'd be nothing?

'When I was nine,' said our father, 'I made Tower Bridge from matchsticks. A beautiful thing, it was. Should have been in a museum.'

'They made a model of the *Queen Mary* for Dreamland,' said Lawrence. 'The funnels let out smoke and everything. It looks just like a real ship, only it's a building.'

213

It was as if he hadn't spoken. Our father said, 'My teacher told my parents they had a very clever boy on their hands and they should try to give me the best education possible. They nodded and smiled, of course – yes, sir; no, sir; three bags full, sir.' Another brief laugh. 'They did give me an education, though. By Christ they did.'

'One minute,' said the butler.

Our father leaned closer to the partition, his breath making ragged patches on the glass.

'When you go to your families,' he said, 'be on your guard. Families are not always kind. Mothers will humiliate; they will lie. Fathers will beat, and worse. It's the way of things.'

'I really don't think—' the Minister began, but our father said, 'Be on your guard: I can't stress that enough.'

'Mothers do lie,' blurted William.

'Through their teeth,' agreed our father. 'Till they're blue in the face.'

'And we've got three of them.'

'You poor little sods. How you've turned out so well is quite beyond me.'

William beamed at him again.

'Would I really have to kill animals if I became a vet?' said Lawrence.

'The sickest ones,' said our father. 'The hopeless cases. You wouldn't let them suffer.'

'No. No,' said Lawrence.

'Maybe there's a drug,' said William. 'Something for your heart, to make you better.'

'A drug?' said our father. 'For my heart?'

'It would be quite safe. They would have tested it.'

The Minister was staring at William, and I thought she was going to say something – but before she could speak the butler announced that time was up. He took our father by the elbow and led him through the door underneath the clock. How weak he must be, we realised. He raised a hand in farewell as he disappeared. 'Nice knowing you,' he called.

We were barely back in the car before the Minister was asking William what he meant about the heart drug, the drug that would have been tested. William nudged Lawrence, who nudged me.

'Go on,' whispered Lawrence.

So I told her we knew about the drug trials.

'And how do you feel about that?' she said, turning around in the front seat.

Everyone had been lying to us, we said. Including her.

She said she was glad we knew, because it hadn't sat well with her. That was why she'd been pushing to close the Homes and end the trials, even though Dr Roach was hanging on till the bitter end. There wouldn't be any more medicine once we'd been rehomed. She'd insisted on it.

'Why should we believe you?' said William. 'Our mothers, our very own mothers, have lied to us for years. Given us pills and injections and syrups to make us better when there was nothing wrong in the first place.'

'I know,' she said. 'It's been a terrible state of affairs.' Which wasn't a proper answer.

'The boys who died,' said Lawrence. 'The medicine killed them, didn't it?'

'I'm afraid I'm not familiar with the records of particular participants—' she began, but William cut her off.

'Stop it!' he yelled, leaning forwards so he was an inch from her face. 'Stop pretending!' His fingers curled into fists.

'Everything all right, Minister?' said the driver.

'Yes, thank you,' she said.

I reached across to move William away from her. 'She's trying to help us,' I said.

'Those boys,' he said in a quiet voice. 'Was it the medicine?'

The Minister turned away to look out of the window as we

crossed the river. 'I believe so,' she said. 'Heroes, every one of them. But you don't know anything about this – I've not breathed a word. Do you understand?'

Lawrence and I nodded, unable to speak.

'They weren't heroes,' said William, slumping back in his seat. 'They were animals.'

She sighed. 'I understand this is difficult to take in – but the new government is committed to righting the wrongs of the past. This is why we are finding homes for you all. Yes?'

'How long will it take, though?' I said.

'Not too long now, I hope. The television clip should do the trick.'

'And will we . . . Will we be able to stay together?'

'Oh, quite likely,' she said, her gaze sliding off out of the window. 'Yes indeed.'

We crossed the second river, or the same river, and soon we were back at the terminus. I fell asleep on the coach on the way home and dreamt of our father in a tiny airless room – so tiny he couldn't stand up. He was trying to talk to me, but the glass partition muffled all sound, and the more he spoke the more the glass fogged, until I heard only the hush of the ocean and couldn't see him at all. Then I was in the woods again, running after the girl with the tangled black hair, the birds calling to me in their human voices as I called to the girl: *Slow down! Stop! You'll have an accident!* I jolted awake when the coach went over a bump in the road, and I prepared to recite the details of my dream – but of course nobody was there to record it. Everyone around me slept – my brothers, all the other passengers – and on we travelled through the darkness, the great engine growling softly at our feet.

Mother Night was waiting for us when we returned. She'd laid out our pyjamas and put toothpaste on our toothbrushes as if we were little boys again. Drowsily we checked our beds for Margate brochures, then pulled our jumpers over our heads and shrugged off our shirts. I tried to focus on Mother Night's face as she folded back our blankets. The same and not the same. The same but older. But then, weren't we all older?

As she tucked me in and kissed my forehead I whispered in her ear, 'I want to know what happens in *Ulysses*.'

She smiled, shook her head. 'Goodness me,' she said, turning out my bedside lamp, 'you're already in dreamland, aren't you?'

The Minister of Loneliness

At quarter to eight in the morning, her driver arrived to take her to her constituency. Usually she didn't engage in conversation with Evans – she tried not to waste the dead hours in her day, putting any travelling time to good use. That morning, however, she asked after his wife – Sheree, she was almost positive the name was Sheree – who was pregnant with their second child. Oh, said Evans, she's big as a house and a week overdue. Can't get comfortable, and I can't do anything right. Poor thing, said the Minister, but surely it can't be much longer? Another week and they'll induce, said Evans, only Sharon (that was the name) said every day felt like a month, and she couldn't bear it, she wanted the thing out, gone, separate from her, and yes she knew how that sounded. The Minister glanced at her watch and said Sharon was perfectly entitled to feel that way, and were they hoping for a girl or a boy and had they chosen names? But of course it didn't matter as long as Baby was healthy and everything was where it should be. On she chatted, and by the time her watch showed eight the conversation had turned to poor Lord Mountbatten, killed by an IRA bomb in Sligo, and what a disgrace, said Evans, when the man was retired and simply pulling up his lobster pots. The Minister said oh indeed, an absolute disgrace, and it had set the clock back many, many years. Another glance at her watch – but keep talking. Keep talking. The funeral would be a magnificent affair. Horses. Regalia. A chance to make a real statement. She refused to think about the hangman who would have come for Powell by now. She refused to think about the unlocking of the condemned cell, the walk to the execution chamber. She refused to think about how quickly the hangman would finish his job, how the quickest hanging at Strangeways had taken only seven seconds from the opening of the cell to the snap of the rope. Nor would she let herself think about Nancy Liddell, still lost, lost for good, because Powell had gone back on his word after he'd met the boys, of course, and of course the Minister should have insisted he divulge the location of her body before she brought them to him, and how gullible was she? Gullible and cowardly, even now making up stories for the boys rather than telling them what they were, rather than according them basic human rights. *Verité Sans Peur*, she thought. An image drifted into her memory: Vincent's drawing of the mattress factory. All the children laid out in their rows, eyes closed, fast asleep. Well, she supposed they were asleep.

One by one her constituents came to her with their concerns. A pedestrian crossing was needed on a busy suburban street: there'd been dozens of near misses in the last six months alone, and the Minister must realise that children's lives were at stake, it was only a matter of time. And something had to be done about the ethnic minorities flooding in and taking all the jobs when they couldn't even speak the language, not to mention the fact they insisted on cooking with some very pungent and frankly quite disgusting ingredients. And could she please look into the marking of the English Literature O-level exam, because the Unseen Poem question seemed discriminatory to those pupils who, through no fault of their own, had never laid eyes on the work before. The Minister thanked them for taking the time to visit her office; it was important to her that they felt heard, and even if she couldn't promise to deliver on each and every request – because they must understand, she received hundreds – she certainly would take their thoughts on board.

All day she kept herself busy, barely stopping for a cup of tea or a bite to eat, but all day the images kept coming to her: the door to the condemned cell opening; Powell, hands pinioned, being led to the execution chamber; the hangman placing the noose around his neck. The drop, the snap.

And another image, too: Nancy Liddell, buried deep in some lonely place, and sinking deeper all the time. Turning into dirt.

The news showed the crowds thronged outside the prison that morning, craning their necks as if they might be able to see through walls twelve feet thick. Sending up cheers at eight o'clock.

Nancy

They rose early on the morning of the party and dressed in their best clothes: Nancy's father in his funeral suit, her mother in her shantung silk and Nancy in the seafoam dress. Soon, Nancy thought, they would be free – whatever that meant. She turned her earrings to keep the holes open. Her mother pulled the spiky curlers from her grey hair and sprayed herself with the atomiser that sat on her dressing table, squashing the tasselled bulb to scent her wrists and neck. When they came to the sitting room they found everything just as they had left it the night before, the model village festooned with all the miniature streamers, paper chains, garlands and bunting that Nancy and her father had made. The tiny Chinese lanterns hung from the wire trees, their cellophane flames shining in the sunlight. Nancy had made full-sized streamers too, and they spiralled out from the ceiling lamp to the four walls, so closely spaced that the room seemed transformed into a big-top tent. Any minute now, the fearless trapeze artists; any minute now, the lady walking the tightrope. Nancy's mother flicked the switch on the cuckoo clock to turn the sound back on, and Nancy's father began blowing up the balloons, handing one to Nancy because she begged for a turn and he could never refuse her. He showed her how to stretch it first in all directions to make it easier to inflate, how to pinch the neck shut between breaths, then how to tie a knot in the neck when she'd finished. She managed two and a half balloons; after that she had no more air, so he told her she could fill the open wagons of the model train with sweets. Her mother went to the kitchen to finish preparing the food – devilled eggs and vol-au-vents and meringues, brandy snaps and mini trifles and dainty tomato sandwiches. She arranged it all on the card table she'd set up next to the plastic-covered sofa, and very festive it looked too. They wouldn't need breakfast today. When the cuckoo clock sounded the half hour, she almost dropped the chocolate éclairs. 'Oh!' she laughed as she stopped the plate from toppling to the carpet. 'Calamity averted!' Her voice too high, too tight.

'Will the guests be here soon?' said Nancy.

'What do you mean?' said her mother.

'Barry Sedgwick. Other people.'

'The *plumber*?'

'It's just us, love,' said her father.

'The same as ever!' said Nancy, slamming her hand against the sofa. 'How is that free?'

'Don't get yourself all worked up. You'll tear your frock.'

Nancy took a long, slow breath. Then another.

'Good girl,' said her father.

Her mother had let out the seafoam dress the week before, unpicking the bodice and waist with her sharp little seam ripper and plucking free all the bits of broken thread. A quality garment, you see, she'd said to Nancy, showing her the good spare inch and a half of fabric hidden inside. Pulled open, pulled apart, it hadn't looked like a garment at all, the pieces of filmy tulle and organza slumped over the back of a chair and shaped nothing like a girl. But her mother had sprayed the old needle holes with water and run her fingernail across them, scratching away the puncture marks until they all but vanished, and then she'd sewn it back together again, that dream of a dress, and they'd squeeze another year from it, surely. All the same, as they prepared for the party, Nancy was aware of the stitches pulling if she stretched too far or took too deep a breath. Once, she was certain, when she bent across the model village to reattach a length of bunting that had fluttered free, she felt – she *heard* – stitches tear open. She hardly dared check if anyone had noticed; her mother would be crushed, she would sink to the sofa and burst into tears, and Nancy would have ruined everything . . . but when she glanced over her shoulder her mother was humming to herself, removing the replica Tiffany lamp from the occasional table to make room for the cake.

The cake. How spectacular it was, the way it rose up and up on fluted columns that seemed too slender to hold it. Nancy's mother had kept the three tiers wrapped in tea towels and foil after she'd cooked them, and every week she fed them with the brandy from the fruit, poking holes in the top with toothpicks to let it soak right in. After that she'd iced them, first with a layer of marzipan, then with fondant smooth as soap, and then with royal icing piped into rosettes and beads and stars and fleurs-de-lis that dried bone-hard, and the thinnest of strands that hung from the sides in impossible looping swags, as precise as anything Nancy might draw with her Spirograph wheels. The flowers her mother had made by hand, mixing in two or three drops of colouring to turn the sugar paste pale yellow and pink, then cutting out petals with a scalpel and shaping them in her cupped palm. When she carried the towering confection into the sitting room step by careful step and lowered it onto the occasional table, Nancy and her father clapped until their hands stung: it was a work of art, they said. And wasn't it too pretty to eat? Wasn't it a shame to cut it? But her mother readied the knife, and the three of them sat on the sofa and watched the cuckoo clock, the white hands moving too slowly to see . . . almost at eight o'clock now, almost. And when the little door opened and the pinecone weight dropped and the woodsman swung his axe and the cuckoo flew out to sing its eight notes, Nancy's father lit a cigar, and her mother took the knife and pushed it tip-first into the thick white icing. Nancy shivered as the blade caught the light, and her hand fluttered to her neck, though she could not say why.

Her mother cut them each a slice, and the inside was dark and moist as deep earth, and Nancy didn't really want to eat it, but her mother was handing her a cake fork and spreading a serviette over her lap to protect the dress. In the background, the model train pulled the sweets around and around the tracks, buzzing like a trapped blowfly. Shards of royal icing scraped the roof of Nancy's mouth, and the wet cake clogged her throat. Her father popped open the two bottles of real Babycham that glistened with condensation on the *Swan Lake* coasters, and he poured Nancy a small glass, saying, 'Under the circumstances, Marjorie?' and her mother said, 'Under the circumstances,' because eight o'clock had come and gone and now they were free, whatever that meant. And the Babycham took away the earthen taste of the cake, sort of, and the bubbles burst against Nancy's tongue and turned into nothing. Then she was allowed to help herself to the rest of the food, and she ate a chocolate éclair first, and then a vol-au-vent and a meringue, and then a second éclair. Her father blew smoke rings – she'd never known he could do that; they sailed through the air like smudgy little lassos – and her mother cut herself another thin sliver of cake, picking up a sugar rose that tumbled onto the occasional table and eating it whole.

Nancy waited by the train tracks, snatching sweets as the wagons passed by and stuffing them in her mouth – a wine gum, a liquorice allsort, the red Smarties, a wine gum – until her cheeks bulged and she could hardly chew. The Chinese lanterns trembled on the wire branches. Nobody else was coming.

'Do you feel any different?' she heard her father ask in a quiet voice, and after a pause she heard her mother say, 'I don't believe so, no.'

'Nor do I,' he said.

Nancy took another red Smartie from the wagon. The red ones were her favourites, though they tasted no different from the others. When the Smartie wagon came around again, she grabbed a green and a yellow, closed her eyes and ate them one at a time.

Identical.

She still preferred the red, though.

After a while she noticed that her parents had fallen silent, and she turned, expecting to see them enjoying the party food too. But her mother held her face in her hands and wept, and her father sat slumped in the corner of the sofa, the lit cigar almost touching his funeral-suit trousers as if he might burn himself up.

'What's happened?' she said. 'What's changed?'

Nothing at all, they said.

Her mother cleared away all the food, tipping plate after plate into the big bin outside. Even the cake. The tiers collapsed as it fell, the fluted columns kicked out from under it. Nancy's father pulled down the streamers and undecorated the model village, and soon the party – the very idea of the party – seemed like a dream. Her parents spoke no more of it, nor of being free, and only the tiniest scrap of red crepe paper remained taped to the ceiling lamp, which was proof of something, Nancy thought, though she wasn't sure what.

Two nights later she sat wedged between her mother's knees on the carpet, having her hair brushed for bedtime. On the television the news presenter was talking about plans for the funeral of Lord Mountbatten, who'd been blown up by a bomb in Ireland.

'Maniacs and monsters,' said her father. 'Ice in their veins.' He had a tray on his lap and was twisting lengths of fine wire together to make a new tree.

The funeral would be an occasion of national mourning not seen since the death of Prime Minister Halifax, the news presenter intoned. There was to be a procession through the streets of London all the way to Westminster Abbey, and large crowds were expected as people turned out to pay their respects.

'National *mourning*, is it!' Nancy's mother said, separating a strand of Nancy's hair. 'Their *respects*! They'll all just be jostling for a good gawp.'

'After the service,' said the presenter, 'Lord Mountbatten's body will be taken by special train back to Romsey Abbey, where he frequently worshipped with local townsfolk.'

'Ow!' said Nancy, wriggling away from the hairbrush.

'Well, excuse me, but it's a bird's nest,' said her mother, easing the bristles through a knot. 'High time we gave it another trim.'

Nancy studied the photo of Lord Mountbatten, all medals and gold braid, that appeared on screen. 'Will they put him in a suitcase?' she said.

'Beg your pardon?' said her father, bending the lengths of wire into branches, snipping here and there with his pliers.

'To take him on the train. I've seen it on TV – you need a suitcase if you want to take something big on a train.' Surely he'd be very heavy to carry, she thought – but then again, maybe he weighed a bit less since he'd been blown up.

'They won't put him in a suitcase, love,' said her father. Little offcuts of wire peppered the tray on his lap; he was careful not to let any fall on the carpet, because they were extremely sharp and also extremely difficult to see.

Her mother started at the bottom of each strand of hair and worked her way up, gripping it above the snarls so that she did not hurt Nancy, but Nancy could feel her scalp tugging all the same. 'We could just cut it short,' she suggested, half turning around, but her mother gently pushed her back into position and said, 'Nonsense. It's your crowning glory,' which was what she always said.

When she'd finished, she brushed the hair in long, smooth strokes. Nancy liked that part, the light pressure travelling down over her scalp and shoulders and back. On certain days, depending on the weather, wisps of her hair rose from her head of their own accord and floated in a fly-away haze about her. She pretended she was a fairy then, or a mermaid – some wondrous creature not quite human – and she twirled this way and that in front of the bathroom mirror and wondered what powers she might possess.

Then the news presenter said, 'Police are still appealing for any information about a series of letters and a recorded message sent to them by a man claiming to be the Yorkshire—'

And her father was lunging for the television set and turning the sound right down and blocking the view of the screen, and her mother was saying, 'Would you fetch me a cardigan, Nancy? I'm feeling rather cold.'

'Why can't I see those stories?' she said. 'What are you not telling me?'

'I don't know what you're talking about,' said her mother.

'You keep things from me!' said Nancy. 'Those sad stories on the news! And you never let me out, and you never let other people in. Not a single guest at the party. Why not? *Why not?*'

'The world is a dangerous place, love,' said her father. 'It's better this way.'

'This isn't our Nancy,' said her mother. 'So angry, so accusing. This isn't our darling girl.'

Nancy felt a little ashamed of herself then – ashamed of hurting her parents. She knew she had; she could tell from their faces.

'I'm still cold,' her mother said in a soft voice, so Nancy did as she'd been asked.

When she returned to the sitting room, her mother thanked her and made a show of wrapping the cardigan around herself, shivering as she did up all the buttons, though the early September evening was mild. Nancy settled in next to her on the sofa, resting her head on her mother's shoulder and letting their breaths fall into step. Quietly, so quietly Nancy could only just hear it, her mother hummed snatches of a song that she used to sing when Nancy was a baby and wouldn't go to sleep. *Early one morning, just as the sun was rising* . . . And perhaps Nancy was not so much hearing her mother as feeling the thrum of the words, the notes, transferred from her mother's body to her own. *Oh, don't deceive me, oh, never leave me* . . . Barely moving her fingers at all, Nancy picked out the tune on her imaginary piano. She could just make out the scrap of red streamer on the ceiling lamp high above.

Her father, who had turned the sound back up and returned to his armchair, said, 'Look at the pair of you. What did I do to deserve you, eh?'

On the television a middle-aged lady in a chiffon blouse with a big floppy bow at the neck was saying, 'I believe every British child deserves an equal chance,' and, 'You'll never regret a good deed,' and, 'You have the opportunity to change a child's life.' Then a different lady who was younger and had dead-straight long brown hair was saying, 'Let's invite our special guests on now,' and three boys around Nancy's age came and stood with the first lady in front of some ferns. They were triplets, Nancy realised – identical triplets, impossible to tell apart. The younger lady asked if they wanted to say hello to Britain, and they looked right through the screen, right into Nancy's house, and said, 'Hello, Britain.'

Nancy's mother had stopped humming the song, the old lullaby, and Nancy felt her stiffen and catch her breath. She was staring at the three boys who were staring at her. She blinked a few times, frowned at some private question running through her head. Then she said, 'Kenneth,' in a voice low and full of warning, as if she didn't want to wake a wild animal she'd only just noticed in the corner of the room, and Nancy's father looked up from his wire tree. 'Do you see it too?' she said. As he took in the boys, shock flooded his face; his eyes widened, and his pliers fell clattering to the tray, making all the little offcuts jump.

'What's the matter?' said Nancy.

The triplet boys were shaking their heads because the younger lady couldn't get their names right, and then the middle one started talking about vulgar furniture.

'Oh God oh God oh God,' whispered her mother, hand over her mouth, trying to catch all the air rushing out of her.

'Mum?' said Nancy.

Her father was halfway out of his chair but didn't seem to know what to do with himself. He picked up his pliers again and gripped them in his fist, and his knuckles were white, his veins thick and dark.

But he didn't turn down the sound, and he didn't block Nancy's view of the screen, because the story wasn't a sad story, after all. So why were her parents acting strangely, as if they were watching something terrible?

'It can't be,' muttered her father. 'Can it?'

'I think so,' said her mother.

'Three of them, though? You wouldn't credit it.'

'Just think,' the younger lady was saying to the boys, 'perhaps your families are watching tonight.'

'What does she mean, *families?*' said Nancy's mother.

'That's the idea,' said her father. 'Release the lot of them. It's been in the news.'

The boys leapfrogged around the grounds of a huge old white manor house, and then they were inside, hoovering the passageway and doing the washing up.

'They look . . .' said her mother as the boys put away the clean plates and cups. 'They look . . .'

'Ordinary,' said her father.

Vincent

I couldn't wait to tell Jane about our father – our actual father, alive and kicking, who lived in a castle and had his own butler to help him keep track of time.

'When will the young ladies visit again?' I asked Mother Afternoon.

'Whenever the Ministry tells us.' She pulled a scrap of paper from her apron pocket and peered at it: an old Spot the Ball coupon she'd never posted, all her guesses marking the newsprint sky like dead birds. She was supposed to be showing us how to make a spice rack for Craft Day, but we could see that her heart wasn't in it; she simply gestured at some bits of wood and unlocked the Equipment Cupboard, and when we asked how big the rack should be, and how many shelves it should have, and how many jars each shelf should hold, she said we should show some initiative, because in the *real* world, when we were matched with our *families*, we wouldn't have someone telling us what to do step by step. We looked at one another. A spice rack. A rack for spices. Well, hadn't our father made Tower Bridge when he was just nine, good enough to be in a museum? And hadn't we ourselves already completed several successful woodworking projects? The ornamental goat watched us from the Library windowsill, its glass eyes aglow in the sunlight, the wires that held them in place pushed all the way inside its head.

We went to the Kitchen to count the jars of spices in the pantry and measure their height and depth. Cardamom, paprika, ginger, nutmeg, mustard, the cinnamon that Mother Morning sometimes let us sprinkle on our porridge as a treat . . . but what about salt? Was that a spice? We poked at the fine white crystals in the terracotta salt pig. It certainly wouldn't fit on a narrow little shelf, and besides, salt was nothing special, whereas spices – we knew this from The Book of Knowledge – spices were so important they could provoke wars, determine the rise and fall of states. Salt, we decided, was not a spice but a condiment, and therefore did not belong on a spice rack. But pepper? And herbs? Were herbs also spices? Things were much more complicated than we'd realised.

You probably wonder why we persevered with Craft Day at all. I think the routine felt like safety to us. We decided to make the spice rack big enough for extra jars should our mothers want to add them. They'd find a spot for it in the Kitchen, on the wall next to the cooker, perhaps, where it would be within easy reach. It was comforting to imagine that the three of them would remain at Captain Scott even after we'd left, continuing to turn out fondant fancies and Dundee cake, saving the dripping from the joints of roast meat, cooking Chicken on Chicken Day and Corned Beef on Corned Beef Day. Wiping the leaves of the philodendron plant. Dusting the china horses. Everything normal, everything safe. That was what we imagined, because imagining anything else was too frightening.

I cut some thin, flat pieces of wood to serve as the shelves and sides, while Lawrence measured up the dowelling that would stop the jars from falling to the floor and smashing. I made sure to mark the exact spots for the screws, but even so, William drove the first one in crooked and it broke through the surface of the shelf.

'Look what you've done!' said Lawrence. 'You've ruined it!'

'You sound like a little girl when you're upset,' said William, twirling the screwdriver in his fingers.

'You look like one!'

'Then so do you, idiot.'

Mother Afternoon glanced over but didn't bother to tell them to stop bickering. She'd withdrawn into herself more and more, no longer sewing our buttons back on or mending our sheets, no longer keeping the dust from settling in the Gun Room, no longer reminding us of the importance of clean fingernails or pointing out the beauty of the changing seasons on a Nature Walk. Mother Night seemed to have given up too; she hardly showed herself, and we'd begun to wonder if she'd disappeared entirely. Once, when I crept down the passageway in the small cold hours, I found the Upstairs Common Room empty, the gas fire dead. An open bottle of furniture polish sat next to Mother Night's usual chair, a rag abandoned on the console: one of our old vests sliced down the chest, the armholes gaping slack-mouthed. I checked the label inside the neck: Tom Walker. A slight, pale boy who'd wet the bed most nights, yet he and his brothers still got to go to Margate. And there he was, down the far end of the console – or there was his name, at least. I had the sudden feeling that if I stared at it hard enough, it would light up. I screwed the lid back on the furniture polish. The air smelled of beeswax and turpentine. The stuffed pike was eyeing me.

We stood back and looked at the spice rack. It really was quite smart, with its scalloped trim that I had drawn and Lawrence had hacksawed. I'd turned over the shelf William had damaged so you couldn't see the splintered bit.

'It's still there, though,' said Lawrence.

'But invisible,' I said.

'Not if you crouch down.'

'Why would you crouch down?'

'To see all the mistakes,' he said. 'All the things people have tried to hide.'

'We should paint it,' said William. 'Then it'll look like a proper spice rack.' He rummaged around in the Equipment Cupboard and found a few tins, spread out an old bedsheet.

'Mother Afternoon?' I said. 'What colour would you like?'

'It doesn't matter,' she said.

We prised open the tins to find puddles of black that lay on the surface like oily mould.

'It's gone bad,' said Lawrence. 'We can't use it.'

William stuck his finger into the red tin and stirred. 'It's just separated,' he said, and he was right; as we watched, the black split into long hooks like the blades of a dozen scythes, and then it disappeared.

We each wanted to paint the spice rack our own colour – green for Lawrence, red for William, yellow for me. We lunged for the Equipment Cupboard, pushing one another aside to grab for brushes, and slopped the paint onto the raw wood without caring about splashes or drips. As the colours mixed under our chaotic strokes, they turned a sludgy brown. At one point William painted over my hand, so I painted over his. He glared at the slick of yellow across his knuckles, then rammed his wet brush against my mouth, twisting it back and forth so the bristles splayed.

Lawrence laughed – for once he wasn't on the receiving end. 'You look like a vampire,' he said. 'A werewolf.'

I ran to the Bathroom, and when I saw the creature that was my reflection I recoiled: smears of red covered my lips and chin and even my teeth, as if I'd done something very bad. I washed my face, scrubbing hard, and rinsed out my mouth, but even so an aftertaste of paint remained – chalky, metallic – and the wet-animal tang of the bristles.

Back in the Library, my brothers had abandoned their brushes, and the spice rack lay muddy and glistening on the old bedsheet like something dragged from the earth.

Mother Afternoon said, 'Is it finished?'

Yes, we said, it was finished.

No praise. No exclamations over our attention to detail. 'Free Time until tea then.'

Out in the garden the light had turned to gold, like the golden grapevines surrounding the open-mouthed fish at the door to the Big House.

We forgot about the spice rack until the next day; by then it had dried to the bedsheet, and we had to rip the fabric to get it off. How grotesque it looked, this thing we had made, the paint all clotted and dull, fuzzy with lint. How pointless a task it had been. The only reason we still had Craft Day, we decided, was to keep us busy and stop us from asking questions. I nudged the spice rack with my toe, then so did William, but a bit harder, and I suppose that's what gave us the idea. Before we knew it, we were jumping on our creation, snapping the dowelling and the slender shelves, turning it over and stomping on it to break its back. For one brief moment, as I launched myself from a chair, I thought I saw Mother Afternoon watching us from the doorway, white-faced – but when I looked again she had gone.

Only Mother Morning was maintaining her routine, still insisting on recording our dreams every day. Now and then they featured the girl running through the woods, but for a bit of fun we began to make things up: flagrant stories of mothers who lied to their children, put poison in their stew and broken glass in their porridge. A mother who gave her children pills to eat in place of real food – pill sandwiches, pill soup. A mother who filled the bath with medicine and dunked her children in it, holding them under until they stopped squirming. Mother Morning pursed her lips, and we could tell she didn't believe we had dreamt these dreams, but she wrote them all down as usual, and kept up our Lessons from The Book of Knowledge: Queer Cactuses and Their Lovely Flowers; Fire: Friend and Enemy of Man; The Adventures of a Lump of Sugar. The one thing that changed was the medicine – no more canary-yellow pills, no more checking under our tongues and inside our cheeks to see if we were deceiving her. Starting to feel a little bolder, we asked why, and she shrugged and said it hadn't been her decision.

'But you realise you have no protection now,' she told us. 'You'll need to be very careful. The Bug could take you any day.'

'There is no Bug,' we said, and we felt giddy and hollow and light; we'd never dared speak like that to a mother.

'That's very wicked,' she said, pushing back our curtains with no care for the rotten patches that might tear.

'Yes, it is,' we said.

'You know,' she went on, opening the window so the cold air flooded in, 'one day you'll look back on your time here and long for it. You'll realise how lucky you were. How loved.'

Bolder still, we laughed and ran from the room, leaving our beds unmade and our teeth unbrushed, and we slid down the banister in our pyjamas, shrieking like monkeys as we smashed against the griffin at the bottom.

'Boys, boys!' called Mother Morning, rushing down after us. 'You should be ashamed of yourselves!'

But already we were scrambling outside, haring across the wet grass, whooping and beating our chests. William grabbed a spade abandoned on the Grounds Beautification Project, and I snatched some apples from the trees and bowled them to him on the cricket pitch. He bashed them in all directions, the juice flying. One of them flew right over the flint wall. One of them hit Lawrence in the shin. 'And he's bowled him! He's bowled him!' shouted William. 'Those aren't the rules!' said Lawrence. He hurled the apple back, and it splatted against William's hair. William caught it and took a great wet bite from the good side, at least half the fruit disappearing into his mouth. For no particular reason I roared and ran at Lawrence, knocking him off his feet, and William joined us as we rolled over and over, a snarling beast made of boys.

'Do you really think you can do away with the good manners we've taught you?' said Mother Morning, standing over us so she blocked out the sun. 'Acting like hooligans. Destroying your Craft Day project – oh, don't worry, I know all about that. I've written it up. The families will send you straight back here once they realise they have little animals on their hands, you know.'

We sat panting in our dew-soaked pyjamas all muddy and streaked with grass stains. Suddenly we felt cold.

She was probably right. We'd be sent back here.

'Sorry, Mother Morning,' we said, untangling ourselves.

We went inside and dressed, and then we made our way to the Library, where we learned about The Fantastic Realm of Magic – primitive beliefs that still flourished in some backward races. One by one we inspected the picture of a calf's heart studded with pins and thorns and twigs of witch hazel.

After tea that evening, when we'd cleaned our teeth and put on our dressing gowns, Mother Afternoon unlocked the door that led to the North Wing of the house and ushered us through to their private quarters. We passed the bedrooms, each with its narrow bed and plain chest of drawers. I caught a glimpse of stockings hanging on a clothes horse like shucked skins. A tin of sweets on a bedside table; a glass-eyed doll in a crochet dress, holding out its arms as if it wanted to be picked up. A poster of a ballerina pinned to a wall. Pictures of the royal family cut from the *Woman's Realm*.

Mother Morning and Mother Night waited in their Sitting Room, Mother Morning already in her own dressing gown and slippers, Mother Night in her smart houndstooth skirt and her silky blue blouse. She seemed to shrink away from William when he sat next to her. In the corner, the black telephone lay off its cradle.

Mother Afternoon shifted her sewing basket from a chair to clear a space for me. She brought us each a drink of orange squash, placing it on the low glass table; she was trying to make it a special occasion, but I felt uneasy. She kept looking at her watch while we took sips of our drinks and checked one another's tongues to see if they were turning orange, and before long it was time: on went the television. At first the picture was gritty, just spatters of white and grey, and Mother Afternoon fiddled with the antenna on top of the set, moving the long knitting-needle arms a fraction this way, a fraction that, while we squinted to see if we could recognise ourselves.

'You're making it worse!' said Mother Morning. 'We'll miss it!' She shooed Mother Afternoon away and began adjusting the antenna herself. 'I did tell you we should switch it on in plenty of time.'

'I beg your pardon,' said Mother Afternoon, 'but I for one do not want to keep hearing about poor Lord Mountbatten.'

Mother Morning twisted her face, as if that might help the picture – but then, finally, it came right, and we saw the top half of a man in a suit, and behind him a picture of the Home, our Home.

'We can't hear anything,' said William.

Mother Night glanced at him; did she shudder?

'In a minute,' said Mother Morning. She waited until the man had finished talking and the Minister of Loneliness had appeared on the screen, and then she turned it up.

We had watched television before: every Christmas our mothers brought us through to their Sitting Room for the Queen's message, in which she talked about unity and family and hope with a large brooch pinned to her shoulder. This was different, though. The Minister was on the screen, but somehow, somehow, she was also in our garden, and we knew that we were viewing our past, or a dream of our past, and we had the strangest feeling that if we looked out of the window we would see the Minister standing in front of the fernery, and see ourselves playing cricket and leapfrog and picking apples, and if we opened the window we would hear ourselves saying *The world, yes, the world*, and the boys in the television were ghosts of a sort, and at any minute they might dissolve back into the ghosts of our own memories.

'They didn't show us making our beds,' said Lawrence when it was over. 'I did such a good job. Perfect hospital corners.'

This was a shame, we agreed, but on the other hand they hadn't shown William being rude, and surely we should be grateful for that?

'They did tell us they wouldn't use all the footage,' said Mother

237

Morning. 'They said they'd cut out a bit of you here and join it to another bit of you there. Remember?'

And that was exactly what they'd done, and we hadn't even noticed the joins. We drank our orange squash, which was a bit strong and made our tongues flinch almost painfully at the edges, but we finished it anyway. We begged to be allowed to stay up late, to watch a bit more television – the top half of the man in the suit came back and said, 'Finally tonight, football,' which sounded interesting – but Mother Afternoon said we couldn't stay, and our other two mothers agreed: we couldn't stay. Mother Afternoon switched off the set, and the picture shrank into a shining white dot in the middle of the black screen, like an after-image when you blink, like the only star left in the sky, and then it vanished.

We had little time to prepare for the next Socialisation Day. When Mother Morning announced that the young ladies would be there after lunch, we cleaned and tidied as quickly as we could, shoving things in cupboards and under beds, telling ourselves it would all be fine as long as nobody looked too hard. Mother Afternoon didn't bother with refreshments, so Lawrence arranged some Digestive biscuits on a plate, along with the last of the milk-teeth sweets from the bag in the pantry. Then, before we knew it, Mother Afternoon was showing the young ladies inside to where we waited in the Playroom, our hands more or less clean and our shoes shined on the backs of our trousers. In walked Diane, her eyes bigger than ever behind her spectacles and smeared with silvery-blue shadow like she was part mermaid. Behind her came Karen, though she had lost so much weight in the three weeks since the picnic that it took me a second to recognise her. A striped jumper hung baggy on her body, and her neck looked too slender to support her head.

'How do you do,' she said, staring past us at nothing in particular – the shelf where we kept the Mona Lisa jigsaw and the Stickle Bricks, it seemed. We hadn't played with them in ages; they were for little children.

'Won't you sit down?' I said, and Lawrence shifted a cushion on the daybed to hide a mark – an old orange-squash spill, perhaps, or something worse left by one of us when we were poorly. Jane must be in the passageway, I thought, arranging her dress or unbuttoning a cardigan. Smoothing her hair because she wanted to look nice for me. As soon as I could manage it, I needed to ask her about their volume of BOO–CRO. Whether it too was missing page 504.

Mother Afternoon lifted the lid of the radiogram and put on her Irish Rovers record. It was one of my favourites, though a lot of the songs were sad songs if you paid attention.

'Are we to dance?' said Diane, whose rash had gone completely from her hands and face, but Mother Afternoon said no, we wouldn't be dancing, we'd just be listening, because many people enjoyed listening to music for its own sake.

'We do that on Music Appreciation Day,' said Diane. 'I enjoy Glen Campbell, who sings about the dreams of the everyday housewife. Except, when the housewife closes her eyes and touches the housedress and it suddenly disappears, where does it go? Is she just standing there with no clothes on?'

We didn't know Glen Campbell, so we weren't sure about the disappearing housedress but agreed that it sounded unclear. I glanced at the door to the passageway: no sign of Jane. The Irish Rovers, who lived in Canada, were singing about the extinction of the unicorn. Diane tapped her foot in time to the tune.

'My family has a large collection of records,' she went on. 'I expect they own many Glen Campbells – I didn't have time to check – but if they don't, I expect they'll purchase them for me based on my interests.'

'Your *family*?' said William.

'Oh yes. I did a home visit last week.'

'What was the butler like?' said Lawrence. 'Will he teach you to swim in the indoor pool?'

'They don't want her,' said Karen. 'After careful consideration, they've decided they're not a good fit for her, but they wish her the best in her future endeavours.'

'I expect they'll change their minds,' said Diane. 'We all wear glasses, so we have that in common. And they said I was very clean and had excellent pronunciation.'

Why had nobody mentioned Jane? Where *was* she? I peered out into the passageway.

'Refreshments?' said William, offering the plate to the young ladies.

Diane took a Digestive and Karen one of the milk teeth. How strange the sweet looked in her fingers – how real, with its pale-pink gums and its perfect incisors. As if she'd just pulled it from somebody's mouth.

The Irish Rovers were up to the bit where the unicorns realise that the ark has left without them, and they have made a terrible mistake, and they look up from the rocks and cry. I had a bad, bad feeling.

Then Lawrence peered out into the passageway too and said, 'Where's Jane?'

'Oh, *Jane*,' said Diane, rolling her eyes. She took a bite of Digestive biscuit, and chewed and chewed and swallowed. 'She went to Margate.'

Margate isn't Margate, you must never go to Margate.

And the waters were rising and the unicorns were scrambling for their lives as the ark drifted off with all the other animals who had behaved sensibly rather than hiding and playing games when the rain started to fall, so the unicorns – reckless creatures – had only themselves to blame for their extinction, and Noah was quite justified in leaving them behind to drown. That was what Mother Afternoon always told us on Music Appreciation Day.

'Margate?' I said, my voice all reedy and weak.

Karen was struggling with her milk teeth; she'd bitten into them, but they would not give, instead stretching horribly out of shape.

'Last week,' said Diane. 'Lucky cow.'

'Excuse me?' said Mother Afternoon.

'Thing,' said Diane. 'Lucky thing.'

'Have you heard from her?' I asked.

'*Heard* from her?' said Diane. 'You don't *hear* from people who go to Margate. They're too busy riding the Sky Wheels at Dreamland. Shooting up into the air, higher than the Big House. Or crashing into other people as hard as anything on the Dodgems, only it doesn't hurt because the cars have rubber bumpers and everyone is quite safe.'

'But you were best friends,' I said. My scalp felt too tight, my chest hollow.

'I expect my family will take me to visit her in the Big House,' said Diane.

'They don't *want* you,' said Karen. 'You *know* that.'

'Right then,' said Mother Afternoon. 'Today we're pretending to be Good Samaritans. Who wants to go first?'

'What's a Samaritan?' said Lawrence.

'A person from Samaria, I expect,' said Diane.

'Where's that?'

'Israel. It doesn't exist any more, though.'

'What happened to it? Where did it go?'

'Let's stick to the task at hand,' said Mother Afternoon. 'We need a Good Samaritan and an injured person.'

'But we're all fine,' said William.

'We're pretending,' said Mother Afternoon. 'We're practising.'

'Why are we pretending to be Good Samaritans if we're not from the ancient kingdom of Israel?'

'Goodness me, it's just an expression!' said Mother Afternoon. 'The origins are lost to the mists of time, but it just means someone who helps others.'

'Are there bad Samaritans?' said Diane.

Mother Afternoon ignored her. Glancing around the room, considering each of us in turn, she settled on William. 'You're the Good Samaritan,' she said. 'And let me see . . . Karen, you're the injured person.'

'I don't want to be the injured person,' said Karen.

'Just pretending, remember?'

'I don't want to pretend.'

Mother Afternoon sighed. 'Diane, then. It doesn't really matter. Lie down on the daybed – you've sprained your ankle. William, you're walking past and notice she's hurt herself. Off you go.'

I looked out into the passageway again, though I knew Jane was not there – but perhaps everything was fine. Mother Afternoon hadn't batted an eyelid when Diane mentioned Margate, and wouldn't a person show some kind of reaction to bad news?

And yet.

'Is something the matter?' William was saying. He was leaning over the daybed and Diane was whimpering. 'Have you hurt yourself?' He felt under her arms and around her neck, the way Dr Roach did when he examined us. Then he palpated her stomach.

'It's my ankle,' moaned Diane. 'Though I'm a bit peckish too.'

'Digestive biscuit? Milk teeth?' said Lawrence.

'*I'm* the Good Samaritan,' said William. He offered the plate to Diane. 'Digestive biscuit? Milk teeth?'

'I'd prefer a Scotch egg, if you have one.'

'Sorry,' said William. 'But let's take a look at your ankle.' He touched it with his fingertips, and Diane flinched.

'Ouch! Ouch!' she wailed, helping herself to the last two Digestives.

'Oh dear,' said William. 'This seems serious. What did you do?'

'Roller skating,' said Diane. 'I'm actually the Under-18 Female British Champion, but a jealous rival threw pebbles in my path and I went flying.' She munched on her biscuits.

'What a horrible trick to play,' said William. 'If I can just loosen your shoe . . .'

'Roller skate,' said Diane. 'Ouch.'

'Roller skate,' said William. Gently he unbuckled it and removed it from her foot. Laid his hand on her ankle as if to warm the sprain.

Diane sighed a slow sigh and fell silent, and the two of them stayed like that for a long moment. Then Diane said something we couldn't make out, so we asked her to repeat herself.

'Will there be another family?' she murmured, keeping her eyes fixed on William's hand as it rested on her ankle. Her eyelids shimmered ocean-blue.

'Of course,' said Lawrence, though none of us believed him.

Mother Afternoon was gazing out of the window at the scraggy buddleia and the browning hydrangeas that nobody had bothered to deadhead, the bald patches on the gravel driveway that nobody had bothered to rake. Wouldn't that reflect badly? But our mothers seemed to have stopped caring about such things. The Irish Rovers were singing about children and flowers being their sisters and brothers.

'I think we need proper help,' said William. 'Can you put any weight on it?'

'I don't know,' said Diane, and she seemed really hurt now, not pretending any more.

William put his arm under her shoulder, and she shifted to the edge of the daybed, and then, leaning on him, tried to stand. 'I'll take you to hospital,' he said. 'You might have broken something.'

He'd been to hospital once himself for a broken bone, so he knew about such things – when we were nine, he'd leapt from a high branch to ambush Lawrence and had shattered his wrist. All night he had whimpered, cradling his crooked limb, and by morning it had turned black. Dr Roach took one look at it and bundled him into his Jaguar, and Lawrence and I and a couple of other boys who still lived there stood and watched as they disappeared through the gates. William had all the luck, we said, and Mother Morning, who was listening, told us that William was not lucky, he was a very silly creature, a very irresponsible creature, whose actions would have to be written up in The Book of Guilt. But when William returned, he confirmed his luckiness himself: Dr Roach had bought him a Cornish pasty and a Swisskit bar that he didn't have to share with anyone, and on the way home Cynthia had fallen asleep on his lap and hadn't even woken when he'd folded one of her ears inside out. The hospital, he said, was full of people who'd hurt themselves, and they were not reprimanded, and their families sat with them and held their hands and talked to them in soft voices, and everyone thought Dr Roach was his grandfather, and Dr Roach had not corrected them. For six weeks Lawrence and I had to help him do up his buttons and cut up his food like we were his slaves. The cast began to stink of decay, and when it came off his arm was pale and soft, smaller than the other one. The arm of a younger boy, the arm of a girl. For the first time, we looked different. But it didn't last.

Together William and Diane picked their way across the Playroom. He guided her away from the hard corners of the radiogram and pointed out the edge of the rug where she should take care not to trip, and she clung to him, wincing, trying not to cry, and they disappeared into the passageway.

Lawrence and I clapped – because hadn't William done well? Hadn't he been kind? Karen didn't join in, but she was holding the half-finished milk teeth, too polite to put them back on the plate.

'Yes, very good,' said Mother Afternoon, still gazing out of the window. 'Very convincing.'

Then the record started to skip. *What happened to us happened to us happened to us*, the Irish Rovers stuttered.

Mother Afternoon flew to the radiogram and lifted the needle. Holding the record by its thin edges between her palms, she tilted it back and forth, the rings of song shiny as liquorice straps. 'Someone's been interfering,' she said. 'Someone's been putting their mucky fingers where they shouldn't.' And she began to cry.

We looked at one another. Nobody knew what to do. Mothers didn't cry; mothers were the ones who persuaded us of the pointlessness of crying. William and Diane sidled back into the room and stood by the daybed, unsure whether to sit down. For one irrational moment I thought Mother Afternoon might take our fingerprints and compare them to the marks on the record. Have it tested for DNA evidence.

'I'm sure it's just a bit of dust,' said Lawrence. 'Where's your velvet cleaning pad?'

'Look at it,' said Mother Afternoon. 'It's *scratched.* You can't clean away a *scratch.*'

Lawrence leant over the record. 'I really can't see—'

'It's *ruined.*' She began to sob again, so Lawrence put his arm around her.

'We'll go to the shops,' he said. 'To the big shops in the city, where they sell records. We'll find this one again for you.'

'What?' she said, sniffling.

'We'll replace the record. Come on, come with me. Perhaps we'll see Princess Margaret – she likes shopping, I believe.'

'What are you talking about?'

'Well,' said Lawrence, frowning, 'I'm being the Good Samaritan. I thought it was my turn to pretend.'

'Pretend?' said Mother Afternoon. 'Do you think I made the record jump for the purposes of some stupid game dreamt up by the Minister?'

'I . . . I don't know,' said Lawrence.

'Do you think I scratched it *myself?*'

'No,' said Lawrence, slumping. He was only trying to be kind. She looked around the room at the rest of us.

'No,' we said.

Of course she hadn't scratched it. We knew how carefully she handled her record collection, how she planned to take it with her to the little cottage she'd buy when she won Spot the Ball. But sometimes damage just happened, and nobody could stop it or fix it. Nobody.

Nancy

The large brown envelope dropped through the letterbox in the front door with the rest of the post that morning. When Nancy's mother picked it up from the mat she let out a cry as if she'd injured herself, and she placed it on the kitchen table where she could keep an eye on it as she paced back and forth in her quilted dressing gown and spiky curlers. Nancy could make out the words *On Her Majesty's Service* running across the top, and in smaller letters, in the bottom left corner, *Ministry of Loneliness: London*. She nudged it with her fingertip when her mother went off to get dressed and fix her hair. Shook it the way she shook her Christmas presents. Sniffed the flimsy paper, held it up to the light. No telling what was inside, though it felt thicker than a letter. All day her mother skirted around the thing, glancing at it as she wiped up the breakfast crumbs, shooing away the cat when he sprawled himself across it in a patch of afternoon sun. Now, after tea – beans on toast, which Nancy's parents insisted she loved, and butterscotch Angel Delight as a special treat – they sat on either side of the cleared table, the envelope between them.

'Shall I do the honours?' said her father.

'One of us should,' said her mother. She was twisting her hands, which were still red and soft from the washing-up water, and Nancy was drying the last of the cutlery with a sodden tea towel.

'Pass me the butter knife, there's a good girl,' said her father, but when she handed it to him he scrutinised its blunt edge and said, 'Do you think it's the right tool for the job? Marjorie?'

Part of a dream from the previous night flashed into Nancy's memory: a blade in her mouth, a thin steel tongue.

From across the table Nancy's mother also considered the butter knife. 'We don't want anything too drastic,' she said. 'We don't want to damage the contents.'

'Don't we, indeed,' he said.

'Kenneth,' she warned.

'All right, all right. But at the same time, it needs to be sharp enough to glide cleanly through the paper. No trouble, no mess. Look, I can't even get under the flap with this.' He jabbed at the corner of the envelope with the round-tipped knife.

'What about the one from the cheese board?' said Nancy's mother. She searched in the cupboard where they kept all the things they never used – the musical cocktail shaker, the nutmeg mill, the electric kettle that was supposed to switch itself off but always forgot. Right at the back she found a board with an inlaid tile decorated with a sunflower – that was for the cheese to sit on – and a slender wooden-handled knife with a curved blade that split in two at the tip, like a snake's tongue. Again, fragments of the dream shivered through Nancy.

'Oh,' said her mother, 'I'm not sure that will fit under the flap either. I could have sworn it had just the one sharp point.'

This was an easy mistake to make, because the cheese board was something to be used when visitors came, and no visitors ever came.

'Two points are the convention,' said Nancy's father. 'They allow you to pick up the bit of cheese once you've cut it, and then transport it to a cracker.'

'Yes, I see that now,' said Nancy's mother.

'But you're quite right. That's not going to work on the envelope either.'

'No.'

'No.'

'We have a proper letter-opener, though,' said Nancy, and her parents looked up as if they'd only just noticed she was there. 'The one you brought back from Luxembourg.'

'Luxembourg?' they said. 'Pardon?'

They had all but forgotten that trip, taken when they were still so young; young and travelling the world after the Treaty had ended the war and made things better for everyone. But Nancy had seen the photos, the proof of another life – her mother in cat's-eye sunglasses biking along a canal, her father grinning a lopsided grin as he held up a croissant moustache. Her mother on a camel, her father on a ski lift, her mother using chopsticks, her father pitching a tent. Ruined castles and fields of tulips, striped sun umbrellas on stony beaches, bear cubs begging for food at the window of their car. Rowboats and waterfalls, churches carved into rock, cities bright white in the sun and spilling all the way down the cliffs to the blue, blue sea. A lizard on her father's shoulder. Their names written in sand. Years before any hint of a baby.

Nancy went to the credenza in the sitting room and opened the bottom drawer. 'Here,' she said, handing the letter-opener to her father, and he ran his thumb over the medallion on the bronze-look hilt: the Pont Adolphe in Luxembourg, its elegant arches reaching across the river. Nancy imagined her parents standing hand in hand on the bridge, looking out across the city, perhaps nibbling on a pastry or a pretzel of some description – whatever one nibbled on when visiting Luxembourg.

'Just the ticket,' said her father, and he eased the blade underneath the flap of the envelope and ran it precisely along the crease, no trouble, no mess.

The catalogue seemed to slip out of its own accord, making a soft hush as it brushed across the kitchen table. On the cover a young girl sat on the grass with a fox terrier in her lap. She beamed up at the camera and so did the dog. Both wore daisy-chain crowns.

'She seems sweet,' said Nancy's mother.

'Let's not get sidetracked,' said her father.

Nancy peered over their shoulders as they began to turn the thick pages. Each showed pictures of a child – a close-up of the face as well as a full-length shot, all in colour. Some of the children came in twos and threes, and looked identical apart from their clothes and names.

'No expense spared,' murmured her mother.

'Ten-year-old Matthew enjoys growing vegetables and mowing lawns,' read her father. 'An intelligent boy with a flair for maths, he remains even-tempered in the face of any challenge.' Over the page were Elizabeth, a bubbly eight-year-old with beautiful table manners, and her twin sister Claire, who possessed a truly angelic singing voice and always volunteered to dry the dishes even when it wasn't her turn.

'Who are they?' said Nancy.

'Nobody,' said her mother.

'Surplus to requirements,' said her father.

Nancy thought of the other catalogues that came in the mail, their pages bursting with beautiful items. Her mother sending off her orders, wondering where she might display the new thing – and then, when she unwrapped it, announcing it wasn't as nice in person. Shutting it away in some dark corner.

Perhaps the children wouldn't look as nice in person either.

'Are they . . . for sale?' said Nancy.

'No, they're free,' said her mother.

'Free,' said Nancy.

'Yes, free.'

They were more than halfway through the catalogue now.

'Karen's a big girl, isn't she,' remarked her father.

'Fat,' said her mother. 'Karen is fat. Though I suppose that might appeal to an overweight family.'

'Her hobbies include hoovering, cleaning windows and hanging out washing. You have to be quite fit for those.'

'That's why they've mentioned them.'

'Mmm.'

The girl on the next page – Jane, whose serious expression belied her compassionate nature, and who was a safe and reliable supervisor of younger children – had a word stamped in large red letters across her face: *WITHDRAWN.*

'She does seem a bit shy,' said Nancy, and her parents stopped turning the pages and looked around at her. Neither of them spoke; they seemed to be trying to figure something out.

Then her mother said, 'You're quite right, poppet, but in this case – and I might be wrong, of course – in this case I think they mean she's unavailable.'

'Oh,' said Nancy.

'Another family has already taken her,' said her father.

'Oh,' said Nancy. She paused. 'Is that what we're going to do? Take one of them?' A sister. A brother. A friend.

But her parents were poring over a page near the back, huddling together as if to tell secrets, and her mother was drawing in her breath, and her father was tapping the page with his forefinger as if to say *Here it is. Here's the thing we've been searching for.* The letter-opener wobbled with the force of the tapping, and its blade swivelled to point at the open window. Once more Nancy's dream of the knife in her mouth returned to her. She moved to her mother's side to see the catalogue – and there he was. One of the boys from TV.

'Lawrence, aged thirteen, is a gentle boy who has a special love of animals,' read her father. 'A sound sleeper and fastidiously clean, he performs all chores without complaint and in excellent time.'

'Pfft,' said her mother.

Over the page, the two other triplets: Vincent, who showed a remarkable aptitude for woodwork and could be trusted with independent errands, including shopping; and William, a vivacious all-rounder in possession of a delightful sense of humour.

'A sense of humour,' said Nancy's father. 'Vivacious.'

'I think we can read between the lines,' said her mother.

'Are we going to take one of them?' Nancy asked again.

But neither of her parents replied.

Vincent

I was brushing my teeth one evening when I heard William yelling from the bedroom. At first I thought he'd hurt himself, so I ran down the passageway, my mouth frothy with toothpaste, Mother Afternoon's withered ikebana arrangement falling to bits as I thundered past – but when I reached our room I found him jumping on his bed, not a thing wrong.

'Stop it,' I hissed. 'You'll get us all into trouble.'

Bed-jumping was strictly prohibited; in the past, before we could remember, a boy had crashed right through his steel-mesh bed-base and a piece of broken metal had severed the major artery in his leg. That was the story, at least – we never could find the incident in The Book of Guilt, though we looked back through many volumes. But then, we reasoned, if he'd died, surely he wouldn't have been written up? Surely the death itself would have been the punishment? For a time, in secret, we'd checked the floorboards under every bed in the house, scrutinising the grain of the wood and the cracks in between for traces of blood. But the accident – if it had happened at all – had been cleaned entirely away.

'Look!' William yelled at me now, launching himself off the bed and waving a sheaf of paper in my face.

No, not just a sheaf of paper.

A brochure.

I ran to my own bed – and there it lay on my pillow at last: *Welcome to Margate*. The children screaming on the wooden roller-coaster. The boy buried up to his neck in sand. The merry-go-round with the giant swan, its great white wings spread wide.

'Can you believe it?' said William.

I shook my head. I swallowed the remains of my toothpaste; it felt hot and caustic as it slid down my throat.

Lawrence appeared at the door then too, still wet from the bath, holding a towel around his waist. 'What's happened? What's the matter?'

William dragged him into the room and, linking arms, swung him around in a wild dance. 'We're going we're going we're going,' he sang.

'Going where?' said Lawrence, pulling his arm free and grasping at the ends of his towel.

I pointed to his pillow, and he froze, then crept to the edge of his bed and slowly, gently sat down. He stared at the brochure, not daring to touch it, as if it might disintegrate should he move any closer. 'Is it real?' he said.

In the distance we could hear the water from his bath choking its way down the plughole.

William was already flinging open drawers, pulling out clothes to take with him. 'We won't need vests,' he said. 'Or jumpers. Or even long trousers, probably. I suppose they'll give us swimming trunks when we get there . . .? And swimming lessons too, I expect.'

'Yes,' murmured Lawrence. 'We'll need swimming lessons.' He'd picked up the brochure now, and a smile spread across his face. 'I wonder which floor of the Big House we'll be on. Quite high up, don't you think? By this stage?'

'High enough to see where the water ends,' said William.

'We'll feel like birds!' said Lawrence, swooping his brochure through the air, making the pages flutter.

'I don't know that we should go,' I said.

The two of them looked at me. 'What?'

'I keep thinking about what Mother Night told me when I was sick – the old Mother Night. Well, the young Mother Night. Margate isn't Margate, she said. We must never go to Margate.'

'You dreamt all that,' said Lawrence.

'You were out of your mind,' said William. 'Bonkers! Mental! Remember?'

'What if I wasn't? Why don't we ever hear from boys who've left? Not even a postcard.'

'Well, it's like Diane said – they're too busy on the Sky Wheels and the Dodgems. Too busy having fun.'

'They lied to us about the medicine. How do we know they're not lying about Margate?'

'The brochures, for one thing,' said William. He pointed to the girl offering candy floss to the Tyrannosaurus, the friends waiting to see Mademoiselle Yvette the Headless Lady: Alive and Human. 'Those are real photos of real people. And Margate is a real place. It's in The Book of Knowledge.'

'So?' I said.

'So they haven't made it up.'

'That doesn't mean—' I began, but Lawrence said, 'Who made you the expert? Why are you trying to ruin everything?'

He dumped his wet towel in a heap on the floor – something he never did – and yanked his pyjama bottoms up over his legs.

On the back of my brochure a boy stood at the edge of the sand and looked through a telescope, pointing it out past the beach, out past the busy pier to the empty horizon. *Come to Margate, where children can have the time of their lives just being children.*

'Anyway,' said Lawrence, who had started to choose his own clothes to pack, 'aren't you forgetting something?'

'What?' I said.

'Jane. Jane's at the Big House. In the room next to ours, probably, since she's only just gone.'

'I bet your beds will share a wall,' said William. 'She'll be inches away.'

I wanted to believe I would see her soon. At the beach we could paddle in the shallows together, and then, when we'd both learned to swim, we could venture further out, trailing our fingers through ribbony seaweed, feeling the soft brush of fish against our bare legs. We'd visit the Dolphinarium and watch Britt, Turk and Speedy leaping from the water to sound a note on a horn, walking on their tails, talking when their keepers asked them questions – actually *talking*. That's what the brochure said. At Dreamland we'd see the mischievous monkeys scurrying about, and the bright-green parakeets riding their tiny bicycles. We'd visit the Shell Grotto, too, and marvel at the intricacy of the mosaics in the curious underground tunnels, and we'd come up with our own theories about who might have made them. Children, we'd decide; a secret society of children had fixed the four and a half million shells to the tunnel walls, because children had hands small enough for such delicate work.

I peered at the photograph of the boy with the telescope. The waves washed over the golden sand; the pier took aim at the horizon. I searched for the thing the boy was watching, but all I could make out was the flat blue sea, the empty sky.

'Do you really think she's there?' I said, lying back on my bed. The water stain on the ceiling reached almost to the light fitting now, its brown edges frilled like some strange fungus that had sprouted as we slept.

'Where else would she be?' said Lawrence.

I did not know.

William had a nightmare just before dawn the following day – the skinny girl and the woods and the knife again. As the girl ran through the trees, he said, the leaves began to shiver and fall until it was raining leaves, pouring leaves, and the air turned red. A bird followed behind her, flitting from branch to branch, calling its awful call: *cut-cut-cut*. And then someone was digging a hole, slicing through the wrist-thick roots of the trees with the knife, unearthing all the beetles and worms that lived in the ground. Down deep and deeper, until the hole began to fill with water, and the level rose and rose like a bath left running, a bath made of dirt. And William was trying to rinse the knife clean in it, only the leaves were falling so thick and fast he could not see his own hand in front of him.

He woke shaking, shouting. No one came. Not Mother Night, and then not Mother Morning either. We turned on the light and reminded him that the girl wasn't real, that he was right here with us in our bedroom. We all three settled back into our beds, lying quite still under the blankets, and waited.

'Just tell her you can't remember what you dreamt,' I whispered.

'Say you were dreaming of Margate,' whispered Lawrence.

Margate! Of course, today was the day we were going to Margate, and how had we forgotten? We'd spent our last night ever in our old room. Now, as we looked around, we noticed its shabbiness: the dingy rag rugs on the scuffed parquet, the chipped paint on the bedsteads. The marks on the wall from old drawings and calendars. We could hear the clinking of crockery coming from downstairs – Mother Morning preparing our breakfast. Had she forgotten to come to us with The Book of Dreams? But Lawrence said, 'Remember when that boy four rooms down went to Margate? Stephen, was it? She didn't ask him for his last dream. He lay there waiting till nine o'clock, and by then he'd missed breakfast, but he said he didn't care because soon enough he could eat toffee apples all day.'

Yes, we thought we remembered him – Stephen, or maybe Simon – and then we remembered other boys boasting on the day they went to Margate that they hadn't reported their last dreams either.

We climbed out of bed and put on our clothes. Lawrence pulled down the pictures he'd drawn of Cynthia and the ponies, the pins flicking out of the wall and into his bed, which no longer mattered, because he'd never sleep in it again. But what time was it? How late was it? We'd waited and waited for Mother Morning, and now eight o'clock had come and gone, and the Van would arrive at 10.30

because that was when it always arrived. We hurried downstairs without brushing our hair or teeth and without even touching the griffin's wings: no time, no time.

The Refectory smelled of fried eggs and bacon and sausages and mushrooms, and Mother Morning brought out treat after piping-hot treat and let us help ourselves to as much as we wanted. Scrambled eggs, too, and racks of toast to slather with butter and jam. Porridge with brown sugar and cream. Slices of black pudding that we wolfed down even though William insisted it was made of blood – Lawrence said he didn't believe him, and I said I didn't care.

We were cleaning our plates with the last of the toast when Mother Morning joined us at the table, her floral housecoat a little creased, her auburn curls a little greasy.

'A big day,' she remarked.

Mouths full, we nodded.

She toyed with the salt and pepper cellars that had S and P punched in holes on the lids. 'You know,' she said, not really meeting our eyes, 'one must always be mindful of the greater good, difficult as that may be at times to understand.'

We nodded again, not understanding, and watched as she lined up the P next to the S. People who wrote letters put that at the bottom when they wanted to add something else, we knew.

'We have tried to give you the best life we could,' she continued, 'under the circumstances. But though to you we may have seemed in charge of the whole operation, I want you to know that we were not free to act in the way we might have chosen had things been different. Yes?'

'You mean the drug trials,' said William, and she looked up at him as if he'd pinched her, the heel of her hand knocking over the salt cellar.

I kicked him under the table. Now was not the time to be making mischief.

'You know, in a way,' said Mother Morning, seeming to consider every word very carefully, 'we've had just as little control as you.'

She swept up the salt that had spilled onto the checked tablecloth and threw it over her shoulder to avert bad luck. 'But you have felt cherished,' she added. 'Loved. Because we have done our best, under the circumstances.' Then she stood and began to clear our plates even though I had a bit of mushroom left on mine that I wanted to finish. 'Go upstairs and pack,' she said, still not meeting our eyes. 'The Van will be here soon.'

The Van. We'd seen it come for other boys: a grey, blunt-nosed vehicle with double doors at the back, and tinted windows, so if you tried to peer inside all you saw was your own dark reflection. It looked like the village butcher's van that delivered meat to people – pork sausages and lamb chops, sirloin and silverside, sweetbreads that weren't actually bread. The butcher's van didn't have the tinted windows, though.

Three small rucksacks waited in our bedroom. They wouldn't hold much – but then we wouldn't need much. Underwear, a few shirts, a couple of pairs of shorts. Our hairbrushes and our tooth-brushes. I would have taken my plastic soldier with the torn parachute and my Strepsils tin of feathers and stones, but for my own good Mother Morning hadn't returned my confiscated items. William said it didn't matter; I'd be able to start a whole new collection in Margate – feathers from seabirds, and stones from the beach which would be much nicer than the ones I'd found in our garden. And seaweed, maybe, I said, tracing the lines of the antler that rested on the windowsill. Shells too, said Lawrence, and all sorts of other things that the sea washed up, things we couldn't even imagine.

Then we caught a movement at the corners of our eyes – some-thing outside at the gates – and we ran to the window. Was the Van here already? Was it time to go? But no, the Van hadn't come – not yet. A pony had wandered into view and was nuzzling at the wrought iron, turning its head sideways to poke its muzzle through the bars. Two more ponies appeared and did the same, and we said how curious it was that they were trying to get in just as we were preparing to leave. Outside our window the day was pearly white.

We hooked our arms through the straps of our rucksacks and headed back downstairs. I was beginning to regret how much breakfast I'd eaten; I felt a bit sick as we descended, each step jolting everything I'd swallowed. We passed the portrait of the family who had first lived in the house, the woman letting the little girl stand on the afternoon-tea table, the boy in a dress restraining the gun dog, the father with his hand on the head of the other boy in a dress. The real fire leaping inside the fake-marble fireplace. This time we did touch the griffin's wings; they were smooth as glass.

'Should we take the Stickle Bricks?' said Lawrence. 'And the Mona Lisa jigsaw?'

We looked at one another. We'd have so much to do in Margate, we said, that we wouldn't need our old things, which we'd definitely outgrown. We'd be swimming at the beach. Exploring the Shell Grotto. Gazing up at the *Queen Mary* building as night fell, wondering if it might float out to sea, a shadow ship. Watching the motorcyclists ride the Wall of Death – backwards, sideways, no hands – and maybe even training to ride it ourselves. We'd be getting to know the other children in the Big House, meeting up with the Captain Scott boys and remembering all the names we'd forgotten. Burying one another in sand.

But then, it wouldn't hurt, would it? To take our old things? And we had the room.

Lawrence slipped the Stickle Bricks into his rucksack, and I slipped the Mona Lisa jigsaw into mine.

Then we were ready.

We sat and waited in the Entrance Hall, perched on the bottom stair. We could see ourselves in one of the old dark mirrors, our reflections all silty and indistinct, submerged in dirty water.

'How long is the trip?' said William.

'A few hours, I expect,' said Lawrence.

'Maybe more, if we stop to pick up other children,' I said.

On the table just in front of us one of Mother Afternoon's shallow vases stood empty. We could see the flower frog in the base – the block of metal spikes that held the stems upright when she made her ikebana arrangements. It looked like a Stickle Brick piece, only much harder and sharper. Normally it was invisible.

We fell silent. The air in the house seemed to clot around us as we sat with our rucksacks on our backs.

Mother Morning would be making us a packed lunch to take in the Van, we decided. That was where she must be.

At quarter past ten – although it wasn't anywhere near time for her shift – Mother Afternoon came downstairs carrying our pillows.

'Take them,' she said. 'You'll be more comfortable that way. It's nice to have something familiar with you, isn't it. Look, I've put clean pillowcases on.' She was holding them around their middles, hugging them to her chest. A sob flew from her mouth as she handed them to us. We didn't know what to say. Above us we heard the telephone ringing in the distant North Wing. Our pillows smelled of fresh air, and we leaned against them as we waited.

Then Mother Night appeared at the top of the stairs, and we worried that we had woken her and she would growl at us and write us up in The Book of Guilt – but no, we hadn't been running about like mad things; we hadn't been yelling and screaming. She passed between William and me, her satin dressing gown brushing across my cheek, and she whispered something in Mother Afternoon's ear. Glancing back at us, Mother Afternoon followed her in the direction of the Kitchen.

Well, said Lawrence, it was normal that Mother Night should come to say goodbye, even at this inconvenient hour, because she had known us our whole lives.

Yes, we nodded. Our whole lives.

And, despite everything, we were feeling gracious now that we were going to Margate – generous, even – and we would allow our mothers to put their arms around us if they so wished, and kiss our foreheads, and tell us they would gobble us up.

But it was nearly 10.30, and where were they? What if the Van arrived at the gates and nobody was there to let it in? I went and watched through the front door to make sure we did not miss it. The Van was always very punctual.

At one point we heard raised voices coming from the Kitchen – Mother Morning shouting over Mother Afternoon, we thought, though we couldn't be sure. Then, just like that, they stopped.

'Should we take something to read?' said Lawrence. 'GERM–LOCK, because it has Graceful Birds of the Sea Coast? Or SEV–ZWI, because it has British Shells of Land and Water?'

'Won't they have The Book of Knowledge at the Big House?' said William.

'They definitely will,' I said. 'Maybe other books too.'

'*Other* books?' said Lawrence.

'What sort of other books?' said William.

'I don't know. Something by Shakespeare, whose work has the ease and careless grace of all masterpieces. Or . . . or James Joyce, who is remarkable for a style verging sometimes on incoherence. We don't really know what it'll be like, do we?'

And my brothers agreed: we didn't really know.

Lawrence took off his rucksack and double-checked he'd remembered his toothbrush. William got up and poked at the flower frog in the bottom of the ikebana vase, pressing against the spikes and inspecting the marks they left behind.

'Be careful,' I said. 'You'll hurt yourself.'

Our mothers returned to the Entrance Hall then, and Mother Morning cleared her throat.

'It appears there's been a change of plans,' she said. 'It appears that a family in Exeter – a married couple – is interested in meeting you.'

'But we're going to Margate,' said Lawrence. 'Exeter's in completely the other direction.'

'Yes,' said Mother Morning. 'We'll have to cancel Margate, I'm afraid.'

'You can't cancel it!' said William. 'It's our turn!' He was holding the flower frog in his fist now, pushing the sharp side into the flesh of his hand.

'I know this will come as a disappointment,' said Mother Morning.

Mother Afternoon and Mother Night flanked her, and all three wore the same expression: yes, a disappointment, but nothing to be done.

'The thing is, we got the brochure,' said Lawrence, reaching into his rucksack and pulling it out to show them. The boy clutching the throat of the swan; the boy buried up to his neck. 'See? Whoever gets the brochure goes to Margate. That's how it works.'

'I know how it works,' said Mother Morning, 'but Margate is off, at least for the time being.'

We could hardly believe it. William was grasping the flower frog so tightly he'd started to bleed, but he seemed not to have noticed. He was looking at each of our mothers in turn, waiting for a proper explanation.

'Your hand,' I murmured, and he glanced down at the blood.

Mother Morning sighed and said, 'Must you, William?' She passed him a handkerchief from the pocket of her housecoat.

'We've had word from the Minister, you see,' said Mother Afternoon. 'She telephoned just now and spoke to Mother Night.'

We'd heard the telephone ring, so perhaps it was true.

Mother Night nodded and said, 'Fletcher is their name – a Mr and Mrs Fletcher in Exeter. They're very keen to arrange a home visit with a view to taking one of you.'

'Only one of us?' I said.

'I'm sure there will be other families before too long,' said Mother Night. 'The Minister will be arranging it.'

'And we must do as the Minister asks,' said Mother Morning. 'Every little thing, even if we had other plans – better plans – in mind.'

'Exeter was besieged by William the Conqueror but held out valiantly, admitting him at last on honourable terms,' said Lawrence.

'Yes,' said Mother Afternoon. 'Very good.'

Then the Van pulled up at the gates and tooted its horn, waiting to be let in. Mother Morning made her way down the driveway but opened only one gate, and we could see her motioning to the driver to wind down his window and shaking her head a few times as she explained. Shielding our eyes from the glare of the pearly sky, we tried to see in through the windscreen, past the driver in his grey cap. And surely behind him we could make out half a dozen other children? And surely they were peering through the windscreen too, trying to see us? But then Mother Morning closed the gate, and the Van disappeared into the white morning.

The Minister of Loneliness

And finally, just over a week after the television clip aired, a call came: a childless couple in Exeter were interested in the New Forest triplets and wanted to look into adopting one of them. They realised they were older than most parents – both fifty-eight – but they hoped this wouldn't count against them, because they truly believed – they *knew* – they could offer one of those poor creatures a stable and loving home.

The Minister put down the phone and allowed herself a self-congratulatory whoop. A social worker would have to pay them a visit, of course, and arrange for a background check . . . but these things could take weeks to put in place. So mightn't she expedite the process? Conduct the visit herself, for instance? (And – a fleeting thought – take all the glory.) Yes, she needed to move things along as promptly as possible. With one family on board, she had something to work with – something that could generate excellent publicity around the rehomings. Pictures of a happy, well-adjusted, perfectly normal boy with his new parents – flying a kite in the park, perhaps, or running through drifts of autumn leaves, or feeding ducks. Now, surely, the tide would turn. Everyone would want a Sycamore child. They'd be queuing up.

*

The boxy, pebble-dashed bungalow lay on the outskirts of Exeter in a quiet cul-de-sac. The Fletchers must have been watching for her car, because they opened the front door before she was halfway up the path and said, 'Welcome to our home. How kind of you to travel all this way. Won't you come in?'

A concrete birdbath stood in the front garden, topped with a boy, a girl and a whimsical basset hound taking shelter under an umbrella. Inside, the house was spotless. Plastic on the three-piece suite to protect the brown velour, coasters to protect the tables, doilies underneath all the lamps and the bowl of perfect fruit in the sitting room. Net curtains at the windows, a draught excluder shaped like a caterpillar at the bottom of the front door. The place smelled faintly of furniture polish and bleach and – less faintly – cooked fish.

'I do apologise,' said Mrs Fletcher. 'We had cod last night, and it's lingering. We should have thought.'

'Not at all,' said the Minister. 'I enjoy a nice piece of cod myself.'

'We eat fish once a week,' said Mr Fletcher. 'For the good of our health,' he added. 'We're not Catholic or anything.'

'Not that we mind Catholics,' said Mrs Fletcher.

'My goodness,' said the Minister, taking in the miniature village that filled two-thirds of the sitting room, 'what's all this?'

'Kenneth's pride and joy,' said Mrs Fletcher.

'Keeps me out of mischief,' said Mr Fletcher.

The Minister studied the tiny houses and shops. The detail was remarkable – slate roofs made from the thinnest slivers of wood overlapped row on row and painted dark grey; windows and doors that could open and close; dozens of tiny trees, no two alike; a gushing stream that looked so real she couldn't help but touch the water.

'Dried glue,' said Mr Fletcher. 'One of the tricks of the trade.'

'You built all this yourself?' said the Minister.

'Every inch.'

'You must be a very patient man.'

'I suppose I am.'

'We thought it might appeal to one of the boys,' said Mrs Fletcher. 'It might be a nice hobby for him – something he and Kenneth could do together.'

The Minister caught the note of wistfulness in her voice. 'Yes,' she said. 'I think it's exactly the sort of thing that would appeal.'

While they made afternoon tea, she waited on the plastic-covered sofa. She glanced at the magazines in the wicker rack, all mail-order catalogues: Empire, GUS, Littlewoods, Kays. A framed wedding photo on the mantelpiece showed Mrs Fletcher slender in white satin and a Juliet cap, Mr Fletcher clasping his hands awkwardly in front of his double-breasted suit. They looked about sixteen. Would it be intrusive – would it be *wrong* – to take a quick look at the contents of the sideboard? She eased open the top drawer: a set of binoculars, a box of garish placemats, an oversized hourglass, a second set of binoculars. How still the house was, as if the Fletchers had gone out and left her there quite alone. Through the net curtains she could see a sparrow in the birdbath; it shimmied its tiny body and flicked its wings, splashing the concrete children underneath their umbrella – but this was no time to be watching birds.

The drawer stuck a little as she eased it closed, and the bowl of perfect fruit wobbled. She caught a pear before it fell – wax, she realised. Wax apples and wax bananas too, and a single wax orange dotted with hundreds of microscopic pores, just like a real one. Her parents had owned a similar assortment when she was growing up; her father had bought them for her mother's birthday, explaining when she unwrapped them that they'd add a bit of colour to the place, besides which they'd never rot or attract fruit flies. For years they'd sat on the kitchen table, and her mother had pretended to like them – but such things were quite old-fashioned now. As the Minister replaced the pear she noticed a gouge in its side, and for one awful moment she thought she might have done it herself – grasped it too tightly, pressed her thumb into the wax somehow.

But no. No. She couldn't have caused such damage just by holding it. She peered at the dull white wax where the skin was missing – nothing like the inside of a real pear – and then she made out the tooth marks. Someone had taken a bite.

She thought she heard the Fletchers' footsteps, so she returned the pear to the bowl and took her seat on the sofa once more. When they didn't appear, she held her breath and listened hard – and there was the sound again, just through the wall behind the sideboard. Not footsteps but a tapping, a pattering, like the first uncertain drops of rain before a downpour.

'Here we are,' said Mrs Fletcher, bustling in with a tray of tea and biscuits. 'Kenneth, the safari-animal teaspoons, please.'

Mr Fletcher went to the sideboard and opened the top drawer, and the Minister felt herself blushing. Had she left everything as she'd found it? Would he know, somehow, that moments before she'd been rummaging through their belongings?

'Lion, elephant, zebra, giraffe, cheetah or gazelle?' he said, offering her the case of spoons.

'Oh,' she said. 'Let me see . . . well, I think the zebra.'

'Quite right,' he said.

She wasn't sure what that meant.

'Marjorie?'

'I'll be the cheetah,' said Mrs Fletcher.

He took the elephant for himself. 'Just a bit of fun,' he said. 'We make a point of finding fun.'

After a few sips of tea, the Minister took her notepad from her handbag. 'Perhaps you can tell me what prompted you to look into adoption,' she said. 'You won't mind if I jot a few things down?'

Oh, of course not, of *course* not, they said. They understood that there were certain procedures, and they were more than happy to answer questions on any topic at all. They were an open book.

She asked them where they grew up and how they met, whether they were religious and how they resolved disagreements and what role extended family played in their lives, if any. Would they say they were stable, financially speaking? How many hours a week, on average, did Mr Fletcher work at the engraver's? Was he fulfilled in his job, was he happy? What about their health – any issues there? Any niggles that could turn into issues? And where did they stand on discipline? If a behavioural challenge arose – a physical altercation, for argument's sake – how would they deal with it? Could they describe a typical weekend? Could they describe a typical breakfast, lunch and supper?

Outside in the birdbath, at the feet of the concrete boy and girl and the mournful basset hound, the sparrows washed themselves clean.

'Now,' said the Minister, 'I realise that this may be a sensitive subject—'

'Ask away, please,' said Mr Fletcher.

'Nothing is off limits,' said Mrs Fletcher.

'Well,' said the Minister, 'perhaps you can tell me why you never had children yourselves.'

'We wanted to,' said Mrs Fletcher. 'And I did fall pregnant. I did. Except it never lasted. We couldn't manage to keep the babies.'

'We saw doctor after doctor, and not one of them could find the cause,' said Mr Fletcher. 'But clearly something was very wrong.'

'And you didn't consider adoption then?'

Mrs Fletcher rubbed her thumb back and forth over the cheetah on the end of her teaspoon. 'For a long while,' she said, 'I couldn't look at a baby. Not even on television.'

'Yes, I see,' said the Minister. She heard the soft pattering again on the other side of the wall. Could it be mice? Rats? Furtive, gnawing creatures hidden away? Maybe that explained the bite mark in the wax pear. 'I do apologise,' she said, 'but I need to ask – do you have a rodent problem?'

'A rodent problem, Minister?'

'Some kind of infestation – only I keep hearing noises behind that wall. *In* the wall, perhaps.'

All three of them looked over at the sideboard and listened.

'I can't hear anything myself,' said Mr Fletcher, 'but it would have been Cloud, our cat. She squeezes herself into all sorts of places.'

'Yes,' said Mrs Fletcher, 'she's a very naughty girl, but we love her to bits.'

The Minister was still listening so intently that she just about bit her tongue when a cuckoo clock sounded; really, she needed to pull herself together. Apologising, she suggested they show her the rest of the house.

There were two modest bedrooms – a master and a spare – with nylon bedspreads and furniture in the Queen Anne style. A carpeted bathroom with a khaki-green bath and basin and a gold soap dish shaped like a shell. A third bedroom set up as a sewing room, the machine tucked away under a patchwork cover decorated with cockerels. A paper pattern pinned to a length of dark-blue corduroy lay across the bed – and yes, a cat padded across the mustard carpet, stretched, then brushed against the Minister's tights. At the back of the house, off the dining room, a conservatory; Mr Fletcher said they'd had it installed to add value, and so they could sit inside but feel as if they were outside. Begonias and geraniums and African violets bloomed in pots, and two wicker chairs, brittle from the sun, faced out to the small private garden.

Mrs Fletcher pinched off a dead leaf from a begonia and, gazing at it, said, 'Could you give us an indication of what our chances are, Minister, do you think?'

'Only we've our hearts set on meeting the boys,' said Mr Fletcher.

'Would you be available for a home visit next week?' said the Minister. 'You'd need to take a few hours off work, Mr Fletcher.'

Certainly, certainly, they said. And their chances . . .?

'I can tell you that your application is very strong,' said the Minister. 'But I wouldn't want to get your hopes up before we've organised the home visit.'

'I suppose you've had quite a bit of interest in them,' said Mr Fletcher. 'What with them being on television.'

'Yes,' the Minister found herself saying, 'we've fielded several inquiries about the triplets.'

Well, and what did it matter if she gave the impression the boys were in hot demand? If it convinced the Fletchers to take one of them, where was the harm?

The night-time carer sounded quite flustered when the Minister phoned.

'The boys have been poorly,' she said. 'I don't think they're up to travelling.'

'It's only to Exeter,' said the Minister. 'I'm sure they'll be all right by Wednesday.'

'Wednesday?' said the carer. 'You mean the day after tomorrow?'

'Yes, Wednesday,' said the Minister.

'The thing is, we've been very concerned about their health. Concerned enough to contact Dr Roach.'

'What's wrong with them?'

'Hard to say. Some sort of serious reaction.'

'You've stopped all medication, though?'

'Of course, as directed. But occasionally, as you know, the side-effects can be long term. Fatal, even.'

Flustered, thought the Minister, and very tense. Possibly on the verge of tears. 'I think I understand what's going on,' she said.

'Oh?' said the carer.

'You've become close to the boys over the years. That's only natural. Only *human*. But now we need to let them go.'

'Let them go,' said the carer.

'Yes,' said the Minister.

Silence on the other end of the phone.

'Are you still there?'

'What if something goes wrong?' said the carer. 'Undesirable behaviour that might . . . reflect badly?'

'Nothing will go wrong. We've taken special precautions to ensure that. The Socialisation Days, for instance.'

'What if something undesirable happened on a Socialisation Day?'

'We'd look into it.'

'And if nobody reported it to the Ministry?'

'That would be a serious omission with serious consequences.'

Another silence.

'*Did* something happen?'

'No,' said the carer. 'I was just wondering.'

'If you can make sure the boys are ready by ten o'clock on Wednesday, then – that'll get us to Exeter for lunch.'

'They'll need proper supervision,' said the carer. 'Not just on Wednesday. The people should keep a close eye on them.'

'I'm confident they'll make excellent parents to whichever boy they take,' said the Minister.

And then she thought the strangest thing: I hope they don't take Vincent.

Nancy

One morning, a few days after her parents had browsed through the catalogue of children, they told her a lady was coming to the house. Ladies were far rarer than men – men like Barry Sedgwick. Nancy wasn't sure what the purpose of her visit might be. Could ladies fix things? Stop a flood, prevent a fire? 'Is something broken?' Nancy asked, but her parents said no, everything was perfect.

When the lady was due to arrive, Nancy crawled into the wardrobe with her sandwich and her mother shut the door. For a moment she couldn't see a thing, not even her own hand, not even the white of the bread, but slowly her eyes adjusted, and she began to make out the shapes of the skirts and dresses that hung about her head, empty and soft. She'd brought her Spirograph set with her, and she pinned the largest plastic ring to a sheet of paper, then felt for the saw-toothed wheels and coloured pens. She couldn't tell what she was creating, but that was half the excitement – only when she emerged from the wardrobe would she see what she had dreamt up in the dark.

Soon she heard a knock at the front door, and her parents were inviting the lady inside and showing her through to the sitting room. Their voices were a little clearer there, and Nancy pressed her ear to the wall.

'. . . a nice hobby for him,' her mother was saying. 'Something he and Kenneth could do together.'

Her parents were calling the lady *Minister*, so perhaps she'd come to talk to them about God. They didn't believe in him and pitied those who did; usually if such people knocked at their door, they explained in their most apologetic voices that he was not real.

The conversation had stopped, and Nancy could hear nothing but her own breathing. Inch by inch she turned around, careful not to make the Spirograph wheels clatter or the clothes hangers jangle. She pressed her hands to the wall until her imaginary piano took shape beneath her fingertips, the keys smooth and cool, and she began to pick out a tune – the song from *Jim'll Fix It* about a letter being only the start of it, only the start of Jim fixing whatever you asked him to. Back and forth she swept her fingers, up and down the notes, singing the words in her head. Sometimes the root of her tongue ached to sing out loud – to shout or even scream – but she knew she mustn't. At such moments, to distract herself, she counted all the buttons on the clothes and always got one hundred and nine. She started on the far left today, with the duffle coat's long wooden toggles: one, two, three, four . . . Then she heard someone on the other side of the wall opening a drawer in the credenza, shifting things around, and it might have been her mother or her father, but it also might have been the lady, the Minister. Nancy sat perfectly still, as if she were not a real girl, just an empty dress like all the other dresses in the wardrobe. Her jam sandwich felt damp on her bare knee.

Eventually the person closed the drawer and retreated, and Nancy breathed out and began the *Jim'll Fix It* song where she'd left off. If she could write to him, she thought, what would she ask him to fix? How would you ever decide? On the last episode she'd watched, two girls spun around, and in a flash of light both turned into Wonder Woman. Anything was possible.

When the voices started up again, the lady wanted to know all sorts of things, private things, as far as Nancy could tell, and she made out her father saying *she's an owl and I'm a lark, but we've*

273

learned to accommodate it and *we're comfortable but careful* and *a bit of arthritis when it's cold.* Nancy's mother said *I suppose we'd withdraw to a safe place*, and after that she was rattling off *porridge, tea and toast; sausages, peas, mashed potatoes, and maybe a nice apple crumble; something lighter in the evening – I've been experimenting with cheese soufflé.*

Nancy didn't understand the next thing the lady said, and thought she must have misheard. *Perhaps you can tell me why you never had children yourselves.* She flattened her ear to the wall to hear her parents' reply, but they didn't put the lady right. *We wanted to*, said her mother. *And I did fall pregnant. I did. Except it never lasted. We couldn't manage to keep the babies.*

The words pelted through the wall. What had happened to these babies that hadn't lasted, that they hadn't managed to keep? And if they hadn't kept any, what did that make Nancy?

The cuckoo clock sounded three o'clock, and the lady let out a shriek.

I'm terribly sorry, she said. *That took me by surprise.*

Later, when Nancy's father came to let her out, her leg had gone to sleep and she couldn't walk properly.

'Oopsy daisy,' he said, grabbing her arm before she fell.

She blinked in the glare of the bright afternoon.

'Did you draw some nice pictures?' her father asked.

Nancy looked down at the patterns she'd made with the Spirograph, the lines all off-kilter, none of them meeting up where they should. The pages were creased too, and smeared with jam. She thought she'd been so careful.

'It's *The Generation Game* tonight,' he said. 'Shall we watch it together?'

'All right,' said Nancy.

'Good girl.'

They made their way into the sitting room, and she steadied herself on the credenza. The bite mark was showing in the wax pear, and somehow she could taste it, the inside of the fruit too white, too hard, like the candles they kept for emergencies.

'Ah, there you are,' said her mother, as if Nancy had been lost for a time.

'I was just remarking that it's *The Generation Game* tonight,' said her father. 'We're going to watch it together. See if we can remember all the prizes on the conveyor belt.'

'That'll be nice,' said her mother. 'It's amazing what people win, isn't it. My goodness, if I had half a chance.'

Nancy thought of the things tucked away in the credenza – tucked away all over the house. Maybe one day her mother would have packed the place so tightly there'd be no room left for any people.

They'd have to move. Start again somewhere else.

Free.

She closed her eyes and breathed in all the fresh air she could hold, then tried to walk on her own. Still her leg felt dead; it would not support her.

'Give it a moment, love,' said her father. 'You'll come right.'

Vincent

'Just be yourselves,' the Minister said in the car on the way to Exeter. 'They want to get to know the real you.'

My brothers and I sat in the back seat, Lawrence in the middle and William and I on either side. It was pouring, and the windscreen wipers kept missing a patch. The raindrops clustered on the glass, now pulled together like mercury, now blown into long fingers of water.

'This better be good,' said William. 'As good as Margate.'

'I'm sorry?' said the Minister.

'It was our turn,' I explained. 'We were all packed and ready to go – the Van was on its way.'

'What van?'

'The Van to take us to Margate.'

Lawrence pulled the brochure from the back pocket of his good trousers – he'd kept it with him the whole time, even slept with it.

Wordlessly the Minister turned the pages, examining the photographs of the Dolphinarium, the Shell Grotto, Dreamland, the Big House, trailing her finger over the boy buried in sand. *This young chap's in trouble when the tide comes in!* 'I see,' she said at last.

'Have you ever been?' I asked.

'No,' she said, watching me with her pale-blue eyes that seemed to see everything. 'I don't know Margate at all.'

There was a strange look on her face as she returned the brochure to Lawrence, who folded it in half again and tucked it back in his pocket.

'We still might get to go,' he said. 'If the families don't want us.'

'Yes,' said the Minister. 'You still might.' She hesitated, then took a small card from her handbag, wrote something on it and passed it to me. 'In case you ever need to get in touch,' she said quietly. 'Day or night. That's my home number at the bottom.'

Then we were turning into the Fletchers' street, and we peered through the rainy windows at the small, neat houses and the low fences, the family cars parked in the driveways, and we tried to imagine what it might be like to live there. But we couldn't.

'What a dreadful day!' said Mrs Fletcher as she opened the front door. 'I'm so sorry!' She was a fine-boned woman, completely grey, with rouge rubbed into her sallow cheeks.

'She thinks she controls the weather,' said Mr Fletcher with a smile. He had laugh lines around his eyes, and black-rimmed glasses, and a bushy moustache but little hair.

They shook us each by the hand as if we were important.

'I hope you're hungry,' said Mr Fletcher. 'My wife's made enough to feed a dozen of you.'

'Doesn't it smell delicious?' said the Minister.

Yes, we agreed, very delicious.

We took off our anoraks in the passageway, and Mrs Fletcher hung them up by their hoods. The house was much smaller than Captain Scott: no panelled entrance hall hung with old dark mirrors, no grand staircase, and the ceiling so low above our heads that we thought we might have to duck – but the carpet stretched wall to wall and felt like a pelt of moss beneath our feet, like the softest eiderdown, and the air was warm as midsummer. We could hear something clattering, something humming and clicking, and when we entered the sitting room we saw it: a model train passing through a village that sprawled across table after table, hardly leaving room for the lounge suite. We ran to it, unable to believe our eyes. We'd always wondered about such toys – seen the occasional advertisement in the *Woman's Realm*, overheard the boys in the village talking about their brake vans and coke wagons – but we'd never dreamt of something on this scale. There were entire streets of pretty houses; rows of shops; a church and a school. A rushing stream, its grassy banks dotted with primroses. Little plastic people with painted-on clothes and faces – and a forest, a whole green forest, with oak, hazel and birch trees covered in spring leaves, the foliage so dense we couldn't see the forest floor. Here and there, birds no bigger than apple pips. Even a tiny nest of pale-blue eggs high in the branches. Everything bursting into life.

'Careful,' said the Minister, who had taken a seat in a plastic-covered armchair, but Mr Fletcher smiled a kind smile said, 'They're all right. Let them enjoy it.'

He showed us how to operate the train controls – reverse, forward, full speed, stop – and how to reroute a train to a siding so another could pass without disaster. We could load the wagons with cargo – little logs, bags of mail, sacks of sugar and flour – and sound the horn as we approached a level crossing to make sure nobody was on the tracks. We gasped when the lights went on in all the shops and houses, and we asked Mr Fletcher how he'd done it. Magic, he said, but we knew there must be some hidden switch that he was keeping from us – something he would share only with the chosen boy. We gasped, too, when we heard the cuckoo and the chiming bell, and at first we thought it must be part of the model village. We checked the tiny birds in the trees to see if they were singing – and then we saw the clock in the shape of a chalet on the sitting-room wall, and the cuckoo calling from its eaves. We rushed over to it, but by the time we got there the bird had shut itself away.

'Can you make it come out again?' asked William, and Mrs Fletcher looked at Mr Fletcher and said she supposed that would be all right, wouldn't it? And he said yes, that would be all right, so she reached up and nudged the hands back a couple of minutes.

'Wait for it. Wait for it,' she said, and we stood there without a word, barely daring to breathe in case we somehow scared the bird away, and we waited for it. At twelve o'clock it shot out, and each time it called a little man at the base of the chalet swung an axe at a log. We laughed and clapped our hands and wanted to see it again, but the Minister said we couldn't keep asking poor Mrs Fletcher to turn back the clock or we'd be there all day.

'They have a TV set too!' whispered William, pointing to the far corner of the room where the television sat on its square legs.

'Have you seen colour TV before?' said Mr Fletcher. 'What's your favourite programme?'

We didn't know, we couldn't think, and we felt stupid, and they might not want a stupid creature who couldn't answer an ordinary question.

But Mrs Fletcher said, 'Plenty of different ones to choose from. It's just a matter of finding out what tickles your fancy.'

And we nodded and said yes, yes, we'd love to have the chance to find out what tickled our fancy.

We returned to the model village, and Mr Fletcher began to move the plastic people around and invited us to do the same – perhaps this gentleman in the checked cap was on his way to church, or perhaps this lady with the shopping basket needed to pick up some grocery items. Lawrence placed a boy and a girl outside the sweet shop, looking in at the jars of lemon drops and pear drops, and I put a baby in a pram and set it in the shade of an oak tree while its family lounged in deckchairs nearby. William assembled a group of more than a dozen outside the hospital – doctors and nurses, children and parents, and a couple of patients on stretchers with bandages around their heads.

'What are they doing?' said Mr Fletcher.

'The hospital's on fire,' said William.

'How imaginative!' said the Minister.

William wedged the hospital door open with a plastic man, laying him face down on the ground so he was half in and half out of the building. Trying to escape, perhaps. Or perhaps not any more.

Mr Fletcher made no comment. Instead, pointing at the train as it passed by, he said, 'See the engine? That's real coal it's carrying in its tender, smashed down to the right size with a hammer.'

'On my dining table, I might add,' said Mrs Fletcher from the plastic-covered sofa.

'My husband once used my face flannel to polish his shoes,' said the Minister.

They both laughed and shook their heads at the hopelessness of their husbands.

'Plastic people but real coal?' said William.

'Check for yourself,' said Mr Fletcher, so when the train circled back again William grabbed a piece of coal, and I did too. It was shiny and smooth at first glance, but the more I looked, the more layers I saw: black horizons piled one on top of the other; lengths of satiny black hair.

'When we burn coal, we're burning the sunshine of long ago,' said Lawrence.

'Are we,' said Mrs Fletcher.

'Yes. Heat is energy, and that energy was collected from the sun by trees and plants which grew long before Man appeared on earth.'

Black dust smudged itself across my fingertip, the remains of a long-dead forest.

In reality, of course, said Mr Fletcher, the train wouldn't loop around the village – it would carry on to other places – but, as we could see, he didn't have the room to build those other places.

'I put my foot down,' said Mrs Fletcher, who was only pretending to be annoyed.

Mr Fletcher winked at us. 'She loves it as much as I do,' he said. 'She made all the mailbags, and all the bits of washing on the washing lines.' There really were tiny clothes pegged up in the gardens – vests and socks and trousers and skirts, and white bedsheets that fluttered in the currents we made as we loomed above the model village like gods, lifting cars with a single hand, plucking up whole families at once. I had a sudden desire to open a mailbag and check inside for letters no bigger than postage stamps, the writing too tiny to decipher with the naked eye. Round and round the train went, never really going anywhere. Never really leaving.

At lunch my brothers and I sat on one side of the table and the Fletchers sat on the other so they could watch us and decide which one they wanted. The Minister sat with them and exclaimed over the quantity of food, and said she would have to restrain herself or suffer serious waistband-related consequences, which was a roundabout way of saying she would get fat. The chairs were not Refectory chairs; they were covered in cushiony dark-gold brocade and must have cost a lot of money. Six placemats showed six different Celebrated English Inns. Mr Fletcher swished the carving knife across the steel and cut glistening slices of roast pork, and we helped ourselves to crispy potatoes and parsnips, and peas with mint, and carrots sliced on the diagonal so they looked fancy though they tasted the same as normal carrots. We kept our elbows off the table and held our forks the proper way, not the way little savages hold forks, and we made sure not to speak unless our mouths were empty. At one point I spilled my peas across the tablecloth that was patterned with brown flowers like they were all dead. I stared at the peas, and my brothers stared at me staring at the peas, and then I picked them up one by one and put them back on the edge of my plate and was careful not to eat them, because only people with no manners ate food they'd dropped.

'Save room for jam roly-poly and custard,' said Mrs Fletcher.

'Jam roly-poly!' said the Minister. 'And *custard*! What are you trying to do to me, Mrs Fletcher!'

We all laughed.

Then, as I was lifting a piece of pork to my mouth, I saw a line of white hairs along the skin. Perhaps I faltered – perhaps the disgust showed on my face – because I could sense Mr and Mrs Fletcher watching me to see what I would do. And of course the polite thing would have been to place the meat in my mouth, then chew it and swallow it, giving no indication that I could feel the bristles poking the flesh of my tongue, scratching my throat as they slipped down inside me. That would have been the polite thing. But the hairs were too real; they looked like pale eyelashes, like the fuzz on Cynthia's muzzle. I thought of the cockroach I'd swallowed for William, all the medicine I'd swallowed for our mothers. I lowered my fork and carefully cut the skin away, pushing it to the edge of my plate with the dropped peas. Then I ate the piece of meat. And when I stole a glance at Mrs Fletcher, an expression crossed her face so fleetingly I later wondered if I'd imagined it. For a split second her eyes narrowed and her mouth curled down, and I saw it: pure loathing. And I saw, too, Mr Fletcher placing his hand on the back of his wife's – to comfort her? To stop her from saying something? – before returning to his own meal. In the distance I heard the cuckoo sound one o'clock.

After lunch my brothers and I sat on the plastic-covered sofa while the Fletchers asked us about our hobbies. We liked Morning Exercise, we said, because it helped us to start the day with a healthy attitude, and we enjoyed crafts such as papier-mâché and woodwork. Only recently we'd made a very fine spice rack, and once we'd knotted a macramé owl for Mother Afternoon which she assured us she'd hung in her room in the North Wing.

'An owl!' said the Minister. 'From macramé!'

There was a short silence, and then Lawrence said we knew how to find food in the outdoors – mushrooms and watercress and things that were perfectly safe to eat. I said we were good at tidying up after ourselves – making our beds and putting away our clothes and doing the washing up. Oh, and cricket! said William. Yes, we agreed: cricket was probably our principal hobby. Our father had been good at it, and in fact at one time had thought he might be able to do something with his cricket, so it must be in the blood. We liked football too – not as much as cricket, but sometimes I helped Mother Afternoon with the Spot the Ball contest.

'Your father?' Mr Fletcher said pleasantly, and I was about to explain that although he'd had a heart attack, it turned out it wasn't fatal – but then the Minister cut in and said she'd seen us playing cricket, and we really were very good. And I understood that we shouldn't mention our father, because the Fletchers might want to be our parents – or the parents of one of us, at least – and they wouldn't want to know about other parents.

We shifted a little on the sofa, trying to think of more hobbies, and the plastic squeaked underneath us. Then a white cat strolled into the room, glanced at the three of us in turn, and jumped into Lawrence's lap.

'Hello, you,' he said, scratching it behind the ears and under the chin, and it purred and closed its eyes. I remember thinking that Lawrence had passed some kind of test – that he'd already been chosen.

'Would you look at that,' murmured Mrs Fletcher. 'She hates just about everybody.'

'I'm going to be a vet,' said Lawrence.

'He'll have to kill some of them, though,' said William.

'No I won't.'

'It's the kindest thing.'

'I *won't*.'

'Anyway, that's all in the distant future,' said the Minister.

The cat rolled onto her back and stretched out her paws, and we stroked her exposed belly. It was the softest thing I'd ever touched, much softer than Cynthia's coat. I scratched her chin, and I could feel her tiny frame vibrating as she purred, as if she had an engine inside. I would have liked to bury my face in her.

'Would she sleep on a person's bed?' asked Lawrence. 'If you left the door open, say, would she creep in and jump up on the bed and stay there all night?'

'She would,' said Mr Fletcher. 'She does.'

Lawrence beamed.

And then I'm not sure what happened – one of us must have

touched her in a painful spot, I think – because she flinched and twisted and leapt away to the corner of the room, where she sat licking a paw.

'Hey,' said Lawrence, approaching her with his hand out. 'I'm sorry. I'm sorry. Did we hurt you?'

She flattened her ears and hissed, glaring at him with her goblin eyes. I thought Lawrence might cry.

Mrs Fletcher picked her up and put her outside through the French doors. The cat sat on the other side of the glass, on the other side of the net curtains, just a white blur now, like something we couldn't quite remember.

I said, 'The Egyptians tamed the wild cat, *Felis ocreata*, to protect their stores of grain.'

'Did they,' said Mr Fletcher.

'Some people,' I went on, 'notably the French, believed that witches could turn themselves into cats, so they often cruelly killed these charming creatures.'

'I wish I could turn myself into a cat,' said William. 'I'd be an ocelot. No, a serval.'

'Built for speed over short distances,' I said. 'Lives on small quadrupeds in the jungle.'

'Mm,' said the Minister. 'It's fun to play make-believe, isn't it.'

Lawrence had returned to the model village, and Mr Fletcher said, 'Good idea. Come on, boys – all aboard!' He started up a train for us again – the passenger train this time, full of people he must have manoeuvred into the seats with tweezers – then asked the Minister if he could tempt her to a Harveys Bristol Cream.

'Just a thimble, thank you, Mr Fletcher,' said the Minister. 'Half a thimble, even.'

'Marjorie?'

'You'll be the ruin of me.'

'What happens if there's an obstacle on the tracks?' said William. He was leaning in to try to read the tiny newspaper headlines outside the corner shop.

'Well,' said Mr Fletcher over his shoulder, unstoppering a cut-glass decanter, 'sometimes the train pushes the obstacle aside, and sometimes the obstacle pushes the train aside.'

'Derailment?' said William.

'Potentially. But it's very rare.'

Lawrence was unlatching a garden gate and lifting a plastic man on a bicycle out onto the pavement. He set a little brown dog in the basket on the front, then moved them along, stopping to let the man chat with his plastic neighbours – a woman in a striped apron, a boy and girl in school uniforms. They didn't speak actual words; Lawrence just waggled them from side to side and made humming sounds – deeper for the man on the bicycle, higher for the woman and the children. Off the man went again, his knitted waistcoat picked out in diamonds of grey and green paint, even a pair of bicycle clips painted around his ankles. He biked past the school, where the teacher stood at the doorway as the class filed in, their satchels slung over their shoulders. He biked past the Post Office, where a lady balanced three parcels wrapped in paper and string. Nearing the level crossing and the red sign that said *STOP*, he looked to the left at the approaching train, decided there wasn't enough time to cross safely, and balanced on his bike to wait for the carriages to rush by. Lawrence let go of him then, and William swooped his hand down and gave the man the tiniest flick, and he tumbled forwards onto the tracks, the little dog spilling from the basket. Too late to save either of them: the train struck the man in the back of the head, colliding with his jaunty cap, while the dog glanced off the wheel and went flying. The bicycle flipped upside down and the train pushed it along, dragging the man across the sleepers, clunk-thunk, clunk-thunk, until he disappeared underneath it. William laughed while Lawrence just stood there, his hand covering his mouth as the engine collapsed on its side and lay like a shieldbug kept too long in a jar.

None of the adults had noticed the disaster. They sat sipping their glasses of Harveys Bristol Cream, the Minister murmuring that they should take some time to decide, by all means, but she'd hate them to miss out so they shouldn't take too long.

Lawrence went to retrieve the little dog, but William got there first, enclosing the figure in his fist. 'Is this what you want?' he said, waving it under Lawrence's nose. 'Come and get it, then! It's right here for the taking!' He uncurled his fingers to let Lawrence glimpse the dog, then snapped them shut again. Lawrence kept snatching at William, and William kept dancing out of reach, just as he always did. Nothing could touch him. Finally, growing tired of the game, he pitched the dog into the thickest part of the forest, where it dropped through the canopy and disappeared.

'Why would you do that?' said Lawrence. He tried to part the trees, but they stood so close together he couldn't see through them. The tiny blue eggs shook in their nest. He really was starting to cry now, so I helped him search for the dog. It couldn't have gone far, I said; it would be somewhere just here. It wasn't *lost* lost. As I reached my fingers down through the wiry branches, I felt something, and peered in – but it wasn't the dog. A little wooden cross marked a spot at the base of a birch tree. Invisible unless you were looking right there.

'We'll never find it!' said Lawrence, his voice cracking. 'It's gone!'

Only then did the adults notice that anything was wrong. Mr Fletcher leapt to his feet, and in a few strides he'd reached us. 'What's up, chaps?' he said. Then he saw the train. The collapsed engine, the zig-zagged carriages, all the passengers thrown from their seats. 'Oh my God,' he said. 'How did this happen?'

'Lawrence was being irresponsible,' said William.

'No I wasn't,' sobbed Lawrence. 'He pushed the man on the bicycle onto the tracks.'

'Shut up,' said William, shoving him.

'Yes, let's just leave it,' I said, not because I wanted to defuse things for Lawrence, but because I was worried for William. Always William.

'Now then,' began Mr Fletcher.

'And he threw the little dog into the forest,' added Lawrence.

'I did not!' shouted William, shoving him harder.

'He did it on purpose.'

Another shove, and Lawrence fell backwards. William was on top of him then, hitting him, holding him down by the throat. Ruining everything.

'What is going *on*?' said the Minister. 'William, stand up!'

Lawrence was starting to turn purple.

'I said stand up!'

She tried to catch hold of him, but he was twisting and bucking as Lawrence struggled. At her touch, William let out a low growl, so I grabbed him by the back of the collar and hauled him off Lawrence, who lay on the mustard carpet and gasped. For a moment no one spoke.

Then Mr Fletcher said, 'My brother and I used to get up to high jinks too.'

And Mrs Fletcher said, 'Would anybody like a fizzy drink?'

In the background, the wheels of the train still buzzed like flies.

'I doubt they've ever encountered a model train set before,' said the Minister. 'Have you, boys?'

No, we said, shaking our heads, we'd never encountered one. We took small sips of our cherryade; we'd never encountered that before either, and the bubbles filled our mouths with tiny shocks and crawled down our throats.

'We became a bit over-excited,' the Minister went on. 'Yes? A bit exuberant?'

Yes, yes, we'd become over-excited and exuberant.

'So I think we can all agree we're very sorry,' she said. 'Can't we.'

'Sorry,' said Lawrence.

'Sorry,' said William.

I said it too, even though I'd had nothing to do with the fight, because I could see the way the Minister was eyeing us.

Mrs Fletcher waved a hand. 'Really, there's no need,' she said.

'No need,' echoed Mr Fletcher.

'Well, I'm sure the boys will tidy up the mess and find the little dog,' said the Minister.

'They're our guests,' said Mr Fletcher, smiling his kind smile, the lines around his eyes crinkling. 'Guests don't have to tidy up.'

I finished the last of my cherryade and said I could show him the exact spot in the forest where the dog had disappeared.

But again he said no; he'd sort all that out later.

They held open our anoraks for us when we were leaving. 'There we are now,' said Mrs Fletcher, helping us slip our arms into the sleeves, untucking the hood of mine when I got it caught under the collar. 'It's been so lovely to meet you all.'

'A real pleasure,' said Mr Fletcher.

'I'll be in touch, yes?' said the Minister.

As our car pulled away, they stood at the gate and waved, and when they could no longer see us the Minister slumped in her seat and closed her eyes. 'That could have gone better,' she said.

William stared at his knees. 'Did I ruin everything?'

'Let's just wait and see what happens.'

'Will you have to tell our mothers?'

'We'll keep it to ourselves.'

'Stupid, *stupid*,' he muttered, punching himself in the head.

'Don't do that,' said the Minister, but he kept on punching himself.

The driver turned around at the end of the cul-de-sac, and we passed the Fletchers' house again – and there they still stood at the gate, waving and waving, framed by the thick hedge. The driver tooted the horn.

Then, a few houses further down the street, Lawrence let out a cry.

'My brochure!' he said, checking all his pockets. 'It's gone! It's gone!'

'Never mind,' said the Minister. 'I'm sure—'

But Lawrence cut her off. 'We waited years,' he said. 'Every night we checked our beds, hoping it might be our turn. I *want* my *brochure.*' It wasn't like him.

'All right,' she said, motioning for the driver to pull into the kerb. 'We'll find it.'

We looked on the floor and in the crack at the back of the seat, and we lifted the mats, and Lawrence checked his pockets again. He even asked us to check our pockets. I found the Minister's card tucked against my breast, but there was no sign of the brochure anywhere.

Then I remembered how Lawrence had fallen when William had shoved him, and how the two of them had struggled on the carpet.

'It must have slipped out when you were fighting,' I said.

'They'll throw it away!' said Lawrence. 'They'll think it's rubbish!'

'No no,' said the Minister. 'We'll get Vincent to run back, shall we? Vincent?'

I let myself in through the gate in the hedge. At the base of the birdbath the white cat trained her goblin eyes on me and twitched her tail. I knocked on the front door, and when nobody answered I turned the handle.

'Hello?' I called. 'It's just me.'

Mr Fletcher appeared from a room off the passageway. He stopped, and I was certain a look of revulsion passed across his face.

'Just me,' I said again.

He shut the door behind him. 'Who is it?' he said, and I was confused – couldn't he see me? Then I realised that my anorak hid my yellow shirt. He didn't know which one I was.

'It's Vincent,' I said.

'What can I do for you?' he asked, smiling.

'Lawrence lost something, we think – a brochure. We think it fell out of his pocket when William . . . when they were on the floor.'

'A brochure?' said Mr Fletcher.

'Yes, a special brochure.' I felt a little foolish, coming back to ask for such a thing.

'Let's have a look then.'

In the sitting room Mrs Fletcher was scouring the sofa with a wet cloth, so intent on her cleaning she didn't hear us enter.

'Lawrence forgot something,' said Mr Fletcher, and she jumped then, and tried to hide her cloth behind her back.

'What did you forget, Lawrence?' she said.

'This is Vincent,' said Mr Fletcher.

'Vincent, yes,' she said.

I could see the damp streaks on the sofa, all across the back and over the seat, across the rolled arm where I'd rested my hand when I held my cherryade. 'Just a brochure,' I said.

Mr Fletcher knelt down and hunted under the trestle tables that supported the model village, pushing aside the curtains that screened off cartons of tools and parts – and there it was, between two shoeboxes of unpainted people. On the back page, the boy with the telescope gazed into the dark.

'Margate,' said Mr Fletcher, unfolding it. 'My parents took me there once. A donkey ate my ice cream, and they wouldn't buy me another.'

'You poor little love,' said Mrs Fletcher.

'Admittedly, I was teasing the donkey.'

He was still holding the brochure. I cleared my throat.

'Well, here we are. Was that everything now?'

'Yes, thank you.' I folded the brochure in half – the cover was starting to turn soft and furred, and to show tiny splits – and slipped it into my back pocket where it fitted me as neatly as it fitted Lawrence.

I don't know what made me look back at the house. As I approached the gate, I thought I sensed movement behind me, and I turned around, expecting to see . . . the white cat? The birds in the birdbath?

But the cat had disappeared, and the birdbath was empty, and the Fletchers had not come outside to wave me off this time; I was quite alone. Then I saw it – a net curtain stirring in the window to the left of the front door. As I watched, a white hand pushed the curtain aside, and then a white face appeared behind the glass. Long black hair, skinny shoulders. The girl we'd dreamt about, all shimmery and strange, living and breathing right here – wasn't she? She looked terrified to see me, and I had to stop myself from screaming. We stared at each other for a moment, neither of us daring to move, and then she mouthed a single word. And the word was *Run*.

I fumbled with the latch on the gate; the hedge felt low and close around me as I passed through to the street, and what if the car had disappeared and I had no way of getting home? What if I had to go back to the Fletchers, to the house with the ghostly girl? But there was the car, a few houses down, waiting for me with its engine still thrumming. And Lawrence must have seen me sprinting for it, because the door opened, and I climbed in.

'Are you all right?' he said.

'Of course.' I wanted to turn around to check if the girl was behind us, snatching at the back of the car, her black hair flying, but I forced myself to look straight ahead.

'Did you get it?'

'Did I get what?'

'My *brochure*.'

'Yes.'

'Where is it, then?'

'In my pocket.'

'Well, can I have it?'

I had a bad feeling, like the bad feeling I'd had about Jane. I gave him the brochure, then reached up and locked the passenger door.

PART THREE

The Book of Guilt

Nancy

After the lady's visit, Nancy couldn't stop thinking about the babies her parents hadn't managed to keep. When her father was at the engraver's and her mother was at the shops, she started poking about. People took photos of their babies, didn't they? And kept bits and pieces to remember them by? The cupboard in the sewing room was filled with all the pictures her parents had taken of her, and locks of her hair tucked away like dead moths, and teeth that rattled inside an old film canister. A carton covered with embossed wallpaper held little woollen things she'd worn – a musty bonnet, its ribbons dotted with rust; booties as soft as Cloud's ears. Surely, if they'd had other babies, they'd have kept mementoes of them too?

She started in her parents' room, searching the shelves at the top of the wardrobe where they stored their summer clothes when it was winter and their winter clothes when it was summer. She looked under their bed and in their drawers, pushing aside her mother's fawn underwear and her father's socks balled into fists. In the sewing room, apart from her own things, she found only offcuts from the skirts and blouses her mother had made for her, the pieces bright and unworn; the tin of buttons she used to use for money when playing shops with her dolls; the stacks of paper patterns with the pictures of girls holding baskets and beach balls and tennis rackets and skipping ropes, shading their eyes with their hands, laughing with other girls who were their friends. Nothing unexpected in the credenza either, or in the kitchen cupboards and drawers – just the placemats and travel clocks and novelty hourglasses her mother had ordered.

Then she thought of the loft.

She'd only once seen her parents open the hatch. They'd thought she was asleep, but she'd heard strange noises and had got up and crept to her bedroom door – and there in the passageway her father was pulling down a folding ladder and climbing into the ceiling. Her mother had noticed her then and had taken her back to bed, and when Nancy had asked about the ladder her mother had explained that the roof was leaking and her father was fixing it, but that Nancy must never be tempted to explore the loft herself, because it was a dangerous place for children and she might come to grief.

'What's up there, though?' Nancy had asked.

'Nothing but dust and spiders,' her mother had said.

Nancy listened now for the sound of her mother's car, but everything was quiet. Tucking a torch in her pocket, she dragged a dining chair into the passageway, making sure to rub away the track marks in the carpet, then balanced a stool on the padded seat. Carefully, carefully she climbed up, reached for the hook and pulled down the ladder.

The loft looked rough and unfinished, not a proper room at all. The timber holding up the roof was splintery, pitted with knotholes, and Nancy could see nails poking out here and there, as if the whole thing might collapse when the wind blew. She inhaled the dry, motionless air; it smelled like the lawn in summer, when the grass shrivelled away and you could see the dirt underneath trodden down hard. In the torchlight she could make out spiders with legs as skinny as a single hair, and dust caught in soft whorls like dandelion clocks. The space was empty apart from two suitcases that stood a few feet from the hatch, their leather straps worn and their clasps rusty.

Slowly, so she didn't come to grief, Nancy crawled across the gritty floor. The larger case was heavy and thudded as she laid it flat, sending up shivers of dust. Inside, packed in three neat piles, were photograph albums with thick black pages soft as felt. The first one was filled with pictures of herself that she recognised from the albums down in the sewing room: there she was as a dark-haired baby in her flouncy bassinet, and as a little girl crawling across the floor in nothing but a nappy, and as a toddler squashing stewed apple with her fingers. Leafing through them, however, she noticed that all the photos were black and white rather than colour – and then, when she looked more closely, she realised that while her poses and hairstyles and clothing were familiar, the pictures weren't quite the same as the ones she knew from downstairs.

She grabbed another album and saw herself as an older child on a swing. In the next album she was stroking a white cat, and in the next she was blowing out the candles on a cake shaped like a castle. She opened album after album as if in a fever; they all contained slightly different versions of the pictures she knew. The rooms weren't quite right – the swirls on the carpet, the stripes on the wallpaper, the unprotected sofa – and nor were the patches of garden. A tree where there should have been a shrub. A gravel pathway instead of paving stones. The hedge was too sparse, the cat too thick-set, and the clothesline stood in the wrong place. And what was it about her parents? She shone the torch on them, peering at the faces she knew so well, and the strangest feeling came over her – the feeling that time was whirring backwards. Her mother's hair was long and dark rather than short and grey, and her father wasn't bald. They looked decades younger – but how could that be? Strangest of all, though, were the photos of Nancy with other people, taken in places she'd never been. A group of children in party hats and Nancy beaming in the seafoam dress, the glass studs glinting in her earlobes. A grey-haired lady holding her hand outside a church. Two girls sprawled either side of her on what appeared to be a park bench. The same two girls with their arms around her shoulders in front of a cage of monkeys. And, impossibly, photos of the spots she recognised from her parents' travel albums, only she was there too – sitting between her mother and father on the steps of Notre Dame; holding her father's hand on a ski lift. One of the pictures fell out as she turned a page: herself and her parents paddling in shallow water. On the back, written in pencil, *Corsica, July 1950.*

Nancy dropped the torch, and it bounced and switched off, and in the dark she tried to gather her clattering thoughts. July 1950. Impossible. Impossible. But was that a car engine she heard? Or just her own breaths? Her mother couldn't be far away, surely. How long had she been gone? How long had Nancy been up here in the airless loft? Ten minutes? Twenty-nine years? She should climb back down the ladder, close the hatch and never think about the strange photographs again. She felt around for the torch, then angled the beam across the floor so it caught the album, but when she tried to return the Corsica photo to its spot, her hands kept shaking: each time she managed to secure one corner, another popped free. Eventually she gave up and packed all the albums back in the suitcase as quickly as she could, slamming the lid shut, clicking the rusty clasps into place and pulling the straps tight. She sat there, watching the gigantic shadow of herself cast on the sloping roof. She turned the studs in her ears, which still hurt. Then she opened the other suitcase.

The smell of newspaper rose around her, earthy, woody, and she lifted out the stack of cuttings. The top one was a full page, only a couple of months old; she unfolded it and smoothed it flat and ran the torch across the headline: *BUTCHER OF BIRMINGHAM TO SWING AT LAST.* Underneath that, a grainy photo of a light-haired man around her father's age. He had a bushy beard, and he stared at the camera with a blank expression as if he'd just woken up. *Thanks to the recent reinstatement of the death penalty*, the story read, *one of Britain's most dangerous men is to face the executioner 15 years after his sentence. Arthur Powell was convicted in 1964 of the brutal murder of 11 schoolgirls in the West Midlands region over a 16-year period. Luring his victims to his car by stopping to ask for directions, he then forced them into the vehicle and drove them to nearby wooded areas. Here he assaulted them with a hunting knife, severing their tongues and other body parts before slitting their throats. He escaped the noose when capital punishment was abolished shortly after his conviction, and has languished in Strangeways Prison ever since. Now, however, at 8 a.m. on 31 August, he will finally pay for his crimes. But who is this monster that roamed amongst us?*

Nancy's dream of the knife in her mouth returned to her then: the blade a cold tongue between her teeth. She slid the torch further down the page to a picture of a white-haired baby on the lap of an unsmiling lady with long dark hair. Another picture showed a little blond boy sitting in a wooden cart just big enough to hold him, one bare foot dangling over the side, the road stretching steeply downhill. *Born to Henry and Agnes Powell in 1923,* the article continued, *Powell's childhood was marked by frequent violent disputes between his parents. These most often concerned his father's drinking, the family's financial difficulties and the love affairs his mother was conducting with a variety of other men, including her own brother-in-law. Powell was a troubled boy prone to sudden fury, and he began to engage in criminal activity at an early age, breaking into neighbouring properties to steal goods ranging from radios to jewellery to bicycles. However, rather than selling these items, he gave them away to local petty criminals in an attempt to curry favour with the individuals he was determined to emulate.* Another grainy photo of Arthur Powell: as a young man with a neater beard now. And wasn't there something familiar about him? The pale eyes, the blond curls pushed back off the broad forehead? And another picture of him, though she couldn't tell much from this one; he was holding a jacket over his head as two police officers guided him up some steps.

The beam of the torch landed on a cluster of photographs – the faces of eleven girls, all with long dark hair. This man, this Arthur Powell, had *forced them into his car, taken them to the woods and tortured them with a knife, then slit their throats and watched them die.* It was too horrible; she didn't want to read any more . . . and yet she kept reading. The body of his third victim, it said, was never found: *only the index finger, earlobe and tongue were recovered of Nancy Liddell, 12 years old, who disappeared just outside her home in Church Lane, Redhampton, on her way to school.* Nancy swallowed – and there, at the bottom of the page, a picture of this other Nancy wearing gingham pedal-pushers and a white blouse, her hair caught up in a satin bow.

And Nancy recognised the clothes, because they were her own clothes that hung downstairs in her wardrobe, and she recognised the pose – cross-legged, her chin resting on her left fist – because it was the pose her mother had asked her to strike when she photographed her in the garden back in June.

And she recognised Nancy Liddell's face, because it was her own face.

Heart smacking against her chest, she snatched up a cutting from 1964, fifteen years older than the first: *DEATH SENTENCE FOR POWELL.* A photo showed the same light-haired man, this time without a beard, and again Nancy felt she might know him from somewhere. *The man dubbed the Butcher of Birmingham is to pay the ultimate price for his crimes*, the cutting read. *Arthur George Powell, 41, was found guilty today of what Mr Justice Robin Carmichael called '11 cold-blooded, premeditated, unspeakably barbaric murders'.*

The verdict and sentence came after a retirement of 3 hours 16 minutes by the jury, who had considered the evidence on 12 separate charges. Powell pleaded not guilty to the murders of Lilian Clarke (15), Doris Taylor (12), Nancy Liddell (12), Veronica Bennett (13), Rita Davies (13), Christine Lloyd (11), Jill Bradley (10), Eileen Westwood (14), Joyce Lowe (11), Denise Cooper (12) and Wendy Morris (10). He also denied the charge of abducting Pauline Morgan (14).

After listening to the Judge sum up the evidence for nearly four hours, the jury retired at 1.40 p.m., but they were back just over an hour later with a question for the Judge. This concerned the absence of the remains of Nancy Liddell; aside from the finger, earlobe and tongue identified as hers by genetic testing, her body has never been recovered. The court reassembled, and the jury's question was settled in a few minutes by Judge and counsel.

Soon after 5 p.m. Powell mounted the 18 steps into the dock for the last time.

As the victims' families watched from the public gallery, the court clerk read the charges to the jury foreman. The answers came swiftly: Powell guilty of murdering Clarke, Taylor, Liddell, Bennett, Davies, Lloyd, Bradley, Westwood, Lowe, Cooper and Morris, and guilty of abducting Morgan.

The Judge told Powell he would pass the only sentence befitting such depraved crimes. Weeping was heard from the gallery. Powell, who seemed unmoved, walked down the dock steps flanked by two prison officers.

The Judge then turned to compliment the police. The murders, he said, had been brought to light by investigations of 'the utmost skill'. The careful questioning of Pauline Morgan, resulting in a detailed description of Powell's appearance and vehicle, was the sort of thoroughness which had led to today's conviction.

Outside the court, Mr Keith Liddell, father of Nancy Liddell, told journalists that he and his wife just wanted to lay their daughter to rest. 'If anybody knows where she might be, please contact the police,' he said, adding that she was their only child, and they were unable to have any more.

The trial lasted 10 days.

Nancy spread the cuttings out around her and skimmed the torch over them. Here and there her parents appeared, her mother with masses of dark hair piled high on her head, her father without his glasses years before he went bald. Her parents, yes – but with different names. Again and again she saw the picture of herself in her gingham pedal-pushers.

SNATCHED IN BROAD DAYLIGHT. HAVE YOU SEEN NANCY? PARENTS' WORST NIGHTMARE. HAS THE BUTCHER STRUCK AGAIN? NANCY LIDDELL STILL MISSING. BUTCHER SUSPECT ARRESTED. WHERE IS NANCY?

I'm right here, she thought. Haunting the attic.

She heard an engine then: her mother's car pulling into the driveway. She pocketed the first cutting – the one only a couple of months old – and shoved the rest back in the suitcase, then scrambled down the ladder and folded it away. By the time her mother appeared, she was sitting at the dining-room table, drawing a new pattern with her Spirograph. She felt the tiny plastic teeth clicking together and watched her pen describe loop after loop of a many-petalled black flower.

'You've cut yourself, poppet,' said her mother, bending down to dab at Nancy's knee with a handkerchief.

Only then did Nancy notice the sting, the creep of blood down her shin. She must have scraped herself on the ladder. 'I was chasing Cloud and tripped on the back steps,' she said. 'I didn't realise I was bleeding.'

'You must look after yourself,' said her mother. 'You're too precious to be having accidents.' She produced a pretty new blouse from a shopping bag and held it up to show Nancy. 'For you,' she said. 'Since you're growing so fast. The blue will bring out your eyes, I think.'

That night, when she was supposed to be asleep, Nancy crept to the wardrobe and took the newspaper cutting from her skirt pocket. Where did she know Arthur Powell from? Because she was sure that she knew him. That her body, her muscles knew him. She studied the photos: the little boy sitting in the wooden cart about to career downhill; the young man with the beard and the pale eyes; the hidden man flanked by policemen, a jacket held over

his head. The curly hair; the long tapering fingers. Something in
the slant of the nose and the fullness of the mouth.

As she was drifting off, they came to her: the three identical
boys she had glimpsed on TV – the triplets from the catalogue of
children. The man in the cutting looked like a grown-up version
of them. Something else came to her then too, and she turned on
her bedside lamp and checked: *Now, however, at 8 a.m. on 31
August, he will finally pay for his crimes.* Eight in the morning.
The 31st of August. The exact time her parents had thrown the
party with the cake and the Babycham.

'Don't you think the blue brings out her eyes, Kenneth?' said her
mother.

'Oh yes, very much so,' said her father.

They were eating their tea on trays in the sitting room, her
parents on the sofa and Nancy on the floor, *The Two Ronnies*
playing on the television. Nancy pushed some beans and soggy
toast onto her fork and raised it to her lips. She paused, lowered
her fork again.

'Not hungry, love?' said her father. 'It's your favourite.'

'I keep telling you: I don't much care for beans on toast,' said
Nancy.

Her parents stared down at her. 'You've loved them since you
were a scrap of a thing,' said her mother. 'Hasn't she, Kenneth.'

'At least since then.'

Nancy pushed her tray away; she'd had enough. She folded her
serviette and drew it through the silver ring engraved with an *N*.
Ask them, she thought. *Ask* them. She said, 'Who was Nancy
Liddell?'

Her mother gasped.

'How do you know that name?' said her father.

'Who was she? Am I her? Am I a ghost?'

'A *ghost*?' said her mother. 'Oh, poppet. You're as real as we
are.'

'How do you know that name?' repeated her father.

Nothing for it. 'The loft,' she said.

His knife tumbled to the floor. 'It's dangerous up there! We've told you so many times!'

'Is that how you hurt yourself?' said her mother. 'Not chasing Cloud?'

Nancy nodded. 'But it was just my knee. I didn't come to grief.'

'We don't tell lies, poppet. You know that.'

'We don't keep things from each other,' said her father.

'No?' said Nancy, thinking of all the photographs and cuttings just above them, hanging over their heads for years. Two whole suitcases of things kept from her. She imagined them cracking the floor of the loft, splintering the ceiling and crashing down onto the mustard carpet.

Her parents exchanged glances.

'She was our first daughter,' said her father. 'We had her when we were both still children ourselves, at the start of the war. The dearest little baby, never a grizzle . . . I hated having to leave her when they posted me to Burma. By the time I came home she'd grown and changed so much, but still with the same sweet nature – and she knew who I was, no question. She knew I was her dad. A friend of mine, his girls didn't recognise him when he walked through the door. Not Nancy. She ran to me and threw her arms around my legs and wouldn't let go. And later she came with us on our travels – Spain, France, Corsica – when Europe was putting itself back together again. Oh, she was game. She ate snails and hopped on a ski lift and learned how to ask *How much is that?* in four different languages . . . she drank in the world. Then, when she was twelve . . .' His voice began to tremble, and he retrieved his knife from the carpet and cleaned it with his serviette. 'When she was twelve, we lost her.'

'She was walking down our street, on her way to school,' said her mother. 'Just like every other day. She should have been able to walk to school without . . .' She broke off.

'Arthur Powell,' said Nancy, and her mother let out a cry as if she'd burnt herself.

'We don't speak his name in this house,' said her father.

'Ever,' said her mother.

On the television the smaller Ronnie held up an olive and said, 'That's about the size of it,' and the larger Ronnie said, 'Is it really?' Nancy eyed the uneaten beans on her plate, the garish puddle of sauce.

'We had the party the day they hanged him, didn't we,' she said.

'Can you blame us?' said her father.

'All the paper chains and streamers. The sweets, the éclairs. The real Babycham. None of it helped.'

He sighed. 'No, none of it helped.'

The three-tiered cake dropped in the bin, its delicate swags snapping.

On *The Two Ronnies* a quartet crooned about a snooty little cutie, a kissy little missy, a vain little Jane. Nancy stared at the screen. 'What am I?' she said at last.

Again her parents exchanged glances.

'For many years,' her father said carefully, 'we didn't want another child. We couldn't take the risk a second time. We moved away and changed our names – people had been so intrusive, feeding off our grief, and we thought we'd try to put the past to bed. But also, also . . . we loved her so much, we wanted her back. The house was too quiet, too empty, no matter how we filled it with things. So we decided to have you.'

'And give me her name, and dress me in her clothes,' said Nancy. 'Tell me I love beans on toast when I don't. Take photos of me posing as her.'

'You're so alike,' said her mother. 'You're our miracle.'

Nancy went over to the model village and crouched down to read the street signs. 'Church Lane,' she said. 'That's where you lived. That's where he took her from.'

Her parents did not deny this.

The larger Ronnie was pretending to suffer from a bad memory and couldn't recall his own name. From his pockets he produced all kinds of things to help him remember: a knotted handkerchief, a brick, a hammer. The audience laughed and laughed.

'Which house?' said Nancy.

'Number 33,' murmured her father.

There was the tiny moulded girl with long black hair and a school uniform painted on, and she was closing the gate behind her, returning home.

And there on the far side of the village, the dense forest. Nancy ran her hand over the treetops, making the branches quiver.

'We weren't wrong, were we?' said her mother. 'To have you?'

'You can't blame us, can you?' said her father.

The television audience roared with laughter as the larger Ronnie began substituting *banana* for words he had forgotten.

'The catalogue boys are his sons,' said Nancy. 'And you're ordering one of them.'

Side by side on the wipe-clean sofa, her parents nodded. They only wanted to put things right, they said. To take back what was taken from them. Didn't that sound fair?

When the lady had brought the boys to visit, Nancy had been made to hide in the wardrobe. She could hear them in the sitting room, exclaiming over the model village and the whirring trains and the cuckoo clock. If they all spoke at once she could make out three voices, but she couldn't tell which boy was which – Lawrence, who had a special love of animals, or Vincent, who showed a remarkable aptitude for woodwork, or William, a vivacious all-rounder. One of them said *The hospital's on fire*, and another one – or perhaps the same one – recited some interesting facts about coal. When they'd moved to the dining room, Nancy had unwrapped her cheese and ploughman's pickle sandwich – it was a bit stale, but her mother had promised to save her some jam roly-poly – and the only sound was the cuckoo clock striking the half hour. She played her imaginary piano on the back wall of the wardrobe, until she became aware of her left index finger. The way it lifted itself and tapped the silent notes almost of its own accord. She held it to her cheek: warm. Alive. The root of her tongue ached, and she could have called out, she could have screamed – but she raised herself to her knees and began to count the buttons on the clothes. One hundred and eight today; one less than usual. Perhaps a button had come loose; perhaps it had fallen into the toe of a shoe or even into a pocket. She tried counting from the other end, and this time she got one hundred and seven.

When the boys returned to the sitting room they talked about their hobbies, and cats that lived in the wild, and something about their father being good at cricket but nothing about him being dead. The model trains started whirring again, and one of the boys shouted *We'll never find it! It's gone!* and maybe the same boy or maybe a different one shouted *He threw the little dog into the forest*. Then she heard a thump, and someone shrieked and someone growled, and a few moments later her father said he used to get up to high jinks with his brother – Nancy hadn't known he had a brother – and her mother offered everyone a fizzy drink.

Finally, the front door clicked shut and she heard her parents in the sitting room again.

'I think I'm going to be sick,' said her mother.

'Brawling right in front of us,' said her father. 'Didn't take long for the rot to show itself.'

'At least we know which one to choose.'

'By Christ, I wanted to do it today. I could *see* myself doing it – pinning the little shit to the floor, knee to the throat, then one two three with the carving knife—'

'I know, I know, but let's make a proper job of it. Draw it out the way he drew it out. Ugh, what did they touch? I'll fetch a bucket and cloth.'

'What *didn't* they touch, more like.'

Silence for a bit, and then her father called, 'Couldn't we dispatch all three? We'd be doing the world a favour.'

And a moment later her mother, back in the sitting room but her voice just a murmur: 'One we can explain. He flew into a rage, we couldn't control him, he ran away never to be seen again. But three?'

Her father heaved a sigh. 'I'll go and let her out.'

Nancy heard his footsteps approaching the wardrobe. 'It's safe now, love,' he said, but she stayed where she was. 'Nancy, it's safe now,' he repeated, so she crawled out and stood up, and his face looked like his normal face, and she couldn't tell exactly what her parents had meant by *one two three with the carving knife* and *we'd be doing the world a favour* and *draw it out the way he drew it out* but she knew they'd meant nothing good.

'What a mucky pup,' he said, scraping a bit of ploughman's pickle from the front of her blouse, though there was no scraping away the stain; her mother would have to soak it.

'We saved you some jam . . .' he began, then paused. 'Was that a knock?'

'I'm not sure.'

'Hello?' called one of the boys. 'It's just me.'

Her father smiled an apologetic smile and whispered, 'Won't be a tick,' and it wasn't safe now, not at all. *Let's make a proper job of it.* She heard the boy say his name – Vincent; it was Vincent.

For the first time ever, Nancy didn't crawl back inside the wardrobe to wait until the visitor had gone. Creeping to the passageway and into her parents' room, quietly, quietly, her stock-inged feet sinking into the lush carpet, she gazed through the net curtain. After a few minutes, Vincent emerged and made his way down the path. She couldn't see his face – not until he was almost at the gate, when he turned and looked back at the house. She knew she wasn't supposed to push back the curtain, but she wanted to tell him, somehow, what her parents had said – wanted to warn him, she realised. *Couldn't we dispatch all three?* And then she was bunching up the filmy net in her fist and staring through the glass straight at him, and he was staring straight back at her, terrified, and he was the boy in the catalogue and at the same time the man in the cuttings, and the only word she could think of was *Run*. So he did.

The Minister of Loneliness

'I am quite certain the Fletchers will take one of them,' she said, 'and then other families will follow. It's only a matter of time.'

The Prime Minister folded her hands on the green leather desktop and regarded the Minister with her soft grey eyes. 'Of course, we'd hoped for far greater interest by this point,' she said.

'Of course, yes,' agreed the Minister. 'But we have been working tirelessly behind the scenes to build public confidence. To quash misinformation and rumour.'

'So I hear.'

Was that a joke? The Minister gave a half-smile just in case. She always felt a little on the back foot here in this sumptuous room with its gold draperies and its silver-topped inkwells. 'Once the first boy is placed,' she said, 'which I expect to happen any day now, we'll be able to take advantage of that – get some pictures of him out and about with his new parents. A kite. Autumn leaves. Ducks.'

'Ducks?' said the Prime Minister.

'That sort of thing.'

'No concerning behaviour at the home visit, then?'

The Minister recalled the way William had shoved his brother. The way he'd pounced on him, held him down by the throat until Lawrence began to turn purple. Did the PM know something? Had the Fletchers been in touch with her office, perhaps? 'None at all,' she said. 'They were perfect little gentlemen – a credit to the Scheme.'

'Thank goodness for that. Any *hint* of Flamborough and the rehomings are off the table.'

'Not a hint of a hint,' said the Minister, trying to push from her mind the growl William had made when she'd lunged for him. Scarcely human, surely. But then, what did she know of thirteen-year-old boys? Weren't they rough creatures, always playing rough games? Hadn't Mr Fletcher said that he and his brother were the same?

Except it wasn't just the fight. *This young chap's in trouble when the tide comes in!*

'Well, thank you for the update,' said the Prime Minister, rising from her desk, which meant the conversation was over.

'There was one other thing I've been wondering about,' said the Minister, also rising to her feet.

'Oh, yes?'

'The boys have mentioned it a few times now, and I've no idea what they mean.'

'And what's that?'

'Margate.'

A frown passed over the PM's brow.

'What have they said about Margate?' she asked, smiling now.

'They seemed to believe they were moving there – a kind of reward. Why would they think that?'

'I really couldn't say.'

'They told me it was their turn. They were to live in a place called the Big House with dozens of other Sycamore children – all their old departed friends – and could visit the amusement park whenever they pleased.'

'You know how children are.'

'You mean they made it up?'

'Oh, quite likely. Think about the nature of the children involved, after all.'

'But they showed me a brochure they'd found on their beds. Pictures of happy boys and girls splashing about in the water, playing in the sand. Enjoying the rides at Dreamland. And a whole page about the Big House. A van was on its way to pick them up and take them there, they said – but then I telephoned.'

The PM gazed at the Minister. She drew in a deep breath, held it, sighed. Gestured for the Minister to sit down. Light from the window behind her illuminated the French twist held high on her head by some complicated and invisible architecture. 'As you know,' she said, 'due to their unpredictable temperaments, the Sycamore children have been strictly monitored – every instance of violent or antisocial behaviour recorded, along with every dream. Time and again over the years Alastair Roach's studies have borne out the value of such monitoring. While it is not possible to calculate how many harmful events have been avoided – naturally, one cannot quantify events that have not happened – it is safe to say that his methods have averted many, many Flamboroughs. Thanks to them he has been able to predict, with great accuracy, which residents pose a threat, and to recommend appropriate action.'

The Minister nodded. 'Have them talk to a trained social worker. Withdraw certain privileges in order to modify the undesirable behaviour.'

'Mm,' said the PM. 'In the early years, those were the favoured approaches. But as time went on, and the residents became more unruly – which was hardly surprising, given the origins of the later cohorts – a more reliable solution was needed. Something permanent.'

All the air in the room seemed to press against the Minister's chest, her eardrums, her throat. 'Permanent?'

The PM shifted a crystal water carafe away from the edge of the desk. 'Dr Roach recommended that any unstable elements be removed from the Scheme for the safety of all concerned.'

'How?' said the Minister, the word barely a whisper, barely a breath.

'Well, typically the carers weaned them off the drugs – gave them placebos instead, so the side-effects disappeared. They recovered, in effect – the afflictions that bother most Sycamore children left them, and they were promised a spot in Margate. When the van came, they boarded it happily, of their own free will. After that it was very gentle. Very humane.'

The Minister swallowed. 'And nobody questioned this?'

'It was very gentle. Very humane,' repeated the PM.

'But these are more enlightened times,' said the Minister. 'That no longer happens.'

Somewhere in the distance a telephone rang and rang.

'No,' said the PM.

What did that mean? 'Why did the New Forest boys have the brochure?'

The PM waved a hand. 'They must have found some old ones. Gone poking about in a supplies cupboard, I expect.'

'Only they seemed very certain they were leaving for Margate.'

'Margate,' said the PM, 'is irrelevant. We needn't concern ourselves with it.'

'I want your assurance that my children are safe.'

'*Your* children?'

'The children. The residents.'

'They are to be rehomed, according to your plan.'

'And I have your word on that.'

A pause. 'You have my word.'

The telephone was still ringing.

'However,' the PM continued, 'we must remember what they are. We must bear in mind that they are not the same as you and me. Valuable, yes, but not the same. It is vital we remain dispassionate in this regard. I hope I haven't made a mistake in appointing a woman to Cabinet.'

'I know what they are,' said the Minister.

The PM glanced at the pale-yellow rose in a bud vase on her desk; she had a fresh one every day. 'Autumn Delight,' she said. 'It blooms well into September.'

'It's very lovely,' said the Minister.

'Gardening is an excellent solution when one is under stress. Gardening, fresh air, a short break in the countryside. I myself like to walk up a hill for a bit of perspective. There's one near Chequers – you can see for miles.'

'How nice,' said the Minister.

'A hill can really sort everything out.'

'Yes,' said the Minister. 'A hill, yes. Thank you, Prime Minister.'

Vincent

When the car dropped us back at Captain Scott late that afternoon, nobody was there to let us in. At first we thought we'd have to shout for one of our mothers to come and unlock the gates for us, but they swung open when we pushed them, and we found the key in the lock on the other side. We waved goodbye to the Minister and locked the gates behind us.

'Hello?' Lawrence called in the chilly Entrance Hall. The old dark mirrors showed us from all sides. Alone.

No clattering from the Kitchen. No smell of roast chicken, even though it was Chicken Day and we always had the leftovers for tea. In the Gun Room the china horses stared at the chintz sofa while the philodendron plant drooped its dusty leaves, and in the Library our work on the French Revolution lay where we'd left it – the passages we'd written about the Paris mob, our drawings of the storming of the Bastille. Lawrence had started a sketch of Marie Antoinette that was really very good, her gown catching the light like the gown of the lady who'd first lived in our house.

'Hello?' we called. 'Anybody home?'

We wandered into the Playroom, where a plate of bitten-down sandwich crusts sat on the rug and a half-finished glass of milk soured on the windowsill. William flung himself across the daybed and said, 'I couldn't care less if they choose me or not,' which

Lawrence and I knew was a lie. We'd seen the way he'd marvelled over the model village and the colour television, the way he'd laughed and clapped his hands at the cuckoo clock.

'You might still have a chance,' said Lawrence.

We knew that was a lie too.

'I don't want to be chosen,' I murmured, and my brothers turned to stare at me.

'What?' said Lawrence.

I blinked at him. Nudged the plate of crusts with my toes. All the way home I'd been planning to tell my brothers about the girl I'd seen in the window – really I had – but now something stopped me. My own fear grabbing me by the throat, choking the bad feeling out of me. I remembered again how they'd laughed when I told them about Mother Night visiting me while I was delirious. How William had leapt about, contorting himself, then leering in close. *He's bonkers! He's mental!*

'What do you mean?' he said now.

Surely she was just a trick of the light. A ghost I'd raised. Why mention her? 'Nothing,' I said.

'It's a weird thing to say, though.'

And maybe I would have elaborated – I think I would have – but we heard a thump from upstairs, followed by a cry. When we raced up, we found the door to the North Wing wide open, and we looked at one another, then entered our mothers' quarters.

Mother Morning lay sprawled on the floor beside her bed, her hair messy and her housecoat all askew. The room smelled sweet, over-ripe, like windfall apples left to rot, and we saw the bottle tipped on its side, the last sticky contents leaking onto the parquet.

'There you are,' she said, and laughed a loose laugh. 'I'm seeing triple.'

I helped her up – her hand felt soft and small – and she sat on the edge of the bed and said, 'Will they let me clean lavatories, do you think? Or will I have to work my way up to that?' Another laugh.

'Where's Mother Afternoon?' said Lawrence.

'Packed her bags,' said Mother Morning. 'Gone.'

'Gone where?' said Lawrence.

'To her little cottage?' I said.

'Oh, I expect so,' said Mother Morning, but I didn't like her tone. 'Yes, I expect she's sitting in front of a roaring fire, a pet of some description on her lap, listening to Richard Clayderman.'

'She can't have just gone,' said William.

He ran down the passageway to check her room, so we followed: empty. A dead ikebana arrangement, its bracken and roses dry as paper. Nothing on the chest of drawers but dust. Nothing in the wardrobe but an old raincoat.

Mother Night's room was the same – just a pair of laddered stockings on the floor and the ballerina poster sagging from the wall, the dancer's legs bending where they shouldn't. On the windowsill a dented sweet tin and only the left-over sugar inside.

We cooked our own tea – not chicken but scrambled eggs made with too much milk and too little butter. We ate them anyway, scraping the watery mixture from the burnt pan and hoping we could fix it with pepper. Every few minutes we glanced at the Refectory door, expecting to see our mothers.

'Do you really not want to go to the Fletchers?' Lawrence asked me.

I shrugged. 'They won't choose me anyway.' Still that bad feeling.

'They'll choose *Lawrence*,' said William, pushing a bit of soggy egg around his plate. '*Lawrence* turned on the tears.'

The next day, when Mother Morning found the burnt pan soaking in the sink, she called us to the Kitchen and said, 'You have to keep stirring the eggs. Don't you know anything?'

She tipped out the greasy water, chipped away at the black crust with the sharp edge of the egg slice, scoured it furiously with a Brillo pad, but rough patches remained. Mouth set in a tight line, nostrils flared, she flung the pan back into the sink. 'Ruined,' she said. 'Just like everything else.'

317

'Are we finishing The Story of the French Revolution today?' said Lawrence. 'Only I want to know what happens to Marie Antoinette.'

'They chop off her head,' said Mother Morning.

Then she went back upstairs to the North Wing.

'What do we do now?' said William.

Lawrence was standing motionless in the Kitchen doorway, staring at the space Mother Morning had occupied.

'Lessons, I suppose,' I said, so we made our way to the Library as usual.

It felt comforting to take up our work again, and I began to colour in a plume of smoke above my drawing of the Bastille. On my back I could feel the eyes of all the boys in the photographs – all the boys who used to live here too.

Lawrence grabbed the FACT INDEX and looked up Marie Antoinette, then found her main entry in LOCO–ORE. 'Somewhere about noon,' he read, 'on 16 October 1793, a cart rumbled slowly through the Paris streets amid the howls and jeers of the populace. In it sat a woman in a ragged white dress, with hands bound behind her yet with traces of majesty in her stricken bearing and of beauty in her wasted face.' His voice began to wobble. 'At the Place de la Révolution the victim alighted, then mounted the steps of the scaffold, and laid her prematurely whitened head beneath the knife of the guillotine. Such was the end of an empress's daughter, once the gayest and most beautiful princess in Europe.' He closed the Book, shut away the awful story. 'I don't like that ending.' He screwed up his drawing of Marie Antoinette, then immediately regretted it and tried to smooth it out again.

'Here,' said William, offering him his own picture of her: flouncy sleeves, feathers in her hair and a ribbon tied around her throat. The proportions off, the eyes crooked. 'You can keep it – I don't mind.'

He could be kind, you see. He really could.

I flicked through LOCO–ORE for a new topic. *They Carry*

Their Searchlights with Them, read the heading above a drawing of strange, unnerving fish that glowed from their gills and spiny bodies. *Man would solve a major problem if the secret of the luminescence of these fish which dwell in the ocean depths could be discovered.* William slithered his fingers along the back of my neck, and I shoved him away as he smiled his beautiful smile at me. I took up the FACT INDEX and looked for something else.

Right at the back of the volume I found a list I'd never noticed before: Additions and Corrections. *An editor of any such reference book as this would be a bold man indeed if he dared to claim that his book had succeeded in reaching a standard representing 100 per cent accuracy. For all the constant checking and re-checking of millions of facts, occasional small slips seem to be almost inevitable, and some of these are noticed too late for any correction to be made to the printed page. Then the only amends that can be made to the reader is to admit the mistakes, with real regret, and to correct them at the end of the book.* I scanned the list: fate should be gate; James I of Scotland should be James VI of Scotland; 10,625 gallons should be 10,625 million gallons; July should be June; the radius of the moon should be 1,080 miles, not 108; it is not Ferdinand who says, 'The isle is full of noises', but the evil monster Caliban. These were significant mistakes; some of them were vast. What else had slipped through undetected?

We let our stomachs tell us when to stop for Break Time – nobody had wound the clocks – and William cut up the cubes of cheese and pieces of apple while I tipped the raisins into the little blue bowl. Everything perfectly normal. Everything as it should be.

Then Mother Morning appeared and said the Minister's office had just telephoned, and the Fletchers had chosen William; he was to go to them the following Friday.

'*Me?*' he said.

'Yes, you,' said Mother Morning, and William let out a whoop.

'But he pushed the little man onto the tracks!' said Lawrence. 'And threw the little dog into the forest!'

319

'What are you talking about?' Mother Morning said, then held up her hand. 'Never mind. I have a headache.'

'He attacked me!' said Lawrence. 'Right in front of them! Why would they choose him?'

Mother Morning was already walking away.

'I'll get to drive the train whenever I want!' said William. 'And drink cherryade! And watch TV! *Colour* TV!'

Lawrence squashed a cube of cheese between his fingers. I knew he was trying not to cry. 'It makes no sense,' he said at last.

We knew he was right – but maybe the Fletchers had seen something good in William, something they could love. Or maybe they felt compelled to give the most troubled boy a home. Either way, the person I loved most in the world was leaving me. I couldn't bear it. I wanted him to stay at Captain Scott forever; I wanted nothing to change. And yes, and yes, I kept thinking of the girl, or the ghost, or whatever she was. *Run.*

'You don't have to go,' I said in a small voice.

He frowned at me as if I'd said the most ludicrous thing. 'Why wouldn't I go?'

'Because . . . because I'll miss you.'

'Because you don't deserve it,' said Lawrence.

William just laughed and threw a handful of raisins into his mouth.

I looked at the clock, which was still wrong. 'It's Thursday,' I said. 'It's time for Ethical Hour.'

'We don't have to do that any more,' said William.

'Please?' I said. For a little longer, I could pretend everything was normal.

He sighed. 'We have no question.'

Lawrence found a stub of chalk and wrote on the blackboard: *Should the French have spared Marie Antoinette?*

'I have a better one,' I said, and I took the chalk and wrote: *Should William go to live with the Fletchers?*

'That's easy,' said William.

'Yes, it is,' said Lawrence.

They were both wrong.

We were finishing lunch the following Friday – sausages, which we'd managed not to burn – when Mother Morning came to the Refectory to remind William to pack his last few bits and pieces, since the car would be there at three o'clock.

'How will we know when it's three?' I said.

'The car will come,' she said.

Then she glanced at the stopped clock and said she was going off duty because it must be well after one – but we knew she was just guessing and she couldn't be certain about the time.

Our rucksacks stood at the foot of our beds, packed from when we thought we were going to Margate; we hadn't had the heart to put them away, and Mother Morning no longer cared. I unbuckled mine and looked inside: the lid had come off the Mona Lisa jigsaw, and the pieces had fallen out. I upended the bag and shook everything onto my bed – my summer clothes, my sandals, all the chipped and peeling pieces of the puzzle – and a page fluttered from the base of the jigsaw box. Along its edge, a note in blue ink, scribbled in a hurry: *I thought you should know – Mother Night (Frances).*

I picked it up by a single corner, smoothed it flat on the bed.

Page 504.

The missing entry from BOO–CRO.

And the heading, in thick black letters, right after *Copper* and right before *Coral*, was not **Copulation**.

While Lawrence and William argued over whether the jigsaw and the Stickle Bricks should stay at Captain Scott or go to the Fletchers', I began to read.

Copy. A copy is the term used for an exact replica of a human being that is identical in every physical way to the original person. Most often the process results in two, three or even four copies of each donor – identical twins, triplets and quadruplets, essentially – but in some cases just one copy survives.

321

After Swiss chemist Friedrich Miescher first identified DNA in 1869, scientists such as Walter Sutton, Theodor Boveri and Phoebus Levene made steady progress in unlocking the key to our makeup. As early as 1902, using a noose fashioned from a strand of baby hair, Hans Spemann separated the cells of a salamander embryo to create identical twins – the first successful vertebrate copy. However, it took Briton Alastair Roach to produce the first copy of a mammal: a rabbit that lived for six months.

Dr Roach sitting us on his lap when we were small. *Shall I have a look at you, my little rabbits?* His hand cool at the back of our necks.

A method refined during World War II and shared with Allied scientists as a condition of the Gothenburg Treaty allowed Dr Roach to create Britain's first generation of human copies in 1946. Drawing on the same source material, he created her second in 1950, and so began his trials of new, potentially life-saving paediatric medications. In collaboration with the State, he established the Sycamore Homes to house the resulting populations in the most efficient manner. Although still children now, by the early to mid-1960s the surviving members of both cohorts will be old enough to care for subsequent generations or take on other menial work, thereby ensuring the Scheme's cost-effectiveness.

Like all great scientists, Dr Roach has made adjustments to his method in order to resolve early teething troubles. At the time of printing he is working to source fresh material for a third generation of copies; it is his hope that they and future generations can be used to improve the lives of all Britons.

Grown in laboratories, these creatures cannot be considered fully human and therefore cannot possess the same rights as we do; it may be helpful to think of them as 'conscious tissue'. However, the fact that the physical makeup of copies corresponds exactly to that of real people means that British doctors can be confident of some truly remarkable medical breakthroughs.

Below the text, a photograph of a group of boys lined up in

a row, like the photographs that hung on the back wall of the Library.

My whole body started to shake. I could feel every tooth in my jaw, every fingernail and toenail juddering in its bed. The churn of the marrow in my bones.

'Look,' I said. It was all I could manage, but something in my tone made my brothers stop bickering and kneel with me on the rag rug beside my bed. As they read, I pressed my knee hard against Philip Cole's knotted scraps. I could sense the knowledge taking up residence in my brothers' bodies, lodging in their chests, sticking in their throats. Lawrence gave a small whimper, and William exhaled as if he'd been punched.

'So . . .' he began. 'So . . . is this what we are?'

'I think so,' I said.

'And Dr Roach made us?'

I nodded. 'Made us to use us.'

Lawrence was re-reading the entry, holding the page close as if he might find something we'd missed. His fingers worried at a piece of the Mona Lisa puzzle – a patch of the distant water behind her head – and eventually he slumped back onto his haunches and said, 'We're not real?'

'We're copies of someone real,' said William.

'Our father,' I said.

'Is he even our father?'

I couldn't answer that. I touched the note from Mother Night: *I thought you should know.* Scribbled in a hurry.

'I want to ask Mother Morning,' said Lawrence.

'She's off duty,' I said, but even as I spoke I knew that the old routines, the old rules, no longer applied.

We knocked on the door to the North Wing and waited, and when she didn't answer we hammered with our knuckles. Finally, we heard footsteps and the door opened.

'Well?' she said, a glass of something milky-brown in her hand.

No housecoat, just a skirt and blouse. 'Has someone broken a leg? Is the place on fire?'

I cradled my knuckles to my chest.

'We know,' said William.

'Know? Know?'

I held out page 504. I think I'd been expecting her to deny it, or to snatch at the evidence and insist we needn't bother with such nonsense. Instead, she hesitated, then took the page from me gently, as if accepting a gift. She read Mother Night's note at the bottom, gave a small sigh and motioned for us to follow her. I noticed that the hem of her blouse had come untucked at the back and she wasn't wearing stockings. I'd never seen her bare legs, and the sight of them, pale as grubs, made me wary somehow.

In the Sitting Room she turned off the television and cleared a space for her drink on the glass table. It was smeary with finger marks and covered in all sorts of things that didn't belong in a Sitting Room: a hairbrush tangled with strands of auburn hair, a single rubber glove with a torn fingertip, a scrunched-up flannel, a wooden spoon, a small pile of clothes that needed ironing, a tin of talcum powder – Yardley's English Lavender, which we bought for her every Christmas with money she gave us from her purse. The curtains were drawn, and the room smelled unaired. The telephone sat on the floor, stretched to its limit.

'Is it true?' we said. 'Are we made from someone else?'

'Everyone is made from someone else,' she said.

'But our father isn't our father? We are our father?'

She rubbed her chapped lips, gave another sigh. 'None of it matters at this point,' she said, 'but you are *not* your father. We did our best to ensure that.' Her eyes flicked to William, and she gulped a mouthful of her drink. It was true, she said, that Dr Roach had made copies of people, but that was nothing to be ashamed of; quite the contrary. We should feel—

'So he made us to use us,' interrupted William.

Mother Morning held up her hand and said she wouldn't hear

a word against Dr Roach – the man was a genius, even a god; he had given us life, *life*. Would we prefer the alternative?

We considered that as she refilled her glass from a bottle that said *Baileys*.

The first two generations were the nation's great hope, she went on. A chance to test wonderful new paediatric medicines on living subjects. Twins, triplets and quadruplets, all raised in Homes that provided them with a solid grounding in the things that mattered: frugality, hard work, nice manners, good morals. They might not have had parents in the traditional sense, but they had dozens of siblings, and at a time when many British children were still living amongst the ruins of the bombed-out cities, the Sycamore boys and girls had wanted for nothing. Nothing important.

'And the later copies?' I said. 'Are they – are we – the nation's great hope too?'

She frowned at me. 'Well, of course,' she said. 'You can rid human children of disease. You can make miracles happen.'

'But have we?'

'There's Mr Webb's grandson. Although . . .' She twirled her finger in a circle beside her temple: the sign for crazy.

'Is he the only one?'

'There has been significant progress in several areas, I understand.'

'No other miracles to speak of then,' said William.

'*You* are miracles,' she said. 'Don't you see?'

No, we said. We didn't.

'If it's nothing to be ashamed of,' said Lawrence, 'why couldn't we know what we are?'

Mother Morning picked up the brush from the glass table and started pulling out the auburn hair. The first two generations did know, she said, but after that there were complications.

'The teething troubles?' I said. 'The adjustments to the method?'

She rolled the hair between her palms until it made one long matted strand: a length of coarse string, a rat's tail. 'The public had

325

no idea, but the first copies were sourced from the dead,' she said at last. 'The stillborn, the never born. All the little lives that failed to start. And isn't that a beautiful thing, if you think about it? A second chance to live. A resurrection.'

It didn't sound beautiful, but we said nothing.

She swallowed her Baileys. Stared across the room at the blank television. I could see the four of us reflected in its opaque screen – the shadows of a family acting out a very strange story.

'A first-generation girl was recognised,' she said. 'She'd been made from a stillbirth, but the hospital had failed to pass on the fact that the original was an identical twin – and the other twin survived. A member of the extended family saw the copy at the shops one day a few years later and started asking difficult questions . . . then the newspapers got hold of it. The upshot being that Dr Roach was forced to look elsewhere for donors.'

'So we're not made from dead babies?' said Lawrence.

'Our father's not a dead baby, is he, idiot!' said William.

'Prison populations offered a wealth of freely available material,' said Mother Morning. 'And, unlike ordinary people, prisoners asked no difficult questions – they were quite happy to sign away a bit of blood, a bit of plucked-out hair in exchange for a few cigarettes. All perfectly legal, even if they didn't know the full details – only that they were making a meaningful contribution to society.' Her words were beginning to stumble into one another. 'I imagine that was very attractive to those wanting to mend the error of their ways. And attractive to Dr Roach, too, who'd long been interested in studying the origins of evil.'

I thought about the building where our father lived – the castle we'd visited. How much it reminded me of the picture of the Bastille in The Book of Knowledge.

And the Bastille was a prison.

'He's a criminal?' I said.

'He took a wrong turn,' said Mother Morning.

'What did he do?' said William.

She waved a hand, tried to drink from her empty glass. Poured a fresh one, spilling it over the sides and onto the rubber glove with the torn fingertip. 'Dr Roach became increasingly focused on nature versus nurture,' she said, gazing at the television as if she'd forgotten we were there. 'If the children were protected from the knowledge of their backgrounds, could the right upbringing negate any criminal tendencies? Hence the mothers. The Lessons. But often' – and here she glanced at William again – 'blood will out.'

'What does that mean?' said Lawrence, though he sounded like he didn't want to know.

She told us anyway, the Baileys loosening something new and reckless in her that made us uneasy. Out the truth lurched: the violent attacks by Sycamore children over the years – on their mothers, on each other. The deaths. Oh yes, deaths. We'd got off lightly at Captain Scott. That was why Dr Roach had introduced The Book of Dreams and The Book of Guilt – to better understand how evil can develop. With close monitoring and reports from mothers, he believed, he could predict undesirable behaviour and organise appropriate treatment. It was the mothers' responsibility to avoid at all costs bringing the Scheme into disrepute. At all costs. And she, Mother Morning, had fulfilled that responsibility for years . . . Then three members of the public were killed in Flamborough, and the press made a meal of it – but how was any of that her fault?

I watched the strand of hair on the glass table. Had it moved of its own accord? Had it quivered just a little? I kept my eyes on it. 'And Margate?' I said, so quietly I hardly heard myself.

But Mother Morning had started crying, and her freckled face had turned all blotchy, and we were so shocked that we asked no more questions. We looked at one another, making the smallest of gestures with our heads, our eyebrows, our chins, each of us signalling to his brothers that someone should comfort her. That would be the kind thing to do, wouldn't it? But none of us moved. In that darkened room, in that house of stopped clocks, nothing seemed real any more.

We didn't learn until later that *appropriate treatment* meant Margate. That once a mother had reported serious warning signs about a copy – William's attack on Karen, for instance – that copy was earmarked for disposal. Any siblings had to be destroyed too, because if one turned bad, sooner or later the others would follow: it was in the blood. A placebo was given for a week or two instead of the usual medicine, so the copies seemed to recover from the Bug, and then the brochures were placed on the pillows, and then the Van came. The doors and windows locked so the gas couldn't escape. The ashes dumped into waterways to be washed out to sea.

We didn't learn until later, either, that a handful of people managed to order unofficial copies, paid for via bribes, to replace loved ones who had died. Humans as well as animals, just like Cynthia.

And we didn't learn until later that the dream of the skinny girl was a genetic memory, a gift from our father. Dr Roach had come to understand that copies from the later generations could inherit memories from their donors – often violent events, expressed as dreams. That really spooked people – if we could re-enact crimes in our sleep, mightn't they spill into our waking lives? – but it paved the way for valuable research into human memory. So Dr Roach and his team maintained.

We sat there motionless, the three of us, wishing Mother Morning would stop crying. When she did, she continued to gasp and shudder like something dying but not quite dead.

'I always thought they would reward us,' she said. 'If we just worked hard enough – if we were loyal to the Scheme. I thought they would grant us citizenship one day. The right to vote. Dr Roach intimated as much.' She let out a small, hard laugh. 'We were so young when we became mothers – only sixteen, in my case. And I was fiercely proud to be part of it. To be doing my bit.'

I think all three of us understood at the same time. 'You're a copy too,' I said. 'The same as us.'

She shook her head. 'Mothers are first or second generation. Quite different donor material.'

'They replaced Mother Night, didn't they,' said Lawrence. 'Because she wanted to tell us the truth.'

'She was warned more than once,' said Mother Morning. 'We tried to talk her round, but she refused to listen.'

I remembered sitting with her in the Upstairs Common Room, asking about her childhood while the gas fire breathed its warm breath and the fire surround really did look like marble. She'd told me about her sister Emma and their cat Honey who had scooped their goldfish from the pond, which was terrible but also just the way of things. They'd played croquet and skittles, she'd said, and knitted gloves on toothpicks for their dolls.

'What happened to her?' said Lawrence.

Mother Morning shrugged. 'She was warned more than once.'

Nobody spoke for a few moments. Mother Morning smeared her finger around the inside of her glass to get to the last drops of Baileys.

Then the car came for William.

Nancy

In the evening, when Nancy's father was in the bath and her mother was shut away in the sewing room, Nancy took a sheet of writing paper and an envelope from the box in the credenza.

Dear Jim, she wrote.

Please fix it so my parents don't hurt the boy they have ordered. He is being delivered next week. I always wanted a sister or brother because I've never been past our hedge but I think they will cut him into pieces.

Yours sincerely,
Nancy Fletcher

That night she slipped the envelope into the pile waiting by the front door – all the order forms her mother had filled out for an electric clothes-brush, a scientific calculator, melon dishes in the shape of wedges of melon, decorative beer steins that said *Ein Schatzerl und ein Edelweiss sind des Jägers Ehrenpreis*. Every day she listened for the post dropping through the letterbox, and darted to the door to fetch it, but no reply came.

The boy arrived in the early evening, her parents' voices too cheerful as they let him in the front door: *Welcome, William! We're so happy to have you! Are you hungry? Let me take your bag!*

Her mother brought Nancy's tea to the bedroom and told Nancy that she could eat it at the dressing table rather than in the wardrobe – a special treat for a special occasion.

'What are you going to do to him?' Nancy asked.

'You needn't worry,' her mother said. 'Tomorrow we'll look after everything.' She was bright and flushed, as if she couldn't wait to give Nancy a special present. The same as the morning of the party.

'Can't you just let him go?'

'Let him go?' said her mother. 'He's a monster. A *murderer*.'

'No he's not! What are you talking about?'

Her mother pressed her lips together. 'There are things you don't understand. Trust me, that creature can't be allowed to tear another family apart.'

'They'll put you in prison,' said Nancy. She'd seen it plenty of times on television.

'Nonsense,' said her mother. 'He went berserk and ran off – no idea where. We were merely defending ourselves.'

When her mother had left the bedroom Nancy sat in front of the mirror and let the steam from her cream of mushroom soup mist the glass. She turned the little glass studs. They still hurt.

That night she couldn't sleep. In the excitement her mother must have forgotten to switch the cuckoo clock to silent, and Nancy heard it calling ten times, eleven times, twelve, each more urgent than the last, it seemed, until it dropped back to a single plaintive call. She rose from her bed and crept across the passageway to the sewing room. Her parents had locked the door, leaving the key in the lock. Silently she entered.

On the table by the window she saw the outline of the sewing machine hunched under its patchwork cockerels. Usually the dress-making scissors sat next to it, and the book of needles with its red flannel pages, and the tin that held the nest of glass-headed pins – but her mother had taken away all the sharp things and hidden them somewhere.

The boy's breaths were slow and deep. How beautiful he looked in the soft orange glow from the streetlight; it filtered through the curtains like the glow of a vast candle, and Nancy longed to stroke his pale curls – to touch someone other than her mother or father. Kneeling down next to the bed, she whispered, 'William . . . William . . . you're not safe here.' Then she heard her parents' bedroom door open and her father's heavy tread in the passageway. She held her breath as he walked past the sewing room; had she closed her own bedroom door behind her? She could not remember, and if her father noticed it ajar . . .

Something soft moved against her fingers. Her hand had come to rest on the boy's hair, and he was stirring. Looking at her through barely open eyes.

'You're a dream, aren't you?' he murmured.

'I'm Nancy,' she said, but the boy and the room and the candle-light glow and even her own body seemed unbelievable. Unbelievable to be talking to someone else, to feel the warmth of him so close. Not just a shape on the television, one of the *Jim'll Fix It* children made from dots of light, but a real live person, here beneath her hand.

The toilet flushed. Her father might not have noticed her door ajar before, but he'd be more awake now. She heard him turn on the tap to wash his hands, and knew she had only seconds to get back to her room. 'You're not safe here,' she whispered to the boy, whose eyes had closed again. Then she slipped away.

In the morning her mother roused her; she must have overslept after lying awake for so long. At first she couldn't pinpoint the reason for the fear that clotted like mud in her chest – and then she remembered the boy.

Her father sat reading the paper at the kitchen table, the same as usual. 'Morning, sleepyhead!' he said, finishing his cup of tea.

Nancy shivered in her nightie; she hadn't thought to put on her dressing gown, and the cool air crept up her legs. She cleared her throat. 'Could I . . . could I see him?' she asked.

Her father looked at her mother. 'Well,' he said. 'I suppose that would be all right, just for a moment, don't you think, Marjorie?'

'I suppose so, yes,' she said.

Nancy followed them to the sewing room where the boy sat slumped in a strange position on the bed. Was he asleep? Surely, yes, just asleep.

'Is there anything you want to say to him?' her father asked. 'Arthur. Oi, Arthur.'

'He's William,' said Nancy.

Her father shook the boy's shoulder, and the boy opened his eyes, but he seemed even drowsier than he had in the night.

Nancy said, 'Hello.'

He looked up at her. 'You?' he said. Then his head lolled back against the wall.

'What's wrong with him?' she said.

'Nothing,' said her mother. 'We just popped a bit of something in his breakfast to relax him. He'll come round.'

'You can give him a kick if you like,' said her father. 'Slap him across the face. He won't feel it.'

'No thank you,' said Nancy.

'Look,' said her father, flicking his finger hard against the boy's forehead. Twisting the flesh of his forearm. 'I could get used to this.'

'Stop it!' said Nancy.

'He's not human, love. You're looking at pure evil.'

Nancy stepped back, and her foot sank into something clammy and smooth. She screamed.

'It's just the hot-water bottle!' said her mother, picking it up. 'See?' It lay heavy in her hands, like a dead lizard. The insides sloshing. 'There's some porridge in the pot. You can help yourself, can't you? Only we've a lot to prepare here.' Already she was checking a list she'd written.

'What are you going to do to him?' Nancy asked.

'You don't have to watch,' said her father. 'Why don't you see what's on television?'

'But what are you going to do to him?'

Her mother hesitated. 'Only what he did to you.'

'He didn't do anything to me! He's not Arthur Powell, and I'm not Nancy Liddell! You'll go to prison!'

'Now then, now then,' said her father. 'Let's not get all worked up.' He put his arms around her, and she inhaled the smell of him – Brut 33, wood shavings, milky tea – and she wanted to stay there with her cheek pressed to his chest. He was wearing one of his oldest shirts; bits of paint from the model village stained the over-washed fabric.

'You must trust us, poppet,' said her mother, who had also dressed in old clothes – her gardening trousers and a matted jumper. Clothes that didn't matter. Clothes that could be thrown away afterwards.

'When are you going to do it?' said Nancy, her voice muffled by her father's chest.

'He'll know all about it, don't you worry,' said her mother. 'We'll wait till after lunch, when he's wide awake.'

'Now off you go and amuse yourself,' said her father. 'We'll be busy for quite a while. Don't be scared if you hear anything – turn the television up if it's bothering you, yes?'

They were both beaming at her, nodding.

'Yes,' said Nancy.

In the kitchen she served herself a bowl of porridge topped with swirls of cream and melting brown sugar. Mechanically she ate it, all the while thinking three words: *Who can help? Who can help? Who can help?*

She sidled back down the passageway until she reached the telephone table outside the sitting room. The door to the sewing room was shut, but she could hear the rustling of plastic, the ripping of lengths of tape. Easing the telephone book from its narrow recess, she looked under P for Police – and there was the number for emergencies, right above her shaking finger. She knew how to work the phone; she'd seen her parents use it, and once, when her father was at work and her mother was gardening, she'd answered it herself. She hadn't spoken a word to the man on the other end, and he'd said *Hello? Hello? Is anyone there? Are you there?* and finally he'd hung up. If she just lifted the receiver now, and dialled 999, and explained that something terrible was going to happen, they'd send policemen to break down the door and aim their guns and shout *Freeze! You're under arrest!*

And what then?

Then they would take her parents away and put them in prison.

A card fell from the back of the telephone book: *Barry Sedgwick, Plumber. 24-Hour Assistance.* She remembered the day he'd come to the house to unblock the kitchen sink. *Thank goodness you're here, Mr Sedgwick,* her mother had said, and he'd said *Got yourself in a spot of bother, have you, sweetheart?* He'd sounded so nice – and then, when he was leaving, Nancy heard him say *Give me a ring if you need me again, sweetheart, and I'll come and sort it out – but remember, these problems are easy to avoid if you do the right thing in the first place.*

Perhaps Barry Sedgwick could help. Perhaps he could come and sort it out.

Keeping her eye on the door to the sewing room, Nancy picked up the receiver and dialled.

'Barry Sedgwick,' said Barry Sedgwick.

'You don't really know me,' whispered Nancy, 'but you unblocked our sink once.'

'What's that?' said Barry Sedgwick. 'I can hardly hear you.'

Nancy pressed her mouth to the black receiver. 'The Fletchers' house. You said to ring if we needed you again.'

'You'll have to speak up, sweetheart,' said Barry Sedgwick.

'My parents are going to hurt a boy,' she whispered. 'Mr and Mrs Fletcher, at 18 Belgrave Close. I need you to come.'

Then she saw the handle turning on the sewing-room door, and she hung up the telephone and leapt to her feet, already two steps away by the time her father came into the passageway.

'Did you want something?' he said, smiling.

'I was just going to get dressed,' said Nancy.

'Only I thought I heard you talking.'

'Cloud was clawing the carpet. I told her not to be a naughty girl.'

As if she'd heard her name, the cat appeared in the passageway. Rubbed against Nancy's legs.

'Well, we'd best keep at it – we've a lot to get through before lunch,' said her father. 'You go and see what's on television, all right?'

As he let himself back into the sewing room, Nancy saw the swathes of plastic sheeting spread across the carpet, covering the sewing table and the machine, reaching up the wall to the window-sill as if the room had turned to ice. She saw the lengths of rope coiled beside the bed. And on the plastic-covered table, lined up in a row, every sharp knife in the house: the small, pointed paring knife, the serrated bread knife, the boning knife, the cleaver, the carving knife, the cheese knife that split in two at the tip like a snake's tongue. The folding knife her mother had ordered from a catalogue and never used, all the secret tools tucked away in the handle: the corkscrew, the bottle opener, the toothpick, the tiny scissors.

Nancy snatched her warmest clothes from her wardrobe and pulled them on, gave her hair a few quick strokes with the brush and pulled it into a ponytail. Slipped the newspaper cutting about Arthur Powell and Nancy Liddell into the back pocket of her trousers. In the sitting room she turned on the television, then began to flick through the magazine rack. Where was it? Where was it? She shoved aside catalogue after catalogue until she found what she wanted: the catalogue of children. And there at the back, where her parents had turned down the corner of the page, the triplets. Captain Scott Home for Boys, Ashbridge, Hampshire.

Quietly she opened the front door, and quietly she closed it behind her. As she hurried to the gate in the hedge she recalled, for some reason, the lump of muck she'd seen in the kitchen rubbish bin after Barry Sedgwick had unblocked the sink: fat and hair and scraps of food left over from their meals, all rinsed down the drain by her mother and rotting away in the dark.

Out on the street the power lines sliced the air to ribbons, and the sky went on forever. It was too vast, too high, and Nancy couldn't tell which way to go. In the end she ran downhill, away from the top of the cul-de-sac, because she could see that led only to other people's houses – and other people might not be kind like Barry Sedgwick was kind. Other people might ring the police. She picked up speed with every step, the concrete pavement jolting her bones, and faster and faster she ran until she thought she might lose control of her body and either fall or fly. A boy in orange shorts said, 'Hello, what's your name?' as she hurtled past his garden; when she looked back he was craning his neck over the gate to watch her disappear.

The road at the bottom of the hill was wider, and every so often a car passed, forcing a shock of cold air against her. The drivers seemed to know which way to go, so she ran in the same direction, and the next road she reached was wider still, and busier. She'd seen people on television waiting on the sides of such roads for someone to give them a ride – they just held out their thumbs. She turned to face the traffic.

The first few drivers barely glanced at her, but then an older lady in a dented yellow car slowed down, stopped a little way ahead and opened the passenger door.

'Where are you going, pet?' she said. She wore a dark-green anorak and wellington boots, and her car smelled of mud and damp wool.

'Ashbridge,' said Nancy. 'In Hampshire.'

The lady peered at her. 'How old are you?'

'Sixteen.'

'Sure about that?'

'Of course. I know when I was born.'

The lady pushed an old newspaper off the passenger seat. 'I can take you as far as Dorchester, if that's any help.'

'Is Dorchester close to Ashbridge?'

'It's about halfway.'

Nancy climbed in.

'I'm Ruth,' said the lady.

'Nancy.'

'Pleased to meet you.' As Ruth pulled out into the traffic she said, 'Buckle up, there's a good girl.'

'What?' said Nancy, flinching at the cars that whipped past them – surely they were coming too close. Surely they would crash into the yellow car.

'The safety belt,' said Ruth. 'Behind your shoulder,' she added, looking puzzled as Nancy searched around her waist for a belt.

Nancy remembered then: people on television strapped themselves in. She pulled the belt across her chest and fumbled with the clasp until it clicked.

'Everything all right?' said Ruth. She had thin grey hair pulled into a plait, and tiny lurid veins scribbled their way over her cheeks.

'Yes, thank you,' said Nancy, eyeing the cars that kept surging past.

As Ruth picked up speed Nancy gripped the edges of her seat. Her breaths were catching in her throat. She tried to concentrate on the view, but it changed and changed: now a row of trees, now a patch of scrub, now grassy hills, and now, vanishing so quickly she might have dreamt it, a petrol station with a gigantic yellow scallop shell that seemed to hang in mid-air above it.

They drove for a while in silence, then Ruth said, 'What's in Ashbridge?'

'I'm going to visit a friend.' That was what people did, wasn't it? What they said they did?

'There's a bag of bullseyes in the glove box if you're interested.'

Nancy didn't know what a bullseye was, or a glove box for that matter. 'Thank you very much,' she said.

'Go on then, pet, don't be shy.'

'Yes,' said Nancy.

Ruth gave another puzzled frown, reached across and opened a compartment just above Nancy's knees. She pulled out a gaping paper bag. Small black-and-white orbs glistened inside, and Nancy let out a cry.

'What's wrong?' said Ruth.

'Are they real?'

'What do you mean?'

'Are they real eyes?'

The lady began to laugh. 'No, love. Why would I be driving around with a bag of eyes? They're sweets.'

Nancy could see that now. Blushing, she took one from the offered bag. She would have to be more careful. Ask no stupid questions; pretend she knew how the world worked. She held on to the safety belt but felt no safer.

'My daughter and I used to play a game,' said Ruth, popping a sweet into her own mouth. 'We'd see who could make their bullseye last the longest. She always won – I'd give in and crunch mine to dust every time. No self-control.'

Nancy could hear Ruth rolling the bullseye against her teeth, and a moment later she was shattering it – but Nancy held hers on her tongue, letting the cool peppermint fill her mouth.

'You're made of stern stuff, I see,' said Ruth.

'Am I?' said Nancy.

'Oh yes. I can tell.'

On they drove, and Nancy tried not to imagine what her parents were planning to do to the boy, and how much time she had left to help him. *We'll wait a few hours*, her mother had said, *till he's wide awake.* The bullseye grew smaller and smaller until finally it was blade-thin. Then it broke in two, and at last it disappeared.

'Thomas Hardy country,' said Ruth as they passed a sign for Dorchester and veered onto a smaller road.

Nancy nodded, though she had no idea who Thomas Hardy was.

'Do you know *Tess of the d'Urbervilles?*'

'I think I met her once,' said Nancy.

Again Ruth laughed. 'What was she like?'

'I don't really remember.'

'I could never stand her,' said Ruth. 'Deadly boring and too fat! Hah!' She pulled over to the side of the road, stopping next to a low stone wall that looked as if it might fall to pieces. 'This all right, love?'

'Yes, thank you,' said Nancy. 'What time is it, please?'

'Just after 10.30. Look after yourself, won't you?'

Nancy wanted to tell her everything then – beg her to turn the car around and come home with her to save William, but already Ruth was reaching over to slam the passenger door shut and driving away.

She held out her thumb again, but car after car rushed by. If Dorchester was halfway, Nancy thought, she'd need at least another hour and a quarter to get to Ashbridge, and then a bit longer to find the Home, and then . . . she wasn't sure what would happen then, but with every passing moment she felt the clot of fear thicken in her chest. She forced herself to smile at the swooping traffic. Just an ordinary girl on her way to see a friend.

Finally a car stopped, and a man opened the door. 'Hop in,' he said. 'Where are you headed?'

'Ashbridge,' said Nancy. 'In Hampshire.'

'Easy,' said the man, who told her his name was Anthony but she could call him Ant. He was a lot younger than her father, with blond hair that hung down past his collar, and he wore a bobbled grey jumper and a pair of jeans. She'd never seen jeans in real life.

His car smelled of warm plastic, and a rabbit's paw hung from the mirror.

'My lucky charm,' he said when he saw Nancy looking at it.

'Is it real?' she said.

'Course it is. You can touch it if you like.'

Nancy reached up and felt the soft cool fur, the smooth claws. 'And does it work? I mean, does it make you lucky?'

'All the time,' he said, winking at her.

She could hardly bear the way the car shook and roared, eating her alive. Ant kept glancing over at her as he drove.

'How old are you?' he said.

'Seventeen,' she said.

'No you're not.'

'I know when I was born.'

He laughed. 'A feisty one! I like that. But you're not seventeen.'

She had the feeling he was looking right through her clothes and skin to the inside of her. She shifted in her seat, and the newspaper cutting crinkled in her back pocket. 'I'm thirteen,' she said, staring at her lap.

'You could pass for older, though. Bit of lipstick. Wear your hair loose.'

She didn't know what to say to that.

'You're very pretty,' he said.

'Thank you.'

'Do your parents know you're out on your own?'

'They don't care,' said Nancy. 'They let me do whatever I like.'

'Lucky you,' he said.

He turned on a radio that was built right into the car, and all of a sudden a lady was singing about someone with a heart of glass and being lost inside adorable illusion. She sounded like she couldn't really be bothered with anything; like she'd just woken up. Ant tapped his fingers on the steering wheel in time to the drifty music. He had hair on the backs of his hands, soft and downy-looking, like the rabbit's foot. Strange that it was gingery, thought Nancy, when the hair on his head was blond. She couldn't stop looking at it; she'd only ever seen her parents' hands in the flesh. Maybe the man had been pieced together from bits of different people. A hand here, a head there.

Still he kept glancing over at her. 'Do I know you?' he said at last.

'No,' she said.

'I'm sure I've seen you before, though. Are you famous?'

'I'm nobody. What time is it?'

He checked his watch – the same strange gingery hair curled over the edges of the strap – and said, 'Almost half eleven.'

'We must be nearly there, mustn't we?' said Nancy.

'Seems like you're keen to get shot of me.'

'I . . . I'm just in a hurry.'

'Right. Only it seems like you can't wait to escape.' He turned off the radio.

'I need to get to Ashbridge,' she said. 'It's important.'

'Is it a boy?'

'Yes!' she said, relieved that he finally understood. 'A matter of life or death.'

He gave a single laugh. 'Someone needs a good seeing-to.'

'What?'

'Do you know, Nancy,' he said, speeding up to overtake the car in front, 'boys aren't all they're cracked up to be. I expect you're in for a big disappointment.'

He was overtaking another car, and another. Nancy felt her body pressed into the back of the seat as if by invisible hands. 'Can you slow down a bit?' she said. 'You're scaring me.'

'Aren't you in a hurry?'

'I don't want to have an accident.'

'We're good, we're good,' he said.

She could have cried when she saw the sign for Ashbridge, but Ant seemed to speed up, not slow down. 'This is it,' she said.

'I can read,' he said in a low, quiet voice she did not like.

She thought he was going to zoom right past the exit, but at the last minute he turned off at top speed. The rabbit's foot jerked on its thread.

'Anywhere is fine,' she said as they entered the village.

He parked outside a bakery; in the window a little mechanical man in a white hat and apron nodded his head and tapped a spoon on the glass. Nancy scrambled to free herself from the safety belt, but she couldn't figure out the clasp.

'This boy,' said Ant, unhooking it for her, his hand pushing at her hip, 'be careful with him, all right?'

She nodded. She just wanted to get away, but he was holding her by the forearm now, staring at her hard in the face.

'Boys can do terrible things to a girl. Terrible things.'

'I know,' she said, and she saw something in his expression change.

'You look like that girl,' he said.

'Who?'

He let go of her arm. He'd turned quite pale. 'That murdered girl. Nancy Liddell.'

'I don't know her,' she said. She could feel the cutting folded up in her back pocket.

'One of Arthur Powell's victims,' he said. 'The only one they never found. She was all over the papers when I was a boy.'

'See?' said Nancy. 'That's far too long ago.'

'And then, when they hanged him this year, she was in the papers again. Posing in her tight little trousers. You could be her twin.' He was shrinking from her, pressing himself against his door.

'I've never heard of her,' said Nancy. 'Thank you for the lift.'

She climbed from the car, and as it accelerated away she saw Ant watching her in his mirror. He looked terrified.

Nancy took in the pretty street with its red-brick buildings that stood shoulder to shoulder, its hanging baskets of flowers, the deep-blue face of the clock. But how could it be quarter past two already? She hurried around the base of the clock tower, and each of the four faces told a different time, and she couldn't find anybody to ask. The little baker tapped his spoon on the window at her, regular as a heartbeat. For some reason she thought she might see the plastic people from her father's model village grown to life size.

343

The lady with the stack of parcels would be exiting the corner shop, perhaps, or the man in the tweed suit would be walking his dog past the church. The girl from *Jim'll Fix It* would grab her hand like a friend. *Morning, Nancy*, she'd say. *Lovely day, isn't it?* She felt a warm breath on the back of her neck then, and something nudged her shoulder blade. When she turned, she found herself nose to nose with a pony, its black muzzle whiskered with fine hairs that quivered as it sniffed at her.

'Oh,' she breathed, reaching out to stroke the white star between its eyes. 'Oh, aren't you beautiful.' She'd never seen anything like it in person – never come anywhere near such an animal. In the garden at home she sometimes spotted hedgehogs, and occasionally Cloud brought her mice and sparrows, and once a perfect but dead baby shrew . . . but the pony, huge and sleek and lithe, seemed to have chosen her. And now that she looked, she noticed other ponies too, further down the street – a group of three stood in the shadow of a bus shelter, and a mother and foal were crossing in front of a car, its driver patiently waiting for them to pass.

'Don't touch it!' cried a voice. 'Step back!' A lady in a grey overcoat and knitted hat shoved Nancy's hand clear. 'You mustn't touch them, you know. They can cause serious injury.' She seemed more annoyed than concerned.

'Sorry,' said Nancy. All she wanted to do was press herself against the black pony, listen to the beat of its great heart, but the lady was shooing it away.

'They're not pets,' she said, taking up the handle of her tartan shopping trolley. 'You can't just come here and treat them like your personal property.'

'Yes. No,' said Nancy.

A second lady with a knitted hat and a tartan trolley walked past. 'Dorothy,' she said.

'Judith,' said the first lady, who pulled her hat further down and started to move away just as the clock chimed eleven.

'Wait!' said Nancy. 'How do I get to Captain Scott, please?'

'Why on earth would you want to go there?' said the lady, but before Nancy could think of a reason, she said, 'Cross the bridge just past the corner shop, then follow the road along the edge of the woods.' And she nodded ahead, where the pony was leading the way.

The verge was wet from recent rain, and Nancy took care not to land in a rut and twist her ankle as she ran. Trees arched across the road from both sides, making a tunnel of green that was almost black. The pony seemed made from shadows – and then they were out in the open again, where conkers and acorns gleamed in the grass, and the hedgerows were tangled with rosehips. A rich, sweet scent filled the air, rising from the tiny yellow apples that lay all about the roots of a hollowed-out tree. In the fields, rooks picked over the dark dirt. Nancy's breaths came in gasps as she pushed herself on. She looked to the left and right, but the farmhouses were small and squat and nothing like the manor house where the triplets lived – the place she'd seen on television. Were her parents hurting William at this very moment? Had he woken up properly now, so they could *draw it out the way he drew it out*? Were they already *doing the world a favour*? She willed him to stay asleep a little longer. Up ahead, the pony stopped to nuzzle up a crab apple with its soft mouth – and there, where the hedgerow stopped, a wall began.

Nancy ran its length, trailing her fingers across chunks of glossy stone that looked like the bits of veal her mother set in aspic. She couldn't see over it, but if she stepped back she could make out shards of broken glass on the top. And finally, a gap in the wall – gates – and behind them, at the end of a long driveway, a large white house, white as the cake her mother had made and thrown away. A sign, painted in neat black letters, read *Captain Scott Home for Boys*.

She tried the gate, but it was locked, and she was too big to squeeze between the bars. The pony, still munching crab apples, gazed at her as she approached with her hand out. 'I won't hurt you,' she said. 'It's fine. Everything's fine. Will you help me?' She stroked the star between its eyes again, moved her hand to its strong spine. Pressed. Then, taking an ungainly run-up, she pulled herself onto its back.

The pony gave a small whinny but did not try to buck her off. She sat there stroking its mane, scratching the base of its ears the way she scratched Cloud to make her purr. Gradually her gasps slowed to panting. How incredible to feel the warm, solid animal beneath her own body. 'Good,' she said, keeping her voice gentle. 'Good. Now I'm going to stand up, but I promise not to hurt you.' Leaning against the wall for balance, she rose to her feet and stretched herself as tall as possible – and if she planted her forearms along the top edge of the wall and pushed herself off the pony's back with every muscle in her legs, she could hoist herself up.

A corner of glass jabbed through her trousers as she dragged her knee over the top, and she sucked in her breath. She crouched there for a moment – then, gritting her teeth, she scrambled across the shards and dropped to the ground. Stay asleep, stay asleep, she thought, as if willing herself not to wake to the sting of her bleeding palms and knee. And truly, she felt she'd dropped into a dream: the huge old oaks and chestnuts soft and hazy green, and the scraps of mist that hung like little ghosts above the grass, and the bone-white mansion with its rows of dark windows. And in the distance, sitting beside a patch of ferns, a boy. Although he had his back to her, she knew he was one of the triplets.

Vincent

I'd taken GERM–LOCK out to the garden; since the truth of our origins had come to light, I found I could barely look my brother – my *copy* – in the eye, and all I wanted to do was lose myself in reading. I settled down next to the fernery and opened the volume to All the Knots and How to Tie Them, pulling my crochet blanket around my shoulders since the day was chilly. *It is important to know how to tie knots properly*, I read. *Such knowledge saves much time and trouble, and sometimes even lives depend on it. The sailor aloft in a ship's rigging, the cowboy roping a wild steer, the steeplejack dangling high in the air, all of them know what will happen if a knot slips.* I browsed the pictures of knots – only nine different kinds. Was that really all of them, as the title claimed? I thought of the list I'd read at the back of the FACT INDEX – the Additions and Corrections. How many knots were missing? How could I ever know?

Some knots are valuable because of the speed with which they can be made. But the best are those that hold firmly without slipping, yet do not bind so tightly that it is hard to untie them.

My father's dextrous hands. The fingernails longer on his right.

I must have been sitting very still, because a blackbird appeared at my side and began digging for worms. It was so close I could make out the thin ring of yellow around its eye and a single white feather on its wing. Then something shifted in the surface of the gazing ball, and I saw her reflection but did not believe it: the girl from the window in Exeter. The girl from our dreams, coming straight for me. Slowly, slowly, I turned around, and she stood not a foot away now, as real as the blackbird with the strange white feather, as real as the worm it was tugging from the earth. As real as myself – wasn't she? A drop of blood ran down her finger and splashed on the ground.

'Lawrence?' she said, panting. 'Or Vincent?'

I wanted to run but I couldn't move. The blackbird fluttered off, the worm twisting in its beak. 'I'm . . . I'm Vincent. But who are you?' I said, holding The Book of Knowledge to my chest as if it might shield me.

'William's in trouble. I need your help.' She was almost out of breath. Another drop of blood fell from her fingertip.

'You're bleeding,' I said.

'You have to help us,' she said.

'What?'

She wiped her hand on her trousers and knelt down. 'William's in trouble,' she repeated. Then she began gabbling about her parents putting something in his food to make him sleepy while they set everything up, because his father – *your* father, she said – had killed her elder sister, who was called Nancy, which was her name too.

I didn't believe her story – didn't even understand it – until she pulled the newspaper cutting from her pocket and thrust it at me: *BUTCHER OF BIRMINGHAM TO SWING AT LAST.* Our father, it claimed, had murdered eleven schoolgirls back in the 1950s, including someone called Nancy Liddell. I looked from the photograph to the girl crouched next to me, and they might have been the same person – only Nancy Liddell had died twenty-eight years earlier. Then I noticed another photo – our father as a young boy, sitting in a go-cart at the top of a hill. And his face was my face, our face, and I knew this was the picture – the full version of the picture – that the jay had dropped in our garden. *At 8 a.m.*

on 31 August, he will finally pay for his crimes. We'd visited our father the day before.

'He's dead?' I said.

'Yes, yes, he's dead,' she said, impatient, as if it didn't matter.

'And . . . he killed your sister Nancy, and you're also Nancy?'

Yes, she said; her parents were so heartbroken at losing their firstborn that they'd had her, Nancy, many years later, which was a miracle, and when she, Nancy, looked so like her sister, they'd given her the same name. And they loved her so much that they couldn't bear the thought of anything happening to her, and because the world was a dangerous place they'd kept her inside all her life, apart from the times when they let her into the garden.

I knew then that she was a copy, and I wondered if I should tell her so – but she was clutching my sleeve with her bleeding hand and saying, 'They want revenge, do you understand? They planned a whole party to mark your father's hanging, with streamers and cake and real Babycham, but afterwards they felt no better at all, so now they think they'll feel better if they kill William.'

That couldn't be right, I said; they couldn't mean him harm. They'd let us play with the model trains, and turned back the cuckoo clock, and said it was a real pleasure. They'd given us jam roly-poly and fizzy drinks. But Nancy was sobbing and digging her fingers into my arm and saying she'd seen a row of knives all lined up, and they'd told her they were going to do the world a favour, draw it out the way he drew it out.

I recalled Mrs Fletcher scouring the sofa with the wet cloth when I went back to the house. Rubbing away every trace of us.

'They'll *kill* him,' said Nancy, and I believed her then.

'We'll ring 999,' I said, jumping to my feet. 'That's the number for emergencies – I've seen it in the telephone box in the village. You ring 999 and say where you are, and the police come and fix everything.'

But she said no, the police would put her parents in prison, and then they would hang them, because that was what happened to people who killed other people, everyone knew, and didn't it say so in the newspaper?

'You love them,' I said.

'Of course I love them. They're my parents.'

Maybe that makes sense to you. I suppose I understand it now, but at the time I had no idea what to do, and every second I stood there panicking was a second later.

'We'll ask my mother,' I said at last, my voice trembly and hollow.

'You have a mother?' said Nancy, running along behind me as I hurried to the house.

'Yes and no,' I said.

The door to the North Wing was locked, so I pounded on it and called for Mother Morning, and finally we heard her footsteps.

'What is it?' she slurred through the door. *Whadizit?*

'William's in trouble,' I said. 'The Fletchers are going to kill him.'

She laughed. 'You're telling fibs. I'll write you up.'

'Can you let us in, Mother Morning? Please!'

Something thudded and slid against the door. 'I need a new bottle,' she said. *Needuhnewboll.*

'Let us in, and I'll get you one!'

'Mmm,' she murmured.

After that I couldn't get her to answer at all, let alone open the door.

'I don't know—' I began, turning to Nancy, but she was looking down the passageway.

'You must be Lawrence,' she said.

My brother stopped dead in his tracks. Took in the blood smeared on her trousers and across her cheek. 'Get away from me,' he shouted. He ran for the staircase, stumbling over his feet, and a moment later we heard the front door slam behind him.

'Is it because I look so much like her?' said Nancy. 'Do people think I'm a ghost?'

'Something like that, maybe,' I said.

She frowned, regarding me. 'You know something I don't.'

I licked my thumb and wiped away the blood on her cheek. 'Come on,' I said. 'I know who can help us.'

In my bedroom I yanked open the chest of drawers and found the card the Minister had given me – in case we ever needed to get in touch, she'd said, day or night. Then I ran down to the Library, grabbed our woodworking tools from the Equipment Cupboard and raced back upstairs.

'A Minister came to our house,' said Nancy, studying the card. 'She asked my parents why they'd never had children.'

'But where were you?'

'In the wardrobe, with a jam sandwich and the Spirograph.'

There was no time to ask her what she meant. I knocked on the door to the North Wing one last time. 'Mother Morning?' I called.

No answer.

I began to drill.

I made a row of holes next to the door handle so I could slip in a hacksaw blade and begin cutting. Soon enough my fist could fit through. I reached for the key and turned it – except the door still would not give. Desperate now, I kicked at its base and Mother Morning groaned from where she must have been slumped against it.

'Can you use your hands?' I said to Nancy.

She hesitated, then nodded, and together we pushed with all our might against the door. Inch by inch, it opened.

Mother Morning had vomited on herself. It was in her hair and on her crumpled blouse, lodged in the creases of her neck, even in the whorl of an ear.

'Is she all right?' said Nancy.

'I don't know,' I said, stepping over her.

The sitting room smelled sweet and sharp. Dirty plates covered the floor – ham sandwiches mossy with mould, a halved pear rotted to slush. I thought I saw something scuttling away under the television. Nancy drew back the curtains and threw open the windows while I hunted for the telephone, shifting piles of unwashed clothing and old newspapers, a stained eiderdown, a tablecloth with an iron mark burnt into its middle. I found the phone muffled under a mound of pillows, its spiralling cord lumpy with knots, and I dialled the Minister's number.

A man answered.

'Have I made a mistake?' I said.

'Who is this?' he said.

'I don't know. I thought I was ringing the Minister of Loneliness.'

'I mean, who are you?'

'It's Vincent,' I said. 'From Captain Scott.'

'How did you get this number?'

'She gave it to me. Please, it's an emergency.'

He paused, sighed. 'One moment.'

I thought I heard a whispered argument, but I couldn't make out any words apart from *our home life, Sylvia*.

Then the Minister came on the line and said, 'Vincent, how can I help?' and I knew I had telephoned the right person. I told her everything as quickly as I could – that I knew we were copies, that I'd seen the cutting about our father, that Nancy had come all the way from Exeter to find me, that she was the secret sister of Nancy Liddell, and that her parents were going to hurt William very, very soon. I stopped short of saying that she was a copy, since she was standing right there with her torn trousers and her bloody hands, looking as if she might collapse.

'What do you mean, the secret sister?' said the Minister.

'Yes, and identical,' I said, eyeing Nancy.

I heard the Minister breathe in and slowly out. 'She's also a copy?'

'I'm certain of it.' I smiled at Nancy as if everything would be all right now, and she touched the back of my hand.

'No police, remember?' Nancy whispered, so I explained that too.

'Leave it with me,' said the Minister.

The Minister of Loneliness

There goes my career: that was her first thought, far ahead of any concern for William. What sort of person was she? But she knew her reputation would never recover from the scandal. She had failed to put in place adequate checks to ensure the Fletchers were trustworthy. She should have had social workers screening them, and the police poking about too – except she'd wanted to control the whole operation. Take all the glory. And now, the very first placement – the only placement she'd managed to organise – was about to go terribly, terribly wrong.

Her husband didn't believe a word of it. Nancy Liddell, copied and hidden away in Exeter for years? Her parents living under assumed names? The story seemed so far-fetched, the Minister admitted . . . and yet. Why would Vincent make it up? He'd sounded genuinely distressed on the phone. And hadn't she heard something behind the wall of the Fletchers' sitting room? They'd said it was their cat, but what if it was a copy, an illegal copy of their dead daughter?

She raced upstairs and searched through the stack of work on her bedside table, looking for the folder she'd brought home a few weeks earlier. She hadn't taken it back to her office, had she? Left it to be filed with the rest of the Sycamore Scheme material? But no, there it was at the bottom of the pile – the collection of cuttings about Arthur Powell. She'd pored over them in preparation for her visit to Strangeways. Ghoulish to bring him to bed, her husband had remarked.

The Minister flicked past the more recent pieces, working her way back to the ones from 1964, when Powell was tried and convicted. She hadn't paid much attention to the few small photographs of Nancy's parents, but now she bent close, scrutinising each of them in turn. And there in the grainy reproductions of Keith and Mary Liddell she could just make out Kenneth and Marjorie Fletcher.

Oh God. She sat very still on the edge of the mattress, the satin bedspread suddenly cold beneath her. The PM would have her head . . . and a child was in danger, of course. Do something, she scolded herself. *Do* something. *Verité Sans Peur.*

She picked up the telephone and rang the police, outlining the situation as concisely as possible, and then she lay down on the bed and closed her eyes. She must have fallen asleep, because she dreamt she was back in her friend Beatrice's potting shed, and she was daring Beatrice to open the tin of slug pellets and have a little taste.

'Sure you want to watch it?' asked her husband, his hand poised to switch the television set off.

'Yes,' she said. 'No. Wait, yes.'

It was the lead story, of course. She half turned her head away, looking out of the corner of her eye.

'Following a tip-off that a child's life was in danger,' said the newsreader, 'police today raided a home in a quiet Exeter cul-de-sac where they found a range of knives, lengths of rope, plastic sheeting, quantities of the sedative methaqualone, and a male copy aged thirteen years. The home is believed to belong to Keith and Mary Liddell, the parents of schoolgirl Nancy Liddell, who was murdered in 1951. Last month her killer, Arthur Powell, was hanged for his crimes, but sources suggest that he left behind three copies, and that Sylvia Dalton, the Minister of Loneliness, was in the process of placing these individuals in the community as part of the winding down of the Sycamore Scheme. While police are remaining tight-lipped about today's incident, it appears that the Liddells, using the name Fletcher, had been approved to adopt one of the copies.'

Footage of the house appeared on the screen – the birdbath in the front garden, the net curtains covering the windows. No interior shots, but the Minister had been briefed about the room swathed in plastic. The streaks of blood on the bed, the bloodied knife on the floor.

'They keep to themselves,' a neighbour was saying. 'Friendly enough if you see them on the street, but they'd never invite you in. I borrowed their lawnmower once and a wheel fell off, and they were very good about it.'

'We saw him carried out on a stretcher,' said a second neighbour. 'He was absolutely covered in blood, all over his face and neck. We were ever so relieved when we found out it wasn't an actual boy.'

'Police arrived at the address in time to prevent fatal damage,' said the newsreader, 'but the copy had been significantly vandalised. Sylvia Dalton was unavailable for comment today.'

The Minister groaned, covered her eyes. Her husband moved closer to her on the sofa and rubbed her back.

'You'll have to talk to them eventually, my love,' he said.

'We need to be armed and ready,' said the Prime Minister. 'The press have already got wind of the Liddells owning an illegal copy of the daughter. It's only a matter of time before they break the story.'

The Minister blinked. She'd assumed the PM had summoned her to sack her; to suspend her, at the very least. 'It's my fault,' she said, staring at the blotter on the PM's desk, trying to make sense of the scattered dots of ink. 'All this could have been avoided if I'd involved the proper experts from the start.'

'Avoided how?' said the PM. 'You couldn't have travelled back in time to stop them from ordering a copy of their dead child.'

As if the girl were the most problematic part of the whole sorry mess.

'What's to become of her?' said the Minister.

'Who?'

'Nancy, of course.'

'I've no idea. And she's not Nancy, remember.'

'Just as William is not Arthur Powell.'

'Mmm,' said the PM, fiddling with the rose in the bud vase at her elbow.

'What does that mean?'

The PM spread her hands. 'They chose him because of his obviously disturbed temperament. They didn't want a child, they wanted a . . . a sacrifice. And you've not had a flicker of interest from any legitimate applicants. I think it's time to abandon the rehoming programme.'

'I can't *abandon* it,' said the Minister. 'What about the children?'

'They can be absorbed into the clinical programme, perhaps. One way or another, they'll be looked after.'

'Looked after,' repeated the Minister.

'Exactly,' said the PM.

'I just wonder . . .' said the Minister, and the PM sighed. 'I just wonder how successful it's been – the Scheme. How many actual medical breakthroughs it can claim. Whether we can ever justify the cost.'

'The clinics will be much cheaper to run,' said the PM.

'I'm not talking about money.'

The PM sighed again. 'Medical research requires living subjects. You know that. And in the wake of the dreadful experiments in the camps during the war, Dr Roach came up with an alternative solution – experimentation on conscious tissue, identical to the human body but devoid of . . . well, you might call it a soul.'

'There is *no* difference between the copies and us,' said the Minister.

'Exactly – they're physically identical.'

The Minister closed her eyes for a moment. Took in a deep breath, then released it. 'Surely gene modification would have been a better solution,' she said. 'A more humane solution.'

'It doesn't work for all diseases,' said the PM, glancing at her watch. 'At any rate, what we must focus on right now is how to make this look right.'

'I find it hard not to come to the conclusion,' said the Minister, 'that Dr Roach has been allowed to forge ahead with his research quite unchecked.'

'Not at all,' said the PM. 'No new material has been produced in close to a decade.'

'Material?'

'Subjects. Residents. Let's not get bogged down in semantics.'

'But the clinical programme's waiting in the wings, isn't it? And Roach has continued to experiment on the remaining children, even after news of the closure of the Homes! The man has a God complex!'

'He has changed the face of modern medicine,' said the PM.

'He's also made hefty donations to those in power over the years.'

'As have many individuals.'

'But what miracle drugs has the Scheme produced?'

'There has been significant progress in several areas,' the PM said, and waved a hand: topic concluded. 'Now, the business in Exeter . . . we need to stress the human-interest angle. The Liddells, driven mad by grief for their lost daughter, took action that nobody – *nobody* – could have predicted.'

'They tortured and mutilated a thirteen-year-old child,' said the Minister.

'Well, a copy,' said the PM.

'They drugged him and severed his tongue. His finger and earlobe would have been next, and then his throat, the same as Nancy.'

'It's not ideal, I agree, but—'

'They were planning to *murder* him,' said the Minister.

'Can one murder a copy, though?'

'What? They'll be arrested, won't they?'

The PM smiled, tilted her head in that way she had. 'No crime has been committed,' she said. 'Now, an ordinary British mother and father, put through the most unimaginable ordeal . . .'

An aphid clung to the rose in the vase, the Minister noticed. Exactly the same green as the stem; almost impossible to see.

'The important thing at this point,' the PM was saying, 'is to focus on the fact that the public – the community – is absolutely safe.'

'Of course the community's safe!' said the Minister. 'The children pose no danger at all! It's the *community* we need to worry about!' She could feel her voice rising, her face flushing.

'I can rely on you to handle this in the proper way, can't I, Sylvia?' said the PM.

The Minister stared at the aphid as it sucked out the sap.

'Sylvia?'

'Of course, Prime Minister.'

A day later she was sitting in front of a mirror that showed her every wrinkle, the thinness of her short brown hair.

'I haven't been sleeping well,' she said, gesturing in a hopeless way at her reflection.

'Never you mind,' said the makeup girl. 'We'll soon have you looking fresh as a daisy.'

She went to work on the Minister, pressing the foundation into her pores, smoothing her out. The Minister could smell her perfume – cheap and synthetic – and below that the peppery musk of the girl's skin. There was something so intimate about being made up – letting a stranger touch your lips, your eyes.

'When you were a child,' the Minister said, 'was this what you saw yourself doing?'

'It was, actually,' said the makeup girl, scouring the cake of foundation with a damp sponge. 'I used to put my mum's lipstick and eye shadow on my dolls. Made a terrible mess, but she always told me how pretty they looked. How clever I was.'

'She sounds lovely.'

'She is.'

The Minister took her seat in the studio. She could feel the tag of her blouse itching the back of her neck, and she longed to tear it out, but already the cameras were rolling and the interviewer was opening fire.

'Isn't it the case, Minister,' he said, 'that you visited the Exeter house on more than one occasion?'

'I did visit the Fletchers—'

'Except they're not the Fletchers, are they?' said the interviewer. 'Are we really to believe you had no inkling of their true identity?'

'I saw nothing to suggest—'

'Not to mention the copy of their murdered child hidden away in the wardrobe!'

The Minister scratched the back of her neck. 'I think what we need to remember,' she said, 'is that we're talking about an ordinary British mother and father, put through the most unimaginable ordeal.'

'It's not a very good start to your rehoming programme, is it?'

She scratched her neck again, harder. 'Driven mad by grief for their lost daughter, the Fletchers – the Liddells – took action that nobody – *nobody* – could have predicted. But I can assure you that they posed no danger to the community at any time.'

'But – pardon me, Minister – I think you misunderstand my point. The fact is, when he regained full consciousness, the copy lashed out. Keith Liddell suffered scratches to his face, and Mary Liddell had a handful of hair torn from her head. Is it any wonder you've had no takers for these creatures?'

'William was fighting for his life,' said the Minister, but the interviewer spoke over her.

'Just how much of the public purse has your office spent on the programme?'

'Well, I don't have the exact figures in front of me, but—'

'Thousands of full-colour catalogues. Professional photographers. Trips all over the country.'

'And on those trips I have met many Sycamore children, and never once have I come to any harm.' Which was true, despite all her misgivings. She scratched furiously at her neck. 'What people need to realise,' she said, 'is that the behavioural issues displayed by some of the children resulted from their inhumane treatment, not their genetic inheritance.'

But on the interviewer went: it wasn't just the Sycamore children the community needed to fear; who knew if any other illegal copies might crawl out of the woodwork? With no schooling in ethics, no Socialisation Days, wouldn't they be even more unpredictable? Hadn't a young man who'd given the Liddell copy a lift to Exeter come forward to say that she'd seemed a very unstable individual?

When it was finally over, the Minister found the makeup girl and asked her to cut the label from her collar.

'You've scratched yourself,' said the girl. 'You're bleeding.'

'Have I? Have I really?' She looked at her hand and saw blood under her nails. But how wonderful to be free of the irritation!

The Minister told Evans she'd make her own way home, and then she began walking. She passed rows of shops – a chemist, a betting shop, a hair salon, a place that repaired bicycles – and terraced houses with wide bay windows. A few people glanced at her as if they recognised her, and one man stopped and said she wasn't really going to let all those little hoodlums out, was she? Because that was the worst idea he'd ever heard, and had she forgotten Flamborough? Thank you for your comments, she said, and on she walked, past travel agencies and fruiterers, dry cleaners and Italian restaurants, pet shops and television shops and banks, then across the murky Thames until at last she reached Kew.

The Palm House rose like a glass cathedral, opalescent in the watery afternoon light, and when she stepped inside she could imagine herself somewhere else entirely. Somewhere tropical and lush, rustling with vast dark leaves and scented with the rarest of flowers. She ran a finger over a spiky palm, a pendulous white trumpet, the strange roots of a banyan tree. Carved into a stem of bamboo, a wobbly heart.

When she climbed the spiral staircase that wound itself into the sky, she could see the arching struts holding the whole impossible structure aloft, all the hundreds of panes of glass suspended above her. The air was closer up here, humid and hot, and she heard water dripping. Around the narrow balcony she moved, hovering above the rainforest like a bird, taking in the endangered and the extinct. Everywhere, shoots and tendrils pushed their way through the railing, determined to survive. Drops of water splashed on her face and hands, and the view to the outside was foggy. The wrought iron bloomed with rust, all the rosettes and palmettes and chrysanthemums covered in it, even the iron walkway beneath her feet, as if seized by some unstoppable blight. She thought about what the Liddells' neighbour had said on television: *We were ever so relieved when we found out it wasn't an actual boy.*

Vincent

Of course I felt terrible about the attack, and wished I could turn back time – go to the Liddells' in my brother's place. I would have done that for him, I told myself. I would have.

He was in hospital for two weeks, and when they brought him home he refused to look at me. They gave him a notepad for writing things down that he wanted to say, but he wouldn't write anything for me, no matter how I begged. He took his pillow and his crochet blanket and lay on his side, staring at the wall. With the stump of a pencil he drew a tiny picture of the merry-go-round swan at Dreamland. The slender neck all wonky.

'Can I bring you anything?' I asked.

He shook his head, held his hands over his ears.

Mother Morning had gone by then – nobody told us where – and a new lady came to look after us instead. She worked no particular shift, so we didn't know what to call her; Mother, we supposed, because she was there all the time, like a real one. But no, she said – there had been enough confusion in that regard, and we should call her Miss Ream. She was cheerful and kind and very large, with fleshy arms that stretched her sleeves tight as sausage casings and an upper half that seemed all bust. Her hands were permanently chapped, and she rubbed them with coal-tar ointment and slept in cotton gloves; each washday their hollow fingers fluttered in the breeze. She put us to work waxing the parquet and linoleum, cleaning the spatters from the cooker and the smears from the light switches. 'Poor motherless lambs,' she murmured. 'Poor wee bunnies. Jesus has a plan for you.'

Other children began to arrive too, from the closed Homes – more than twenty of them, girls as well as boys. They brought with them games we'd never seen before: draughts and Ludo, a bag of chipped marbles that wouldn't roll straight, a Battleship game with a picture of a father and son sinking each other's ships while the mother and daughter beamed over the washing up. When Diane and Karen arrived with a set of twins from Edith Saunders, I found myself looking for Jane – until I remembered. By that time, we all knew what Margate meant, and we discussed it as we cleaned the house: would the children have *realised*, at some point? Did it hurt? Did anyone escape? A boy from Sir Isaac Newton said that any ashes dumped in the Thames or the Lea or the Medway or the Stour would make their way to Margate eventually, so that was something, wasn't it? Nobody replied. Diane said she had no doubt Jane had escaped – she would have given them the slip and dashed off into the crowds at Dreamland, or hidden underground in the Shell Grotto and waited till night-time. Buried herself in sand, maybe. A girl from Elizabeth Fry said didn't Diane know that they never even went to Margate? That Margate was never real? Well then, said Diane, what about the Van? Why would a van pick them up, if not to take them to Margate, which was a long way away and would require such a vehicle? When Miss Ream overheard us she said, 'Now then, now then, that's all in the past, my chickens. You are not going anywhere. You are the lucky ones.' And we kept wiping away the spatters and the smears and counting our blessings, which she assured us were many.

'Are you like us, Miss Ream?' we asked her.

'We are all God's creatures,' she said.

'But are you a copy of someone who did something wrong?'

'We are all perfect in God's eyes.'

The girls slept downstairs and we slept upstairs, and we ran in and out of one another's rooms. It felt almost like the old days – but as Miss Ream served us our beef stew that first week she said that while it was fun to make new friends, and while it was fine to visit a friend's room during the day so long as we left the door open, there was to be no funny business.

'Are we not allowed to tell jokes?' Diane said to me, poking at a chunk of mushroom. 'Only I've a very good one up my sleeve.'

I said I didn't think that was what Miss Ream meant by funny business.

'What does she mean, then?' said Diane.

'Copulation,' I said, louder than I'd intended.

Karen glanced over at us from two tables away; she never sat with me and my brothers, or so much as spoke to us.

'What does *that* mean?' said Diane.

I thought again of the picnic in the woods. Karen at the foot of the beech tree, her blouse torn and her trousers pulled down. She'd lost even more weight since the last Socialisation Day; I could see her skull pushing through the shallow planes of her face.

Diane put up her hand.

'Yes, dear?' said Miss Ream.

'What do you mean by funny business?'

'I mean girls sneaking into boys' rooms and boys sneaking into girls' rooms under cover of darkness.'

'To do copulation?' said Diane.

Miss Ream said, 'Our bodies are a gift from God, and we respect them, and we also respect the bodies of others.' Which didn't really answer the question.

Diane raised her hand again, but Miss Ream said, 'I think we'll have a reading from the Bible now.'

She went and fetched her thick book with the gold-edged pages. On its brown vinyl slip-cover Jesus stared at a cloud, perhaps thinking of the plan He had for us. Miss Ream had been teaching us about all the miraculous things He had done, such as casting out demons and raising the dead. He had saved her life, she said, and He could save ours too.

Karen listened intently when Miss Ream talked about Jesus. She took to reading the Bible herself, copying out certain passages and pinning them above her bed. According to Diane she knelt down every night and prayed, muttering away for ages. It was very annoying.

Diane and I were in the room they shared, and I was admiring a blue glass bottle she had unearthed in the vegetable patch at Edith Saunders. It had been scaly and dull and choked with dirt when she'd found it, but now it gleamed like a jewel.

'I don't show it to many people,' she said. 'Obviously, it's a target for thieves – see?' Down its length, in raised letters, ran the words *NOT TO BE TAKEN*.

'I think that means it had poison inside,' I said.

'Don't be stupid. It's very valuable and rare, and therefore is not to be taken. Don't you know anything?' She snatched the bottle back from me and returned it to her bottom drawer.

I peered at the scraps of paper pinned above Karen's bed, the handwriting tiny and crowded. *And now a leper approached him, bowed low, and said, 'Sir, if only you will, you can cleanse me,'* read one. Another read *His feet were wetted with her tears and she wiped them with her hair, kissing them and anointing them with the myrrh.*

'I'd quite like to swap her for Tina from Elizabeth Fry,' said Diane. 'Tina can do French plaits and is going to teach me how. It's extremely complicated, but Tina says she has every confidence in me.'

'I don't think you can just swap her,' I said.

'She stole a chair.'

'What?'

Diane pointed to a dining chair beside the door. 'She took it from the Refectory, which she shouldn't have, obviously, because the chairs are for everyone and not just her.'

'We have dozens of Refectory chairs,' I said.

'Didn't you pay *any* attention in Ethical Hour?' Diane put her hand on her hip. 'I haven't told on her yet, but I could if I wanted. She wedges it under the door handle at bedtime, and she won't sleep if it's not in place.'

'Why would she do that?' I said, but I knew. I knew.

'Because of the funny business, I expect,' said Diane. 'It's very inconvenient if I need to go to the lavatory. Once, when I was out of the room for about two minutes, she wedged it under the handle again, and I couldn't get back in. I had to knock. On my own bedroom door!'

She was waiting for me to say something. 'How terrible,' I murmured.

'Which reminds me,' she said. 'Knock knock.'

'What?'

'Knock *knock*.'

'Um . . .'

'You say, "Who's there?" I'll start again. Knock knock.'

'Who's there?'

'Luke.'

'Um. Luke who?'

'Luke through the keyhole and find out!'

She was doubled over, killing herself.

'Do you know where you come from, Diane?' I asked after a moment.

She straightened up. 'I told you ages ago,' she said. 'My parents died in a car accident.'

'But where you *really* come from.'

Some children had discovered their origins when the Homes closed – they had asked their mothers, and their mothers, beyond caring, had told them the truth at last: that they came from criminals who'd just wanted some free cigarettes and who didn't even look at what they were signing. One boy, Terry, announced to us that he was a copy of a bank robber from Liverpool who had blown open the safe with dynamite and bludgeoned to death a bank employee who tried to stop him. 'He just kept hitting the guy,' he said, 'until his face was a bloody pulp.' Terry, grinning, mimed the blows for us, *pow pow pow*, but we could tell he was wondering what he carried inside him. What he really was.

Other children didn't ask their mothers.

'My parents died in a car accident,' Diane repeated. 'And Jane is in Margate. End of story.'

Jane on the Sky Wheels at Dreamland, spinning higher and higher, whirling into the stars. Jane underground, wandering the shell-lined passages, searching for a way out. The sea seeping drop by drop into the walls. All the world above her going about its business.

'You must feel very guilty about William,' said Diane. 'Will he ever be able to talk again?'

A shivering, a scuttling inside me. 'Why would I feel guilty?'

'Because he was attacked and you weren't.'

'That was nothing to do with me.'

'Well, you must have noticed something odd about those people.'

'No.'

'Nothing at all?'

Nancy mouthing *Run* through the window. The bad, bad feeling I'd had.

'He went of his own free will,' I said. 'He wanted to go. They had a train set and a cat.'

'Can you talk without a tongue?'

'I don't know.'

'You can't. Or taste food.'

'He wanted to go,' I said. 'Nobody could have known.'

'Mm,' said Diane. 'I doubt he'll ever forgive you. He stares right through you like you're empty air. Like you're nothing. You'll have written yourself up, I expect.'

'Why would I write myself up when I didn't do anything wrong? And anyway, we're finished with The Book of Guilt.'

'No we're not.'

She was right. Although Miss Ream had told us that things would be different now, I knew that some of the children – many of them – kept to the old habits. They sat on one another's beds each morning and asked for the details of dreams, jotting them down just as Mother Morning used to. Assuring one another they saw no cause for concern in the visions of flying and falling, of hidden rooms and injured animals and people who started out as one person and turned without warning into someone else. 'All completely normal,' they'd say. 'No need to send you to Margate.'

They made entries in The Book of Guilt, too, fetching it from the Library if anyone stepped out of line. *17 October 1979: Susan Cook ate the last Garibaldi biscuit when she'd already had three*, they noted in their best handwriting. *19 October 1979: Denis Thompson asked to see Julie Green's pants. 19 October 1979: Julie Green showed Denis Thompson her pants.* And some children wrote themselves up, taking a strange comfort in recording their misdemeanours. *22 October 1979: I, Clare Roberts, left a disgusting ring around the bath. 23 October 1979: I, Ian Turner, made up a song about Michelle Johnson's buck teeth and sang it to her till she cried.*

One or two came to the door of our bedroom and asked to see Lawrence's Margate brochure. They cradled it on their laps and touched their fingertips to the swan and the parakeet, the River Caves and the Wall of Death, turning the pages slowly, slowly, as if they couldn't bear it to end.

The Minister called in to see my brothers and me one day. We sat in the Gun Room, where the bristly roots of the philodendron plant were bursting like insects through the holes in the pot. The Minister clasped and unclasped her hands, and finally she said, 'I must apologise, William, for the terrible events of September. I should have looked into things more closely. I'm so sorry.'

Miss Ream said, 'It takes a big person to own up to her failures, doesn't it, boys?'

My brothers stared at the floor and did not respond.

'Thank you, Minister,' I said.

She gave a sad smile. 'I'm not a Minister any more. My decision – that's the official story, anyway.'

'God will direct you to the right path,' said Miss Ream.

The Minister started fiddling with the safety chain on her cameo brooch; the tiny pin had worked its way loose of her lapel. 'I've been thinking,' she said, 'and I want to help. In light of what's happened, I want to try to do something about the rights of . . . of people like you.'

'Copies,' I said.

'Well, yes,' she said.

'Rights?' said Miss Ream.

'The right to decent work,' said the Minister. 'The right to vote. The right to citizenship.'

'My goodness me. You'll have a fight on your hands.'

'And I mean to shut down the clinical programme. There has to be another way.'

'Is it true they're starting from scratch? With babies?'

The Minister sighed. 'If people knew what went on in the Homes – I mean really *knew*—'

'The thing is, people did know – or they suspected. They just didn't care. They still don't, by and large.'

'I think that can change, over time.'

'Do you know when the rot set into our souls?' said Miss Ream. 'After the war. The Gothenburg Treaty. We signed a pact with the Devil – helped ourselves to the research from the camps, no questions asked.'

The Minister let go of the safety chain; it swung back and forth for a moment. 'Dr Roach had already produced the rabbit,' she said. 'It was only a matter of time before they moved to humans.'

'Poor innocent souls,' said Miss Ream, shaking her head. 'I shall pray for them – and for you, my dear.'

The Minister hesitated, glanced at my brother. 'I hope, William, you might be able to forgive me one day . . .?'

He glowered at her, then scribbled a note on his pad – and I saw what he was writing, and I wanted to snatch it away and tear it to pieces, but already he was handing it over:

I'm NOT William.

Confusion spread across the Minister's face. 'Not William?' she said. 'Who are you, then?'

And out it all came – what I'd seen. What I knew. Mr Fletcher's fleeting look of revulsion when I returned for the brochure. Mrs Fletcher scouring the sofa clean of every trace of us. The girl – Nancy – watching from the window, warning me to run. How terrified I'd been, but how I'd kept it to myself until I knew which one of us the Fletchers – the Liddells – wanted.

'And why did you tell your brothers what you'd seen once you knew they wanted William?' said the Minister.

'He was trying to protect me,' said William – the real William. 'What's wrong with that? We talked it all through in Ethical Hour – whether I should be the one to go.'

I remembered the three of us sitting around the table in the Library. My brothers at first had refused to believe in the girl. William had turned pale and insisted that she wasn't real, that I'd simply seen a shadow on the glass, remembered a bit of a dream – or that I'd made her up. *You're trying to frighten me! So I won't want to go, and you get to go instead, and have the train set and the TV and the fizzy drinks all to yourself!* Then Lawrence had announced that he wasn't scared – that he hoped she *was* real, and as pretty as he dreamt her.

'Lawrence wanted to go,' I told the Minister. 'And as William said, we talked it all through, ethically speaking. I put the question to them – if there was even a chance this girl existed, this figure from William's nightmares, was it fair to send him to her? Especially when the solution was staring us in the face?'

'The solution?' said Miss Ream.

'Lawrence wanted to go,' I repeated. 'I pointed out that he could just put on William's clothes and take his place.'

The Minister gasped, and I started to cry, and William kicked the leg of the sofa.

'You suspected something was very wrong with the Fletchers,' said the Minister, 'but you talked Lawrence into going?'

'The Liddells,' said Miss Ream.

The Minister ignored her. She held my gaze with those pale-blue eyes, and I couldn't shake the feeling I had failed her somehow.

'Yes,' I said in a quiet voice.

'Why would you do that? When you thought it might be dangerous?'

'I don't know.' I did not say: Because I loved William better, always had loved William better, despite his cruel streak. But both my brothers knew it.

Lawrence scribbled on his pad, tossing it to the Minister before leaving the room: *Vincent did this to me. It's all his fault.*

'He is still your brother,' said Miss Ream, scurrying after him. 'Wait, William – I mean Lawrence. Come back and let him apologise.'

But he'd gone.

As the tears poured from me, the Minister opened her arms, and I laid my head against her chest and sobbed for the things I could not undo. For the creature I knew I was.

We sat like that for a time, William doodling ripples on the notepad, lines that spread out and out from Lawrence's words. The Minister rocked me like a baby. I could feel her cameo brooch under my cheek, and later, when I looked in the mirror, I saw the shape of the goddess of Night pressed into my skin as if someone had carved her there.

Nancy

'I'm not your miracle, am I,' said Nancy. 'I'm your copy.'

'We had you because we love you,' said her mother.

'You didn't have me. You bribed a lab worker to make me. What did you use? Nancy's hairbrush? The bits of her they found?'

'*What?*' said her mother.

'We couldn't lose you, love,' said her father. 'Not when we knew it was possible to get you back.'

'To get *her* back,' said Nancy. 'What did you use?'

'We don't think of you as a copy,' he said, putting his arm around her. 'You're our Nancy. The same girl. Every cell of you the very same.'

'Don't touch me.'

'Please,' said her mother, beginning to sob. 'Please.'

'Tell me what you used. What I'm made from.'

Her father looked at her mother, who hesitated, then nodded. 'We gave them some of her baby teeth,' he said.

Nancy stood up from the plastic-covered sofa. 'I'm going outside for a walk.'

'On your own?' said her father.

'Yes.'

'It's pouring,' said her mother.

'I know.'

'Shall we come with you?'

'No thank you.'

'How long will you be?'

'I'll be home when I'm home.'

Nancy shut the front door and strode down the path to the gate. She felt the blood pulsing through her body, her muscles buzzing with every step. Beyond the hedge, the other bungalows in the cul-de-sac sat squat on their plots: brown and red bricks, pebble-dashing, net curtains, strips of shrubs – how lovely they were. How lovely the gutters that shone with water. The dead leaves leather-smooth. The abandoned footballs and the pavement cracks and the distant pylons, the fat drops of rain that pattered across Nancy's umbrella, the streetlights that would burst into beacons soon, when dusk fell. From a window a man watched her, his face expressionless even as she waved. A lady emerged from the house opposite to place her empty milk bottles on the doorstep – and then, noticing Nancy, hurried back inside. A car pulled into a driveway, and a girl a little younger than Nancy climbed out; when she started to say hello, her mother said, 'Katie, what have we spoken about?'

But the girl raced over to Nancy and said, 'Do you like hopscotch?'

'I . . . I don't know,' said Nancy.

'You have pretty hair.'

'Thank you.'

The girl squeezed under the umbrella and fingered the ends of Nancy's ponytail. 'I'm the hopscotch queen. I'll teach you if you like.'

'Katie,' called the girl's mother. 'You'll catch your death.'

'Come back at the weekend.'

'All right,' said Nancy.

On she walked, and the people in the cars peered out at her as they passed, the tyres raising water from the road, and the water made fabulous shapes: ostrich feather fans, the fins of leaping fish. Nancy waved at every car, and a few people waved back, and she ran down the street with the umbrella resting on her shoulder, catching great scoops of air. Perhaps she would stay out until well after dark. Find a patch of woods to explore, a river to swim. Perhaps she would hitch another ride – to Redhampton this time, where she could wander the life-size village. Linger on the train tracks, knock on the doors of strangers.

Nothing could harm her. She was made from teeth, and she would devour the world.

Vincent

When he turned fourteen, Lawrence ran away. The police searched for a few weeks, so they said, but found no trace of him. We had to learn to accept God's will, said Miss Ream, and perhaps He had a special plan for Lawrence that would reveal itself in the fullness of time. So we waited. For a year, and then another.

It was the Minister – Sylvia – who told us he had fallen in with a bad crowd in London and was living on the streets, breaking into people's houses to fund a heroin habit. That made no sense and couldn't be true, I told her; he hated needles. She said she was sorry.

Many times, over many years, I went to the city and tried to find him, looking under bridges and in parks, in alleyways and doorways, looking into the faces of the lost for my likeness – but he had vanished. Empty air. Nothing.

I told myself that he turned things around eventually. That he volunteered for the RSPCA and then trained to be a vet. That he opened a practice somewhere in the countryside and could heal any animal without ever needing to speak a word, fixing fractures and closing wounds and making tumours disappear under his kind hands. He had a pretty wife and a house full of dogs, I told myself.

Those sorts of things – marrying; a proper education and a proper job – were becoming possible for us by then. If a copy applied for a legal birth certificate, all doors opened, in theory, even if *Father:*

Unknown and *Mother: Unknown* were a giveaway. Nancy had found work in a fashion boutique, and I had managed to train as a librarian. I'd built shelves in every room of our flat for all my books, fitting them around Nancy's piano in the sitting room; she joked that soon we'd have to sleep in the broom cupboard.

'He might have fallen on his feet, though,' I said to her.

'You never know,' she said.

But William, who was visiting us that day, poked me in the ribs and said, 'I bet he's doing unspeakable things for money.' He mimed sucking the air above his fist.

'You never know,' I repeated.

'Yes you do,' he said.

He showed up at our place without warning from time to time, only ever staying long enough to say something cruel.

'Don't you worry he'll turn on you?' he asked Nancy once. 'You know what they say – blood will out.'

'He's not his father,' she said.

I'd taken pains to make myself look different from Powell – glasses, no beard, my curls close-cropped – and Nancy, for her part, bleached her hair and wore it short. We'd never been recognised, despite the pictures that had been in the papers and on television, and we were grateful for that.

'He's exactly the same, though,' said William. 'Every cell of him.'

Then he left, and Nancy said maybe we shouldn't see him any more, as usual, and I said maybe, as usual.

But I longed for his visits. I longed for the past. I dreamt of Captain Scott – the scuffed parquet, the shimmer of the gazing ball, the blue velvet curtains full of dust and rot. The griffin's wooden wings smoothed by hundreds of hands. I dreamt of Lawrence, too; he kept trying to speak to me, to accuse me, his mouth a silent cave that washed me down a river to the sea. Yes, some part of me had known the Liddells would hurt him, and yes, I could have let William go – but then I would have lost him. So does that prove I am capable of great evil? Or of great sacrifice, great love?

Nancy told me she dreamt of her street. Running along Belgrave Close, no breath left inside her, the road tugging at her soles. Her driveway cracking, the pebble-dashed bungalow a stony beach washed up by a violent tide, everything hard, hard, and my father crawling past in a rusty car, something thudding in the boot.

As for our mothers, I heard that they took on whatever work they could find: cleaning jobs, waitressing, driving taxis. Once, at the cinema, I thought I saw Mother Night again – the real Mother Night. She bought a ticket and a packet of Opal Fruits and made her way into the theatre, and I followed and sat behind her. I watched as she removed her winter coat, polished her glasses. Then, before the lights went down, I tapped her on the shoulder, and she almost jumped out of her skin. 'It's me,' I said. 'It's Vincent.' But she said, 'I'm sorry,' and although her voice was the same, I could tell she didn't know me. Still, I sat through the whole film thinking she would come to her senses and remember; I could barely follow the story. The shape of her head right there in front of me like a memory, the shadow of a memory. At the end of the film, when I caught her eye again, she repeated, 'I'm sorry,' and I knew that she was not Mother Night: she was just a copy.

It wasn't until I heard about the exhibition that I decided to go to Margate. Nancy and I caught the train there, passing by stubble fields filled with sunlight, the rows of dead stalks tapering to vanishing point. We were staying in the old town, just a minute's walk from the museum, and posters about the exhibition lined the street.

'Ready?' said Nancy, lacing up her shoes.

'We don't have to see it straight away,' I said.

She gave me one of her looks, but she took my arm and we strolled in the other direction.

We visited Dreamland first, where the air smelled of sugar and rancid oil and the wooden rollercoaster shuddered beneath its shrieking passengers. Nancy hooked a rubber duck to win a stuffed bear with its mouth stitched crooked, and I tested my strength with a hammer I could hardly hold. It was the last day of the season, and already some of the stalls were packing up. We went for a ride on the Dodgems, our steering disastrous, quite out of control, and we screamed as we hurtled down the rollercoaster tracks. On the edges of the grounds we found the old cages they'd kept lions in. How cramped they were: scarcely room for the animals to turn around. But where was the *Queen Mary*, its funnels breathing out real smoke? And the merry-go-round with the great white swan? Where was the Magic Garden with its electric snowdrops, its glass oranges glowing on the trees? The parakeets riding bicycles? The roaming dinosaurs?

A woman waiting at the hotdog stand overheard us. 'They haven't been here in decades,' she said. She was with a boy who must have been her grandson; he tugged at her sleeve and said he was starving.

The man selling the hotdogs heard us too. 'You want to steer clear of the likes of them,' he told the woman. 'They're what's left of the Sycamore Scheme. Been coming through all season, looking for what's not here.'

'Oh,' said the woman. She gave us an awkward smile, then took her grandson's hand and, holding on tight, asked if he wanted tomato sauce.

Before we left, we stopped at a glass box with a turbaned figure inside: Zoltar the fortune teller, with his glued-on beard and his crystal ball made from a light shade. Although we knew he was not real, we both flinched when he started to move and speak, asking us for money, promising to tell us our fortune. I pushed in a coin, and he said, 'Zoltar, the great Gypsy, is here to give you ancient wisdom for your happiness.' Soon a card emerged from a slot, and I tore it off and read the message, the ink blotchy and indistinct: *Open the envelope of life and your dreams will come true, you have the courage to pursue them, do not fear the future. Love is strong around you and someone special is close.* Then another card emerged, and another, and something must have gone wrong with the mechanism that we couldn't see. We kept tearing the cards off and reading – *You are the lucky one, you were born lucky and luck continues to follow you* and *Beware the mask of lies that some people wear to look attractive* and *The road to happiness is in front of you* – until we couldn't keep up with the fortunes spiralling around our feet. Nancy thought it was funny, but I dragged her away; I didn't want to get into trouble.

At the Shell Grotto I bought her a shell lady with crinkled scallop skirts and a cockle bonnet and black eyes painted on a cowrie head. The woman at the desk told us to try the whispering trick: a secret breathed into the wall underneath the Dome would carry right along the Serpentine Passage. We could say whatever we liked, she assured us – summer was over, so we had the place to ourselves, apart from the ghosts.

'She was joking, wasn't she?' whispered Nancy as we made our way to the stairs.

'Just a story for the tourists,' I said.

Down we went, and the air cooled around us, and then we were underground, alone in the muffled gloom.

'Are you all right?' I asked Nancy, who preferred to avoid confined spaces.

'I said I'd come with you.' She took my hand.

The walls swarmed with scallops and cockles, whelks and mussels and oysters, four and a half million shells fixed to the chalk passage-ways. I caught my breath as something brushed past my leg, but it was just a tabby cat, camouflaged against the mosaics. They were quite grimy, coated with dust – too fragile to clean – and they'd lost their colour over the years, fading to tooth-white, bone-grey. We longed to touch them, but we refrained because touching was not allowed, although some visitors must have done so anyway; a few patches of shells gleamed. Instead, we moved our fingers through the air to trace the patterns we thought we could discern: a womb, an anchor, a tree, a serpent, a setting sun, a skeleton. And perhaps the grotto followed the journey of the soul through birth and life and death, ending in rebirth amongst the stars, just as we had read in The Book of Knowledge.

'Is it how you thought it would be?' said Nancy, and I said no, but it was beautiful all the same.

Here and there, missing shells had left impressions in the mortar like fossils. We stood beneath the Dome that was open to the sky and looked up at the disc of light high above us, every inch of the curving vault studded with rings of white and rings of grey. Then, while Nancy stayed put, I walked on down the Serpentine Passage, and when she whispered into the wall I could hear her ghostly voice transmitted by the shells that filled the space between us like so many mouths. *It's not your fault. Not your fault.* Nancy's voice, I told myself. Nancy's. But I stayed there a moment longer, and when I closed my eyes and listened hard I could hear another voice, and it was young but also old now, decades distant: *Sometimes I think about running away.*

In the final room – the Altar Chamber – we wondered at the ornate pedestal and the arched niche cut into the wall. For candles? For sacrifices? We took in the moon, the stars, the setting sun. I listened again, hard, but heard only my own breath.

After lunch we went walking along the seafront – past the arcades with their flashing lights and their robotic claws that dangled prizes for a few precarious seconds, past the pavilion where T.S. Eliot sat and looked out at the water and wrote of connecting nothing with nothing – and then I saw it. I must have gasped or made some sort of noise, because Nancy said, 'What's the matter?'

'The Big House,' I said, pointing.

It really was – or at least, it was the building from the brochure. The same blue and white awnings, the same windows with a wide view of the bay. At the front door, the same stained glass depicting the open-mouthed fish, the golden grapevines. And just for a moment I thought: all the children are in there. All the ones who recovered from the Bug and set off in the Van, their rucksacks light on their backs. Frank Harris, who drew me the picture of the

Dolphinarium, which was long gone too, and the Carter brothers – or perhaps the Connor brothers – who scratched their initials into the skirting board . . . and Jane, with her long plait and the faux pearls that shone at her throat.

But the place seemed deserted, the glass cracked, the awnings filthy and torn. The fish gasping. A bright-green bird alighted on the windowsill and studied me with its glossy black eye before fluttering away. A parakeet, wasn't it? Escaped from somewhere; gone wild. I thought I could see shadows out in the bay, shifting under the water; clouds of ash. Further in the distance, wind turbines waved their white arms.

'We should get to the museum,' said Nancy.

Yes, by then we were running out of time. We headed back to the old town and found the place – a series of cramped rooms housed in the former police station. The volunteer at the desk asked if we had any personal connection to the subject of the exhibition. 'Yes, no, prefer not to answer?' he said, his pen hovering over a form. 'It's for statistical purposes only,' he added when we glanced at each other.

'No,' we both said.

We knew he didn't believe us.

We looked at the seaside memorabilia first: pictures of the Miss Margate contest, the women lined up in bathing suits and high heels; a fake donkey, lumpy and splay-legged; a Punch and Judy show, the unmanned puppets staring from their booth; a lifebuoy. We poked our heads through a board painted with a faceless couple at the beach, and a volunteer took our photo. In a cabinet, cups and plates painted with beach scenes read *Souvenir of Margate*, and dainty china shoes burst with brittle flowers.

'Aren't they pretty,' said Nancy, and I nodded – but they were not what we had come to see.

Finally, we went to the cells.

'You can go in,' said a volunteer, smiling at the entrance to the first one. 'We won't lock you up.'

The space was tiny; Nancy and I stood shoulder to shoulder, the bars of the open door at our backs, and we read the placards fixed to the brick wall.

The Sycamore Homes were established after World War II to house the Copies bred for Sir Alastair Roach's Sycamore Scheme. These individuals, used in paediatric drug trials, were initially sourced from abortions and stillbirths, but later generations were derived from criminals. For this reason they were strictly monitored for certain indicators that might predict undesirable episodes, especially following the discovery that Copies could inherit 'genetic memories' of their donors' crimes, most often recalled in dreams. In order to thwart any similar tendencies, all dreams were recorded, as were all instances of violent, dishonest or cruel behaviour.

I remembered Mother Morning touching us on the shoulder to wake us, The Book of Dreams on her lap. The blue velvet curtains full of dust.

Located on the fringes of small towns and villages across Britain, the Sycamore Homes allowed these later generations no contact with ordinary people; at the time it was believed that this would protect the community. In 1971, in the face of scant evidence for the success of the Scheme, the government called a halt to the production of any further generations. However, Roach was permitted to continue his research with the remaining individuals, including ongoing studies into memory, inherited character traits and the origins of evil.

The Copies themselves were not made aware of their backgrounds or purpose in case this knowledge adversely affected their development, but in 1978, a flailing minority government made the decision to allow the Sycamore children to go on errands in the nearby villages. Some members of the public, defying the laws of the time, informed the children of the truth – and in the wake of these revelations, a small number of Copies committed significant acts of violence. However, statistical analysis shows that, per capita, Copies committed far fewer violent acts than any normal population.

After the closure of the Homes in 1979, the problematic treatment of their residents came to light. Many died as a result of the highly experimental medications administered by carers – 'mothers' – under the direction of Roach. His ethos, and the prevailing attitude of the era, was that these children could be sacrificed for the greater good, although the number of successful treatments developed as a result remains small. In recent years some researchers have claimed that Roach became obsessively focused on the elimination of individuals regarded as dangerous, and that successive governments turned a blind eye to this 'culling' because of the substantial donations Roach made to their parties. Most shocking is the revelation that unknown numbers of Sycamore children were exterminated in gas vans – vans they boarded willingly, in the belief they would be transported to a dream life here in Margate.

The Carters or the Connors, who left behind their scratched initials.

Frank Harris, who drew the Dolphinarium for me, and told me that soon it would be my turn.

Jane.

Ordinary people knew nothing of this scandalous practice. It was brought to the public's attention by the tireless work of Sylvia Dalton, who campaigned for decades to secure equal rights for Copies – a decision that cost the former Cabinet Minister her political career. Now, in 2019, Copies can vote, own property, obtain an education and hold a British passport. They can marry, and not just their own kind. They can apply for any job they please – although many employers still find reasons to exclude them from the workforce. Sadly, despite the closure of the Homes and the cancelling of the clinical programme that was to follow, Copies face continuing prejudice, and it may be many more years before this changes. This exhibition seeks to speed that process by casting light on a shameful period in our nation's recent history, the full truth of which was kept from ordinary people. For those of us proud to call Margate home, it also seeks to erase the stigma unfairly attached to our lovely town.

'Are you all right?' murmured Nancy.

I nodded and read a tiny footnote at the bottom of the placard: *At the age of ninety-three, Sir Alastair Roach died in his sleep at his Buenos Aires home, his fox terrier pup Cynthia by his side.*

We moved to the next cell, where two women were peering at a book displayed in a cabinet. I recognised the picture on the open page from The Immortal Story of Captain Scott in The Book of Knowledge. *'I am just going outside and may be some time,' said Captain L.E.G. Oates, a member of Captain Scott's last Antarctic expedition. Both he and his comrades knew that he was going to his death when he left the tent and walked out into the blizzard that was then raging.* Below it, the FACT INDEX, its map of the world unfolded. The two Russian peninsulas. The two New Zealands.

'Imagine thinking that some outdated children's encyclopaedias hold all the knowledge in the world,' said one of the women.

'If that's what you're led to believe . . .' began the other.

The first woman shook her head. 'They're just not very bright. Something to do with the copying, I've always thought. Fiddling with Mother Nature.'

'Kevin at the Aldi's nice.'

'He's a trolley boy, Carole. In his late fifties.' She tapped at her temple. 'Halfwits, the lot of them.'

'Yvonne! You can't say things like that any more.' But she giggled.

I stared into the other cabinet in the cell, which also contained a book. A handwritten book. *27 May 1975. – Fiona King: I'm at the Dolphinarium in Margate, and I trail my hands in the water, and Speedy comes swimming over to me. I give him a fish, and he says, 'Thank you, Fiona, you're very kind.' I ask how he knows my name, and he says, 'We remember you,' but I don't think I've been here before. – Timothy Simpson: I'm trying to find something in The Book of Knowledge, but the pages fall out when I touch them, and I know I'll get into trouble even though I didn't mean to destroy anything.*

'Listen to this,' said Yvonne, reading over my shoulder. 'Andrew Reynolds: A little girl asks if I want to play, so I say yes, and she throws me a ball. Only it's not a ball, it's the head of a fish, and its eyes are staring at me, and then it says, "This is all your fault," and I look over at the little girl, and she has no head.' She shuddered. 'Creepy.'

'It earned him a trip in the van,' said Carole, pointing to the sign above the cabinet: 'Andrew Reynolds was ten years old when he recounted a nightmare to his carer. This was his fifth violent dream in the space of two months, and it sealed his fate: his carers replaced his drug-trial medications with placebos. When he "recovered" a short time later, he was gassed in the van he was told would take him to Margate, where he would live in the "Big House" with all the other departed children, and visit Dreamland as often as he chose.'

'What did I tell you?' said Yvonne. 'You have to be pretty thick to believe a story like that.'

'It's a shame they had to drag Margate into it,' said Carole.

'I'd like to throttle whoever came up with that, really I would,' said Yvonne. 'Property prices through the floor. Dreamland dead in the water for years. Who knows if we'll ever recover?'

They drifted away.

'We'll wait here for a bit,' said Nancy. 'Let them get ahead of us.'

In silence we read all the old dreams, the security camera eyeing us from above. Nancy glanced at the low ceiling, the close walls, her breaths turning shallow and quick.

'Do you need to go outside?' I asked.

She shook her head. 'I said I'd come with you,' she repeated, 'and I'm coming with you.'

Through the cells we moved, taking in the items in the cabinets: a faded game of Ludo, a Meccano rocket ship flaky with rust, a hand-knitted jumper with *Ann Robinson* sewn into the neck. On the walls, photographs: Dr Roach holding three identical babies, Dr Roach showing a mother how to inject a boy's upper arm. Children making collages of milk-bottle tops and dead leaves. Children doing star jumps in a garden. Through the wall we could hear the women remarking on the exhibits. 'Oh, a national disgrace, was it? Pardon me for breathing!'

In the final cell a volunteer sat reading beside a cabinet. She must have been close to seventy, and she looked up when we entered, her brown eyes pale as acorns, her wavy grey hair secured with tortoiseshell combs. I knew her at once, and I thought: This must be a dream. I could feel her watching me as I walked to the cabinet, and I was walking not on cold flagstones but on sand, wet sand. The chill sky lowered itself to me, pressing on my skull, and a seabird's feathers, stiff with salt, brushed at my back. Ahead of me the wide water, clouded with ash. I touched my fingers to the surface. Glass. Yes, glass, and under the glass, another book: The Book of Guilt. I searched for my own name, because I knew it should be there, but I found only the names of other guilty children at some other Home. *25 August 1979. – Lisa Shaw: Stole money from Mother Morning's purse to spend on cigarettes. 26 August 1979. – Sandra Edwards: Tried to start a fire in her own bedroom. 28 August 1979. – Pamela Hall: Concealed a dead fly in the meal of another child.* All the bad things recorded, remembered. *1 September 1979. – Alison Hughes: Bit Mother Afternoon.* And then, squeezed in at the bottom of the page: *4 September 1979. – Jane White: Encouraged a Captain Scott boy to stop his medicine.*

I froze, remembering the day Mother Morning found my saved pills. William blurting that Jane had told me they made us sick.

And William had known only because I had told him.

So Mother Morning knew only because of me.

Mother Morning repeating her name, *Jane, Jane,* tucking it away for future use.

And here it was, her name and her crime, and I knew that this was Jane's final entry, the one that sent her to Margate.

All the other bad things I had done returned to me then. All the times I'd stood up for William, made excuses for him. Denying that he'd stamped on Cynthia's paw. Convincing Karen that he liked her – telling her he'd just made a mistake, played a bit too rough at the picnic in the woods. Talking Lawrence into going to the Liddells in William's place, even though I had a bad feeling about them, a terrible feeling.

You can't blame yourself – that's what Nancy had insisted all these years. But I knew she was wrong. I knew.

I felt my legs buckling under me, and Nancy was grabbing my right arm and the volunteer my left, and she was saying Vincent, Vincent, and she knew my name, she knew me, even though I'd worked hard to make myself different from my father. Come and sit down, Vincent, she was saying, helping me to her chair, and she was Mother Night, the real Mother Night, forty years older but still the same. Across the passageway the two women were shrieking with laughter at something they found funny. Let me look at you, said Mother Night, her fingers light as moths on my shoulder.

'I found the page you left in the jigsaw box,' I said.

She shook her head. 'I should have done more. Shown greater courage.'

'Where did you go?'

'Prison. Ten years.'

'Even after the Homes closed?'

'The courts were so slow to correct these things.'

'I'm sorry, I'm so sorry . . .'

'I was your mother,' she said, her voice breaking. 'I should have protected you. Every one of you.'

She was kneeling before me now, searching my face. I rested my hand over hers.

From the front desk a voice called: closing time.

In the old town we found a café; it was late afternoon, and I was starving. Mother Night – Frances – wanted to pay, she said. As soon as I finished my burger, she summoned the waiter and insisted

I order something else, then watched me take bite after bite. We ended up staying for hours.

Afterwards we headed down to the water, the three of us, where the boats sat askew in the tarry low tide. The smell of mud and brine filled the air – ripe, rank – and below that, too, the stench of tiny creatures stranded on the sand and breaking down. Behind us the clock tower shone shell-white in the last of the sun. The beach was empty, all of your holidays ended. All of you returned to your homes, you ordinary people who knew nothing. No striped umbrellas, no donkeys, no buried boys – but just ahead, a telescope at the edge of the road. Mother Night handed me a coin.

At first I saw only a blur of blue that might have been sea or might have been sky. I turned to face the souvenir shops and pizza restaurants, the cast-iron dolphins twined around the street lamps, the amusement arcades where people could try their luck. Figures passed by, but I could not make them out.

I turned back to watch the water stretch away forever and the waves rush in and in, the sand a tawny wash, the harbour arm a smudge to my right. Gulls wheeled and dived, and something broke the surface and vanished. A little way out, where the water grew deep, the shadows roiled and shook into shapes I thought I knew.

Then my time ran out.

Down on the beach we made our way west, nudging our toes at chunks of chalk drilled by the sea into strange bones. We skirted tangles of black seaweed on the shore, where it seemed to form initials, half-made words. Dreamland's façade rose cinnamon-brown into the autumn evening. Across the top, in yellow letters cut from the sinking sun: *DANCING*. We talked of the past as if we might still change it. We felt we could walk until morning. And at our backs the sea erased our steps, washed up its secrets and then dragged them away again.

A NOTE ON SOURCES

The Book of Knowledge is based on the 1954 edition of *The Book of Knowledge*, edited by Gordon Stowell and published by the Waverley Book Company Limited.

Some of the material in the Margate brochure is adapted from the 1974 promotional booklet *Margate*, published by Margate Corporation Entertainments, Catering and Publicity Committee.

The newspaper cutting Nancy finds is inspired by the 7 May 1966 *Guardian* article 'Life Sentences for Brady and Hindley' by Geoffrey Whiteley.

ACKNOWLEDGEMENTS

Thank you to my editors and their teams: Reagan Arthur (Hachette Book Group), Fergus Barrowman (Te Herenga Waka University Press), Meredith Curnow (Penguin Random House Australia), Kiara Kent (Knopf Canada), Jane Parkin, Nicholas Pearson (John Murray), Christopher Potter and Sarah Ream. Thank you to my agent Caroline Dawnay and her colleagues at United Agents. Special thanks to Virginia Fenton for all her help and companionship during my research trip, and to Kat Aitken, Elizabeth Knox and Sue Orr for their insightful feedback on the manuscript. Thank you to Jennifer Campion, Rowan Deacon, Anne Ferrier-Watson, Hilary Irving, Helen Mayall, Roger Ordish, my colleagues at the University of Waikato, and Dickie Faulkner and Tamara Rattigan at the Dreamland Heritage Trust. I am grateful to Creative New Zealand for funding an arts grant. And thank you, as always, to Alan Bekhuis and Alice Chidgey, who make everything possible.